Here Comes The Muffin Man

David Kirk

Here Comes The Muffin Man.

ISBN 978-80068-826-1

Published worldwide by Crime Central Publishing 2022

https://davidkirkauthor.com/

Acknowledgements

A special thanks to all those who purchased book one in the series and left such wonderful comments on both Amazon and my website. Also, to my long suffering wife, M. Without her support, encouragement, and love, I would have given up long ago.

Chapter 1

4TH DECEMBER 2019

"She will give birth to a son and you are to give him the name, Jesus, because he will save his people from their sins."
Matthew 1:21

IT WAS THREE WEEKS BEFORE Christmas, the start of advent, one of those damp, miserable evenings where the mist had stopped circling and was clinging to the river and the surrounding Ings. There was no wind to move the mist on, and the air was starting to become cold and crisp with the temperature slowly dropping. It would not freeze but would get close to it, and out on the flood pastures of the River Ouse, the breath from the dog walkers and their animals could be seen when they passed under the lights from the bridge traffic.

Chapter 1

In the centre of York, the Christmas illuminations certainly managed to brighten up the spirits of those engaged in the night-time economy, and the usual crowds of underdressed revellers were making their way, lurching and staggering, from pub to pub with the added urgency of the coming hour of eleven, when they would no longer be able to gain entry. Many had settled on their final venue, and more had decided to finish the evening in one of the numerous late-night watering holes thinly disguised as nightclubs. The club and pub doormen were buttoning up their overcoats and stamping their feet to keep out the cold, damp air, and the taxi ranks were filling up with cars waiting for the night-time rush to begin. Little could any of these night workers and partygoers appreciate that this Christmas would be the last free and easy yuletide for some years to come.

Thousands of miles away in China, a new virus was getting to grips with the population in ways that the good people of York could never have imagined. It would change lives and result in millions of deaths worldwide. But, for now, the Christmas merrymakers in the city were oblivious to it and only driven by a hedonistic holiday pleasure-seeking of their own.

The time was just coming up to 11:30, and as it began to drizzle, two households in the city, unbeknown to each other, and unlike the night-time revellers in the city centre, were experiencing their own private concerns. Although both households had never met, the family of Jason Waites and Vitoria Adams, were joined in a sense of worry and distress that both of them found impossible to shake off. The insecurities felt by these families were palpable and slowly building into a state of anxiousness with its own momentum. The alarming rate at which these fears grew was developing uncontrollably, and although the people suffering from these concerns would, in the near future, come together, at this time, neither family was aware of the other's predicament. This was all about to change. Both groups would soon make contact in ways nobody could have predicted, or indeed wanted.

Detective Chief Inspector Victoria Adams's uneasiness at not being able to raise her partner and, as of recently, wife, Mrs Adams-DeSilva, on the telephone was building into a major concern for her safety. The serial killer Jonathan Fahey had escaped from custody. Victoria had apprehended him two years earlier and Dr DeSilva's evidence at his trial had helped in his conviction. The news was seriously playing on her mind and beginning to burrow deep down like some parasite she was finding increasingly difficult to expel. Victoria worked through a range of scenarios, none of which she really wanted to consider. Apparently, while attending an appointment with a specialist at Birmingham Teaching Hospital, Fahey had absconded with the help of a prison officer called Peter Walsh.

Victoria was now recalling her last encounter with both Fahey and Walsh.

She remembered how, at Wellingborough secure unit in 2018, not long into Fahey's life sentence, she suspected that the relationship between inmate and prison officer was somewhat more than inappropriate. The purpose of her visit was to encourage Fahey to disclose where he had buried the remains of one of his victims. But Fahey was giving nothing away. The family of his second victim, Elizabeth Shannon, were still waiting to get some closure on their loss and Fahey was wallowing in the attention this gave him. It was the encounter with Fahey's minder, Prison Officer Walsh, that now troubled her.

She regretted not flagging up her concerns about how Walsh's relationship with Fahey seemed to have overstepped the mark. Walsh's reference to her sexuality and to the friendship that was obviously developing between Fahey and Walsh appeared to her to be highly inappropriate. If only she had said something at the time . . .

Too late now, she thought. Fahey was out and on the run. When she added this fact to the fact that Miriam had been attending a conference on Pathology in the very same city, and at the same hospital, to boot, she was putting two and two together and making twelve. Victoria paced around the kitchen and stopped, placing her palms on the kitchen island. She looked around for a couple of seconds, eventually settling on the smoky-glass doors that exited onto the garden.

When she and her partner Miriam bought this house together last year, it signified a major commitment in their relationship. Marriage followed quickly, and only last year, the decision to go to a private clinic for a round of IVF was a further step in cementing their love for each other. The IVF had been successful. Victoria's visit to the clinic today had confirmed she was indeed pregnant.

Unfortunately, she had not been able to give Miriam the good news and was now running through all the possible scenarios that could spoil their life together. This was not the time for outside forces to disrupt what they had, especially considering what she was expecting to have in eight months.

As she pushed herself onto the kitchen bar stool and took another sip of wine, she thought about the baby inside her and then, placing the glass down, gave her tummy a gentle stroke. *One glass can't do any harm*, she thought. But then pushed the glass way, thinking, *Enough for now.* She took the copy of the test results from her handbag. The letter of confirmation from the clinic said she was around two weeks pregnant. She held it tightly and thought about how everything had seemed to be going in their direction.

Victoria mouthed the words, 'Not now... Please, not now.'

***

Across the city, in the suburb of Badger Hill, another family was having similar worries. The Waites family were going through their own personal hell in a handcart, making copious cups of tea, pacing up and down, and telephoning all and sundry who might have some information about their son, Jason.

It was well after eleven and their thirteen-year-old son had not returned from Thursday's football training. He should have been back home at around six and, understandably, they were becoming more and more concerned. Mr and Mrs Waites had made all the usual phone calls to Jason's mates, who all said he had trained with everyone until about five-thirty and left on his own. The team coach, Phil Southern, had confirmed that Jason had left after training, after turning down the offer of a lift, on his own, and set off in the direction of home. As far as he was aware, Jason was going straight home. Paul and Molly Waites sat looking at each other in the kitchen of their home. They didn't know what to do next.

'I'll make us a nice cup of tea, Moll. I'm sure the lad will be okay. He's big enough to take care of himself. I've taught him that much. And he knows to keep away from strangers and the like.' Paul was trying to be positive and doing his best to calm the situation, losing count of how many cups of tea he had made in the last few hours.

'Oh! You can guarantee that, can you? If he was not coming home straight away, he would have called. He always does.'

'Look, he might have gone to see a girl that we don't know about. You know what lads are like at his age. Shy and full of hormones at the same time. It's a lethal concoction.'

Molly Waites stood and walked across to the large, bi-fold doors at the end of their kitchen diner. Looking out into the dark, she was willing her son to come bounding in through the kitchen door as if nothing had happened, give her a kiss, and ask if she had saved him any tea. Without turning, she spoke as if stating an undeniable fact.

'He doesn't have a girlfriend.'

As her husband was pouring the hot water onto the tea bag in her cup, she was still peering out into the darkness, when the sound of the turning of a key in the front door and the latch opening made them both start. She ran down the hallway just in time to see the front door swing open. Her anxiety lifted for a split second. But as the door was fully open, she stopped in her tracks and turned away, leaning against the wall to allow the visitor to pass in the hallway.

'Oh, it's you,' Molly Waites said in desperation.

'Thanks a bunch, Mum. Good to see you as well.'

Molly's daughter Sam was back from the pub and tried to give her mother a peck on the cheek as Molly turned and made her way back to the kitchen.

'Well, you can't beat a good old family welcome. That's what I always say. What about you, Dad?' Samantha gave her dad a peck on the cheek but immediately picked up on the atmosphere in the house. 'Okay, what's happened? It's not

Gran, is it? Nothing's happened to Gran?' She sat down at the table across from her mother, who stood and went into the living room without speaking.

'No. As far as we're aware, your gran is fine,' said Paul. 'It's Jason. He hasn't come back from football. He should have been home at six and no one knows where he might be.'

'Have you told the police yet?'

Mr Waites gave his daughter a surprised look at the question about the police. 'No,' he said, slowly shaking his head.

'Are you serious? He's this late and you haven't told the police?'

'What? The police? No. Don't be so silly. I don't think we need to involve the police yet. Do you, Moll?' he shouted through to the other room, where his wife had turned up the television. Mrs Waites didn't answer. He tried again. 'Do you think we should tell the police, Moll?'

And he heard Molly Waites begin to cry.

***

When the phone rang, it was answered by Rebecca Standish, who was the civilian desk clerk at Fulford Road Police Station — an efficient woman who was an ex-police officer now working in this new role after her retirement from the job.

'Hello, York Police. How can we help you?'

'Oh, hi. My name is Paul Waites and I want to report my son missing. He's thirteen and — '

Ms Standish cut him off, 'Hold on Mr Waites. How do you spell that?'

'What, Waites or Paul?'

For god's sake, he thought, *they should be able to spell Paul Waites.*

'Your surname, sir. Just so we get it correctly entered.'

'W-A-I-T-E-S. Waites. Have you got that?' Paul was immediately sorry for his exasperation. 'Sorry, but we're all getting a little worried here.'

'Yes, of course, Mr Waites, I understand. Look, rather than you telling me in your words what has happened, could I please ask you some questions? And if you could answer them as concisely as possible, it would help speed things up. In addition, although I can take these details over the phone, I will require you, or some member of your son's family, to come down to the station and speak with an officer before we can take any action.'

Paul did his best to answer all the questions and it was clear that the woman at the other end of the phone was filling out some kind of form. He was becoming more and more agitated with the questions, but also realised the importance of getting all the details correct.

'Why do we need to come to the station? Can't you at least start looking for him now?'

'We need you to bring some ID and a recent photograph of your son. Unfortunately, we must verify that the missing person is a genuine missing person and not some form of hoax.'

Eventually, he agreed to come down to the station as soon as he could. He thanked her and said his goodbyes.

It was agreed at the Waites household that Molly would go to the police station with her husband and Samantha would wait at the house in case Jason returned home. As time went by, both parents could feel the doubt creeping insidiously into their heads for the wellbeing of their son. And, perhaps, they thought, scaling this up and bringing in the police would only hasten the outcome they didn't want.

Chapter 2

It was now almost one o'clock in the morning and Victoria was aware that there was little she could do at this time about her partner's late arrival. She had telephoned the railway station who confirmed that all trains were running to schedule and there had been no major hold-ups anywhere on the line from Birmingham to York. She had resigned herself to the fact that she could do little more, and worrying about something she could not have any effect on was little more than pointless. So she decided to get ready for bed.

She had only just started up the stairs when her mobile phone, sitting on the breakfast bar, started to vibrate and hum. The phone was picked up in less than a couple of seconds and Victoria almost slipped into the counter in her rush to answer it. She glanced at the number to see who it was, and to her utter disappointment, it wasn't Miriam's number, but one she didn't recognise.

'Hello, could I speak to Chief Inspector Adams please?'

'Speaking.'

Chapter 2

'Oh, hello, yes. This is Sergeant Kawasi calling from East Midland's British Transport Police. I have some information for you from your . . . ' He paused for a second. 'Close friend, Doctor Miriam DeSilva.'

'She is somewhat more than a close friend, Sergeant. She's my wife. But please continue.'

He spoke in an accent that Victoria found hard to place; something between somewhere in East Africa and Solihull, she thought.

'I'm just checking that you are she? The doctor has told us that you are her next of kin and we have been given your mobile number by the police at Fulford Road. Doctor Miriam asked if we would telephone you with details of what has happened. Is it in order for me to address you as ma'am?'

'Fine, Sergeant. Just tell me what has happened to her. Is she alright?'

'Er . . . No, ma'am. She is not *alright*. I was just not sure how to address you, if you understand me. I meant no offence.'

Victoria's heart sank and then did a double jump in her chest. She was fighting to hold back the anxiety.

'For god's sake, man, just tell me what has happened.' She could sense her voice was becoming a little shaky as she continued, 'Is she okay? There must be something wrong or you wouldn't be ringing me at this hour.'

'Well, ma'am, I have to report that your wife, Doctor DeSilva, was involved in an assault and what appears to be a bungled attempted robbery at Birmingham New Street Railway Station this evening. She is at present recovering in the West Midlands General Hospital. Her injuries are relatively superficial and are in no way life-changing, although she is understandably quite shaken. I have the telephone number of the hospital if you would like to give them a call. I am sure she is going to be okay after a bit of TLC, as they say.'

The sergeant gave Victoria the number and, after getting his details and when he would be next on shift, she thanked him for calling with the information. Just before ending the call, she had a thought.

'Before I go, are there any details of the assailants involved in the attempted robbery, Sergeant?'

'Well, there's the odd thing about this incident. We would normally expect the assailants to be young, or relatively young, you know, riding bikes for a quick getaway. That sort of thing. But witnesses say the robbers, who, by the way, didn't manage to take any of your wife's belongings other than her mobile phone, were both middle-aged men. The witness statements say the two men were sitting on one of the platform benches and appeared to be waiting for the York train that I assume your wife would have been catching. It looks like one of them got up and walked slowly over to Doctor DeSilva, who then said something to her. She pushed him away and he then struck her in the face. As she fell unconscious, he kicked her several times.

'By all accounts, she was lucky to come away relatively unscathed. She apparently made an attempt to get up and was kicked as she lay on the ground. The other man then rummaged through her handbag and took her mobile phone. Both then walked calmly away and out into New Street, where they disappeared into the pedestrian traffic. When our officers arrived on the scene, they found the victim sitting propped up against one of the benches on the platform with wounds to her face and head. Her travelling companion gave us your details.'

'What do you mean, travelling companion? She didn't have a travelling companion.'

'Well, a lady was travelling with her. A pathologist who was attending the same conference. A Doctor Jane McCormack from Leeds. We have her details as she gave a statement to one of my officers at the scene.'

'Fine. I know Dr McCormack. She and Miriam sometimes work together on larger incidents. I have her details and will thank her later.'

'Would you like me to email you a copy of the report, ma'am?'

'Yes please, Sergeant. That would be good. And again, thanks for passing on the details.' She gave Sergeant Kawasi her work email and ended the call, immediately dialling the hospital. The expected recorded messages played back, asking if Victoria knew who she wanted to speak to, then to dial their number or otherwise hold the line.

As she waited, Victoria worried. Eventually, a female voice came on the line. Victoria explained who she was, and after a round of twenty questions, she was put through to the ward where Miriam was being cared for. The line was answered before the second ring.

'Hello, Ward Sister Shaunessy speaking. Can I help you?' The ward sister had that soft, Irish, lilting accent that immediately had the desired calming effect.

'Yes, hello. I am the wife of Doctor Miriam DeSilva who I believe has recently been admitted. I was wondering how she was doing?'

It still felt a little awkward for Victoria to announce herself as "the wife" and she wondered if this would ever change. Sister Shaunessy told her the major good news; Miriam was doing well and resting at the moment. Although, her injuries were serious enough. It could have been much worse. She had suffered a head injury and lost consciousness at the scene. Because of this, they wished to keep her on the ward overnight for observation. The sister also said that Miriam seemed to be little the worse for her ordeal, other than some facial injuries that would improve with time, bruised ribs, and a headache from hell. She added again that Miriam had been extremely lucky; if the blow to the side of her head had been an inch or so further down, it could have caused serious eye damage.

Victoria asked if it would be possible to get a phone to Miriam. But she was told that it would not be possible as she had been given some strong painkillers and was sleeping at the present time.

'Could I leave my number and ask you to message or telephone me if there are any adverse changes to her condition, please?'

'But of course. That would be no problem at all, Mrs DeSilva.'

Victoria didn't bother to explain that was not her name and decided not to get involved in lengthy explanations. It wasn't relevant, and all she was interested in was how Miriam was doing.

'Before you go, could I ask if the lady who came in with her, Dr McCormack, is still there?'

'No, she left when your wife was settled down. I think she has continued her journey home.'

'Many thanks, Sister, and once again, thank you for caring for Miriam.'

The ward sister gave her goodbyes and Victoria ended the call. She sat in her kitchen mulling over the information and what it meant. Could it have been Fahey and Walsh who had attacked Miriam? And what was their motive in doing such a thing in such a public place? What was a little more concerning was that, if it was indeed them, they now had Miriam's phone with Victoria's texts on it telling her they were expecting their first child.

Victoria wanted to jump in the car and drive down to Birmingham immediately. But she realised there would be little point and she could check back in the morning to see how Miriam was getting on. If necessary, she could then make the journey in daylight after a good night's sleep. That would make more sense. She picked up her mobile and took it upstairs, placing it on the bedside table with its charger plugged in. Eventually, she settled into her bed and was about to drift off to sleep when her phone started to vibrate on her bedside table. She picked it up and the screen showed it was the station.

Oh! For god's sake, what now?

Chapter 3

Mr and Mrs Waites were sitting in one of the small interview rooms that were set aside for families, rape victims, and young people being interviewed under caution. The room was sparsely furnished with four fabric-covered armchairs in burgundy surrounding a small, teak coffee table. The curtains matched the fabric of the chairs and a Canaletto print was the only decoration on the walls. Mr and Mrs Waites were looking agitated and worried when DCI Victoria Adams and DC Varsa Malik entered the room. Varsa was carrying a blue, cardboard folder. Setting it down on the table, she took out of it a double-sided form. Then she placed the form on the table in front of Victoria as they sat down.

The pair smiled a greeting at the worried parents of Jason Waites.

Victoria looked across at them and couldn't begin to imagine what they were going through. Paul Waites was of average height. Possibly in his mid-to-late forties. She thought he had somewhat of a "military bearing" about him, which she noticed immediately, as it reminded her of her ex-boss, Chief Superintendent Sean O'Neill. His hair was neatly clipped, and even at this late hour, he looked like he had taken the time to have a shave. He sat upright with his hands placed on his knees, fists clenched as if having his picture taken in a military group photograph.

Victoria smiled reassuringly.

'Mr and Mrs Waites, I am Detective Chief Inspector Victoria Adams, and this is Detective Constable Varsa Malik. Would it be alright to call you by your first names?' She paused and looked at the form taken from the blue folder. 'Paul and Molly? And you can call us Victoria and Varsa, if that's okay with you?'

She waited and the Waites's nodded their reply.

'Good. Let's begin by going over the details of your son's disappearance. I take it this late homecoming is completely out of character for Jason and that he would normally have made some form of contact by now?'

Mr Waites spoke up while his wife was looking at the Canaletto on the far wall. It was a scene depicting the Grand Canal in Venice and she was counting the number of gondolas and thinking about how she had always wanted to visit the city.

'Yes, he always telephones or makes some kind of contact if he's going to be late. He's a good lad is Jason. Isn't that right, love?'

Molly Waites nodded but didn't speak. She had now moved on to counting the number of people sitting in the gondolas.

'Fine. Could I ask you how often Jason goes to football training, and could you show us which route Jason would normally take home from the training ground?'

Varsa pushed a street plan across the coffee table towards Mr Waites, followed by an attempt to engage Mrs Waites. 'Molly, would you mind making a list of everyone you know at the football club who Jason would normally have had contact with? And, if possible, their addresses and telephone numbers, if you know them? Especially the coach, who may be the best person to fill in any gaps in the list.'

She ignored the request. Paul started to look through his pockets in a gesture to find a non-existent pen that he knew he didn't have. Varsa provided him with one, along with a blank piece of paper. Then he began to write down as many names as he could think of. He started with the coach, Phil Southern, and needed then to switch his phone on to check Phil's telephone number. When he handed the list back to Varsa, it contained over thirty names and numbers, but no addresses.

'I'm afraid I don't know any of the addresses, but I know where they are from picking Jason up and dropping him off, like. Just never taken much notice of the streets and house numbers, see.' He handed the list back to Varsa.

'That's fine, Paul. That's a great help.' She put the list into the blue, cardboard folder. 'And the route Jason would normally take home?' She offered him a yellow highlighter pen and Mr Waites traced the route on the street plan of their estate. The two detectives were about to get up when another woman entered the room.

Victoria stood up, welcomed the woman, and introduced her to Mr and Mrs Waites.

'Paul, Molly, this is Officer Carole Hargreaves who we have assigned to be your family liaison officer. She will be your initial contact throughout and stay with you until Jason is found. We would like it if she could accompany you home this evening, well, morning now, isn't it?'

Everyone finally got to their feet and Victoria and Varsa shook the hands of the two worried and anxious parents.

As Paul and Molly followed Officer Hargreaves, Victoria looked at Varsa and gave a slight jerk of her head. 'Well, come on, you. We might as well get the troops marshalled and get the show on the road. No sleep for the wicked, hey?'

Victoria and Varsa went upstairs to the MIT offices and hit the phones. There was a lot to organise to get the circus on the road for early in the morning. The pair wanted to muster as many officers as possible to assist in the search for young Jason. Victoria started with the search teams and Varsa went on to social media to bring in the volunteers. Over the years, the team had built up a network of volunteers who would do anything they could at the drop of a hat to help out in searches for missing persons. Especially if it was a child.

***

It wasn't light until after eight, but at around five-thirty in the morning the cavalry was arriving at the sports field belonging to the Badger Hill Sports and Social Club. The Police Major Incident van, with its array of computers, toilets, and briefing room was centre stage, with the local uniforms setting up a cordon around the clubhouse and changing rooms. They had taped off a number of parking spaces and had almost set up by the time Victoria arrived for her first look at the area. The club was home to the local cricket club, an indoor bowls club, and a range of local associations and activity groups in and around the suburb of York called Badger Hill. It had also been the home of Badgers Athletic FC for the past twenty years.

After she'd parked her black Audi in one of the spaces, she and Varsa stood by the car and looked at the scene unfolding around them. Victoria had managed to get some sleep, and Varsa had managed a few hours too, before showering and getting over to her boss's house. They had stopped off for bacon butties and coffee on the way to Badger Hill at the café opposite the Fulford Road nick, and then made the short journey in quick time. The morning traffic hadn't built up yet and a mist clung to the sports field swirling around the goalposts. It had rained in the night, which would make it a little harder for the search dogs. But, if nothing else, experience and instinct told Victoria that if the boy was still alive, he would not be too far away. And if he was no longer alive, he would likely be even closer to home.

Victoria and Varsa were finishing their coffees when Sergeants Pete Sinclair and Mal Chambers drove up and parked next to Victoria's car.

'Morning, boss. Early start. I'm assuming the lad hasn't pitched up overnight then?'

'No, Mal, he hasn't come home and no word from him either. We'll be setting up a central control room in the van over there when they get the lines in, and, in the meantime, if you follow me over to the social club, I'll give you the rundown and set the task actions.'

The four members of the team made their way over to the social club where around ten uniformed officers were standing around drinking tea. As the four detectives approached, a uniformed sergeant broke from the group and met Victoria, holding out a hand in greeting.

'Morning, ma'am. Sergeant Hallows. I'll be heading up the search team for the time being. This is all we've managed to muster at the moment, but there will be more arriving later.'

Sergeant Hallows was the epitome of the proverbial "gentle giant." He stood at least six foot six inches and even made Victoria feel small. He had the weight to back up his height and looked every inch the second-row forward. He was well known in the Fulford Road nick and well-liked.

Newbies and seasoned cops all looked up to him. Literally and metaphorically.

'Great, Sarge. If you bring them into the social club, I'll have a quick word with them, but it will be down to you to organise the search areas. I won't need any house-to-house as yet, but perhaps we can use your reinforcements for that later today.'

Sergeant Hallows nodded his reply, and the whole team crowded into the small meeting room in the social club.

'Okay, you lot, settle down now,' Hallows began. 'This is Chief Inspector Adams from the North Yorkshire Major Incident Team, and the guys standing behind her are members of said team. Chief Inspector Adams will be in overall control of the search, although I will be your link to her, and it will be me who will delegate your particular areas of search. As we don't have too many troops at present — more arriving later — we will be relying on a team of volunteers to fill out the numbers. John, Malcolm, Maureen, and Pat, you'll be in charge of a group of these volunteers each.'

'How many will we have, Sarge?'

'Not sure until they get here, Maureen. They could be in their hundreds or tens. We never know until word gets round. It is likely that these numbers will multiply this afternoon, in which case, we will designate some more lead officers. In the meantime, other than those four I have mentioned, the rest of you will work in pairs.' He turned to the two dog handlers. 'Chris, Bob, I would like you two to take the map and work your way down the route we believe was most likely taken by Jason on his way home. You can start as soon as the briefing is over.' The two men nodded and sat down in the corner of the room. 'That's all for now. I believe Chief Inspector Adams wishes to have a word.'

Victoria stood in front of the group of officers.

'Okay, everyone, thanks for getting in this early. It is most appreciated and won't go unnoticed, I promise. We have a young lad called Jason Waites, aged thirteen, who has now been missing from home for around twelve hours. He was last seen here at around five-thirty last night, where he had been training with the Badgers under-fifteen football team. He changed out of his kit and set off for home. He did not arrive home and his parents reported him missing around one o'clock this morning. He sometimes stays out late and his parents were giving him the benefit of the doubt on this occasion. But when he failed to arrive home they came to us with the details. You will appreciate that they are at their wit's end and extremely concerned for his welfare, as are we. As Sergeant Hallows has said, all contacts are to go through him at the moment. This will be our base until the van is operational. And it goes without saying, we need to find this lad.'

She was about to continue when her mobile buzzed in her pocket. She would normally have ignored the vibrating, but this time she could not. She took it out and gave it a glance. It was the saved hospital number from last night.

'Sorry, I have to take this. Sergeant Hallows, could you hand out the photographs of Jason and the list of clothes he was wearing when last seen, please?'

'Of course, ma'am.'

She pushed her way through the crowded room and into the corridor to answer the call.

'Hello, Chief Inspector Adams speaking.'

'Hi again. It's Sister Shaunessy here, from Ward Twelve A, Birmingham Teaching Hospital. I have your wife for you.'

The call went quiet for a second or two then clicked a further connection.

'Hello, you,' said Victoria immediately. 'How are you? How are you feeling? I rang last night but they said you were sleeping. I've been beside myself with worry.'

'Slow down a bit. It's like twenty bloody questions. Where are you? I can hear lots of voices.' Victoria's heart lifted at the sound of Miriam's voice.

'Never mind me for the time being. Tell me how you are.'

'Oh, I'm okay. It's all a lot of fuss over nothing really. They could have let me come home last night, but they gave me something for my headache and it zonked me out. They're going to let me leave sometime today, if they ever get themselves into gear. They are so short-staffed, patients everywhere, and hardly any nurses or doctors. Anyway, once they let me out, I'll get the train back up to York and let you know when it's due in.'

'Hang on a bit, my love. I can come down and drive you back, if you like?'

'Oh, for heaven's sake, there's no need. I feel much better and I'll be back before you can get down here with the car.'

'If you're sure, sweetheart?'

'Yes, of course I am. Now listen. The main reason I wanted to telephone was that I think I recognised one of the two buggers who had a go at me.'

There was a pause as if Miriam was waiting for Victoria to guess who. When there was no guess coming back, she carried on.

'It was only that Fahey bloke, or *Irelande*.' She made an attempt at a French accent. 'Or whatever he calls himself these days. I didn't recognise the other one, but it's what he said that made me lose my rag and slap the bugger in the face. Have they released the mad bastard or what?'

'No, he hasn't been released, but we have been told that he has escaped from custody. The man with him is possibly the one who helped him, a prison officer called Peter Walsh. What do you mean, you slapped him?'

'Yes, I gave the fella one hell of a swipe.'

'Go on, what happened?'

'Are you okay for a moment, Vicky? I can call back later, but I don't have my phone. The bastards nicked it, you know.'

'Yes, I know, sweetheart. I know. So, tell me what happened.'

'Well, I was standing on the platform waiting for the train. I was with Jane McCormack from Leeds. You remember her? We'd been at the conference together and were waiting for the Newcastle train stopping at York. Jane was going to change at York and go on to Leeds. Well, she had gone to get us some coffees, and while I was waiting, these two men got up from a bench they were sitting on and walked towards me. I recognised one as Fahey straight away and I'm sure he recognised who I was. He looked a little older and had put on some weight, but I knew it was him. Well, the other bloke hung back a bit and Fahey came up to me. You know what I'm like with remembering what people say, so I could repeat it word for word.'

'I know what you're like. Go on.'

'Well, he came really close and said, "Miriam, isn't it? How are you these days?" I took a step away, a little taken aback. I didn't want to look scared or anything, but I knew what he was capable of, although I did feel relatively okay with all the people around. Well, he smiled at me and stood to the side slightly and kind of glanced around checking if anyone was watching. He was standing very close and took hold of my left arm, tightly, so I couldn't get any further away. I tried to pull away, but he pulled me even closer to him. Then he whispered very threateningly in my ear . . .'

She paused again.

'What? What did he whisper, for heaven's sake?'

'Well, I don't like to say it here with people listening. It wasn't very pleasant, I can tell you that. If you're okay, I'll just go around the corner out of earshot of the desk.' There was a slight pause and Victoria could hear the chatter of the ward die down a little. 'Well, you're not going to believe it. He said, "Me and my friend here have always wanted to fuck a pair of dykes. I don't suppose you've had a real fuck in a long time. You might enjoy it." Well, my jaw dropped open, I can tell you. He then went on to say that if I was interested, they'd be in touch, and soon. I tried to pull away and he pulled me tightly up to him. I could smell his tobacco breath and BO. He was trying to kiss me, right there on the platform. Well, I just lashed out and whacked him across the face with my free hand. He then let me go but fetched me a right-hander to the chin, which knocked me off my feet. He was a big fella but fortunately, I landed on my bum. I was a bit dazed and as I was trying to get up, he kicked me in the ribs, which sent me back to the floor. I covered my face but then I felt another kick to my head and that's when I must have been knocked unconscious. Eventually, some people helped me up and Jane came back with the coffees. When I looked around, the pair had gone, along with my mobile. I have a shiner of a black eye and a swollen lip, oh, and a few sore ribs. But I've had worse playing in the forwards on the fifteens girls' rugby team.'

'Did you tell the transport police that you recognised one of the assailants?'

'Do you know, I'm not sure, but I definitely did remember him. The smarmy bastard.'

'Okay, sweetheart. It sounds like quite an ordeal. Are you sure you're okay to travel back on your own?'

'Yes, of course. Do you think they might be still hanging around?'

'I'm sure they're not. Fahey might be a nasty piece of work, but he's no fool. I'm sure he'll be long gone. Having said that, if you want me to come down for you, I really don't mind.'

'No, for the last time, I'm okay.'

'If you're sure you're well enough to travel, I'll let you go. I'm up to my proverbial in it at the moment.'

'I can hear that. What's going on? Sounds like you're in the middle of Piccadilly Circus.'

Before answering, Victoria moved outside to get out of the way of the extra uniforms who were arriving. 'We have a missing young lad, aged thirteen, been missing overnight so we are just marshalling the troops at the moment. I'm going to have a word with the parents once I get a shift on.'

'I'll let you go then and call when I know when the train gets in. Love you.' She gave Victoria a kiss over the phone and Victoria reciprocated.

'Love you too and you take care. Oh! You won't have been able to read any of the messages I sent you then, as your mobile has gone AWOL?'

'Nope. Why, was there anything important?'

Victoria smiled to herself. 'No, nothing that won't keep. I'll see you when you get back. Love you again.'

'Love you more.'

And the call ended.

Victoria held the phone, thinking to herself as she leaned on the side of the building. She knew Fahey was a monster, but he was a calculated monster. She should be collecting Miriam herself, but with all this going on, she couldn't just walk off the set and drive to Brum and back. Victoria knew that the golden hour for finding missing kids was the first few hours after they were reported missing. In essence, they were already fast approaching that time. At least Miriam was safe now and didn't seem to have suffered too much from her ordeal. But why would Fahey and Walsh have targeted her in that way? It seemed such a stupid risk to take when he'd only just gone on the run and needed to put some distance between him and the authorities.

A young uniformed officer who worked for the estates team came across from the incident van and informed Victoria that all the lines were now in and set up. So she could move her team in whenever she wanted.

'Okay, cheers for completing all that in double quick time.'

She turned to her small team of Mal Chambers, Pete Sinclair, and Varsa Malik, all of whom had come outside to avoid the crush now developing inside the community centre.

'Right, you lot, let's get this show on the road. We'll go inside the van where it'll be a little calmer and fewer bodies, I think.'

The three officers followed Victoria into the incident portacabin and to the meeting room at the end of a small corridor. The room echoed and sounded hollow, and the fluorescent lighting was already hurting her eyes. When anyone walked, the floor moved slightly up and down, giving the effect of being in a caravan rather than a portable building. In the main room, there was a table that would seat about ten people, a magnetic board, and around six chairs. Although it had windows along both sides, they were covered with an opaque film that dimmed the light. There were electric heaters down one side of the room but they were not yet connected.

'Pete, could you go and find that nice, young guy from the estates team and ask him to rustle up a few more chairs, please?'

'Sure thing, boss. Do you want me to do it now?'

'Yes, please. I'm expecting a visit from the ACC Crime sometime today and I don't want her having to stand.'

Pete left the room and they could hear him outside talking to one of the uniformed officers.

'Varsa, have you got the list of Jason's friends and associates that we got from Mr and Mrs Waites? The one we took last night?'

'Yes, boss,' she said, and handed a copy to Victoria, along with one to Mal Chambers. Varsa sat down in one of the chairs and gave it a little bounce. 'Not bad, but I don't think for a moment we will be spending much time on them.'

Victoria gave her a little frown and a shake of the head as the door swung open and Pete and the young estates officer entered the room carrying more chairs. Victoria thanked him, and as he was leaving, another officer entered the room with a kettle, coffee pot, and tins containing tea bags, coffee, and sugar. He was followed by a female officer carrying a tray of crockery and spoons.

As she was leaving, she turned to the team. 'There you go. Just like home.'

'I hope not,' said Mal. 'My kids would be running all over the place if it was anything like my home.'

The young officer smiled and left the room.

Victoria was looking down the list as she sat down in front of the board.

'Okay, Mal and Pete, I would like you to start with the coach, a guy called Phil Southern. Is that okay? We need the usual stuff. He would have probably been closest to the lad at the club. Details of his last movements and any background on the lad you can dig up. It's sometimes these people who end up knowing more about the kids than the parents do. Varsa, you're with me. We're off to see Mum and Dad. We'll see you back here at twelve-ish?'

Both sergeants spoke as one, 'Sure, boss. No worries.'

Chapter 4

WHEN THIRTEEN-YEAR-OLD JASON WAITES AWOKE, he was enveloped in a blackness he had never before experienced. He could feel an incredible pounding in his head and the bitter cold was causing him to shiver uncontrollably. He wasn't sure which was worse — the headache, the cold, or the darkness surrounding him. The pain in his head reminded him of the time he had drunk too much cider at a party and woken the next day with the headache from hell. The intense cold he felt was akin to when he would come off the football pitch in the winter and couldn't untie his bootlaces because his fingers refused to work. However, the immediate worry was the pitch dark he found himself in. It was impossible to orientate himself. He had no way of telling if it was day or night, how long he had been asleep, or any idea of where he was or how he had gotten there.

Jason realised he was lying on some kind of mattress with his right arm stretched upwards. He tried to pull his arm down and felt some resistance holding it upwards. His wrist was bound with a heavy, metal manacle that had a chain attaching it to the wall somewhere about a metre above and to his right. As he became more aware of his situation, he realised that his right arm had gone numb, due to it being suspended for some time while he had been sleeping. He shifted his body around and sat up, placing his feet off the edge of the mattress and onto what felt like a stone or concrete surface. He didn't have any shoes or socks on and the floor under his feet felt cold and wet.

In a vain attempt to make some sense of his surroundings, he squinted and strained his eyes to try and make out something in the darkness. The mattress he was sitting on stank of urine and he reached out in the dark, moving his fingers to the front and side to check if there was anything close to him. Eventually feeling the wall to his right, he found what appeared to be a large, metal ring set into the concrete. This, he realised, was his anchor point where a chain clasped to his wrist held him fast. He was very thirsty and his lips were starting to crack. He licked them but it didn't seem to help much. As he sniffed the air, all he could smell was the stinking mattress underneath him.

Now he felt the urge to urinate and tried to stand.

As he did this, he sensed a sharp tug at his ankle and looked down at it. It was difficult to make out in the blackness so he ran his hand down his leg to feel what was restraining him. There was some form of metal bracelet around his ankle, a little like the one on his right wrist with a padlock that attached it to a further chain. He ran his fingers along the length of the chain and could feel it wrapped around a thick pipe attached low down on the wall. The chain allowed him a range of movement, but only backwards and forwards along the pipe, and only so far as the restraint on his wrist would allow. But it was long enough to allow him to stand up.

He stood and stretched out as he would have done in training at the football club, firstly stretching his quads and then moving on to his hamstrings and calves. This relaxed him a little, but the urge to pee was now building. As he stood on the damp floor, the cold accentuated his desire to urinate and he could not hold it back any longer. *Oh no! For fuck's sake*, he thought, as the warm liquid ran down the inside of his legs and onto the floor. He realised he was whispering the words, 'Sorry, sorry,' but then felt stupid because who he was saying sorry to? For a moment or two, the warmth comforted him, but then euphoria soon passed and it only served to make him feel somehow more embarrassed and ashamed. It left his legs cold and damp, too, with the strong smell of his own urine now hanging in the air serving only to make him feel humiliated and lonely.

'Hello! Is there anyone there?' he shouted, more a desperate whimper than a shout.

There was no reply and he peered around into the blackness.

Chapter 4

Jason tried to remember what had happened to him. He could recall leaving the training ground at around five-thirty and being offered a lift from his coach, Phil. Oh, how he now wished he'd accepted it. Afterwards, he set off to meet Terry at the layby on Hull Road close to the Black Bull Pub. Terry was five years Jason's senior and an ex-member of the club, someone Jason looked up to. He had picked Jason up in his little van and they had set off back to Terry's flat above the shops in Tang Hall. He could remember going up to Terry's flat at the back of the shops and Terry making him a cup of coffee. They were going to order in some pizzas, play *Warcraft*, and maybe watch a film. But he then had a blank and could remember nothing before waking up here.

He could not remember what had happened to Terry and had no idea why he was being held, locked to a pipe in what appeared to be some bloody dungeon. He sat down again on the mattress and tucked his knees up to his chin, holding his hands at the side of his head. Tears started to well up behind his eyes. He wanted his mum and dad. Jason hoped they were missing him as much as he was missing them. He wanted to feel the soft warmth of his mum's woollen jumper when she held him close and the smell of her perfume when she kissed him on the cheek. She would be worried sick. He wished like hell he had told her where he was going after training.

He could hear his dad telling him to "man up" and not to be such a wuss. But it was hard not to cry and even harder not to be scared. Jason sat for a moment, and in the dark silence, he thought he heard someone else crying. He shook his head, thinking he might be hearing things that weren't there. Then he heard it again. Not a full-on, cry-out-loud cry, but a definite whimpering in the darkness. He looked around, turning his head to the left and then to the right in a vain attempt to locate the sound. He listened hard and could just about make it out again.

'Hey! Hello there! Is there someone there?'

He waited, but there was no reply.

'My name is Jason. Jason Waites from York, Badger Hill. I'm thirteen. I know someone is there. Come on, who is it?'

There was further silence and the whimpering stopped.

'Come on. Speak to me. Who is it?'

Again, silence for a few seconds and then the whimpering again.

'Oh, for fuck's sake, who is it?'

More silence. Then, just before he was about to call out again, he heard a tiny voice just about audible in the darkness, broken by a slight cough and sniffling.

'My name is Thomas Norman Walker and I'm nine.' He paused for a second before adding, 'And I'm from Leeds.'

It came out as if the lad had been practising it for a presentation at school, and Jason gulped and sat back against the damp wall. He didn't know what to think. On the one hand, he was not alone, which gave him some comfort. But, on the other hand, whoever was holding him was also holding another little boy much younger than himself. But why? Shocked and stunned, Jason put his head in his hands, tucked his knees up close to him, and slipped onto his side. He lay like this for a minute or so, thinking about his mum and his sister and his warm house, and he began to cry like the other little boy. His whimpering quickly developed into full-on crying. Then he began to cry deep, long sobs, allowing his body to jerk with each one.

Chapter 5

As Mal and Pete arrived outside the Southern's' home, Phil Southern was just leaving and the pair of detectives stopped him in the driveway. As they flashed their IDs, he withdrew a few steps and squinted.

'Detective Sergeant Mal Chambers and Detective Sergeant Pete Sinclair. Is it Phil Southern?'

'Yep, I was just on my way out. Is this about Jason?'

Mal and Pete nodded in unison.

'You better come inside. I'll get Beth to make us a cuppa.' The three men made their way inside the neat, three-bed, semi-detached house, and Phil Southern called to his wife, 'It's the police, Beth. They've come to ask about Jason. Can you make us a brew?' He turned to the two officers. 'Sit down in here, guys.'

Phil Southern led them into the front room of the house that, although it was spotlessly clean and tidy, looked like it was in need of some serious modernisation and decoration.

Chapter 5

The two officers sat down on a small settee and Phil sat to the side in a matching armchair. 'So, how can I help you both?'

Phil Southern was in his early-to-mid fifties, with a receding hairline and what hair was left slicked back, giving him the look of a Count Dracula character in a movie. He was around six feet tall and skinny in the extreme. The most striking feature of Phil Southern was his beak-like nose. It was hooked downwards and his lack of flesh on bones only served to accentuate the protruding proboscis.

Pete Sinclair was about to speak when Phil's wife Beth came into the room.

Phil stood up. 'This is my wife Beth.'

The two officers stood up to say hello, totally gob-smacked. She was absolutely stunning. She was about five foot seven with blonde, bobbed hair, just enough make-up to look classy and not brassy, and only, at the most, in her late thirties. Her roll-neck sweater clung in all the right places, and her shapely figure filled out her washed-out jeans perfectly.

'So, can I get you guys something to drink? Tea, coffee?'

Once the drinks order was sorted, Beth withdrew into the kitchen with the three men's eyes following her as she went.

Phil turned back to the two officers. 'I know what you're thinking, fellas, that Phil here is punching somewhat above his weight with that one. I don't mind. It's something I have learned to accept over the years.'

'How did you meet?'

'When I was playing for Doncaster Rovers some years back. She was doing some kind of modelling and promotion work at the club and we just sort of hit it off. I was earning quite a bit, fast cars and loose women, that sort of thing, some might say.'

He paused for a moment and Pete gestured for him to carry on.

'Well, we got married, and then after my injury ended my playing career, I thought that was that and she was bound to bugger off, like. But fair play to her, she stuck with it.'

'Do you have any children, Phil?'

Nope. We don't have any kids. Apparently, I've got lazy sperm. We both take an active part in running the lad's team at the Badgers and enjoy it massively.'

'So how did you get into coaching?'

'After my injury in a game against Leeds, the club let me do a bit of coaching on the academy team. But I'd really lost interest in football, not being able to play anymore. Beth suggested I go back to education and I managed to get a history degree and became a teacher.'

'Where did you teach?'

'First job was at Archbishop Holgate's and I'm still there. I love the work, but it's all a bit stressful sometimes.'

'So why the Badgers?'

'I was devastated for quite some years after not being able to play again. It was Beth who helped me through the darker times. It was also Beth who suggested I get back into the game in some limited way. When she saw that the local Badgers under-fifteens were looking for a coach, it kind of made sense. She's one in a million, that woman. She helps on the Saturday games looking after the kitchen, organising meals for the lads, and runs the bar most evenings.'

Beth Southern came back into the room and placed a tray on the coffee table, then sat down on the arm of her husband's chair, leaning her weight on her husband's shoulder.

Mal smiled at her and turned to Phil. 'Could I start by asking you when you last saw Jason, Mr Southern?'

'Well, it would have been around five p.m., and it's okay to call me Phil, by the way. So yes, around five-ish. We train until it starts to get dark and then the lads either get picked up by their parents or, if they're local like Jason, make their own way home. Sometimes, if there's a big match coming up, we might train under the floodlights. But on this occasion — '

Pete looked surprised. 'Flood lights? All a bit posh. Never had anything like that in my day. When it got dark, we stopped playing.'

'Did he get changed before setting off home? Or was he still in his kit?' Mal asked.

'I think he put a pair of tracksuit bottoms on, dark blue ones with Adidas stripes down the side. He would've taken off his boots and put trainers on, and he would've had a hoodie under his puffer jacket. I'm sure his mum and dad would be able to give you more information on his clothes, but I seem to remember that his puffer coat was blue, and he usually wears a grey hoodie under it.'

'Fine. So, he walked off in the direction of home, around 5 p.m.? Did he say anything to you? And how did he seem? Was he distracted, happy, concerned?'

'Well, I asked him if he wanted a lift home and he said no as he wanted to walk off some cramp in his calves. He seemed . . . Well, just Jason really.'

'What do you mean, Mr Southern, just Jason?'

While he was thinking of how to answer, Mrs Southern offered her interpretation of what her husband had said. 'Jason is a quiet lad. You would say he's more thoughtful than the other lads, often not as boisterous or mischievous. He comes over as somewhat sensitive, some might say even withdrawn a little. But he's always polite, respectful, and helpful.'

'What about his playing? You know, how good is he?'

Phil now felt on sounder ground. 'He's no Wayne Rooney or Phil Foden, but he could hold his own at probably a good non-league club, or even one of the league two teams. His main negatives are probably his lack of drive and real enthusiasm for the game. Oh, he talks a good game, but when it comes down to training and playing, he's always *reliable*, if you know what I mean. He always turns up but lacks the ambition. I'll give you an example. We have at least four strikers, including Jason, in his age group, and if I dropped one of the others for a game, they would go ape-shit, asking why, what had they done wrong, telling me they'd put extra effort into it. But if I dropped Jason, for some reason, he would just accept it and that was that. His dad, on the other hand, is a different kettle of fish. He'd want to know exactly why Jas had been dropped. At times, he got quite aggressive about it. Even to the point of coming round here demanding an explanation. To be honest, I think his dad is a lot more interested in Jason playing than Jason is. Have you met Paul, Jason's dad?'

'No, we haven't as yet. Why do you ask?'

'Well, he comes over as nice as pie when you first meet him, but if he loses it, you can stand by. He was in the paras and can be quite an intimidating character. There have been a number of incidents at the clubhouse when he's become a little too aggressive, you might say. Mainly when he's had a few.'

Sergeant Pete Sinclair was busy writing everything down when Beth Southern chipped in, 'Oh, he isn't that bad, He can get a bit rowdy when he'd been drinking, but nothing serious. He is a bit of a ladies' man though. Likes to chat up the women when he's had a few. I'm not sure how Molly puts up with it. But I'm sure he's harmless enough. Quite good looking though,' she said, smiling and still with her arm around her husband's shoulder.

'Is he now?' Phil said, frowning at his wife. He shrugged his shoulders from under her arm and stood up, turning to the two officers. 'Is that all, guys? Or is there anything more you think I can help with? I was on my way to the club to help in the search when you arrived. I'd like to get down there as soon as possible if I can.'

'No, Mr and Mrs Southern, I think we have all we need for now, and I'm sure the teams at the ground will be only too glad of your help. The more the merrier, as they say.'

'Not much to be merry about though, is there?' Mrs Southern chipped in.

***

A couple of miles away at the Waites's home, DC Carole Hargreaves answered the door to Victoria and Varsa.

'Hi, Carole. How are they holding up?

'Not too badly, under the circumstances,' she replied quietly. 'But they're not stupid. They're aware the longer time goes on, the less likely the outcome is going to be a good one.'

The three women went into the hallway of the house. Victoria noticed the military photographs on the wall in the hall. Most depicted groups of men and women at some function or another, the men in mess dress and the women in evening gowns. The Waites's home was detached, well-furnished, and modern. The wide, tiled hallway led into a huge kitchen-diner where Mr Waites and his wife were sitting at a large breakfast bar drinking coffee. When Mrs Waites saw the two officers, she immediately jumped up. Mr Waites remained sitting but turned in the direction of Victoria and Varsa with a look of expectancy on his face.

Chapter 5

'Have you found him then? Please say you've found Jason.'

'No, unfortunately, we haven't found him yet. But the search is in full swing and we have all the officers we can use at our disposal.'

Paul Waites slid off his kitchen stool, pushed it under the breakfast bar, and turned to Victoria. 'Well, if you haven't found him, what the hell are you doing here? We're not hiding him in a cupboard or under the stairs, you know. He's out there somewhere, for Pete's sake.'

'Sit down, love. They're only trying to do their job. Aren't you, love?' She directed the second *love* at Varsa, who nodded her reply.

A mobile phone that was on the worktop started to buzz and Paul Waites picked it up, looked at who was calling, and turned to walk out of the room. 'I have to take this. It's business.'

Varsa looked across at Victoria and she nodded. Varsa moved towards the door Paul Waites had left through and stood within earshot of the telephone conversation.

Victoria turned to Mrs Waites. 'Molly, I can assure you and Paul that we are doing everything we can to find Jason. However, in the meantime, there are a number of things I would like to go over with you both and I would like Varsa here to have a look round Jason's room. If that is okay?'

'Yes, of course. Fire away.'

Before starting to ask any questions, Victoria considered Molly Waites' journey through the stages of grief associated with a missing child. She may need a little time to work through this particular one, Victoria thought to herself. The mother had been through the disbelief, followed by the despair. Now the anger stage was kicking in. *Why couldn't we protect him? We're his mum and dad. We should have stopped this from happening.*

Victoria gave her a moment to settle down before picking up the questioning.

'Well, could we go back to yesterday and just go over Jason's movements throughout the day? I would like you to tell me, in as much detail as possible, what he got up to. Did he go out at all? And where? Any phone calls? Everything you can remember.'

Molly Waites began to recount her son's movements throughout the day until he left for training at around twelve.

'Did he have any lunch before he left? And did he make his own way to the training ground?'

'He had a sandwich, I think. Made it himself. And his dad took him in the car to the club.'

Mr Waites had returned. Varsa looked across at her boss with a nod.

'Would it be okay for you to show Varsa Jason's room, Molly?'

'Aye sure. Follow me. It's at the top of the stairs on the left.' Molly got up and pushed past her husband who was standing in the doorway.

'What do you need to look at the lad's room for?' he interrupted. 'I told you he's out there somewhere, not in the bloody house.'

The two women ignored him and Mrs Waites led Varsa up the wide, open-tread staircase to a first-floor landing. Victoria was left alone with Paul Waites in their kitchen. He took the cups and glasses that were on the island and placed them in the dishwasher, carefully selected a rinse program, and turned it on.

'You have a lovely home here, Paul.'

'Yep, thanks. We had all the extension stuff and new kitchen, etcetera, etcetera, done when I came out of the army a couple of years back. We spent most of my pension lump sum on it all. Look, I'm sorry if I came over a bit sharp before. I didn't mean to. It's just that we're worried out of our brains about him. You can understand?'

'Of course, Paul. Absolutely. Do you mind if I ask some questions about him?'

'No. Shoot. Anything we can do.'

'Okay, firstly, can you tell me how long Jason has been playing for the Badgers?'

'Not too long. I think this will be his second season. He's a good player. No Ronaldo, you understand, but he can hold his own on the team. If only that prat of a coach would pick him. He doesn't know his arse from his elbow and would have difficulty coaching a mouse to a trap with a piece of cheddar. When I left the paras, I was a major. I came up through the ranks and made it to quite a high rank for someone who joined as a private. Quite something, if you know much about the army . . . Quite something.'

'Yes,' Victoria repeated, 'quite something.' She nodded and smiled at him.

He was not a tall man but looked a powerful one. He was broad-chested and his shirt was well-filled. He had his sleeves rolled up to the elbows, showing off his well-muscled forearms, and he looked like he still spent time in the gym.

'So, what made Jason join the club in the first place?'

'Well, to be honest, football wasn't his first love, I think. I was away quite a lot and his mum was the main anchor in his life. She had him going to ballroom dancing classes, would you believe? And the local drama group. He said he wanted to be a dancer like the ones on *Strictly Come Dancing*, or an actor. All a bit bloody effeminate, if you ask me. I wasn't having any of that limp handshake brigade. If you catch my drift? When I got home full-time, I managed to put a stop to all that nonsense and took him to the local rugby club, which he hated with a vengeance. Then we tried the badgers, which he seemed to like.'

'Are you saying that you think your son might be gay, Paul?'

Paul Waites turned to face her and placed his hands on the breakfast bar, palms turned down. '*Gay?* How dare you. No son of mine is going to be a poof. I can tell you that much. He's a normal lad who's been bought up by his mum, who has obviously over-indulged him. That's all.'

Victoria was gobsmacked. She was astounded that, in this day and age, someone who was obviously well-educated could hold such homophobic views. She was about to challenge him when Varsa came into the room, followed by Mrs Waites.

'Well, thanks for your time, both of you.' Victoria cleared her throat. 'We're going to join the teams now at the social club to check on how the search is going along and we will, of course, report back to you both immediately if there is any news.'

Victoria and Varsa shook hands with both of the Waites's and made their way to the front door, where the FLO Carole Hargreaves was waiting. She was holding a laptop under her arm.

'Can I have a word outside please, ma'am?'

'Sure, Carole.'

And the three women made their way out onto the gravel driveway. They stood together on the block-paved driveway.

'So, what is it, Carole?'

'Well, a number of things really, boss. Firstly, I am convinced the lad Jason is gay, and his mother may be aware of that, but his dad is probably not. Secondly, I am also sure that Jason was shit scared of his dad.'

'Scared enough to have run away?'

'Possibly, but I can't obviously be certain.'

'Did his mother tell you that about him being scared of his dad?'

'Well, not in so many words, but from what she was saying about the lad almost being dragooned into playing footie and looking around his room, he was definitely not straight. He had back-dated copies of *Gay Times* and *Drummer* stuffed under his mattress, not copies of *Match of the Day* or *FourFourTwo*, and posters of David Beckham showing off his six-pack and tats rather than him scoring goals. If you catch my drift?'

Varsa looked a little perplexed, as she had never heard of any of these magazines. Victoria half turned and looked back at the house, then turned back to Carole.

'Go on, Carole.'

'Well, I've also had a quick peek at his laptop, which he didn't have protected, would you believe? But it was hidden, pushed under his t-shirts in a drawer. His search history suggests his preferences are male rather than female, shall we say. However, there are some files and emails that are protected, and I can't get at them.' Carole held out the laptop and handed it to Varsa. 'Here you go, Varsa. Something to work your magic on. You're not known as the queen of the keyboards for nothing.'

'What makes you think he was so scared of his dad, Carole?'

'Well, when I found the stuff on the laptop and the magazines, I asked Molly about them and she pleaded with me not to mention any of it to Paul because he would go ape-shit and probably give Jason a good hiding when he came home. I asked her if Jason would be aware of this and she said that he probably would know that his dad would lose it. That it wouldn't be the first time Paul had smacked their son for not really measuring up to his dad's ideals of what a man should be.'

'Okay, Carole, me and Varsa have to get back to the incident room. See if you can tease anything out of Mr Waites that will shed any light on any possible reasons that Jason may have run away, and where he might have gone.' She turned to Varsa and gestured with her head towards the car. 'Come on, Varsa, let's get back to the sports ground. I need you to get to work on that computer as soon as.'

'Sure, boss. Does that mean I'm not riding shotgun for the time being?'

Victoria laughed and tutted. 'Just for the time being, Varsa. Just until we get this lot sorted, hey?' Varsa was duly dropped off at Fullford Road along with her laptop and got down to work on it. Passwords and encrypted files was her speciality and it would not be too long before all of Jason's correspondence would be revealed.

When Victoria's car turned into Badger Hill Sports and Social Club, she saw that the morning crowd of volunteer searchers had certainly multiplied. There looked to be well over a hundred people on the playing fields, in groups of about twenty or so with a number of uniformed officers leading each group of them off in different directions. Many were carrying walking poles or sticks, and the officers were leading them in the direction of their designated search areas. Victoria was certainly impressed at Sergeant Hallows's organisation. A parking space had been reserved for her and she noticed that Mal and Pete's car was already back. Before she was out of the car, she noticed Sergeant Hallows standing waiting.

'All looks good, Sarge. Everything going okay? You look like you have plenty of bodies to work with.'

'Erm . . . perhaps not a good choice of words, ma'am. But we have found something.'

'Oh god. Not the lad, is it?'

'No. Someone has handed in what looks like the lad's sports bag with all his kit in it. It's got his name on the tag and the Badgers' logo on the side. We haven't opened it yet. It's in an evidence bag in the temporary ops room of the portacabin.'

Victoria looked at the pathway across the grass from the tarmac car park to the steps that led up to the door of the portacabin. The foot traffic had turned it into a bit of a quagmire and she turned to Sergeant Hallows.

'Any chance of getting someone to put some duckboards down over there, Sergeant? By this afternoon, it's going to look a bit like the Somme.' Victoria was wearing an expensive-looking pair of patent flatties, and she lifted her right leg to show the shoe to the sergeant.

'Sure, ma'am. I'll get someone on to it.'

Sergeant Hallows went off in the direction of the social club, and Victoria made her way across the wet grass and up the two steps into the portacabin. As she was wiping her feet on the doormat, she turned, and only then noticed the ACC Crime's car parked at the far end of the car park.

'Oh shit. The Hot Chocolate's here. That's all we need right now.' This Sunday was turning into anything but a day of rest.

Chapter 6

ASSISTANT CHIEF CONSTABLE JULIE THORNTON was known to her subordinates as Hot Chocolate partially because of her name being the same as the Thornton chocolate brand, but more critically because of the way she was always made up to the nines. Her auburn hair was always perfectly coiffured and her nails and lips were always matching, usually some shade of flaming red. When in uniform, she looked like she had come straight from a photo shoot for the NPCC (National Police Chief's Council) and when in civies, she probably saw herself on the cover of *Tatler* magazine. She was ambitious in the extreme and didn't suffer fools at all, never mind gladly. She liked to be involved with the minutiae of every detail of a case, not because there may be a possibility of her helping out, but more to do with her not wanting to be caught out by her seniors if asked how a case was progressing. She rarely interfered to any significant degree, but always let it be known that her decision, and hers alone, would be the final one.

Chapter 6

When Victoria entered the meeting room, ACC Thornton was standing in front of the screen with a young man at her side, who was in civilian clothes. Victoria couldn't place him, but he looked early twenties, very early twenties, she thought, skinny and looking like he needed a good dinner. He was what she would call a classic hipster — hair clipped high at the sides with a full beard that didn't meet his side-burns. What confirmed the look was the pale blue suit that looked at least two sizes too small for him, a jacket with all four buttons done up, and the narrowest of trousers at least one or possibly two inches above his pale tan shoes.

Victoria smiled at him with a nod and greeted the ACC with a thin smile and a, 'Ma'am.'

Pete Sinclair and Mal Chambers stood up when Victoria and Varsa entered the room, then sat back down when she gestured for them to do so with a falling palm of her hand.

'How is the search going, Chief Inspector? Any develop-ments?' The ACC was standing in front of the recently found sports bag and obscuring it from view. Victoria realised this immediately and understood that the question was loaded with, *Do you know what's going on? Thank god for Sergeant Hallows telling me about the find.*

'Other than the find this morning of the lad's sports kit, which I believe is behind you on the table, no. No real devel-opments. We have his laptop and Varsa is working on it now at Fulford Road. I have made a first visit to the lad's home and the FLO, Officer Hargreaves, is with them. I am not expecting Varsa to be too long with the laptop, which may flag up other lines of enquiry.

The ACC was nodding. 'Anything untoward with the family?'

'Nothing other than a bit of a homophobic father who possibly scares his son witless, all seems okay. Dad seems to want a "real" son who plays rugby and boxes, not one who dances and acts.' Victoria threw her head backwards scornfully. 'Officer Hargreaves says the family is holding up as well as could be expected at this difficult time and Sergeants Sinclair and Chambers here have been out to interview the chief coach of the football team that Jason plays for. We are yet to have a wee chat about that. So will that be all, ma'am?'

'No, not really. I know how busy you are and the main reason I have come over this morning is to introduce you to Harry here. Harry Burrows.'

The skinny young man nodded a greeting to the rest of the team, and they all nodded back, except for Victoria who looked at the ACC in complete disbelief.

'I wasn't informed we were getting a new member of the MIT. When was this decided, ma'am?'

The ACC could detect the tension rising a little and wanted to avoid any notion of conflict while the team was assembled. She gestured for Victoria to come into the corridor by pulling the door open and jerking her head in the direction of the opening. Victoria obliged, as it was clearly more than a request. She closed the door behind her, leaving the team sitting in silence.

Mal turned to face the new lad. 'So, Harry, long out of uniform, are we?'

'About a fortnight,' he answered with slight nervousness.

This was received with a, 'Humph,' from Mal, who turned to his partner Pete Sinclair. 'Well, I for one am sure Harry here will become a real asset to the team.' A wide, beaming smile came across Harry Burrow's face. 'That is once we get the wrapper off him, of course.'

At this, Pete and Mal laughed out loud, and Victoria turned away so as not to show her grin.

'You could start by making yourself useful and making us all a brew, Harry, if you would be so kind,' Pete continued. 'The boss likes her coffee strong and black. Us two will have a sugar each with a little milk. And Varsa, when she returns, will have a camomile tea with four milligrams of brown sugar and a little coconut milk. Oh, and of course whatever you want for yourself.'

Harry looked somewhat bewildered until Victoria took him by the elbow and led him over to where the tea and coffee were sitting on a side table.

'Don't worry, they're pulling your leg. I'll help you with the drinks, but only this once, you understand.'

As she left the new boy Harry, sorting out the teas and coffees, Victoria turned her attention back to the briefing room, now the ACC had left. Eventually Harry finished the drinks and was handing them round.

'Well, Harry, welcome to the MIT. As you can see, we are a small but well-knit team and, above all, we are fiercely loyal. Do you understand, Harry? Fiercely loyal.'

Harry nodded his head while handing Victoria her drink.

'Don't just nod at me, Harry. It is okay to actually speak. You'll look like a donkey nodding all the while.'

'Sorry, yes, sir. I understand.'

'Good, however, I am not a sir, Harry. As yet, I have not been knighted and I work full-time for a living. But, most importantly, *sir* is a male title, and if you look at these bumps on my chest, they are a bit of a giveaway that I am more likely to be female rather than male. You can call me boss or ma'am. I will answer to either.' She now turned her attention to Mal and Pete. 'So, how did it go with the coach, what's his name?' She looked at the list of names pinned to the board. 'Phil Southern?'

'Well, him and his wife are a bit of an odd pair alright. He looks like a cross between Count Dracula and a white version of Mo Farrar, and his wife looks like a double for Seven of Nine.' Harry looked perplexed.

'Seven of what?'

'Seven of Nine. You know, the blond bombshell from the Voyager Star Trek series?'

All the team turned to look in Mal's direction with Victoria winning the incredulous-look-on-the-face contest by a county mile. Pete was searching on his phone for something, and when he found it, he nudged Victoria and showed her the image.

'Seven of Nine, ma'am,' he whispered to Victoria, who glanced at the image for a second and turned to Mal.

'I take it, from that, you mean Mrs Southern is somewhat more attractive than her husband and that, together, they appear to be an incongruous match? If so, I think, unless there is any relevance to this observation, we should try and keep off the sexist comments. But please carry on, Mal.'

Mal gave a slight cough and took a sip of his coffee. 'Sorry, ma'am. Well, the only reason I mention it was to say that there may be a bit of friction between the two of them. That's Mr and Mrs Southern. Mrs Southern may be playing away from home now and again, if you catch my drift, and her key striker could be non-other than Paul Waites. She mentioned that he was a . . . ' He paused and consulted his notebook. 'A bit of a ladies' man. To which Phil Southern did not look too pleased. He then mentioned that Paul Waites could have a tendency towards violent outbursts, especially when he's had a few.'

'Anything to put Phil Southern in the frame for an abduction?'

'Nope, nothing,' replied Mal. 'He seems a bit of a boring bugger, but that's no crime these days, is it?'

Pete Sinclair looked across at his partner. 'No, because if it was, you'd have been put away long ago.'

'Didn't he have to leave Doncaster under a bit of a cloud some years back?' Everyone looked in the direction of Harry Burrows, who spoke without looking up from his phone.

Victoria took his phone away from him and placed it on the table. 'What are you talking about, Burrows? Who said Southern lived in Doncaster?'

'No, ma'am, not Doncaster the town. Doncaster Rovers, the football club. He used to play for them, and after a playing injury, he was dropped. But the club took him on as a scout for their academy. My brother was signed up by him. Apparently, by all accounts, he was quite a good striker in his day.'

'So, what was the cloud he left under?'

'Well, there were all kinds of rumours, my brother said. Mostly centred around him hanging around the showers a bit too long and getting a bit too close to some of the younger lads who he'd recruited for the club. If you know what I mean? Can I have my phone back now, ma'am?'

Victoria handed him his mobile back and wrote up a few notes under the name of Phil Southern. *Doncaster Rovers. Question mark. Record. Question mark.*

Turning to Mal and Pete, she gave them a quizzical look. 'And did either of you find any of this out when you visited the Southern family?'

'We knew he used to play for Donny Rovers, and he told us he left after his injury, but he said he was a coach, not a scout, and said nothing about any accusations,' Pete

Sinclair said, wincing at the same time and anticipating the flak from his boss.

'So, at worst, he lied, and at best was economical with the truth. I want you two back there this afternoon to find out about what the rumours were, and I want you to check out with the club if there was anything to substantiate them.' Victoria turned to the board and circled the name of Phil Southern in red. 'Let's see what Varsa comes up with.'

She then picked up her phone and called Varsa.

'Anything on the laptop yet, Varsa?' She waited. 'No worries. You can have all afternoon to get it singing. We need all it can tell us about young Jason's life. Okay, speak to you later.'

She ended the call and turned to Harry.

'You will be with me for the rest of the day, and I think it's about time we had a wee look inside Jason's sports bag before it goes off to forensics.'

***

Although Harry was new, a little wet behind the ears, and had not been personally selected by Victoria, he was pleased to be part of the MIT. He knew it would be hard at first to fit in, but he was determined to make an impression. He was suitably impressed by her so far, mainly by her appearance and no-nonsense manner with the team. Anyone, he thought, who could look that good and immaculately turned-out at this time in the morning would be impressive. In addition, Victoria's exploits in the capture of the serial killer Johnathan Fahey were well known across the whole of Yorkshire, and her reputation as a straightforward, down-to-earth cop preceded her wherever she went.

'Gloves, Harry, and get me a pair, please. They are over there on the table.'

Harry fetched a couple of pairs of blue surgical gloves from the box on the table and handed a pair to Victoria. Before struggling to get her hands into the close-fitting gloves, Victoria blew into them one by one. Harry watched and did the same. Once gloved up, Victoria slowly and carefully opened the zip on top of the sports bag. Sergeant Hallows came into the meeting room and stood to one side of the table where the bag was. Before removing anything from the bag, Victoria turned to Sergeant Hallows.

'Where was it found, George, and who found it?'

'Well, there's the odd thing. It wasn't found anywhere within the search area but stuffed into a litter bin in Tang Hall close to the shops. A young lad was chucking his fish and chip papers away and saw the bag sticking out of the bin. He pulled it out as it looked fairly new, found it had some boots and kit inside, and put two and two together and brought it over to us here at the ground.'

'Clever lad. I take it we have his name and address?'

George Hallows gave Victoria a slight frown and a quizzical look. 'I've not just got out of training, have I, ma'am?'

he said, looking at Harry, then handed her a piece of paper with a name and address on it.

'Sorry, George. Didn't mean to come across like that. Just a bit tired at the moment and have some stuff going on that's making me a bit tetchy.' She smiled at him. 'No offence?'

'None taken, ma'am.'

When the bag was opened, Victoria pointed to it and gestured to Harry to do the honours. 'Go on. You can take the stuff out, Harry. There's no way I'm handling a thirteen-year-old's sports kit. Not on your life.'

Harry took a look inside while Victoria held out the first evidence bag. First to emerge from the holdall were Jason's football boots — a pair of muddy Adidas boots thick with winter mud, smelling of autumn leaves and damp. Harry placed them carefully into the open evidence bag. Next to come out was a Manchester United away shirt, also damp and smelling of male sweat. Again, this went into an open evidence bag held by Victoria. Eventually, the holdall was emptied and it too was placed into its own plastic bag.

'Nothing too exciting in there,' Victoria said. She turned to Sergeant Hallows. 'Can one of your team get this over to forensics please, George?'

He picked up the series of plastic bags. 'Yes, of course. I'll tell them it's urgent but don't hold your breath. There have been two separate RTAs on the A64 last night and they are a little up against it.'

Harry was getting himself another coffee and turned to Sergeant Hallows. 'I wouldn't suppose forensics will be able to tell us much about anything from the bag. I don't suppose it matters too much that it has been found anyway.'

Victoria looked aghast at the new team member. 'You are probably correct that all it can tell us is that it belonged to Jason Waites, which, going by the name tag on it, we could have already deduced. However, you don't think there is anything significant about where it was found?'

'I'm not sure what you mean, ma'am. Where it was found?'

'Well, it wasn't found here or anywhere close by. It was found stuffed into a litter bin halfway down Tang Hall Lane. So, what does that tell us, Harry?'

Everyone in the room was now looking at young Harry Burrows. It was making him nervous.

'Erm . . . It could mean that someone found the bag and, after realising it contained nothing of any value, threw it in the bin. Or it might be that Jason threw it away.'

'Not too likely, that one, Harry. Why would he chuck his kit away?' Pete chipped in. 'But carry on. I think you're doing okay.'

'I suppose, if someone took him or picked him up, they could have dumped it. But there could be any number of reasons for it ending up in a bin on Tang Hall Lane.

What about if he was going to see someone? Like a friend from school? And something happened to Jason while he was on his way there or on his way back home, and someone just dumped it?'

Victoria was smiling at him and wagged her finger at Pete. 'Very good, Harry.' Harry returned the smile with what was more of a self-satisfied grin and a nod towards Pete.

'However, as you say, it is not really possible to be certain and we can only surmise how and why the bag ended up in the bin. But what it most likely tells us, Harry, is that at some stage, Jason found his way down Tang Hall Lane to the shops, most likely to meet someone else, and later disappeared in that area, and *not* around the football ground.' Mal looked up.

'Does that mean we should call off the hounds around here and move the search elsewhere, boss?'

'Not for the time being, not for the time being. We keep a presence at the ground until Wednesday, if nothing else turns up.' She turned to Harry. 'Okay, Dirty Harry, you're with Varsa for the time being. Nip back to Fulford Road and see if she needs help in tracing numbers and checking phone records, and in the morning, we're off to the lad's school, Archbishop Holgate's, to speak with the head.'

'Will they see us without an appointment?' Harry enquired.

Victoria gave him a sideways look. 'We are the police, for god's sake, investigating a missing child. We don't need an appointment. Archbishops is only a stone's throw away and it's almost lunchtime, so most of the staff should be free to speak to us. They'll be no one there today on Sunday, other than the caretaker, so there's little we can do. We will need to see Jason's class, or as many as we can, but that will likely have to be Tuesday or later as they'll need to be warned to have a responsible adult with them, and they may want to have a parent as opposed to a teacher.'

'Dirty Harry! I love it. Now that is really going to stick,' Mal Chambers said, shaking his head. 'Detective Constable "Dirty Harry" Burrows. Love it.' Pete and Mal laughed out loud.

Harry, on the other hand, was not laughing but thinking of the ribbing he was going to get from everyone over his new nickname.

'Sorry about that, Harry. It just came out, like,' Victoria said, with a slight grin and a chuckle.

Chapter 7

Archbishop Holgate's School was, prior to the move to a comprehensive system, one of the more prestigious grammar schools in York. It prided itself on its level of school discipline, its academic results, and its ability to retain much of the old grammar school ethos. Like all schools and other places where children were looked after these days, there was the locked entrance door to negotiate. And Archbishops was no different.

Victoria pressed the buzzer. There was no answer. She pressed it again, this time for a little longer. Again, it went unanswered. Two more goes and, each time, she pressed it a little harder. But still, no one answered the intercom. Harry then stepped in front of her and pressed it again, this time letting it buzz continually until a woman's voice crackled over the intercom to the left of the doorway.

'Thanks, Harry. I always think it takes a man to be able to press a buzzer properly,' said Victoria. The sarcasm went above his head as they both listened to the voice.

Chapter 7

'Yes?' was the only word spoken.

Victoria stepped across her DC and spoke directly into the microphone, 'Detective Chief Inspector Adams and Detective Constable Burrows. We would like a word with the head, please, or whoever is in charge if he's not available.'

She waited a second and the door buzzed, announcing they could enter through the set of double doors. Once inside, they passed through a short corridor adorned with student artwork and then through a second set of doors into the reception area. There they were greeted by a formidable-looking woman in her late fifties or possibly early sixties. She was smart and efficient looking in a royal-blue suit, hair in a Margaret Thatcher cut, and sporting a pair of "Nanna Mouskouri" glasses, over the top of which she looked at them. Her name badge identified her as Miss Shaftesbury, with the title "School Secretary" on a second badge underneath.

Before Victoria could say hello, the secretary spoke to both officers but only looked at Harry. 'I am not sure if the head is available to speak to visitors without an appointment. The lunch bell is about to go and he will be required to be on duty here in the reception area or possibly in the dining hall. Thank you.'

Victoria's frown showed she was at a loss to understand why the woman said thank you, but Harry seemed to take it completely in his stride, nodding at the woman behind the counter, who continued speaking.

'At lunch and morning breaks, he usually moves around the school, keeping an eye on the children. After lunch and for the next two periods, he will be over in the sixth form block teaching higher maths, and then the afternoon bell will sound and he will be outside marshalling the evening busses. Thank you. So, you see, it is neither convenient nor really possible for you to speak with him this afternoon. If you allow me to check his diary, I am sure he will be able to fit you in on Wednesday, as he keeps this day relatively free for visitors. I will, of course, need some idea of the purpose of your visit, so he can be prepared. Thank you.'

She spoke almost without taking a breath and her manner was clearly both obstinate and tenacious but, above all, inflexible. Victoria wondered why the woman kept repeating the words *thank you* almost at the end of every sentence, only serving to make her sound like some demented glove puppet. Both Victoria and Harry, although a little taken aback by the secretary's ability to speak without taking a breath, were suitably impressed and nodded at each other accordingly. Harry looked across at his new boss and thought for a moment he could actually see the hairs on the back of Victoria's neck starting to bristle.

Before speaking, Victoria looked around the room for a second or so, to give what she was about to say a little more gravitas and impact. 'I can understand your need to ensure the headmaster's routine is not interrupted . . . ' She looked closely at the badge to ensure she got her name correct. 'Miss

Shaftesbury. And that is to be commended. However, you must understand this is an urgent police matter and if you choose not to tell him we are here now, and I mean now, I will have no alternative other than to arrest and charge you under provisions of the Police Act 1996 Section 89 with obstructing the police in our investigation. An offence which carries a maximum sentence of one month's imprisonment. So, if you could go and fetch the headmaster and tell him that Detective Chief Inspector Adams and Detective Constable Burrows would like to speak with him, that would be most helpful. Thank you.' Victoria gave the school secretary one of her best smiles and waited.

'May I ask what it is in connection with?'

'You can certainly ask, Miss Shaftesbury, but I am afraid I cannot say at this time. Now go and get him, please. We have not got all day.' Victoria's voice was now becoming more than insistent and the school secretary certainly recognised the change.

She picked up the two cards that Victoria and Harry had placed on the counter and turned around. Then she turned back to look in their direction for a moment, and then continued walking in the direction of a door at the back of the reception area. She knocked and entered, closing the door behind her. The two officers could hear inaudible voices coming from inside.

'Well, you certainly put her in her place, ma'am,' said Harry. 'She was just a bit scary. Reminded me of when I was here.'

'You went to this school, Harry? You never thought to mention that?'

'No, ma'am, sorry. I didn't really think it was relevant.'

'And I suppose Miss Shaftesbury was the school secretary during your time here?'

'Aye. Everyone always said she had been here since it was opened by the Archbishop. Sorry.'

'Okay, Harry. Do you know if the head is still the same?'

'I'm not sure, ma'am. Could be. But who knows? It was a Mr Barnes. Baldy Barney, we used to call him.'

Victoria slowly shook her head at Harry. Miss Shaftesbury returned and opened a gate in the reception counter, gesturing for the pair to follow her around the counter. She stood by the door of the head's office and turned to the detectives, now with her air of superiority well and truly back and operating at full speed.

'Mr Barnes will see you now.'

Harry nodded at Victoria, and Miss Shaftesbury continued with her instructions.

'Please knock and go in when the green light comes on above the door.'

She pointed to a pair of lights above the door — one red, which was illuminated, and one green, which was not. She was about to walk away when she turned to face Victoria and Harry.

'Also, please be aware that we operate a strict, and I mean *strict*, security system in the school. If you need to visit any other locations around our school, you will be obligated to wear an identity badge that I, and only I, will furnish you with. This badge must be clearly displayed at all times. When you have finished speaking with Mr Barnes, you may collect the badges from myself. Do you understand?'

Harry nodded, while Victoria, not wanting to give the woman the satisfaction of a reply, knocked and opened the door immediately without waiting for the green light. *Who do they think we are? Bloody parachutists waiting to jump out of a damn plane, for god's sake*?

As the pair entered, Mr Barnes stood up behind his desk—an oak construction of immense proportions that matched the fully oak-panelled room. On the opposite side to where Mr Barnes stood, there were two low armchairs, towards which he gestured for the pair to sit. Harry sat down while Victoria remained standing. There was a power play at work here that she was determined to win and sitting in a chair that barely enabled you to see who was sitting across the desk from you was, in her eyes, going to put you at a distinct disadvantage.

'Welcome to Archbishops . . . ' He looked at the card on his desk. 'Chief Inspector Adams. Hope Miss Shaftesbury hasn't been caught pilfering the stationary again.' He chuckled at his poor attempt at humour.

Sitting down, the headteacher smiled at Victoria and she wondered if indeed he got out from behind his desk as often as Miss Shaftesbury had intimated. Well into his sixties and, she thought, not too far from retirement, the balding Mr Barnes was dressed in a pin-striped suit that had clearly seen better days. He had a waistcoat that was partly opened and straining under an ample paunch, and his unfastened tie, festooned with a neat array of stains, hung on the outside of the waistcoat. What first came to mind when looking at him was that of the absentminded professor who needed looking after. He managed to take his gaze away from Victoria for a second and turned in the direction of Harry.

'And how lovely it is to see you after all these years, Burrows. I see you have done very well for yourself. A policeman. Who would have thought it?' Then, turning to Victoria, he smiled again. 'So, Chief Inspector, how can we be of assistance to the North Yorkshire Constabulary? And please, take a seat.'

Victoria remained standing.

'Well, Mr Barnes, we are investigating the disappearance of one of your students. A lad called Jason Waites. He hasn't been seen since yesterday teatime. We are, at this stage, treating it as a missing persons enquiry. And given the fact he is only thirteen and going missing like this is wholly out of character, we are treating it as a serious incident. I am sure you will understand. We need to speak to his form teacher and all of his classmates, if possible. His teacher today and his friends on Monday. Can that be arranged?'

Barnes rubbed his chin and looked from Victoria to Harry, and then back to Victoria. 'Well yes, of course we can arrange that. Do you suspect foul play of some kind?'

'We are not able to say at this time, but we need to speak with his teacher today and we would ask that you don't mention the enquiry to the students until we arrive on Monday morning. We would need a small room set aside for this purpose, along with one of the teaching or pastoral staff present for the interviews. Would there be any problems with this?'

Mr Barnes recognised this was not really a request. He pressed the intercom buzzer to alert Miss Shaftesbury, who entered the room almost before the buzzer stopped.

'Could you take the two detectives across to the sports hall to speak to Mr Newton and get someone to cover his lunch duties please, Margot?'

She tutted and left the room.

Victoria turned to Mr Barnes and held out her hand. 'Many thanks, Mr Barnes. We appreciate your assistance and will try not to disrupt the working of your school any more than we have to.' After shaking his hand, she placed one of her cards on the desk. 'We would like to start around ten o'clock on Monday morning with the student interviews, if that is okay with you. Also, could you give us some idea of how many students there are in the class? As we may need to bring over some more officers to conduct the interviews in a timely manner.'

'I will need to check on accurate numbers, but in Jason's year, it is not too large a cohort, and there would be no more than thirty in his class and around seventy or seventy-five or so in his year group. Should you wish to speak with all of them?'

Victoria eventually managed to pry her hand away from Barnes's grasp and told him that they would need to speak to the whole year group if possible, so she would be bringing in a team to help. She thanked him again and followed the secretary into the reception.

Barnes offered his hand to Harry. 'Thank you, Burrows, and nice to see you again.'

Harry, who looked decidedly nervous about taking the offered hand, nevertheless shook it. 'Nice to see you too, sir,' Harry lied, and was immediately inwardly kicking himself for calling his old headmaster *sir*. Barnes smiled back at his ex-pupil. Harry had clearly lost this round of the power play and thought he still had a lot to learn from his new boss.

Back in reception, Miss Shaftesbury had the ID badges ready for the pair and pushed a ledger in front of Victoria across the counter.

'Please enter the number on the badge. Thank you. It is in the top righthand corner by the large letter "V" which signifies you are a visitor to the school. Please then sign the visitor's book, both of you, and print your name next to your signature. Thank you.'

Before they had finished signing in, Miss Shaftesbury was around the other side of the counter and gesturing for them to follow her.

'Please come this way and try to keep up. Thank you.'

As she moved at a brisk pace into the corridor, Victoria flashed a look at her new bag man and slowly shook her head. It was clear that when this woman gave instructions, they were the most important sets of orders any individual would be given in their life.

'She hasn't changed one little bit since the day I left,' Harry whispered to his boss. 'Still a real pain in the arse.'

Miss Shaftesbury spoke without looking back or altering her pace along the corridor, 'Did you say something, Burrows?'

'Nothing important, Miss Shaftesbury, and it's Detective Burrows or failing that Mr Burrows, please. If you can manage to remember that?' He paused. 'Thank you.'

Harry licked his index finger and chalked up an imaginary score on the board in favour of himself. Victoria held in a chuckle.

The detectives were led outside into a large, tarmacked play area and across into the school's sports hall — a large, soulless building that was overheated and smelled of human perspiration. Once inside the main hall, the noise was intense. A game of football was underway with mixed teams of around eight or so. Two teams were playing while what looked like a further two were sitting along the edge of the gym. Each team wore different coloured bibs over their shirts and, it seemed to Victoria, were running and darting around like ricocheting bullets. Everyone was yelling at once, in such a way that it was impossible to hear your own mind.

As the two detectives and the school secretary stood on the periphery of the gym floor, the teacher in charge immediately noticed their presence and shouted over to one of the taller girls who was sitting down. He offered her his whistle and gestured for her to take over the role of referee. He was a tall, gangly individual with a clipped beard and gelled hair. Victoria put him at about forty-five trying to look thirty-five, and Harry immediately waved to him with a broad grin that was returned in full. As he approached, he pushed the double door open and ushered them outside into a waiting area, which was decidedly quieter than the sports hall.

'Hi. How can I help?'

Miss Shaftesbury spoke up. 'We are sorry to interrupt your class, Mr Newton, but these two people are police officers and they would like to speak to you about one of your form class. I'll leave them with you. Thank you.' She turned to Victoria and Harry. 'When you have finished, please remember to return your badges to the reception. Thank you.'

Before either of the officers could speak, she had turned away and left them.

'Thanks for taking the time to speak to us, Mr Newton. This is Detective Constable Burrows, who you may remember from his time here, and I am Detective Chief Inspector Adams from the North Yorkshire Major Incident Team. I understand that Jason Waites is one of your form group. Is that correct?'

Chris Newton nodded and smiled in Harry's direction. 'Yes, correct. He's one of mine, but he's not in today so it may be a bit of a wasted journey.'

'We know he isn't in school today, Mr Newton, as he has been missing since yesterday evening. We would simply like a bit of background on him, if possible. How he's getting on at school, friends, who he hangs out with, any girlfriends. You know the kind of stuff. Anything that may help us in tracking him down.'

Paul Newton glanced back through the round viewing window in the double doors. 'Hang on a minute, will you?'

And he turned and returned to the hall. He took a second whistle from his pocket, gave it one shrill blast, and the game came to a halt. 'Mo! Can you get them back into the changing rooms, please? The bell's not too far off and I'll be tied up here for a moment.'

The taller young woman who had taken over the refereeing gave him a thumbs-up and began ushering the children towards the exit.

'Sorry. You might want to stand to the side as they come through. You don't want to get trampled on. It's lunchtime and you know what kids are like when they're hungry.'

Victoria and Harry stood out of the way and the children exited the hall, each one eyeing the pair up and down as they left. When the last one had left the building, Victoria turned back to Chris Newton.

'Jason Waites?' she said.

'Well, where to start? Well, first thing, he wouldn't be having a girlfriend. That's for sure.'

'Why's that then?' asked Harry.

Mr Newton turned to him. 'Because Jason's gay.' Without letting this statement sink in, he continued, 'As for friends, he has many, but none that you would describe as close. He works hard at his studies, is a little quiet, but fits in, as they say, and doesn't seem to have any issues.'

'What makes you say he's gay?' Victoria asked.

'Because he told me so. He asked that I keep it from his parents and, as it didn't seem to be a problem for him and he had managed to come out and tell me, I thought I should respect his request. It seemed only fair to the lad. Anyway, none of my business really.'

Victoria pursued the line of questioning. 'Why do you think he chose you to come and tell?'

'I'm not sure. We get on well together and he just must've wanted to tell someone. I guess he felt comfortable knowing I wouldn't make it common knowledge.'

'And have you done that?'

'Done what?'

'Kept it from common knowledge?'

'Yes, of course. When any of the kids want to tell me anything a bit personal, I always say something like, "Well, you can tell me anything." But if I think there's an issue of protection, I may not be able to keep it to myself and need to pass it on. They mostly get that and tell me anyway. In Jason's case, there was no issue. He did come over somewhat nervous at the last parents' evening, and I thought he might have thought I would let something slip about his sexuality to his mum and dad.'

'Why do you think he was worried?'

'Have you met his mum and dad?'

'Yes.'

'Well, what did you think?'

'Why don't you tell us what you think about them?'

The conversation was interrupted when Victoria's phone started to vibrate, alerting her to a text. As she was expecting to hear from Miriam at some stage, she took the phone from her pocket and gave it a little smile. It was from Miriam.

'Sorry. Do you mind? I need to check this.'

She turned her back and looked at the message, immediately kicking herself for being so stupid. How could it be from Miriam when her phone had been stolen by those two pricks in Birmingham? Nevertheless, she opened it.

Well, hello there. Long time no speak, as they say. How are you doing? It was nice to meet with your other half yesterday, but she's such a grumpy one, isn't she? Anyway, I hear congratulations are in order. You two are soon to be a three. I suppose you are going to need a new wardrobe, aren't you, my dear? But you'll still look hot to me. Even while carrying the youngster around. Take care now and I'll be in touch soon. Love Jean . . . And say hi to Sean for me, will you? xxx

'Bastard,' she said out loud and, feeling a chill run through her, she turned back to the two men, who were looking at her curiously.

Harry spoke first with some level of concern. 'Bad news?'

'No, it's okay.' She appeared distracted. 'I think we're done here. Thanks for your time, Mr Newton, and could you be on hand on Monday when we come to interview Jason's classmates?'

'Yes, of course. No problem.' They shook hands and Mr Newton put his arm around Harry's shoulders as they were leaving the hall. 'Hey! It's great to see you again, Harry. Now you take care and best of luck with finding Jason. He's a good kid, for sure.'

'Yep. We'll do our best. And it's good to see you too, sir.'

He immediately realised, yet again, that seven years of calling someone *sir* is a hard habit to break.

Chapter 8

Outside, Victoria walked over to her car and climbed into the driver's seat, impatiently tapping the steering wheel until Harry eventually came to sit beside her. She switched the engine on and was about to move off when Harry stopped her.

'Hold on a bit, ma'am. The badges. We need to return them.'

She lifted her lanyard over her head and handed it to him. 'Aye. Best not to cause the good Miss Shaftesbury a coronary, hey?'

Harry took both ID badges back inside the school and placed them on the reception desk as Miss Shaftesbury was not about. *Better get while the getting's good*, he thought, and left without signing the visitors' book, which was nowhere to be seen. When Harry returned to the car, Victoria's impatience was clearly visible. Without speaking, she put the car into gear and gunned it, leaving slight skid marks on the gravel car park. No words were spoken on their journey to the Badger Hill Sports ground and on arrival they were greeted by Varsa who had brought her own laptop down to the temporary ops room, eager to be at the centre of all that was going on. Once inside, Victoria pulled up a chair next to where Varsa was busying away at her keyboard.

'Varsa, can you trace where a phone is located if I give you the number?'

'Only if it is switched on, ma'am. If it's off, then no.'

Victoria thought for a moment and opened her phone to show Miriam's contact details. She realised it was a long shot but placed the phone down on the desk in front of Varsa.

'You want me to track your wife's movements?'

'Not exactly. Rather the whereabouts of her phone.' Victoria thought this needed a bit more explanation. 'You see, she lost it and I think someone may be using it, so could you have a try for me?'

'Sure, I'll have a go. Do you want to leave it with me?'

'Any chance you could have a crack at it now?'

Varsa could detect that this was more than just a missing phone. She smiled at her boss and opened up the program to track its whereabouts.

'It might take a while.'

'Sure, thanks.'

Victoria's phone rang and, this time, she double-checked the screen to see who was calling. She didn't recognise the number and felt uncertain as to whether to answer it or not.

'Detective Chief Inspector Adams, North Yorkshire Major Incident Team.'

'Well, get you with the full title.' Victoria recognised Miriam's voice immediately, which lifted her spirits, and she visibly relaxed. 'Hi, sweetheart. How are you? Where are you? What are you doing? And can you pick me up in about twenty minutes?'

'Better now I'm speaking to you. I'm at Badger Hill Sports and Social Club. We're looking for the missing thirteen-year-old lad. And yes, of course. Station?'

'Yep. See you in twenty or so. We've just passed Doncaster.'

'I almost didn't answer your call as I didn't recognise the number.'

'Aye sorry, Vicky. That nice police sergeant from the transport police came to see me, just to check some details of what happened, and he gave me a lift back to the railway station in the centre of town. He hung on with me until my train came, and while we were waiting, he took me to the *Phones R Us* shop on the platform. Sorted out a new phone for me, so I could call if I needed. Such a nice bloke.'

'Oh, wow, that was good of him. He didn't have to do that for you. We could do with a few more like him. See you in twenty. Love you.'

'Love you too. See you soon.'

Victoria turned to Harry before hanging up. 'Harry, would you mind hanging on here until I get back? I need to pop over to the station to pick someone up and drop them off before coming back here. Or Varsa can run you back to Fulford Road, if you like.'

Harry looked at Varsa and then back to Victoria. 'I'll hang on here, if that's okay? I have a few calls to make and I could make a start on the list of names of Jason's teammates here at the club. There may be some that aren't at the school and we don't want to miss any out. I'll also have another word with our young friend who found Jason's sports kit. He may have remembered something from this morning. And anyway, we will definitely need a full statement from him at some stage. Also, I thought it might be worth a shot to contact the local bus services as they all have cameras now. Who knows, the lad might pop up on one of them.'

Victoria smiled at him and winked at Varsa. 'See, Varsa, don't be put off by the gelled hair and sharp suits. The lad thinks as well.'

Varsa nodded an *absolutely*, and Victoria left them both. Harry wasn't sure if he had received a compliment or not from his new boss, but decided to put it down as one.

On her way to pick up Miriam, Victoria thought that it would make sense in the morning to scale down the search around the sports ground, as it was highly likely that the abduction of Jason Waites happened somewhere away from the area in which they were now looking. The scene had been trodden over by too many feet to throw up any useful forensics, and if she was right in her assumptions, there was little to gain from turning every blade of grass over on the football and rugby pitches.

As she pulled into York Station, she checked the time on her dashboard clock. *If it's on time, I can park in the short waiting area.* Before she could get out of the car, there was a tap on her window and the familiar face of Miriam was smiling at her. Victoria wound down the front window on the passenger side and pressed the button that sprung open the boot of the car.

'Wow, that train must have had a following wind. Chuck your bag in there, sweetheart, and get in. I've missed you so much.'

'Missed me? I've only been gone a couple of days, for heaven's sake.'

'I know, but with everything that's happened, I've been so worried.'

Miriam put her bag in the boot of the car and closed the lid. Coming around to the passenger side, she climbed in and pulled down the vanity mirror.

'Well, how do I look? Not too bad when you consider how the other fella ended up. I managed to give him a right good old slap alright. The dirty bugger, saying stuff like that in a public place. I mean honestly, who do these people think they are?'

She turned and looked at Victoria and laughed. Victoria put her arm around her and hugged her close. She always played the tough cop but sometimes just wanted to hold onto Miriam and feel her closeness. She gave her a kiss and then sat back in her seat, taking a quick look in the mirror and checking her mascara was not about to give her away. Eventually putting on her game face, she turned to Miriam.

'I don't really think it's a laughing matter, Miriam. If you're correct and one of them was Jonathan Fahey, well, the man is a multiple murderer, and you've seen what he's capable of. I am pretty sure the other one must have been Walsh, a prison officer who was assigned to look after Fahey on his visit to the hospital. Together they would make up a pretty obnoxious pair alright.' Victoria was still speaking as she pulled out of the station car park.

'Well, I'm dead sure one of them was Fahey. I've never seen the other bloke so I can't say for certain. But Fahey's obnoxious mug will stay with me forever.'

Miriam was searching in her handbag for a bottle of painkillers. 'Anyway, what was it you wanted to tell me? Something about the case you're working at the moment?'

'No. Nothing like that. You need to brace yourself though.'

'Go on, spit it out. What is it?'

Victoria smiled a little smugly to herself and then beamed at Miriam. Savouring the moment a little longer, she eventually gave out. 'We're going to have a baby. Yes, Miriam, a baby.'

Victoria couldn't get the words out properly without giggling and laughing as she spoke. Miriam looked across at her wife and didn't speak.

'Well! Cat got your tongue?' said Victoria. 'What do you say about that? How does it feel to be a Mum-to-be?'

Miriam beamed from ear to ear. 'Pull the car over. Stop. Go on, pull over.'

Victoria pulled into a taxi rank and, almost before she could apply the handbrake, Miriam flung her arms around her, which was not easy while secured by the seat belt. She hugged and kissed her while tears ran down her face.

'Oh, how I do love you. This is the best thing that could have happened. The very best. How long are you? When is it due? Boy or girl? Are you sure? Oh, fantastic. *Fantastic.* How do you feel?'

The embrace and celebrations were interrupted when a man tried to climb into the back seat of the car and ask to be taken to Malton.

'Sorry, mate," said Victoria. "We're off shift now and going off to celebrate big time.'

'Malton is at least a forty-quid fare. You can't turn that down, surely?'

'I think we can, and don't call me Shirley.'

The pair of women in the front seat laughed out loud and Victoria turned around.

'So sorry, my friend, you couldn't possibly afford to pay me enough to stop this celebration. Out you get. Try the next cab.'

He looked somewhat perplexed but got out of the car, tutting and shaking his head, while the two women laughed and whooped together.

They drove on in relative silence, giving each other a glance now and again, accompanied by the wide grins of people who know everything is going to be okay. As they turned onto the ring road on their way home, Miriam asked where they were going.

'I'm taking you home so that you can put your feet up.'

'I thought you were in the middle of looking for a missing little lad?'

'We are, but I need to take you home first.'

'Nope, you can do that later. You get back to the incident room. I can put my feet up later today.'

'If you're sure?'

'Of course I am. So tell me how your new case is progressing.'

'Nothing much to tell at this stage. But you go first. Tell me how you're feeling after the incident, and how it all happened.'

Miriam thought for a moment and looked down at her feet. 'I'm okay, I think. But I would seriously like to see Fahey back behind bars sooner rather than later, if possible. I'm really glad I had Jane with me. She stayed for a while at the hospital and then set off back on a later train to Leeds. I must send her some flowers as a thank you. My head still hurts and I hope this shiner goes down soon. I look like I've just gone ten rounds with Rocky Balboa.'

'Look, I really think I should drop you off at home and then get back to the temporary incident room in Badger Hill.'

'If that's what you want to do. But I don't mind coming with you. I don't really relish the idea of being on my own at the moment, if you understand, sweetheart?'

'Sure I do. I have more or less decided to move the temporary incident room back to Fulford anyway. Although the missing lad was last seen at the Badger Hill sports ground, I think it's a distinct possibility that he travelled some distance before he went missing, and the search teams haven't come up with anything useful. I might give it until tomorrow, but no need for all the portacabins and stuff at the ground. Probably a bit of overkill. We've found his sports bag and that's gone off to forensics. But I don't think it will tell us anything. I say found, but it was handed in by a young lad. Harry's going to have a chat with the boy who found it.'

'Who's Harry?'

'Oh, he's the latest addition to the squad. A little imposition from Hot Chocolate. For once, she seems to have come up trumps. He's slotted in well and, apart from him looking like he's stepped out of the covers of some new-century lads' mag, he seems to know what he's doing. I've even given him a nickname already. Dirty Harry.'

'Oh, that's cruel.'

When Victoria and Miriam arrived outside the incident room in Badger Hill, Harry was bouncing up and down like the proverbial Tigger. He was speaking to Victoria as he was opening her door, and she missed half of what he was saying. All she managed to catch was, 'We've got something. A sighting of Jason.'

'Okay, calm down, Harry. Let's get inside and tell me what you've found.'

Again, he was talking as they climbed the steps into the portacabin. 'We have a sighting on a bus camera on Hull Road close to the Black Bull Hotel.'

'Jason was on a bus? Going in which direction?'

'No, he wasn't on the bus. He was sitting in the bus shelter when the bus pulled up but didn't get on it.'

'What time was this, Harry? And for god's sake, calm down.'

They were inside the building now and Harry consulted his notebook. 'Seventeen twenty-two is the time on the bus camera.'

Varsa had got the projection screen up and running and the video from the bus camera was showing on the large screen. 'Okay, Varsa, play it for us.'

Varsa nodded and acknowledged the presence of Miriam with a look in her direction with pursed lips and a mouthed, "Ouch," at her bruises. Victoria sat down and Miriam went over to the table to make them a coffee. Varsa hovered the cursor arrow over the play button for a second.

'Ready?' She waited before pressing play. 'It's only a short clip taken from the camera positioned above the driver's seat pointing at the door.'

The film started with a shot of the door sliding open and three passengers getting on the bus. The first, a young woman, probably in her mid-teens, who flashed a card — probably a bus pass — at the driver and walked out of shot. The second, a middle-aged woman who paid, took her ticket, and moved away. And, finally, a much older man, who said something to the driver before showing him his bus pass, then also moved on down the bus. Before the doors closed, Varsa paused the film.

'Just before the bus moves off, you can see Jason stand up and walk towards the lefthand side of the shelter before disappearing out of shot.'

She let it play on and Victoria leaned forward to stop it again as the young lad stood up. He was wearing a grey hoodie that could be seen under his blue puffer jacket and what looked like a pair of tracksuit bottoms with Adidas stripes down the sides.

'Look!' she said. 'He's acknowledging someone out of shot. He's raising his right hand to say hello and smiling. It's clearly someone he recognises. I would bet a month of Sundays it's a pre-arranged meeting. He doesn't look surprised, but he does look pleased to see whoever it is.'

Miriam came around to look at the screen and nodded. 'Sure looks like he's greeting someone, alright.'

'But who? For god's sake?' Victoria said. 'We can't see who it is. Have we traced the three who got on the bus at that stop yet?'

'No, not yet, boss,' Varsa answered. 'Harry was talking to the bus company earlier, but they can't say who these three were.'

'So, we're no further on then. All we know is that it looks like he arranged to meet someone at the bus stop at this time, but we don't have a scoobies who it was.' Victoria sat down and took the coffee Miriam had made for her.

'Well, not strictly speaking, ma'am,' Harry said.

'What do you mean not strictly speaking?'

'Well, a number of these buses on routes in York that had experienced RTA set-ups in recent months have been fitted with rear-facing cameras. It's possible that this bus might just have had them. If it did, then we may get an image of who was behind the bus and meeting Jason. It could have been someone in a car or on a moped, or just someone walking.'

Victoria looked at Harry somewhat incredulously. 'Well, if that's the case, what are you sitting here for? Get onto the bus company again and find out.'

'Yes, ma'am. Right away. Am onto it as we speak.' He put his coat on and disappeared out of the door.

After Harry had left, Victoria made the round of phone calls to have the office moved back to the main Police HQ on Fulford Road and scale down the search for Jason around the sports club. It was clear he had moved away from the immediate vicinity of the grounds. As he was last seen at a bus stop some two and a half miles away, the search needed widening. This development meant that it could be coordinated just as well from the HQ in Fulford Road, if not more effectively.

Once all the ends had been tied up, she drove Miriam home in relative silence. The pair eventually settled into their evening meal. On this occasion, neither of them was really up to cooking, so they ordered a takeaway from the local Chinese and washed it down with a bottle of Chablis to celebrate.

'We need to leave it a few months yet before we announce to the world about the coming addition, Miriam.'

'Of course, love. Can I tell my mom though?'

'Yes, I think we can rely on her not to go blabbing the news to all and sundry.'

They'd finished their meal and drank no more than a glass of wine each, sitting with their feet up watching the evening news, when Victoria's phone rang. She glanced at the caller.

'I hope this is good news, Harry?'

'Well, yes and no. The good news is the bus *does* have rear-facing cameras and they were switched on and working that evening.'

'And the bad news?'

Chapter 8

'The guy who's responsible for downloading the traffic cams has gone off sick and no one seems to be able to find the discs.'

'Oh, for god's sake. Have you been down to the bus depot in person? Why can't they contact this bloke and ask him what he's done with the bloody films? It makes no sense.'

'No, ma'am, I mean . . . I've only spoken to them on the phone and I never asked them about calling the guy. I just thought . . . ' Harry paused. 'Do you think I should go there even if the guy's not about?'

'I most certainly do, young man. You take yourself down there now and speak to whoever is in charge. If they can't find the discs, you find out where this fella lives, go and speak to him, even if he's at death's door, and you find the bloody films. Do you understand, Detective?'

'Yes, ma'am. I'm on it right away.'

Victoria ended the call and took a sip of wine.

'You were a bit hard on the lad there, Vics, so you were.'

'Do you think so?' She thought for a second. 'He needs a good kick up the backside, that one. He'll make a good detective at some stage, but he needs a tight rein and a good old nudge in the right direction from time to time. If he comes up with anything, I'll put a smiley face in his report.'

'Oh, you're a hard woman, you are, Victoria Adams.'

It was past ten when Harry eventually rang back. Victoria was about to get ready for an early night. She swiped the screen to answer.

'Go ahead, Harry. What have we got? And sorry for the slight telling off before.'

'Okay, ma'am, no worries. I eventually managed to track him down. The guy who looks after the tapes, like. The bugger wasn't sick at all but taking an extra day before his holidays started. It was a good job I called round as he was flying to Benidorm at four in the morning. But I took him down to the depot and he dug out the CD for the bus we needed on the night Jason went missing. I took the film round to Fulford Road nick.'

'And?'

'And what, ma'am?'

'And don't tell me you haven't looked at it?'

'No. I mean yes, I haven't looked at it yet. Do you want me to look at it now? I'm still at the station.'

'Send it to my email and I will log on from home and have a look. But as one of the detectives on the case, you're allowed to look at it yourself. No one will mind. And good work, Harry. Good work.'

'Thanks, ma'am. I will send it to you straight away. Bye for now, and I'll see you tomorrow?'

'Yep, for sure. See you later.'

The call was ended this time by Harry, and Victoria fired up her laptop and logged on to her work email. There was the usual stack of requests and reminders from Hot Chocolate asking for updates, man-hour calculations, and various reports, some of which Victoria didn't really know what she was being asked to produce. Eventually, the email from Harry appeared with its attachment. She downloaded it, hoping that it had been edited just to show the time sequence at the Hull Road stop.

Thank god for that, she thought. Harry had cut down the recording to just before Jason was sighted at the stop. The film was good quality and she could see the timer on the video clicking away as the bus pulled to a halt. Then nothing. Other than a cat crossing the road about ten feet from the rear of the bus.

Brave animal, she thought, *crossing a dual carriageway in the traffic and in the dark.*

Her hopes began to dwindle that anything useful would come out of the film until a small van pulled up behind the bus. It was a dirty, mustard-coloured Citroen Berlingo and it stopped up close to the bus, obscuring its number plate and the driver. Victoria was again disappointed. However, just as the bus pulled away, it revealed both the number plate of the van and the driver, who then graciously leaned forward and waved to someone on the pavement, then sat back. It was only a split second, but he was clearly visible and could be identified from a still. She then noticed a steady flash of lights as the bus's indicators came on to enable it to pull out into traffic. As it moved slowly into the bus lane, the figure of Jason Waites came into shot.

He gestured to the driver of the van with a wave of a raised hand, opened the passenger door, and climbed in.

His face went out of view, but she could just about see him putting on his seat belt. The problem was that the angle of the camera at the rear of the bus only now showed the van roof, and although you could tell there were two people in it, you could not make out what they were doing. The bus must have stopped to allow some cars to pass on its off side. So the camera was still showing the van stopped in the pull-in of the bus stop.

What happened next made Victoria stop the clip and re-wind it a number of times. As the bus managed to pull away into traffic, the angle of its rear camera adjusted to show the two occupants much more clearly. It was plain to see. As Jason sat next to this other young man, as the driver checked his side mirror and indicated to pull out, Jason clearly leaned across and kissed him on the cheek.

Chapter 9

SOME TIME HAD PASSED SINCE Jason found out he was not alone, but he had no way of telling how long it had been. Having company should have given him some solace and comfort, but it did neither. He thought about his fellow young captive, who was only nine years old, and wondered how lonely he must have been feeling before Jason's arrival.

'Thomas! It's Jason.' *How stupid is that?* he thought. *Who else would it be?* 'Do you know how long you've been here?' *Or where here even is?*

There was a period of silence and Jason could just about hear Thomas moving around. He could also make out the chains scraping along the pipes as Thomas moved a little closer to him.

'Don't know. I started counting when I woke up the first time and got to one thousand, but then fell asleep and I don't know how many sleeps I've had or how long they were. So I don't know how long it's been. I think you came yesterday, but I'm not sure.'

'Do you know why we are here or who brought us?' There was silence from the nine-year-old. 'Well, do you?'

'I don't want to say.'

'What do you mean, you don't want to say? Do you know who is keeping us here?'

Thomas sniffed a little, accompanied by a muffled sob. 'They are bad men. Bad men and they come . . . ' He paused and sniffed again. 'They come sometimes when you are asleep and wake you up.' Again, he sniffed and this time gave a cough. 'And when they wake you up, they give you a needle and then take you away.'

'Where do they take you and what for, mate?'

Thomas didn't reply but began to cry and sniff a lot more.

'Well, what happens when they take you away? They must bring you back afterwards because you're still here.'

There was a further silence and Jason thought that Thomas might be trying to summon up the courage to say more.

'They wake you up and hurt you and it's not nice. Sometimes they take your picture. Sometimes there are more men and they all hurt you.'

Thomas fell silent again and Jason thought it might be best not to press him further on the details of the ordeal. No more questions for the time being. He sat back against the wall and licked his lips. They were dry and cracking by now, and he could feel his stomach rumbling. It didn't seem that long ago that he and Terry were planning to get a burger. He wondered if Terry had also been taken.

What happened to Terry? Is he somewhere else held like this? Or worse?

But his immediate concern was for his hunger and his thirst. What he would give for a coke out of his fridge at home and some of his mum's shepherd's pie. He could almost taste it. He slumped down, listening to the whimpers coming from young Thomas, and put his head in his hands again, determined not to let the despair and hopelessness of his circumstances get the better of him. It was reasonable to assume that whoever his — and Thomas's — captors were, they obviously wanted to keep them alive. At least for the time being. And if they wanted to keep them alive, they would need to give them something to eat and drink. These thoughts had the effect of slightly consoling him, but only for a couple of minutes, as it prompted the question ... *But when? How long will it be before we're fed and watered?*

Thomas was now quietly sobbing in the distant darkness, and Jason wished he would stop. Suddenly, he heard what sounded like a lock being undone, followed by a scraping noise.

Jason looked towards where he thought the sound was coming from. A crack of light appeared high up and to his right. He squinted, but could only make out the light and little else. As it grew, he could see the silhouette of a person standing at the top of what looked like a staircase against an open door. The light was coming through the opening and the person looked to be carrying something that looked like a tray in both hands. *This could be something to eat*, he thought. The shape placed the tray down on the floor at the top of the stairs and then, all too soon, the light was extinguished. Jason clearly heard the door close with a bang, plunging their room into total darkness yet again.

Then a torch flicked on, its beam searching the room. Jason could hear the person coming down the stairs slowly and the torchlight grew in intensity. He realised that it was one of those head torches like his dad had. All he could make out was that the person was tall and rangy, and making his way over to Jason. As the light got closer, he had to look away as it was hurting his eyes. But he realised that if he looked just to one side of the light, he had a better chance of making out what was going on. The person, who Jason was assuming was a man, bent down in front of him and placed a tray on the floor. The torch then illuminated the tray of food.

His heart jumped for joy. On the tray was a Big Mac, fries, and a coke.

Then the person spoke in a kind of sing-song way as if he was reciting a nursery rhyme. 'Here comes the muffin man, the muffin man, the muffin man … Here comes the muffin man who lives down Drury Lane.' Then he gave a little chuckle.

Jason didn't understand.

The man sighed and took a deep breath. The torchlight hurt Jason's eyes again. 'Now eat it all up like a good boy. We're going to need you in good health when all the fun starts. Aren't we, Jason?'

The man gave a further little chuckle and pushed the tray closer with his foot. He turned to face where Thomas was cowering in the corner of his small space.

'Nothing for you, little one, I'm afraid. Well, nothing except one of those little shots you like so much. Now keep still and I promise it won't hurt a bit.'

'What are you doing to him? Leave him alone,' Jason protested.

'Now, you keep your nose out and mind your own business, Jason. Or you'll be next. There was a firmness in the man's voice, but Jason detected it to be younger than his dad's. It was definitely a man's, but that of a younger man. Possibly not too much older than himself.

'What do you want from us? And what are you giving Thomas?'

'I have just told you to be quiet. Now shut the fuck up.'

In the beam of the torchlight, Jason could see the man injecting something into Thomas's upper arm. He stood back to let whatever it was take effect. Jason watched Thomas slump forward a little. The man then took a bunch of keys from his pocket and unlocked the young child, who needed considerable help standing. The man dragged him over to the stairs and helped him climb to the top. Jason estimated there were no more than twenty steps. When the door finally opened and then closed, Jason felt very alone. He hoped above all that his newfound friend was going to be okay.

He picked up the McDonald's bag and opened his burger. Somehow, the fries and burger didn't taste anything like as good as they should. Although the food took away his hunger and the drink quenched his thirst, the feeling of euphoria was short-lived. He could only think of one thing. *What is happening to Thomas?*

Chapter 10

VICTORIA SAT BACK, LOOKING AT the image on the laptop. She decided to ring Harry back. The phone rang a few times and went to voicemail. Victoria decided to leave a message.

'Hello, Harry, it's Chief Inspector Adams here again. I was wondering if you'd managed to have a word with the young lad who handed the sports bag in yet. And if so, what he had to say for himself? Where exactly did he find it and did he remove anything from it? Like possibly Jason's mobile phone?' She stopped for a moment. 'And I don't want to be teaching you to suck eggs, Harry, but have you run a make on the number plate of the van that picked up Jason at the bus stop?'

Before she could end the call, it was answered, not by him but by Varsa.

'Hello, ma'am. No and yes is the answer to both questions. Har's making a brew at the moment. He says he hasn't spoken to the lad who found the bag, but I ran the make on the registration and we have the details. Do you want me to send them over to you, ma'am?'

Victoria was a little taken aback to hear Varsa answer Harry's phone, wondering why, and where they were. 'Yes. Yes, send the details over, Varsa. Thanks.' She paused before carrying on. 'Are you both still at the incident room? It's getting a bit late, don't you think?'

'I gave Harry a lift back to Fulford and we kind of got talking a bit. He's okay when you get to know him. Quite nice really. Do you want us to go and speak to this lad and/or follow up on the owner of the van tonight?'

'No. No, not for now, but send me the info on the van.' Just then, her laptop pinged to announce the arrival of an email. 'And hang on for a minute please, Varsa.' Victoria opened it. Varsa was nothing if not fast on the draw. It read, *Registered Keeper: Terence Greenwood. Address: 115 Tang Hall Lane.* She also noted that this individual was almost nineteen years old, making him more than five years Jason's senior.

Victoria picked up her phone to speak again to Varsa.

'No. Don't make any moves towards either of them yet. I have a feeling we may need to have more than just a word with him and it can hold until morning. Ask Harry if he knows the address exactly, will you? Looks like it could be a flat. Ask him if he knows exactly where the entrance is and the best approach. We will organise a visit first thing.'

The phone was quiet for ten seconds or so, and Victoria could hear Varsa passing on the questions and Harry's reply.

'Got all that, Varsa. Flat on Tang Hall Lane above the Chinese takeaway, with the front door to the left of the shop doorway, and got the details about the fire escape to the rear car park. I think we will pay Mr Greenwood a visit early in the morning. How does six-thirty sound?'

'Okay with us two. Should I alert Pete and Mal to the early get-go?'

'Yep, do that. Briefing at five a.m. in the MIT office, and once again, good work, the pair of you.'

'Cheers, boss. I'll pass it on to Harry.'

Victoria ended the call and turned to Miriam.

'I think there may be something building between Varsa and this new lad Harry. I could be wrong, but stranger things have happened.'

***

Detective Sergeants Pete Sinclair and Mal Chambers hated these early starts, especially in winter. The pair sat at the table in the MIT briefing room, bleary-eyed and clasping their hands around their respective mugs of tea for warmth. When Victoria entered the room with Varsa in tow, both wearing stab vests, the two sergeants looked at each other with raised eyebrows, *what's going on?* on their faces.

'Have we missed something, ma'am? Thought we were just going to have a chat with some guy who popped up on the bus's CCTV?'

'We are, but Varsa has been digging and the lad has form. Possession of knife, aged twelve. Got off with a caution. Assault, aged sixteen. Another caution. And various drugs and minor shoplifting offences on and off since the age of ten. So no chances with him. Sergeant Hallows from the Neighbourhood Policing Team is lending us a couple of heavies with their RAM. They are to go in first by the front door with me and Varsa following, and I want you two to cover the back fire-escape. A simple, quick entry. We will arrest the guy and bring him back here for questioning. We have enough to do that with him clearly having some form of relationship with our missing lad. Any questions?'

Pete and Mal stood, and as they went to follow Victoria out of the room, Mal spoke up.

'What about Dirty Harry? I'm sure he wouldn't want to miss out on the fun.'

Varsa turned and put her hand on Mal's chest, stopping him in his tracks. 'Detective Constable Burrows has been sitting outside the flat on Tang Hall Lane all night keeping it under surveillance, you might want to know. Doing his job.'

Varsa's defence of the team's latest addition came as a surprise to both Pete and Mal.

'Oh, pardon me for asking,' Mal said, as she released him, allowing him to carry on down the corridor.

Outside, the team were met by a couple of uniforms clad in their house entry kit—helmets and visors, hi-vis vests over black overalls, and one of them carrying the big, red door ram. Victoria got them all together and asked the two uniforms to keep it quiet until they were all in position outside the flat. The drive only took fifteen minutes and vehicles were halted well back from the row of shops containing the Chinese takeaway. Harry had spotted the cars arriving and stood on the pavement as each of the vehicles slowly came to a halt.

He walked over to Victoria. 'I've parked round the back, ma'am. Hope that's okay?'

Victoria put her finger to her pursed lips to signal for them all to keep silent and nodded at Harry. Once she had got everyone gathered together, she gestured for them to come close, negating the need to speak louder than absolutely necessary. An early-morning dog walker passed by on the other side of the road, turning his head, not wanting to miss the action that was obviously about to happen.

Victoria checked her watch and spoke to the team. 'Okay, Mal and Pete, get yourselves around the back. Harry, go with them and make sure they know which fire escape is the one up to 115a. We'll give you a couple of minutes to get in position.'

As the two sergeants moved off with Harry in tow, she heard Varsa whisper to him to take care and smiled as he disappeared around the corner. Victoria then turned her attention to the two uniformed officers and Sergeant Hallows.

'I always want to say "Fee Fi Fo Fum" when I'm standing next to you, Sarge.'

Sergeant Hallows gave her a gin and nodded at the two uniformed officers. They nodded back. Victoria gestured to them to get closer to the door.

'Ready, you two, get into position. I will do the knocking and then stand clear for you to do your stuff.'

They both nodded their reply and stood on either side of the door marked 115a.

Victoria checked her watch again and mouthed the question, 'Ready?' in Varsa's direction.

Varsa returned it with a deliberate nod and a mouthed, 'Yes.'

Victoria stood squarely in front of the entrance to the flat and gave the door three sharp bangs with her fist.

'Police!' she shouted. 'Police. Open the door.'

She stood to one side and the uniformed officer carrying the ram took her place. He swung it back and crashed it into the side of the door closest to the lock. Such noise at this time in the morning was deafening, but the door opened with a single crash and hung on one of its hinges. The officers easily pushed it to one side and stormed up the stairs to the first-floor flat. As they climbed the stairs two steps at a time. Followed by Victoria and Varsa, they kept up the shout of 'Police, Police,' while Sargeant Hallows guarded the front door now hanging off his hinges.

The flat stank of dirty washing, sweat, and old food, and was oppressively hot. However, above all, the overriding smell was of a sickly, sticky sweetness, which Victoria and the two uniforms recognised it instantly. It was the smell of a dead body in the very early stages of decomposition.

'Hello, anyone here? This is the police. Terry? Terry Greenwood?'

There was no reply.

Victoria put her forensic blue gloves on. The two uniformed officers were looking in both the kitchen and bathroom, while Varsa opened the door to the lounge.

'God, it's so bloody hot in here. Someone has more money than sense to have the heating turned up this high, and that smell is awful.'

As Victoria slowly opened the door into what was the only bedroom in the flat, she put her hand to her mouth. 'Varsa, stop moaning about the heat and go and tell the other three to tape off the fire escape. Tell one of them to stay there until we can get some more uniforms to hold the fort. We need to secure this place. When you've done that, ask Sergeant Hallows to tape up the front door and call in some uniforms to secure the scene.'

Varsa poked her head around Victoria's side and peered into the darkened bedroom. 'Why, what is it?'

Victoria ushered her out, turning her shoulders and pointing her towards the stairs. 'I thought I asked you to go and tape off the entrance? You may as well call it in as well.'

'Call *what* in?' she asked. She made another attempt to look into the room. 'Oh my god,' was all she could say, and she put herself into reverse. She turned on the top landing and retraced her steps down the stairs and into the street, passing Harry on the stairs and saying nothing.

He appeared at Victoria's shoulder and, without taking her eyes off the scene in the bedroom, she spoke to him, 'Harry, go and check she's alright, will you? Just make sure she has called it in correctly and tell everyone else to stay clear of the flat until we get the SOCOs out here.'

'Do you think it's Greenwood, ma'am?'

'Hard to tell in that position, Harry, but I suspect so. He looks about the right age and height from the CCTV.'

Harry nodded and left his boss standing on the threshold of the small bedroom. She stepped inside and looked around her in an attempt to take in as much as she could. The state of it looked like most young men's bedrooms who lived alone when in their late teens or early twenties. It was an unadulterated tip with stale, half-eaten pizzas still in their delivery boxes, dirty clothes strewn around the floor, and above all, it had the smell of young males hanging in the air and finding its way into the nostrils in a most unpleasant way. *Just like any standard teenager's bedroom,* Victoria thought.

What did set it apart from the standard teenager's room, was the couple-of-days-old, naked male corpse, tied up, face down in a kneeling position with his rear end up in the air. His ankles had been bound together and his wrists had been tied behind his back. He was positioned across the bed and pointing towards the window, with a long piece of orange twine, the type used by farmers, running from his wrists, up, and over his back with the other end tied to the handle on the window frame. This had the effect of lifting his arms and pulling them against his shoulder joints. He had a plastic Sainsbury's bag over his head that had been taped tightly around his neck.

Victoria thought it likely that this would have been what killed him.

She looked slowly around the room. The curtains were closed and she thought about drawing them open but decided they would be best kept closed until SOCO could get the first photographs taken. She moved slowly around to the far side of the bed, treading carefully so as not to disturb any of the clothes that were strewn across the floor. This was no easy task, and as she made it to the far side of the bed, she glanced down at the bedside table. Amongst the debris of pills, chewing gum wrappers, beer, Red Bull cans, and bits of paper towel, the overflowing ashtray was mainly full of roll-ups and stank of a mixture of tobacco and the sweetness of hash. She picked up a half-smoked joint, long since extinguished, and took a sniff. *Yep,* she thought. She'd smelled enough to recognise a good blend when she came across it. This stuff would have cost more than this guy's months' worth of benefits, and some more.

Victoria placed the joint back down on the tray and slowly pulled out the top drawer of the bedside cabinet — full of rubbish, bits of paper, and cigarettes. What stood out were three multi-packs of heavy-duty condoms. She closed the drawer. Time to wait for the SOCOs.

Leaving the door open, she made her way downstairs, out into the daylight and the cool morning air. *Wow, what a relief*, she thought, as she took in a deep breath.

Not too far away, Harry was comforting Varsa and talking to her quietly. It was clear his presence was having the right effect.

Victoria called the team in. 'Okay, everyone. We have what looks like the body of Terry Greenwood upstairs, bound and tied up with a plastic bag over his head. There is little we can do until SOCO arrive so, in the meantime, Sergeant Hallows here will station two officers at the front of the property and one at the rear. The rest of you, make your way back to Fulford Road nick and I'll be along once I have handed over to the munchkins in white suits. Any questions?'

The team nodded and turned for the vehicles.

'Do you want me to stay, ma'am?' asked Hallows. 'We've got the front and back covered now.'

'No, you take yourself off, Sarge. I'll wait around and go over the scene with whoever turns up.'

'Okay, if you're sure. I was going to have a wee word with the lad who handed in Jason's sports bag. He is well known to us. A bit of a scrote. Shoplifting and possession stuff, but I wouldn't put it past him to have kept the phone and be trying to sell it.'

'Fine, Sarge, That would certainly save us a job. Great.'

***

When the SOCOs arrived on the scene, Victoria wondered who might be standing in for Miriam while she was resting at home. She was pleasantly surprised to see Jane McCormack, the Leeds-based pathologist who had been at the same conference where Miriam had been attacked. Jane was in her mid-sixties, a slightly-built woman with close-cropped, grey hair who was efficiency incarnate. Although she was not too far from retirement, she was as fit and agile as a woman half her age. She ran marathons, did a bit of fell running, lots of cycling, and, like Miriam, had that easy but sometimes dark sense of humour.

'Hello, Victoria. This one yours, is it? I take it it's upstairs then? Hope you and your lot haven't been trampling too much over it all since you got here.'

'Just me, I'm afraid. I managed to keep them out of the room where the body is. I'll come up with you, if that's okay?'

'Of course, my dear, by all means. And how is old Jolly getting on after her ordeal?'

'Oh, she's bearing up, you know. I'm sure she'll be back in the saddle before long.'

Upstairs in the flat, Jane's team had set about their work in double-quick time. Cameras clicked away and flashes flashed as the team moved from room to room. Jane McCormack moved to the side as one of the photographers squeezed past, who then turned to Jane.

'Okay to open the curtains, boss? And any chance of turning this heat off?'

Jane checked her watch. 'Yes, to both. Okay, Vicky, follow me. Let's have a wee look at our friend here.' The two women moved around to position themselves on either side of the bed. 'Well, firstly, it looks like the bed has been moved to facilitate getting the young man closer to the window so whoever it was could tie his arms back against the joints.' She ducked under the string and came around the bed. 'Shots of the ligature knots, please.' The man operating the camera duly complied. Jane took out a torch and stood closer to the naked man's rear. She shone the light on his anus as she pulled his cheeks apart. 'Looks like he has had relatively recent anal sexual intercourse and probably not consensual, by the amount of bruising. But we will be able to tell more when we get back to the mortuary.'

'Any time of death? Or will we need to wait for that, Jane?'

'Well, the heat has hastened the purification process, but we can say no longer than two days and no shorter than one. Again, if you can hang on, I will give you a more precise time. Okay, let's cut him down and take off the bag.' Once the bag covering his head was removed, Jane turned to Victoria. 'Looking at the lips and eyes, I would say with some degree of certainty that he died of asphyxiation. But at this time, I can't say if the sex was post or antemortem.'

'Okay, Jane, we have sufficient to be going with there. Cheers. I need to get back now.'

'For sure. PM will be around three-thirty this afternoon, all being well. Will you be attending?'

'Yes. I'd like to say I'll be looking forward to it. But I won't.'

'It's going to take some time to get all this crap bagged up and labelled. We will check for semen and DNA on most of the clothing, and everything else that won't be checked will be boxed and delivered in a couple of days, or even sooner if we can manage it.'

'Lovely, Jane. Many thanks for stepping in and covering for Miriam.'

'Hey, no worries, and don't forget to give her my best wishes. When I left her in Birmingham, she was in a bit of a state. In the ambulance, she was going on about some bloody psychopath attacking her. I must say, it didn't make a lot of sense. I put it down to concussion.'

Victoria thought it better not to go into the details at the moment but said that she was probably right in that assumption. She made her way down the stairs, and nodded to the uniform on the door, who replied with a, 'Ma'am.'

She gave him a smile and set off back to HQ.

***

As soon as Victoria got back, the team assembled. Varsa was introducing Harry to the intricacies of the "Big Board." She was explaining that they usually put the subject of the investigation in the centre, so that would be the image of the fresh-faced Jason Waites in his football strip of the local Badgers team. Harry was nodding attentively and smiling at Varsa. She went on to show him how they would put, on one side of his name, his parents, and, on the other side, his coach and the coach's wife. Because, at the moment, these would be the interested parties. Not suspects or even persons of interest, but at some stage, they could become that. He continued to nod and smile. She then explained that just below Jason, they would put a range of images from the murder scene at the flat showing the body of Terry Greenwood with any close-ups that were thought to be relevant.

'We make links to him with a sharpie and we write the details of who everyone is and their relation to the murder victim and Jason.' She handed Harry the pen for him to draw the lines on the board and fill in the details. At this time, there was little else to add. So Varsa took the pen back and gave Harry a wide grin. 'Simple, see?'

He nodded again.

When she had finished, she announced to the team she was going to make some tea and asked if anyone wanted a brew. Sergeants Mal and Pete were somewhat stunned, as she never made anyone drinks, but they were doubly stunned when Harry offered to give her a hand and the pair set off together for the copier room, where the supplies were stored.

Mal rocked back on his chair. 'Well, you could knock me over with a feather. Who would have guessed that? Never in a month of Sundays.'

'What?' asked Pete.

'Are you totally blind? Dirty Harry and Miss Prim Varsa. Getting it on.'

'You're joking.'

'I kid you not. They're an item if ever there was one. It will do her good to have a bit of love in her life. Have you ever met her mum and dad?'

'No, why? What's up with them?'

'Well, I think they never wanted their little girl to become a copper. A lawyer, doctor, or accountant, yes, but not a copper, and they have sort of disowned her a little. Top that with the fact that last year they found a nice Indian boy for her to marry and she flatly refused. Apparently, she then moved out and took a flat in town. Mum and dad were not best pleased.'

'Wow. Never realised. Not sure how Dirty Harry will go down then.'

Victoria interrupted the pair, 'Sorry to break this up, ladies, but we still have a young lad to find, and if the death of this fella in the flat is linked, which it's almost certain to be, this escalates the urgency of finding him. We do not want this to become a double murder enquiry. Mal, Pete, I want you to go back and have yet another word with the coach, Phil Southern. Ask him if he knew that Jason might be gay and if he's ever heard of this Terry Greenwood. Me and Harry will be checking on the same with the parents.' She called through to Varsa, 'Varsa, could you see what you can dig up on this Terry Greenwood? I want the works — background, employment, bank accounts, as much as you can.'

There was a fit of giggling from the copy room mixed with a reply from Varsa, 'Yep, boss. I'm on it right away.'

Victoria turned back to Mal and Pete. 'It's going to be some time before forensics give us anything from the flat, so let's make ourselves useful in the meantime, hey?'

Varsa and Harry eventually returned to the office carrying a tray of drinks.

'Have we got time to finish these before we set off, boss?' Harry asked.

'Aye. Go on. We need to be off to see Mr and Mrs Waites within the hour though.' She turned to Varsa. 'Do you think we can trawl the information on Greenwood and have another go at Jason's laptop? Facebook and WhatsApp activity. I would like to ask Jason's parents if they were aware of his sexuality and probe a little more into the relationship between Jason and his dad. So while Dirty Harry and I are out, would you mind getting on with all that, Varsa?'

She looked a little disappointed, either at not going with Victoria or, possibly, at Victoria taking Harry away, but she gave a smile. 'Sure, boss. On it.'

Harry downed his tea as if it was a Pepsi and put his coat on. 'Well, I'm ready when you are, boss.' He turned to Mal and Pete, who were grinning at Varsa, and pointed his finger at them both, making a pistol with his hand, and cocked his thumb. 'Well, are you feeling lucky, punk? I know what you're thinking. Did I fire five or did I fire six? Well, in all the excitement, I just forgot. So, do you feel lucky?'

And the whole office erupted into laughter.

Chapter 11

When Jonathan Fahey was incarcerated in Wellingborough Secure Unit, he could never have imagined his good fortune in being sent to that particular institution. Although it housed some of the country's most dangerous offenders, including many serial rapists and murderers, it was considered — even in these enlightened times — a most forward-looking prison. The governor or "Inmate Experience Manager," as she was to be called these days, certainly ran a tight ship, but not so tight that it couldn't be steered in a favourable direction by the more aware inmates, especially by the likes of someone as manipulative as Jonathan Fahey. It was the custom for any new inmate or *patient*, as the Inmate Experience Manger liked to call them, to be assigned a mentor or close advisor who would steer them through the intricacies of the rules and expected standards of behaviour at Wellingborough.

When Fahey first arrived, his reputation arrived well in advance of him. His callousness and total disregard for anyone other than himself made him especially dangerous, and most, if not all, of the staff gave him a seriously wide berth. On the morning of his arrival, all the staff members who were sufficiently experienced to take Fahey under their supervision declined the opportunity. The only offer came from a relatively new member of staff called Prison Officer Peter Walsh.

Walsh was a shy man of 45 years of age, who had somewhat of an obsequious nature that would make Uriah Heep look positively defiant. He was at least fifty pounds overweight and had been on the HMP officers' weight program now for more than two years with little or no improvement. He believed he had been passed over for promotion on numerous occasions and thought all those in charge across the prison service were out of their depth. In fact, in the main, barely better than useless. His thinning, red hair was allowed to grow in long locks at one side of his head then swept across the totally bald expanse, plastered down to his skull with a form of fixative that could secure the Titanic. He never understood why people made fun of his hair and always believed it to be neat and smart. His mother always told him he was as smart as a guardsman. He lived alone in the house he had shared with his now-deceased mother all his life. She had died some eighteen months previously. He had kept all her clothes and her room just the way everything had been when she was alive.

He had brought a girlfriend home once when he was twenty-three, but after a discussion with his mother, who told him girls like her only wanted to be with him so they could inherit the house that would one day be his, he decided not to see her again. After all, his mother loved him and he needed little else in his life. Until, of course, the day she died, and until Jonathan Fahey arrived and took over his life in much more sinister ways than his mother ever did.

It is often said that any individual is capable of doing bad things on their own, but when two damaged individuals come together, their combined levels of depravity and sheer evilness can become more than the total of themselves, and in many cases can escalate with few or no boundaries between them.

When Peter Walsh met Jonathan Fahey, such a partnership was formed. In PO Walsh, Fahey found someone easily manipulated and more than eager to acquiesce to his instructions. Their one-sided friendship developed, with Walsh helping Fahey appear as if he was being controlled by the officer, while all the time not realising that it was him who was being controlled by the inmate. Fahey was very much aware of the need to toe the line in prison, as even in the forward-looking Wellingborough Detention Centre, the system of rewards for good behaviour and sanctions for bad was used extensively. In the case of Jonathan Fahey, his good behaviour and close adherence to the rules only served to increase the institution's belief that their system was working effectively. Little did they realise that it was Jonathan who was using their rules to gain the confidence of Peter Walsh. He would eventually convince Walsh that he was an innocent man who had been fitted up by the police, who had fabricated evidence and managed to get a conviction when all he was guilty of was being in the wrong place at the wrong time.

After a full year of working with Fahey, Walsh was beginning to believe his story. The only way of proving his innocence would be for Jonathan to escape and put matters right.

The plan was, on the face of it, quite simple. However, it would not be sufficient for only Fahey to escape Wellingborough, but also Walsh. Although Jonathan Fahey was, before his incarceration, a relatively successful and wealthy businessman, once outside, he would have no access to funds and would need assistance. In this regard, the only person he would be able to trust would be Peter Walsh. That is where the plan and its execution would take some time to implement. Once Fahey had convinced his newfound partner of his innocence, the rest was easy. Above all, he needed to ensure that Walsh always saw him as his protector and confidante throughout the process.

On the wings of Wellingborough, Walsh was seen as easy meat by almost all the inmates. Even the nonces would have a verbal poke at him and expect to get away with it. That was until Jonathan Fahey arrived. Fahey's reputation was that of a man who had no fear and no remorse for his actions. He made it his objective to become Walsh's protector. And he would always want something in return.

One weekend on C-Wing, Walsh was clearly being bullied by an inmate called Sparky, a man who was serving life for a series of child murders. He got the nickname because of how he killed his victims by electrocution. The man's sentence held a whole life tariff, which meant he could never come up for parole or ever be released. No matter how many psychiatrists came together to tell the world how reformed he was and how he was no longer a threat to the public, he would spend the rest of his life behind bars. These men on whole life tariffs had nothing to lose. They were never coming out, so any offence committed inside would mean, at worst, some restriction of privileges, such as a removal of their televisions or reading material for a period of time. On this particular occasion, Walsh had become trapped in a cell with the lifer, who had taken his handcuffs and secured himself to Walsh. He was threatening to strangle the officer and then kill himself if his books were not returned to him.

While this was going on, in the next cell, Jonathan was contemplating his options. It didn't take him long to decide on a course of action, thinking this would be a good time to build his account with Walsh. Jonathan calmly stepped outside onto the landing and stood amongst the officers, who crouched there armed with batons, shields, and wearing helmets and masks.

'What's going on in there, then?' he asked.

Just then, Sparky called out from inside the cell, 'You lot need to get my books back or I swear I'll top this fat fucker. I swear I will.'

One of the officers turned around and put up a hand to Jonathan, stopping him from going any closer to the cell door. 'Nowt that concerns you, Jonathan. Now you just be a good boy and get back in your cell, hey? Let us deal with this.'

Jonathan shrugged his shoulders and turned to go back into the safety of his cell.

'Well, if you think you can handle it. Sparky is a bit of a nutter and I don't hold out much hope for Mr Walsh being in one piece by the time you get in there. I could get him out in one piece if you let me have a wee word with Sparky on my own. After all, what have you got to lose?'

The officer in charge looked at Fahey and wondered if he had some other motive. He considered that the four officers would eventually overpower Walsh's captor, but in so doing would likely sustain serious injuries themselves. Fahey had been a model prisoner since his arrival. It was probably worth a go. After all, what harm could it do?

The officer in charge beckoned to Fahey. 'Alright. Come here. But don't try anything heroic or stupid. Right?'

Jonathan pushed his way through the scrum of officers and slid the cover of the observation slot in the cell door. He looked in and could see Prison Officer Walsh and Sparky handcuffed together. The inmate had taken the officer's keychain and wrapped it around Walsh's neck, passing it over the metal bedhead that had been turned on its end, with the chain wrapped around Sparky's wrist. All it would take would be for the prisoner to put his weight on his end and Walsh would be quickly asphyxiated within seconds. The chain was already starting to turn Walsh a little blue around the lips.

Jonathan spoke through the door slot. 'Okay, Sparky, my friend, I want to come in and have a wee word. Is that okay with you?'

'No, you can fuck off and tell them to get my books back.'

'Fine. I will do that. But they want me to come in and just check on Walsh for a second. You know the drill, you know how it is. I'm coming in so don't strangle the bastard. Well, not until I get in there, my friend.'

He slowly opened the door and slipped inside, closing it behind him. Once inside, he moved a little closer to PO Walsh and put up his thumb.

'You okay, Walsh?'

Peter Walsh was decidedly not okay but could not speak with the chain tightening around his larynx. Jonathan moved closer, close enough to speak into Sparky's right ear.

He whispered, but loud enough so Walsh could hear what he was saying, 'Now look here, you fuckwit. You know who I am and you know what I am capable of. I don't give a flying fuck about this bastard — if you'll pardon my French,

Officer Walsh — but doing him in is not going to get you anywhere. So you have a choice to make, Sparky, my dear. You have two options. Option one. You can hurt or even try to kill Mr Walsh here and now, but you know I will stop you. And at some time of my choosing in the future, I will hurt you in ways that you could not begin to imagine. I will make sure your life here is spent in abject fear of how and when the next hurt will come. But make no mistake, it will. If this happens, there is a cast-iron guarantee you will not get your books back. While I, on the other hand, will be awarded some form of commendation for my attempt at saving a prison officer.

'Option two. You can choose to release Mr Walsh and let him come out with me. You will not immediately get your books back, but I'm sure the nice Mr Walsh will do everything he can to get them for you as soon as he can. Won't you, Officer Walsh?' Walsh, who was now sweating profusely, nodded as the chain was released a little. 'What do you say, Sparky?'

Officer Walsh was released, unharmed, and was very grateful for the intervention by Fahey, who was given more privileges in the form of extra association time and extra phone call time. This, he sold to the other inmates as he really had no one to call on the outside. Sparky eventually got his books back. And Fahey made sure that his debt owed by Walsh would be collected in full at some time.

It would not be long before this debt, and others, would be called in by Fahey, but not until Walsh had become totally obsessed with him. Walsh had begun to collect press cuttings of the crimes Fahey had been accused of and he had been researching the French Foreign Legion. To someone like Walsh, who had only ever been to Ibiza on holiday for a fortnight, Fahey's life seemed exotic and exciting in the extreme. Fahey had always protested his innocence to Walsh and made a good case, pointing out that much of the evidence used to convict him was suspect and circumstantial. In some ways, Walsh hoped that Jonathan Fahey had murdered those women, along with his inept and truculent parents, as it made him stand out from the crowd and be recognised as notorious and special. A level of recognition he could never hope to attain. He was not too bothered whether Fahey was guilty or innocent. All he wished for was that Fahey recognised him as a kindred spirit.

Some months after the incident in the cell, when Fahey was sure that Walsh was well and truly hooked, he explained his plan for escape. The plan needed flexibility and, above all, attention to detail. There would be a lot of responsibility placed on Walsh's shoulders, which he relished and wallowed in.

When the pair eventually settled on a strategy, Walsh was well aware that when his involvement in the escape was detected, he would become as much a fugitive as Fahey. Then the pair would be on the run together. This did not worry him. In his eyes, it would only serve to intensify the perceived bond between them. At no time did he consider that Fahey would drop him like a stone just as soon as he could. To Jonathan Fahey, the involvement of Prison Officer Walsh was simply a means to an end. What they both realised was that once on the outside, their main concern would be funds. Neither of them would have any opportunity of earning money in any legal way, and if they chose to become embroiled in any further criminal activities, it would only serve to bring them the unwanted attention of the police. So some other method of getting cash would need to be arranged.

It was Walsh who came up with the idea of using money from the sale of his mother's home. The house would go on the market and the pair would open a bank account in the name of a fictitious business. Walsh would arrange for false passports and documentation in false names so they could open the account. He had contacts of ex-offenders who were involved in this work; if the price was right, they could produce any documentation he required.

The house on the outskirts of London was valued at a promising £800,000 and sold quickly. This would provide ample funds to take the pair aboard to the South of France and enable them to open a small bar and holiday letting company. Jonathan's knowledge of the French property market and his excellent French language skills would be a bonus.

If only Walsh had realised then that Fahey had no intention of setting up a home and business with an individual like him. Jonathan despised and loathed him for being so weak and stupid, and he had his own plans for what would happen on the outside.

Once all the plans were in place, they would need some way of getting Jonathan out of Wellingborough for a whole day, and, more importantly, in the custody of Walsh. It was decided that Fahey, over a period of two months, would fake a stomach complaint. He would make appointments with the prison doctor, who would offer a range of diagnoses and medication, none of which would prove to be effective. Over time, the pain would increase. It was suspected that Fahey might have been suffering from some kind of stomach cancer, but the blood tests taken by the prison doctor came back negative. Finally, it was decided to take Fahey, under guard, to the closest hospital, which was Birmingham Teaching Hospital for an appointment with a specialist in gastric cancers. He would be handcuffed to his minder, Prison Officer Walsh, the whole time, and there would also be two extra guards, Prison Officer Brian Strange, who was in overall charge of the trip to the hospital, and Prison Officer Graham Leith. It would be their role to provide backup if required and share the driving.

The four men travelled to the hospital in an unmarked car with Fahey handcuffed to Walsh in the back seat. They were dropped at the entrance and the driver took the car to find a parking space. This had the bonus of reducing the guard to a single person. And the three men then made their way to the oncology department. As they arrived, they announced their presence to the receptionist and were asked to take a seat and told that the consultant oncologist would see them when the patient's name was called.

'How long is the wait likely to be?' asked the guard who was not handcuffed.

'I have no real idea, but Dr Kumar is running a little late. Please take a seat and I'm sure you won't have to wait that long.'

They sat down on the back row of the waiting area and a number of patients turned to look at the newcomer. A man handcuffed and sitting between two uniformed officers was less than a regular occurrence in the oncology department of Birmingham Teaching Hospital.

The guard that was not attached to Fahey stood up. 'Look, I'm going to get a tea from the Starbucks in the foyer downstairs. Will you be okay, Pete? I'll get you and matey here a drink too, if you like.'

Walsh glanced at Fahey. 'We're fine, cheers.'

Fahey looked disappointed. 'I wouldn't mind a cappuccino with some chocolate bits sprinkled on it and two sugars, please. Demerara, if they have it. Thanks.'

The guard stopped in his tracks and turned to face Fahey. 'You'll have a fucking tea like us and like it.' He turned and walked away, leaving Jonathan and PO Walsh on their own with Walsh looking decidedly worried and Jonathan smiling to himself. *It won't be long now.*

A woman turned to look at the pair and stared at the handcuffs with a concerned look on her face. She pulled the child who was sitting next to her close in and Jonathan leaned forward towards her. 'Boo,' he whispered.

She flashed her head back and gave him and Walsh a further look, then decided to move places. Jonathan shifted in his chair and nodded at Walsh, signifying that it was time for them to make their move, when the nurse sitting at the desk called out.

'Jonathan Fahey! Doctor Kumar will see you now.' She stood up and came around the reception desk. 'Would you like to follow me, please?' Then she led them down the corridor and into one of the consulting rooms. The doctor looked at the handcuffs and asked if they could be removed, and Walsh dutifully complied.

'Can you climb up onto the bed here, please, Mr Fahey, while I carry out a quick general examination?'

Before he got himself up on to the bed Johnathan gave little groan of pain and clutched his abdomen. He feigned falling over and supported himself on the corner of the doctors desk and while looking down at the desk could not believe what he was seeing. The image of a woman smiling back at him from a flyer on the desk made him gasp. It was advertising a conference taking place at the hospital, and on the open page of the leaflet was a photograph he recognised instantly. It was that of Dr Miriam DeSilva. He picked up the leaflet and, showing it to the doctor who was about to examine him, asked if he was acquainted with Dr DeSilva. Amazed at this coincidence, he could not stop looking at it.

'Nope, I've never met her. You see, my main thing is trying to keep people alive and, well, hers would be looking at them when my work is no longer required. If you understand?' He took the leaflet from Jonathan and put it back on the desk. 'She is one of the keynote speakers at a conference for pathologists being held today in the main conference hall.' He glanced at his watch. 'But if you wanted to catch her talk, I think you might be too late. She'll have finished and probably have left by now. Why do you ask? Do you know her?'

'We met once, but I wouldn't say I know her in any real sense, you understand.'

'Yes, of course. Could you just climb up on the bench please?' The doctor was really paying no attention to what he considered was his patient's ramblings.

The doctor gave a sideways glance at PO Walsh and asked if Jonathan could pull his shirt up and out of his trousers so that he could feel his stomach. The doctor prodded and pressed around the abdomen and lower down towards the groin while asking if Jonathan could feel any pain as he went. For Jonathan's part, he feigned pain at various prods and pokes, sometimes only slightly and other times grimacing as if it caused considerable discomfort. During the examination, the oncologist asked an array of questions and, from time to time, consulted his notes showing Jonathan's blood and medical records from the prison doctor.

'Okay, you can get down now. It is clear you have some major discomfort and, unfortunately, I am not in a position to tell from this initial observation what might be the underlying cause of your pain. You say that you have passed some blood in your faeces, but there is no mention of this or indeed any samples from your doctor in prison. However, I would like to take some more blood samples, along with some stool samples, and also send you for an MRI scan. This will show up any abnormalities in any of the organs of your lower body. I would like this to be carried out today.' He looked across and PO Walsh. 'Would you have time to do this now or do you need to take the patient back for a specific time?'

'No that's fine, doc. We can do it now. Save going and coming back later.'

'Good. I'll arrange that now. If you would both like to wait outside, the receptionist will let you know when it will take place and point you in the right direction.'

He smiled at both men and nodded at the door — their signal to go.

In the waiting area, they were greeted by Graham Leith, still holding onto his cups of tea. He had only just returned from the café in the foyer and Walsh explained to him that, for the time being, they had finished and all was okay.

However, he told him, it would be necessary to wait until Fahey was given an appointment to return at a later date for more tests. It was imperative, for the time being, that PO Strange and PO Leith both believed they would be soon on their way back to the safety of Wellingborough Secure Unit.

The receptionist eventually handed a folded piece of paper to Walsh. He glanced at the appointment for that afternoon for Fahey's MRI scan, then quickly folded it and put it in his pocket. The doctor had behaved exactly how they'd wanted. All they had to do was overpower Leith and Strange, who believed they were going back to Wellingborough, then Walsh would make the call to the prison telling them they would be late, as they had to wait for Fahey's scan. This would allow the pair time to make their escape without being missed. If the prison doctor checked with the hospital, he would be told about the delay.

Walsh smiled and gestured to Graham Leith to follow them out into the corridor.

'Hey up, Walshey! Aren't you going to put the cuffs back on Doctor Lecter here?'

'Oh! For fuck's sake. Good job you reminded me, mate.' And he re-clipped the black handcuffs around the left wrist of his charge. 'Come on then. Let's make ourselves scarce and get back to the car.'

Once outside, they walked the short distance to the multi-story car park and Graham Leith called PO Strange to find out which level he was on.

'Hey up. Looks like we'll be getting back earlier than we thought. I'll explain when we get back to the car. Where you parked mate?' Graham Leith turned back to the handcuffed pair who were lagging behind a little. 'Come on, you two. He's at the top."

'Any chance of having a smoke before we set off back, Mr Walsh?' asked Fahey.

Walsh looked at PO Leith, who shrugged his shoulders. 'Don't see why not. We've got plenty of time, but it's really up to Brian. He's in charge.'

Once the three men were out of the lift and making their way over the rooftop car park, Brian Strange came across to meet them. 'Wow, you've made good time. There can't be much wrong with the bastard after all, hey?'

Walsh looked at Fahey and then back to Strange. 'Well, he has to come back for some more tests. I have a note here to pass on to the doc at Wellingborough.'

As they moved between a parked grey Volvo and their own vehicle, Brian Strange took out his mobile and pressed speed dial. 'Just need to let Wellingborough know we're leaving now and when to expect us back.'

He didn't get to make the call. There was no way Walsh and Fahey could let him foil their plans for the extra time needed to make their getaway.

Prison Officer Strange didn't see Walsh take out his extendable baton or see it coming down on the back of his head. He hit the ground with a solid thud, catching his chin on the bumper and sending his phone skidding under the car in a number of pieces. Graham Leith stood, open-mouthed, unable to move as if nailed to the spot. The fight-or-flight-mode button had not been pressed in his brain as Fahey, now unshackled from Walsh, turned to face him. The perfectly-delivered headbutt sent Graham Leith spinning and holding his now bloody, broken nose. Fahey took him by the hair and slammed his forehead against the corner of the open car door, piercing his left eye socket, and he slumped onto the tarmac, unconscious. Fahey checked around to ensure there were no witnesses and gestured over to Walsh to assist him in putting the two now comatose prison officers into the boot of the car.

Fahey smiled at his accomplice. 'Easy peasey or what, my friend?'

Walsh was glued to the spot holding his hand over his mouth in shock. 'Come on, help

me get them in. We haven't finished with them yet.'

'What do you mean we haven't finished with them? They're out for the count. We need to make sure they're still okay and can breathe. And Graham's eye needs some attention. It looks bad.'

Fahey looked at him with disbelief. 'Are you kidding me? There's no way we can leave them like this. We tie up all loose ends. We agreed on that. Remember? No loose ends. Did you bring the knife?'

'Yes, of course I did. I'm not an idiot, you know.' Walsh reached inside his jacket and took a large kitchen knife out of his inside pocket and handed it handle-first to Jonathan. Jonathan felt the weight of the knife in the palm of his hand.

'Have you been carrying that around in there all day?'

'Aye, but I thought we'd only need it if we wanted to threaten anyone?'

'Well, it's a good job you didn't fall on it or there might've been three bodies to get rid of.'

Walsh look a little alarmed and Fahey laughed and glanced around the car park to ensure no one was close by. Walsh was still standing looking at the two unconscious men in the boot. Putting his arm around Walsh's shoulder, he gestured to the front seat of the vehicle with the blade.

'If you don't want to look, just go and sit in the front. You need to drive and let me deal with this part. Okay?'

Walsh nodded and went to sit in the driver's seat. He started up the engine. The first of the two officers in the boot to die was PO Graham Leith, husband and father of two. The blade was pressed slowly into his chest, first glancing off the sternum and then straight into the heart. Fahey thought that, for a big man, he didn't bleed that much.

He had to roll him on his side so he could reach Brian Strange.

It was a little awkward to stab Strange in the chest, so he decided to cut the man's throat. Before closing the boot, he stabbed each one three or four more times, just to make sure they were dead. It was important to minimise the spray back from the blood as he didn't want to get covered in the stuff. So, each penetration was done slowly and carefully.

There was still a lot to do before the getaway was complete. Tying up loose ends was his forte. The last thing he wanted was for either of them to start banging on the lid to be let out. Finally, he threw the knife in with the two dead men before closing the boot.

Once inside, seated next to Walsh, Fahey turned to him, still smiling. 'Okay, what're you waiting for? Let's get over to the railway station and pick up the stuff you dumped for us in left luggage.' He fetched Walsh a penetrating stare. 'I hope you managed to do that, Peter. You know how important all the preparation was.'

As part of their elaborate plan, Walsh had been told to deposit suitcases containing a change of clothing for both of them, money, and passports.

'You have left it all haven't you Peter?'

Walsh nodded slowly.

'Well done, Peter. Now you can make that call to Wellingborough. Tell them there's been a delay at the hospital due to me needing a scan and it's uncertain when we'll get back, but not to be too concerned. Oh! And tell them you'll keep in touch on the way back.'

Walsh began the call. When he'd finished, he turned to Fahey. 'All good, Jonathan. All good. Now we have plenty of time to clear the ferry terminal and be in France before we're even missed. Just like the plan.'

As the car pulled out of the multi-storey car park, Prison Officer Peter Walsh thought about the two dead men in the boot and how that wasn't supposed to be part of the plan. He wondered what else he hadn't considered. Of course, Jonathan Fahey's plan was totally different to the one set out in Walsh's head. It didn't include going to France, and it certainly didn't include Prison Officer Walsh.

Chapter 12

When Victoria and Harry arrived at the Waitress's home, Molly Waites and her daughter Samantha were in the kitchen doing the washing up. They had enjoyed a late breakfast. There was no sign of Mr Waites. The FLO, Carole Hargreaves, was sitting on the sofa in the lounge typing on her laptop. Molly Waites came into the lounge to welcome them, although the welcome was somewhat cold and distant.

'Have you come to tell us anything new? Or are you going to trot out the prepared statement of, "We are doing everything we can and we will leave no stone unturned in our search for Jason?"'

'No, Molly, we do have news for you, and some questions thrown up by new sightings of Jason on the night he went missing. Can we sit down please?'

Carole Hargreaves stood up and clicked her laptop closed. 'I'll go and help Sam tidy up, if you like, Molly?'

Chapter 12

Molly Waites nodded and gestured for Victoria and Harry to sit on the vacated sofa. 'So what have you got then? Where has he been seen?'

'Before going into that, could I ask if Paul is in? It would make sense to explain what we have to the pair of you.'

'No, he's out at the moment. I'm not expecting him home for a while,' she said, looking at her watch. She seemed a little distracted.

'Do you mind us asking where he is, Molly?'

'He's just popped out to the pub for a drink. The Black Bull on Hull Road. Said he was meeting some mates and would be back around teatime.'

Harry looked a little sceptical with a slight frown and downturned mouth.

'Okay, Molly,' said Victoria. 'Could I ask you if you know the name Terry Greenwood?'

'No, I can't say I've come across the name. Why?'

Victoria opened her phone and brought up an enlarged image of Terry at the wheel of his van. She turned the phone towards Molly. 'This is Terry Greenwood, Molly. Have you ever seen this young man, either on his own or in the company of Jason?'

'No, I said not already. I've never seen him before. Why? Has he got our Jason? Has he taken him?'

'We can't really comment on that, Molly, but we can say with certainty that this individual is not holding your son Jason at the moment.'

'How do you know that? How do you know he hasn't got Jason? You wouldn't be asking if there wasn't some connection.' Molly stood up and shouted through to the kitchen. 'Sam! Call your dad and get him to come home, will you? He needs to be here.' Molly Waites then sat back down, visibly agitated and disturbed.

'Can I ask you if you ever thought Jason might be gay, Molly?'

'No. Why? What are you saying? I don't think he's gay. No.'

Again, Victoria looked at her phone and brought up the short slip of Jason climbing into the front seat of Greenwood's van. She turned the phone towards Molly and pressed the play button. Molly Waites put her hand over her mouth as the short video clip played.

Then Victoria played it for a second time.

'Jason was picked up at the bus stop on Hull Road close to the back gate of Archbishop Holgate's School on the night he went missing. It's clear that the time on the video shows he was picked up around thirty minutes after the last known sighting of him, by his coach at the club, Mr Phil Southern. You can see that Jason kisses the man in the driving seat, and kisses him in such a way as to suggest they were more than just friends.'

Samantha Waites had come in from the kitchen. She took the phone from Victoria and played the clip again. 'Oh!

For fuck's sake. This is going to kill Dad when he sees it.' She handed the phone back and sat down next to her mum.

'So how can you be so sure this pervert is not holding our Jason now?' Molly said with her hand tightly clasping her daughter's knee.

'We can be certain, Mrs Waites, because the man in this clip, identified as Terry Greenwood, is dead. His body was found early this morning at a flat in the Tang Hall area of the city.'

***

At the same time as Victoria and Harry were interviewing Mrs Waites and her daughter, across the other side of the Badger Hill estate, Sergeants Pete Sinclair and Mal Chambers were speaking to Phil Southern. Phil answered the door in his pyjamas and dressing gown. He had at least a three-day stubble and looked like he had visited the same hairdresser as Boris Johnson.

'Oh, it's you two again. Not found Jason, I expect?'

Mal closed the door behind them and followed Phil Southern into the lounge. Phil sat down heavily in an armchair facing the TV and picking up the remote turned up the volume. He was watching the *Match of the Day* on catch-up. Manchester City VS Liverpool. Pete Sinclair picked up the remote and turned the volume down, so they needn't shout over it.

'No Beth today, Phil?'

'No, she has a part-time job at the Black Bull on Hull Road. It pays peanuts but at least it gets her out of the way while I catch up on the footie.' He spoke without taking his eyes off the screen. 'So, have you found him then, or what? If you ask me, I think he won't be found now, or if he is, he'll likely be . . . . Well, you know. Catch my drift?'

Mal and Pete ignored the requests for information. Instead, they went through the same line of questioning about whether Phil thought Jason might have been gay. He told them it was a distinct possibility, but he wasn't aware of any relationships. However, when they asked about Terry Greenwood, the response was quite different to that of Molly Waites. Phil told Mal and Pete that he knew Terry Greenwood quite well and thought he lived somewhere in Tang Hall. He now turned to the officers fully, who were sitting side by side on the settee.

'Terry used to play for the club some years back, but we had to throw him out for trying to sell drugs to some of the kids. We couldn't stand by while that was going on. He wasn't a bad striker when he was sober and off the pot, but the incidents of him turning up half-cut or high on something or other became more frequent. So, we had to let him go. He came back hanging around the clubhouse and trying to sell his drugs, so we threw him out. Don't tell me Jason has got mixed up with him. Come to think of it, I did see them go off together a couple of times, but I put it down to a bit of hero worship on the part of Jason. Greenwood had managed a couple of trials for York City in the past, but also managed to blow it. They wouldn't stand for his nonsense, not turning up for training and stuff. So, if you haven't found Jason, do you have any leads? And what's Terry Greenwood got to do with it all?"

Mal looked at his partner. 'Well, we can't comment at this time, Phil, but I'm sure it will all come out eventually.'

Phil Southern took that as a yes and hoped that Jason would be okay, while fully expecting he wouldn't.

***

By the time all four officers returned to police HQ, it was after dark. Victoria told them all to go home and get some sleep and she would update the board. The news that Greenwood was known to the football club where Jason was a member was certainly of interest. As was the possible relationship between Mr Waites and Mrs Southern. Both of these issues would need further enquiry, Having thought this, Victoria knew it got them no closer to finding Jason or at least discovering what had happened to him.

Eventually, she decided to call it a night and go home to Miriam.

Miriam was asleep on the sofa and Victoria's key opening the door woke her. She sat up and smiled at her partner through a blurry sleep haze.

'Hey, you! You're earlier than I expected. I haven't prepared anything for a meal.'

Miriam stood up, made her way over to Victoria, and put her arms around her. They kissed and, suddenly, Miriam began to sob.

'Hey! What's wrong, sweetheart? You alright, are you?'

'Yes, of course. Well, it's just one thing after another. I so much wanted to celebrate our good news, and then what with the bastard Fahey getting out and you being so busy . . . Oh, I don't know. Sorry.'

'No need to be sorry. Look, we can send out for an Indian. Bottle of Chablis and a night in. Hey, it's quiz night tonight on the TV. Mastermind, Only Connect, and University Challenge. What do you say?'

'I say we're turning into a pair of boring old buggers. That's what I say. But it sounds great.'

They both laughed and Victoria took out the Indian takeaway menu from the drawer.

'So, what are you having?'

***

The next morning, there was a piece of good news. Jason's phone had been found. Or more accurately, recovered by Sergeant Hallows. He was proudly holding it up in front of Mal and Pete like some prize at a tombola night when Victoria arrived.

'Don't tell me, Sarge. You've got the lad's phone?'

'Aye, that little scrote who handed in the sports bag had it. He was going to try to sell it, but as it was locked, he dumped it in the kitchen waste bin. Would you believe? His dad called us after my visit and said he'd found it. Do you want us to charge the lad with anything? We could have him for wasting police time, if you like?'

'Not for now. He's not going anywhere and we have more important things to be getting on with.' Victoria took the evidence bag from Sergeant Hallows and handed it over to Varsa. 'Varsa, get this over to forensics as soon as you can. I doubt there will be anything of use on it in the way of prints and DNA, knowing how many hands will have been all over it, but you never know. Wait for them to work their magic and then it's your turn to work your magic when you get it back. You know the drill.'

'Aye, boss.'

Each member of the team was putting in their tuppence worth in turn. The suspected relationship between Paul Waites and Beth Southern could have pointed to something, but no one really knew what. Victoria thought it might've held some significance, but it was unlikely to relate directly to Jason's disappearance and may only prove a distraction. However, the details were duly entered on the big wall and silence reigned. Victoria stood back from the wall and spoke to it as if it could hear.

'It is clear that Greenwood is the key here. His death is almost certainly linked to Jason's disappearance, and we all need to focus on that. Greenwood may have been the last person to see Jason before his abduction and Greenwood may have been an accomplice in the kidnapping.'

Vasa had left with the phone and Mal was checking on the background of Greenwood and swapping stories with Pete Sinclair about the merits of Beth Southern's breasts versus her legs when the evidence bags and boxes from Greenwood's flat began to arrive. To say there was a lot of stuff would have been the understatement of the century. A team of uniforms carried them in from a van parked in the back car park, and over the course of thirty minutes, the boxes were piled four high in four stacks with the large bags placed on top. Smaller evidence bags were stacked on the spare desks, and as the final bag was set down, one of the officers carrying a clipboard turned to the team before leaving.

'So, who's in charge then to sign for this lot?'

Victoria spoke up. 'I'm in charge, but Sergeant Sinclair over there can sign for it. Do you need us to check it all?'

'Well, that's up to you, ma'am. I don't really give a . . . ' He stopped himself when he noticed the look on Victoria's face. 'Well . . . It's up to you whether you check it all off or not.'

'Just sign for it, Pete.'

Pete Sinclair took the clipboard and scrawled his signature across the bottom of a slip of paper, paying it little attention.

'Okay, everyone, you have your jobs to be getting on with. I have a PM to attend. Do you want to come along, Harry?'

'Wow! Yes, boss. I mean ma'am. I've never attended one before. I can't wait. Is it Terry Greenwood, ma'am?'

'Yes. Unless you have found us another body somewhere you haven't told us all about, DC Burrows?'

'No, ma'am. I haven't.'

'Okay, then get your skates on. We don't want to miss the first cut, do we?'

***

Jane McCormack always looked somewhat incongruous in her high-legged, heavy-duty, green wellies, apron, and scrubs. Her diminutive size and short, cropped hair did little to alter or improve her appearance that made her look like a child in dressing-up clothes. She greeted Victoria and Harry, both similarly attired, with a smile but no handshake, even though Harry held out his hand as he was introduced.

'Sorry. I'm not being rude, but I've scrubbed and, well, you understand.' Harry and Victoria nodded. 'Well, we may as well get right into it then. Assuming you are both ready.' Jane turned to Harry. 'Hope you've had your breakfast, young man?'

Jane then turned to the two mortuary assistants, one holding a camera and the other arranging the knives, saws, and forceps on the metal tray to one side of the corpse.

Victoria was keeping one eye on Harry and one eye on the proceedings. She was all too aware of how an officer's first PM could end up with him, or her, prostrate on the floor. Jane pulled back the sheet to expose the naked body of Terry Greenwood and was about to begin her initial commentary. She pulled down the microphone that was hanging from a structure that supported the lights over the body and checked it was working okay by giving it a tap. Harry felt a little embarrassed at the sight of the naked Terry. He wasn't quite sure why, but nevertheless, the sight of a dead male laid out for all to see seemed somehow not quite right.

Jane gave one final check to see if it was okay to start, and they both nodded.

'We have the body of an adult male of approximately five feet nine inches in height. Relatively well nourished. Post puberty and I would estimate age around late teens.' She lifted up his right arm. 'Signs of small puncture wounds on both upper arms from what could be a hypodermic needle.' She looked at his legs. 'There are significantly more punctures on his upper thighs and it looks like this young man might have had a serious drug habit. We will, of course, have to wait for the tox report. But I have come across these so many times. It looks like he was a serious heroin, or similar, abuser.'

Jane turned to the two mortuary assistants.

'Can we turn him over, please?'

The two assistants lifted Terry and rolled him over onto his front. Jane surveyed the posterior of the body. 'Ligature marks around the neck and wrists. We have removed the ligatures and they appear to be a brand of plastic twine of the type used in bailing. There is haematoma discolouring to the rear of the upper arms, suggesting that his arms were tied behind him and then pulled forward. We won't know until we do some X-rays, but it might be that his shoulders have been dislocated.'

She walked over to Harry and asked him to turn around and put his arms behind him. She then asked Victoria to lift his arms upwards. Harry cried out and Victoria released him.

'Painful?' Jane asked. Harry nodded and rubbed his shoulders. 'Well, he would have been held like that for some hours before his death. My time of death still stands,' Jane said, as she removed a thermometer from Greenwood's ear and showed it to one of the technicians, who noted the body temperature down on his pad. 'Photos, please, of the posterior ligature marks. Thank you. And when we turn him back over, some of the anterior.'

The camera flashed away.

'Okay, let's have a closer look at you, Terry.' Jane pulled the young man's buttocks apart and looked inside the rectum with a torch. There was extensive bruising around the anal passage and some bleeding that had clotted. Jane let it close and turned to the mic. 'Extensive hematoma injuries to the anal passage and deep into the deceased rectum, which suggests non-consensual anal intercourse before death occurred, possibly with multiple partners and possibly they used of some types of foreign bodies.'

Harry was feeling a little hotter now and undid his tie. 'I don't quite know what all that means, boss, but it doesn't sound pleasant.'

'It means he was raped, Harry, by more than one person and they might have pushed something other than themselves up his rear end.' Harry gave a deep swallow. 'So how did he die, Jane?' Victoria asked.

'Well, looking at the bulging eyes and the colour of the lips and skin, I would say almost categorically . . . asphyxiation. But you know what I'm going to say, don't you?'

'Yep, until you have finished, etcetera, etcetera.'

'Aye, that's right. There may possibly be some semen residue or DNA left on the body. It looks like he may have something under his fingernails. So who knows? No point in you hanging around for the gory stuff. So, you can take your young man for a cup of tea, if you like, and I'll give you a shout in about half an hour if anything significant pitches up. How does that sound?'

Victoria looked at Harry, who was visibly relieved he didn't have to go the whole hog and watch the body being cut up. He was even more delighted when Victoria offered to get the drinks in, and even buy him a rock bun in the hospital café.

As they were enjoying their drinks, Victoria's phone buzzed to announce the arrival of a text. She half didn't want to look at it, fearing it might be another one from her tormentor, Jonathan Fahey.

'Aren't you going to see who it's from, boss?'

She thought for a moment that ignoring texts and phone calls would not help matters and it might indeed help catch Fahey if she could work out where he might be hiding. When she looked, it was from Agnieszka.

Hi Victoria. Miriam has been talking to me about case of missing boy you are working on and I told Sean. He might have something or nothing but if you can come this evening he will tell you what it is about.

Victoria sent a reply back immediately.

OK If I bring Miriam? She can bring you up to date on her boxing skills.

Aggie had no idea what Victoria was talking about but replied anyway.

For sure. It will be good to see you both. About seven? Sean is going to cook.

Victoria smiled to herself.

Oh no. I'm not sure about Sean doing the cooking but we will be there around seven. Love to Sean.

Aggie sent a thumbs-up. Victoria put her phone down on the table and tucked into her rock bun, thinking it would be good to catch up with Sean and Aggie. It had been months since they had gotten together. The only downside was Sean's cooking and his vinyl jazz collection. She smiled across at Harry.

'What?' he asked.

'Nothing, I was just wondering what you would make of our friendly neighbourhood psychological profiler Dr Agnieszka Krystyna Brzezinski. She's a bit of a stunner, you know.'

Harry smiled back, not really understanding.

Chapter 13

When Harry and Victoria arrived back at Fulford Road, they were met by ACC Julie Thornton, who took Harry by the arm and gestured for him to come with her.

'Can I have him back when you're done with him, please, ma'am?' asked Victoria.

'Yes, I won't keep him a minute or two. I just need to pass on some information.'

Victoria thought this somewhat strange but had long since stopped trying to understand how the mind of a senior officer worked. Especially Hot Chocolate.

Julie Thornton took him into a side meeting room and told him to sit down. 'Now, Harry, how's it going? How are you getting on with the team? I hear you've been given a nickname. Dirty Harry, isn't it?'

'Yes, ma'am. I don't mind. It kind of means they've accepted me a bit.'

'How are you getting on with Victoria?'

'Oh, she's great. Seems to know what's happening before it happens, if you know what I mean?'

'Aye, she's a good cop and has her finger on it alright. Just be wary of her impulsiveness. It's got her into trouble in the past and I don't want you getting into anything you can't get out of.'

Harry wasn't sure what the ACC was getting at but agreed to tread cautiously. Just then, Varsa poked her head around the door.

'What are you hiding in here from? Oh, sorry, ma'am. I didn't know you were in here.'

'That's okay, DC Malik, we've finished now. Remember what I said, DC Burrows. Okay?'

'Of course, ma'am.'

When the ACC had left, Varsa stood close to Harry and put her arms around his neck. 'You're not two-timing me with the older woman, are you, Mr Burrows?'

Harry squeezed her around the waist and pulled her close to him. 'Of course I am, but keep it a secret. She has promised to make me a DI.'

They both laughed and Varsa pushed him away with a frown that said *stop teasing*. Both Harry and Varsa returned to the MIT incident room. She returned to her two computer screens and Harry disappeared into the coffee room to make a round of drinks. The pair of them were still giggling.

'What's got into those two?' asked Pete.

Mal gestured with his thumb over to Varsa's desk and sang his reply in a whisper, 'All you need is love, love, love. All you need is love.' And the two men grinned at each other.

'Oh, for god's sake, you two, grow up,' shouted Varsa.

And Victoria added, 'Yes, grow up, will you? And, Varsa, what have you managed to glean from Jason's phone?'

'Well, quite a lot, and not so much.'

'That's a techie for you, double Dutch at every turn.'

'Go on, Varsa. Ignore those two.'

'Okay, well, we have loads of texts between Jason and Terry Greenwood, most of which seem to quickly turn into a passing of dick-pics and/or kisses. He rings and texts his sister on a regular basis. In fact, a lot more than you would expect. They must have been quite close, and from her replies, she was clearly aware of his homosexuality. Next in line is his communication with the coach Phil Southern, who he meets up with fairly often and outside of training sessions. Also, the language used is more like you would use with a mate or friend rather than a coach.'

'Interesting. Can you do a print off of all the texts over the last month along with any searches he'd made?' said Victoria. 'What about his mum and dad?'

'Well, that's what's strange. His contact with his parents at least by text or voicemail is minimal, to say the least. Only two contacts with his mum over the last month and none with his dad.'

Chapter 13

'Okay, everyone. Mal and Pete, when Varsa has run the list off showing the dates when Jason and Phil Southern met up, I want you to get over there and see what he has to say about them. Varsa, you see what more you can get from the phone, and a list of all the searches he has made would also help. Harry, you get the prize. I would like you to begin cataloguing the boxes and evidence bags. Anything you think might be of a higher level of importance, put to one side and we can look over it in the morning.'

Harry was not too happy about this, but nodded his reply with a quick salute and an, 'Aye, aye, boss.'

***

Later that evening, over at Sean O'Neill's flat in the city, Aggie was welcoming Victoria and Miriam. Once all the hugs and kisses were out of the way, and the four were sitting facing each other on the sofas, coffees in hand, Sean spoke up.

'Well, it's so nice to see you both. Aggie tells me you're working on a missing child. Any news or leads as yet?' He stood and picked up a vinyl LP from his collection.

'Look, there's no need to torture us with any Dave bloody Brubeck. We'll let you in on what's happening without the waterboarding, I promise,' said Victoria.

Sean replaced the LP in the rack and sat back down, smiling at his partner. 'I can't understand why no one likes jazz.'

'Nope and they can't understand why you like it. But I love it, sweetheart. Honestly,' Aggie replied, smiling at Victoria and Miriam.

Miriam was bouncing up and down on her chair like she was doing an impression of Tigger. 'Well, before you all get into missing children and horrible murders I, or should I say we, have some good news for you.' There was a moment's silence before Miriam carried on. 'We're going to have a baby.' A stunned silence. 'Yes, a baby. Vicky is pregnant. What do you reckon to that then?'

Sean and Aggie were dumbstruck. They looked at each other, then back to Victoria. Sean's mouth was wide open until Aggie told him to stop catching fish, and then they both beamed great grins in Victoria's direction. Sean stood and formally congratulated the pair of them.

Aggie could not contain herself and spoke like a Gatling gun. 'That's fantastic news, honey. You must both be delighted. When's it due? What do you want, a boy or a girl?' She gave Victoria a hug while Sean hugged Miriam and kissed her cheek.

Victoria blushed a little and gave her partner Miriam a glance that said she hadn't wanted the news broadcasting. But it was out there now. So, what the hell?

Sean sat down and then immediately stood up again. 'Well, this calls for something more than cups of coffee, Aggie. Let's have a proper drink to celebrate.'

Chapter 13

Victoria shook her head. 'Oh, not for me, Aggie. I'm fine with the coffee. Anyway, I got the idea from your text that you had something to tell me about the case we are working on.'

'Well, it's more Sean that has something to tell you, I think. Haven't you, darling?'

'Aye. Yes. Well, it might be nothing really. I can't get over you being pregnant . . . And I take it you've heard about our old friend making a break for it down in the Midlands?'

'Yes,' said Victoria. 'He sent me a text to let me know how he's getting on.'

Miriam put her hand to her mouth. 'You never told me he'd sent you a message.'

'I'm joking, sweetheart,' Victoria covered herself quickly. 'Only joking with Sean.' When her wife turned away, she looked at Sean in a way that made him understand she wasn't joking at all. Sean cocked his head to one side. 'So,' she continued to avoid rousing Miriam's suspicion, 'what about this Mispers case, boss?'

He sat back to give a little thought to what he was going to say. 'Well, two things really. The first is, I'm no longer your boss, and secondly, to be honest, I'm not sure it's going to have much bearing.'

'Well, anything would be a bonus at the moment.'

'Okay, when I was a DC over in West Yorkshire, I worked on a Mispers case of a trio of young lads who had been groomed and then abducted.'

'When are we talking?'

'It would have been around late 1998 or early '99. I was working out of central on Eastgate at the end of The Headrow. The kids went missing from around Leeds and Bradford. They were never found and the case was shelved about eight years after the last one went missing.'

'So, other than them being groomed, how is that similar to our missing lad?'

'Well, they all played for Sunday league footie clubs. At the time, it looked like they had all been groomed by an older kid, who after years of searching, we never managed to trace.'

'Right. I see. How involved were you in the investigation at the time, boss? Sorry . . . Sean?'

'I was only a DC, and it took the SIO some time to link the cases. I interviewed two sets of parents and that was about my level of involvement. The SIO felt all along that it was down to the father of the missing lad in Bradford. But all the evidence was circumstantial and the CPS wouldn't touch it with a barge pole.'

'Who was the SIO on the enquiry?'

'The now retired Chief Constable of Cumbria, Sir Noel Jackson KBE. Back then, he was a detective superintendent. Between you and me, he stifled the investigation. There was some evidence to point to a paedophile ring operating across West Yorkshire that had links to Savile, but in the words of "Stonewall" Jackson, "Fanciful notions and witch hunts seldom bear fruit." So the investigation was effectively kicked into the long grass. He moved over to Cumbria as ACC and eventually retired as a chief constable. There was talk at one time that he was living with our own Julie Thornton, but you know how the rumour machine works overtime sometimes.'

'Do you think it might be worthwhile having a look at the files relating to these missing kids, boss?'

'It wouldn't do you any harm. More similarities might pitch up, once you dig a little deeper.'

'What about having a chat with our retired chief constable?'

'Well, good luck with that. He was a crusty old bugger when I worked with him, so god knows what he's like these days.'

'Aye. We'll keep that for later, but I would like to dig out those files.'

'Yes, and while you are about it, you could have a look at a case Tubby Briers was working on.' Victoria rolled her eyes at the mention of Tubby Briers. 'Apparently, a young lad went missing in Leeds about six months ago. No trace. And he wasn't a footballer, but did come from a household that was not the most *attentive*, shall we say?'

'How did you come across that, boss?'

'Well, Tubby telephoned me last month to ask if he could use the profiling skills of Aggie here on some other case, and we just got chatting.'

Victoria got the attention of Aggie, who, along with Miriam, had re-joined the conversation. 'How did you get on with old Tubby, Aggie?'

'Oh, he's not so bad when you get to know him. I didn't consult on the missing boy. It was about a series of rapes in Leeds and Bradford. Still ongoing, I think.'

Victoria turned to Miriam and gestured for her to finish her drink.

'Can I have a quick word, Sean?' Victoria nodded her head to the hall by the front door of the flat. Miriam stood up and started to put on her coat as Victoria and Sean stepped out into the hallway. 'Sean, I wasn't joking about the contact from Fahey. He stole Miriam's phone and he has been sending me messages.'

'What? How did he get Miriam's phone?'

'It's a long story. It happened on the day of his escape while on a hospital visit.'

'I heard he killed two of the prison guards during the escape. Have you passed on the details of the text to anyone?'

'No, not yet. I didn't want to worry Miriam and I'm not sure what anyone could do about it.'

'What about at least changing your number?'

'I know that would stop the texts but then it would also stop the contact, which might help in tracking him down. It's as if I need to know what he's up to and where he might be to keep Miriam and me safe.'

'I can understand that, Vics, but it might also help him in tracking *you* down. Have you thought about that? At any rate, I think you owe it to Miriam to tell her what's been happening.'

'I know, you're right. Thanks, Sean. I'll tell her later when we're back home.'

Chapter 14

TWO WEEKS BEFORE CHRISTMAS

THE NEXT MORNING, VICTORIA WAS in early and straight on the phone with West Yorkshire police records. She asked them if it would be possible to dig out all the files on the three child abductions in the late 1990s, and that she would be over to collect them later in the day. There seemed to be no problems with the request; the sergeant said he was only too glad to help.

Harry and Varsa arrived together and Victoria filled Varsa in on where they were going and why. The forensics report, the final PM, and tox reports were in, and all would need careful scrutiny. Now that all the items from 115a Tang Hall Lane had eventually been returned from forensics, along with their initial report on fingerprints and DNA, the piles of evidence bags and boxes were immense. Victoria picked up the forensics report and skimmed over the key points. In addition to prints and DNA belonging to both the dead 18-year-old Terry Greenwood and the still-missing Jason Waites, there was a range of other prints found that had come back as not on any database. The bed-sheets had thrown up some traces of semen, but nothing to do with Jason. It was clear Jason had been in the flat, but not necessarily in Greenwood's bed. A further six DNA profiles showed that, sometime recently, they'd visited the flat, three of those having visited the bed for other reasons than sleeping.

Victoria handed the report to Harry. 'Harry, while Varsa and I are over in Leeds, I need you to make a start on cataloguing this lot. You need to compile lists and identify all exhibits as either high or low priority.'

Mal and Pete had been given the task of talking to the parents of Terry Greenwood, who lived in the village of Collingwood near Weatherby and passing on the news of their son's death.

'One or both of the parents will be needed to come over to York to formally identify the body in the next day or so, so make sure you are tactful with them . . . Okay, guys?' she said, then turned again to Harry. 'You'll have the office to yourself, Harry. So make the best of the time.'

At first, he thought this task was somewhat beneath his skill level but was soon put right by Varsa who explained that the boss was allowing him to make key decisions about the level of importance the team should put on any evidence that came out of the flat search. This puffed him up a little and helped psyche him up to the task at hand, no matter how boring it was likely to become. He looked around the room at the boxes that were piled in stacks of threes and fours and stuffed with plastic evidence bags. The boxes were in addition to the large bags containing clothing and bedding from the flat, and there were a further eight of these. He waited until the team had left him on his own before coming up with a plan of action. First on the list was a cuppa. And then the boxes. Once he made his cup of tea, he set it down on a clear desk and turned to the evidence boxes and bags.

Where to begin? he thought to himself. He selected the box marked, "115a Tang Hall Lane box 001. Drawers and bedside tables." *Might as well start at the beginning. Box 001. As good a place as any.* Just like the song from some film he remembered, though its name eluded him.

Inside the first cardboard box, there was a plethora of multi-sized, see-through evidence bags. He picked out the first one which contained what appeared to be a small notebook. At first glance, the little, black notebook, smaller than size A5, was empty. He flicked through the pages, all of which were blank. So he put it down on the desk, wondering why on earth forensics thought it important enough to test if it contained nothing. He looked at it again and picked it up by the spine. Holding it between his thumb and middle finger, he gave the book a shake. A folded piece of paper fell out onto the desk.

Harry picked up the paper and carefully unfolded it. No bigger than a ten-pound note folded down the middle then folded two more times, it had something written, or, more accurately, scrawled in pencil on it. The note was quite faded and difficult to read, and Harry wondered why someone would put it inside a notebook instead of writing the note directly in the book. He held the paper up to the light and wrote on his pad what he could decipher from the scrawling. As far as he could make out, it looked like a location. *Jackdaws, Rosedale E.* Followed by six numbers. He looked at his pad and decided to ask Varsa if it meant anything to her when she returned.

Harry then turned his attention to the rest of the box and began the laborious task of documenting everything before either setting it to one side as something that may or may not be significant or discarding it and returning it to the box from which it came. Each item was recorded on an A4 notepad with the box number it came out of and given a priority code. The problem was that, after about thirty minutes, everything he had looked at, he had given a priority one code. So everything was important. This was not going to work. He decided to have another cup of tea and a think.

Once sat back down with his tea, he picked up the piece of paper with the note scrawled on it and copied it onto a full page of his notepad. *This must have some significance*, he thought. *Why would someone keep this hidden inside a notebook?*

He decided to call Varsa. 'Hey up, you. Are you free to talk?'

'Well, that depends on what you want to talk about. I'm in the car with the boss so I don't want to hear any of that dirty talk, or I'll put you on speaker.'

Victoria was shocked and mouthed, '*WTF*,' at Varsa.

'Sorry, just joking, boss,' Varsa said with a blush you could warm your hands on. 'Don't know what I was thinking of,' she said, with a mischievous chuckle.

Even though Harry was on his own in the office, he too had a crimson face, even noticeable under his beard.

'Er . . . er, no. I mean, I just wanted to pick your brains about something I've found, if that's okay?'

'Yep, of course. Shoot.'

'Well, I was wondering if this means anything to you?' He was about to read out the note as it was written down when the line went dead. He looked at his phone and pressed re-dial. The phone rang out with no answer. He put his phone down on the desk and looked again at the handwritten note. He was about to re-dial when a text arrived.

Hey up you. We are just going into the West York Police HQ. Send me the details of what you need and I will get back to you when we are free.

He dashed off a quick reply.

No worries, it's nothing important. It can wait until you are back. See you later. X

As Victoria, in her heels, clicked her way up the steps into the main reception of West York's HQ, she glanced down at her IT wizard and couldn't help but ask, 'Are you and our Harry an item now then?'

'Is it that obvious?'

'Is the Pope a Catholic?'

'Well, we might be. Would that be wrong or against the rules then?'

'No, not in the slightest, but keep it out of the office if you can.'

The pair made their way into the building and signed in at the desk.

***

Harry was sitting with his feet up on the desk considering what the note might mean and slurping his tea when he heard the sound of a pair of heels clicking down the corridor. The ACC Crime Julie Thornton could just about make out someone through the open door to the MIT office with their feet up on the desk and decided to look in on who it was.

'Well, well, well. Is this how the other half live then?'

Harry jumped to his feet, spilling his tea in the process, and dropping his large notepad with the address on it onto the floor. She bent down and picked it up.

'What's this, Harry? Planning on doing some hiking, are we?'

'Er, no, ma'am. Why do you ask?'

She handed him back his notepad. 'Well, you have a grid reference of one of the loveliest parts of the North York Moors. Rosedale is beautiful at any time of the year but especially when a hard frost and a mist is hanging in the dale. Just thought you were planning a bit of a walk.'

She smiled and walked out, leaving a lingering draft of perfume as she went. Harry looked at the page on his notepad. He remembered something from his schoolboy geography and decided to put the grid reference into Google Maps. Sure enough, it came up with the Ordinance Survey map of the North Yorkshire Moors, or at least the eastern side of the moor, so he assumed the *E* related to the eastern map. He looked at the note again, then back to the map. The six numbers were obviously the six-figure reference and the little pear drop sat smack over some farm buildings called Jack Daw's Farm. *Yes!* he thought. *Now we're getting somewhere. Why would the now-dead Terry Greenwood have this address? It has to be significant.* He called Varsa again and her phone immediately went to voicemail. He tried Victoria's and the same happened. *Shit.* It was only about an hour's drive away, an hour and a half max. He could be back before Varsa and the boss were back from Leeds. *It's got to be worth a shout.* Feather-in-his-cap time was on the cards.

Without further thought, he tore the page from the notepad and folded it up, putting it into his pocket. Then, for some reason, Harry decided to also put the scrap of paper with the scribbled note on it inside his wallet for safekeeping. He grabbed his coat, set his half-finished cup of tea down on the desk, and made his way downstairs. Harry thought about marking the board with where he was going, but as he would be back before the boss and Varsa returned, there would be no need, and the longer he delayed, the longer he would be out. *So off to the lovely, picturesque Rosedale and hopefully Jack Daws Farm*, he thought. Could he really hope to find Jason at the farm? Probably not, but it had to be worth a shout. Once outside, he loaded the address into his satnav, waited for a second for it to activate the directions, and checked his fuel. *Definitely need to fill up on the way back.*

The drive was uneventful and he made it in good time. The satnav took him along the A64 to Malton, then the A169 to Pickering, turning left in Pickering along the A170 until he arrived in the village of Wrelton. Then the route turned him north, along a single-track road called Cropton Lane, for about seven miles, before entering the village of Rosedale. Hot Chocolate really wasn't joking. It was a very pretty village — one pub and a small grocers shop. It even had a babbling brook running along the side of the single-track road through the village. The houses were all built in Yorkshire stone and there were even a few with thatched roofs remaining.

The pear drop on the satnav was sending him off to the left of the main village road onto a narrow, bumpy track with ubiquitous potholes and puddles in plentiful supply. The track climbed a little at first and then began to steepen. He drove for around four to five minutes, climbing steadily up a noticeable gradient, with the occasional scraping of the bumper and sills of his car thrown in for good measure. Every now and again, the front wheels would slip and spin on a bolder or a particularly deep puddle, and his main concern was getting stuck up on the high moor. When the nice satnav lady told him he had reached his destination, he stopped, switched the engine off, applied the hand brake, and just to ensure he didn't roll backwards, put the car in first gear. He climbed out and looked down at his footwear. Flat-soled slip-ons were not the ideal things to be wearing out here. He wished immediately he had put a pair of wellies in the boot.

Looking around, he could see in the distance, probably about three hundred yards away, a group of farm buildings nestling in a hollow in what was, even at this time of the year, a most beautiful spot. The main farmhouse, if you could call it that, was surrounded by a range of buildings, all built on the side of a rocky slope. To the north of the farm and, in places hiding it a little, there was a relatively large copse of mainly Scots pines. There was no farm gate from the lane he had driven up and he wondered how people got to and from it. *Surely they don't bring everything across these fields?*

Chapter 14

He decided to re-trace his route back down the track and ask in the village about Jack Dawn's Farm. It would take all his reversing skills to get back down without hitting one of the dry-stone walls that encroached on either side of the track. If driving up the track was difficult, going backwards down it was the stuff of rally drivers. It seemed to take forever until his car reversed out onto the main road, and he spotted two men speaking together on one side of the track. One of the men was sitting atop a massive, blue tractor, the other holding four terrier dogs on leads. Harry pulled his car off the road and went over to speak with them.

'Hello there. I was wondering if you could help me, please? I am looking for Jack Dawn's Farm. I think I have found it in the hollow over there.' Harry waved and pointed in the direction of where he believed the farm to be. 'The only thing is there doesn't appear to be any entrance to it from the lane here?'

The two men looked at each other and then back at Harry. The man on the tractor smiled at the man with the dogs. 'Go on, George, tell poor lad bad news.'

'Well, aye, lad. I could tell thee how to get in't farm like, but yer see, it's secret. Secret like.' He paused and looked at the man on the tractor. 'If I tell thee, I'll only have to shoot thee later.'

The two men guffawed, which sent the dogs jumping about and barking. Harry was looking perplexed and the two men laughed uncontrollably.

'I think I'm gonna wet meself, George, a really do, thee bloody fool, thee are.' The man called George looped the dog leads around the footplate of the tractor and walked over to Harry.

'Sorry, lad, just havin' a bit o' fun like, hey? No hard feelings?'

'No, of course not. But the farm?'

'Aye, right enough. Well, to start with, it hasn't been a farm proper like since t'fifties. All land 'round 'er is property of the Fitz-Michael Estate like, and the farm was given over to the MOD in t'fifties for use as one of them bunker places. You know, when we all thought end of world was comin' and government, or at least local government and such, would come up 'ere and run stuff from underground bunkers. Supposed to be secret like, so the entrance was taken away. But if you want to go and have a look, you need to drive back down main road a wee bit until you come to a sign that says Fitz-Michael Estates. There is a gravel driveway that takes you up to t'farm. Don't fuss about the barrier that's down, but just lift it and drive on up t'farm buildings. They're all closed up like now, but Lord Fitz-Michael leaves gate open so we can get up to top moor to feed sheep and stuff.'

Harry was making his way back to his car when the man sitting on the tractor spoke. 'What's all the bloody interest in the place then?'

Harry stopped and turned to the two men. 'How do you mean, all the interest?'

'Well, there's been quite a bit of comings and goings just lately. Just lights and what have you, but nowt much like. There was a rumour that the estate manager was going to turn it into a shooting lodge.'

'Oh, right enough. I hadn't heard that.'

They both turned to Harry and spoke almost in union, 'You shoot, do ya, young fella?'

'Nope. Not unless I have to.' Harry smiled to himself and thought, *Touché.*

Harry turned his car around and drove a little way back down the road he had come up when he first arrived in the village. As he approached the entrance to the estate road, he stopped his car and climbed out to open the barrier. Attached to it was a sign.

PRIVATE PROPERTY BELONGING TO THE FITZ-MICHAEL ESTATE. KEEP OUT.

Sure enough, and true to their word, the barrier swung upwards with only minimal effort. Harry climbed back into his car and drove a few feet clear of the gate, giving him room to close it down behind him. *I know how these bloody farmers are about their gates.*

It was now late in the afternoon, and although the light was beginning to fade a little, as he got closer to the group of buildings, he could clearly see that some building work had been recently underway. The main building was surrounded by scaffolding and a couple of skips sat to one side, one partially filled with rubble. The whole place had a rundown and unkempt feel about it. It was a less-than-imposing Victorian or possibly Edwardian structure, two stories high with attic rooms in the roof void. The walls were rendered in a dirty-grey pebble dash that was peeling in places and making it look decidedly that no one really cared for it. Although the main building was set on a slight rise, the trees overhung and made it look dark and somewhat more foreboding than it actually was. The whole place had a sinister air about it that Harry couldn't put his finger on. As he climbed out of his car, in the fading light, he felt a little chill run through his bones.

He shook himself and put it down to the miserable, damp weather. Before venturing any further, he decided to check his phone. No messages and no missed calls. So he returned the phone to his jacket pocket and walked towards the front door of the property. On the front porch, he searched for a doorbell and could not find one. There was a door knocker and the noise created by the three knocks echoed across the driveway and beyond. Still no answer. As he gave a slight push on the door, it was firmly shut.

He was about to take a look around the rear of the property when something told him to go and collect his extendable baton from the car. He wasn't expecting any trouble, but the baton was a useful tool should he need to gain entry. *What am I thinking? Planning to break into a property?*

I must be mad as a hatter. Nevertheless, he went to the car, then made his way around the back, baton in one hand and his small torch in the other.

Under the cover of some trees, he peered through a set of French doors into what appeared to be a large sitting room. He tapped on the glass with his baton, again with no response. Should he or shouldn't he? He decided on the should and gave the glass a sharp tap on the pane closest to the handle of the door. To Harry, the noise of the shattering glass was loud enough to wake the dead, he thought. Then he immediately shook his head. *That is not a good metaphor.* He reached inside the broken pane and turned the door handle.

Stepping inside, he called out to whoever might be there, 'Hello, anyone home?'

He waited for a second or so. No answer.

'Hello, police here. Is anyone about, please?'

Still no answer. He shone his torch around the room in a wide arc and noticed that it looked like some decorating work had recently been undertaken. The furniture was covered in white dustsheets and there was a distinct smell of fresh paint. The floorboards creaked and squeaked under every step, and seemed to get louder as he moved towards the only door in the room. He stopped at the door and thought he'd heard something — some movement, something. *Probably rats.* He gripped his baton a little tighter.

The door opened into a corridor, and he found a light switch on the wall next to the door. When he tried the switch, nothing happened. If he was going to search any further, he would be totally reliant on his small torch.

Harry scanned the light up and down the corridor, debating which way to go and which rooms to look into. There were four doors to choose from. He scratched his chin and was pondering for a second when he thought he heard something that sounded like a cough. It made him jump and he spun around. The sound came, he thought, from behind the door directly in front of him.

'Hello? Who's there? I'm a police officer and I need you to come out.' Harry held his breath. He was in two minds about whether to call it in or go it alone. He gripped his baton even tighter, and then thought about his training. *Hold your baton firmly but not so tight as it slows down your movements.* He let his grip ease a little. Harry looked around slowly, just to make sure there was no one behind him, and felt a slight shiver.

Then came a distinct call. He could not mistake it.

'Help! I'm down here. Help me, please.' Although the voice was muffled, it was clearly that of a young person and sounded male. He tried the door and it didn't budge. 'Help me, please.'

'It's okay, hang on. I'll get you out. You'll be safe now.' Again, he thought about calling it in and getting some backup but decided he could manage. *If it's Jason, Dirty Harry will be the one to get him out.*

He gave the door a heavy shoulder and it gave way easily, almost sending him tumbling down a set of stone stairs. The adrenaline had now kicked in big time and he bounded down the steps into the darkness. As he reached the bottom step he called out, 'It's okay, son. My name is Detective Harry Burrows. Is it Jason? Are you alright? Don't worry, I'll get you out.'

Harry was blurting out words as he made his way through the dark. He trained his torch around the cellar and settled it on the young man who was chained to a set of pipes. The cellar stunk of human faeces and urine, and as Harry got close, Jason held up his hands in a gesture of hope.

'Don't worry, son. We'll have you out in no time.'

Jason was sobbing with a mixture of relief and anticipation of seeing his family again, as Harry came within touching distance. He reached out and hugged Harry's legs as Harry shone the torch and checked Jason's shackles and chains. He noticed that the chains around Jason's wrists had dug in and were starting to leave nasty, red sores. The chains were heavy-duty and the shackles were not going to be broken with any degree of ease. It didn't take long for Harry to realise that this would not be an easy rescue. The chains were secured to the pipes by large padlocks that would need serious bolt cutters to remove them. No amount of tugging and twisting was going to make any difference. Harry tried using his baton to leverage the padlock open, but it was no use.

All the time, he was wondering if they were alone, and he kept looking and pointing the torch up to the open door at the top of the steps. Harry's heart was racing. His previous deliberations about calling for backup were now out of his hands. He was going to need help to get the chains removed.

'Jason, do you know if there is anyone still in the house? Have you seen anyone?'

'I heard someone leave before you came in, but I don't really know how long ago that was.'

'Okay, mate, no problem.' Harry looked around again, feeling discomfort and anxiety, but there was no alternative. 'Look, Jason, I'm not going to be able to get these off without some serious help, so I will have to call for backup.' Jason nodded and Harry checked his phone. 'Shit,' he mouthed. 'No signal.'

He turned to Jason and explained that he needed to go back upstairs to make the call, where he could get a signal, and then he would return and wait with Jason until the cavalry arrived. Jason smiled and nodded at Harry, who put his baton on the floor and gave the young lad his coat to keep him warm. Jason hugged him tightly and clearly did not want him to leave. As he turned to go, Harry glanced back and told Jason not to worry. Help would be on its way soon.

He bounded up the stairs two at a time, just halting to check his phone two steps from the top. 'Great . . . three bars,' he said to himself.

Chapter 14

While looking down at his phone, Harry never saw the ball-peen hammer that hit him squarely between the eyes or felt the stone stairs as he bounced back down into the cellar. Once he had reached the bottom, he also didn't see the subsequent ten blows of the hammer as it crushed his skull to a pulp. He never felt the blows at all, as he was already dead.

Chapter 15

'HELLO, IT'S ME.'

'Oh, for fuck's sake. You know the routine. I told you never to call me. You know how to get in touch, you thick bastard.'

'I know, I'm sorry. But something bad has happened.'

'So, what's so bad that you needed to break the rules we set?'

'I've killed a cop.'

'You've *what*? You've killed a fucking cop? How? Where? Why? You fucking idiot.'

'He was at the house. He found the kid and was going to call for help. I couldn't do owt else, could I?'

'How do you know he was a cop?'

'I checked his pockets and found his card. He's called Harry Burrows.'

'Harry fucking Burrows? You absolute shitfaced idiot. Do you know who Harry Burrows is?'

'No, but he was going to call the other cops. Who is he anyway? He looks a bit young to be anybody important. I hit him with a hammer.'

'Oh, for god's sake. You hit him with a hammer? Are you sure he's dead?'

'Yep, I'm sure. I kept hitting him and he looks dead. Who is he?'

'He's only the fucking nephew of the Assistant Chief Constable of North Yorkshire Police. That's all he is. Oh, for god's sake, man. What have you done?'

'I couldn't do anything else. He was about to phone for help.'

'I know, you said that already. How the fuck did he find the house?'

'He had the note I gave that lad in York, with the address of the house on it.'

'You gave Terry Greenwood a note with the address? Are you kidding me? You braindead moron.'

'I had to. Otherwise, how would he have found the house to bring the kid? You know how he was always on cloud fucking nine half the time with drugs and stuff. I needed to make sure he knew where to bring him.'

'So now all the plod in North Yorkshire will know where we have him.'

'Well, not necessarily. After he found the kid in the cellar, he never had time to call anyone else before I hit him with the hammer. The note was the one I'd written. So maybe he hasn't told anyone where he was going? He was on his own and his car is still out front of the house. You can't see it from the road. I was thinking I could get rid of him and the car at the same time, like? And I was thinking you might be able to check if any of the rest of them have a scooby about the house. You know, with your contacts, like?'

'You should have been doing a bit more *thinking* before you gave the fucking note to Greenwood. How's the kid? Did he see you hit the copper?'

'Yeah, I think he did. Shall I get rid of him too, then?'

'*No!* For fuck's sake, you've done enough to endanger everything, and getting rid of the kid would be like throwing good money down the drain. We might need to move him at some stage, but we have people coming next week who will be paying big bucks for a wee session with the young fella. So leave him alone. Understand? In fact, he'll need cleaning up a bit and feeding.'

'Yeah, right, but he will need to be sorted at some stage?'

'Aye, but not for a while yet, he won't. Now, listen to me. This is what you're going to do with Burrows. First, you get him into the boot of his car. Check there's enough fuel to get to Ripon. I'll meet you on the A61 in that car park, the one in the Quarry Moor Nature Reserve. Do you remember when we met there a couple of years back with those punters?'

'Yeah, it's just south of Ripon, right?'

'I'll meet you there at twenty-three hundred hours. That's eleven o'clock tonight to you. We can torch the car and I'll bring you back to the estate house. I need to check how much they know about the whereabouts of the kid in the meantime and if the MIT are aware of the house or not. It's likely being dealt with by that dyke Adams. So I should be able to get some idea of where they are up to with it. Now, for god's sake, have you got all that?'

'Yeah, got it.'

'Now don't fuck it up. Make sure you avoid any major roads as they'll have cameras running. And make sure the kid is secured. And don't call me again on this number.'

The phone went dead.

Chapter 16

THE CIVILIAN ADMINISTRATOR ON THE desk at West Yorkshire Police Headquarters scrutinised Victoria and Varsa's IDs and checked her list of expected visitors before handing them both a couple of lanyards dangling with visitor passes. She asked the women to wait, explaining that someone would take them down to the records office located in the basement. The pair took a seat on an upholstered bench in front of the window. Varsa looked up into the expanse of the atrium above her; it seemed to go on forever.

'Wow. This is some place alright, boss.'

'Aye. It's certainly undergone some changes over its life. Apparently, it used to be one of the wildest nicks in the country. They used to call it Tombstone.' Varsa was about to ask why but decided against it. 'The old premises were knocked down about ten years back and Buckingham Palace here was built on the site. Makes Fulford Road look like a shoebox.'

The lady from the desk came over to speak to them both. 'I do apologise, but it looks like there is no one available to take you down to records at the moment. Would it be an inconvenience for you to come back later on in the day? Or possibly tomorrow?'

Victoria shook her head in disbelief. 'Yes, it most certainly would. Why do we need someone to take us down to records? I am a DCI and can promise not to get lost. We're also adults who can read and follow signs. I take it the department does have directions?'

'Yes, it does.' She pointed to the large sign that contained a floor plan of each level in the building. 'It's just that the new chief constable has issued a directive that he doesn't want to see visitors wandering around the HQ unattended or unsupervised.'

'I can see that, but we're not on some jolly. We are police officers, and we're working a live case that some of your records held in the archive may be able to help us with. And we would like to get on with this right away, if possible?'

The young woman scanned the reception area as if looking for someone to take the decision away from her. Eventually, she turned back to Varsa and Victoria. 'Okay. Just follow the signs to the basement and when you get down there I think there is a Sergeant Keen on duty who will help you.'

Victoria stood up, thanked the receptionist, and made her way to the stairwell. At the bottom of two flights of stairs, there was a further reception desk. However, this time, it was unmanned and had a buzzer fixed to it with a sign that asked to press for assistance. Victoria pressed and waited. A door behind the desk was opened in less than a second, which made Varsa jump. A short, overweight uniformed sergeant stood in front of the detectives and looked at them over his half-rimmed spectacles. His tunic had what looked like the remains of his breakfast on the lapels and his thinning, grey hair put him well past retirement age. Victoria and Varsa smiled.

'Yes?'

Victoria could see he was a man of few words.

'My name is DCI Victoria Adams from the North Yorkshire Major Incident Team, and this here is DC Varsa Malik. We have come to look at some files pertaining to a case some time ago. 1998 or '99. We're not too sure about the exact dates. However, it relates to a major investigation into missing children in West Yorkshire, none of which have been found to this date.'

He rubbed the stubble on his chin with his thumb and forefinger, and Victoria glanced at the name tag above his right breast pocket. It read Sergeant Keen, IC Records Office. He looked Victoria in the eye with little or no emotion. 'Name of the investigation?'

'I'm not too sure of the exact name of it, but there can't have been many investigations into missing children in the late nineties, can there?'

'So, you're not sure of the year and you don't know the name of the investigation. Do you perhaps know who headed it up?'

She answered immediately, 'Detective Superintendent Noel Jackson.'

'Well, that's not going to be much help. He would've headed up anything and everything at the time. Nope, without the name of the investigation, I can't help you. Sorry.'

Before Victoria could speak again, he had turned around and disappeared back into the bowels of the records office.

Varsa looked at her boss. 'You would be forgiven for thinking we're all on the same side, boss?'

'Yes, you might.'

Victoria dialled Sean's number and he picked up immediately.

'Hey, just a quick question. You don't remember the name given to the investigation into the missing kids back in the late nineties, do you?'

'Aye, of course. I thought I told you what it was called when we met. Odd name really, from some old children's nursery rhyme. It was the Muffin Man Enquiry.'

'Thanks, Sean. We owe you one. And what about that chat we were going to have?'

'How about tomorrow? I'm dropping Aggie off in town and could meet you for a coffee.'

'Sounds good to me, boss . . . sorry, Sean. What about the little café next to the green in Clifton? Ten-thirty?'

'Suits me fine. See you then.' As events were about to unfold their meeting would be postponed until the week before Christmas, neither of them aware of how the case was about to develop.

Victoria ended the call and immediately pressed the buzzer again. Just as before, Sergeant Keen appeared in a split second, almost as if he had been waiting for the buzzer to ring, popping up like a genie from a bottle. It was like Victoria was the keeper of the lamp who could summon him up at will.

He spoke as if it was their first meeting. 'Yes? How can I help?'

Victoria again looked a little surprised but carried on regardless. 'Okay, Sergeant Keen, the enquiry was called the Muffin Man. So, if we could see all files pertaining to that enquiry, that would be most helpful. Thanks.'

The sergeant smiled. 'I hope you have a big boot in your car, Detective Chief Inspector, because there's quite a bit of stuff. If you can follow me, please?'

He led them into a long corridor lit by overly powerful strip lighting. Along each side of the corridor were banks of shelving units that you could expand by turning a wheel at the entrance to each bay of shelves. Sergeant Keen glanced behind him at the two women and gestured for them to keep following him. He eventually stopped and began to spin one of the wheels. The row of shelves slowly opened up to reveal yet another corridor, this one more claustrophobic than the last. There was just enough room for them both to fit inside at the same time. The two women looked back at Keen.

'So which are the files for the Muffin Man Enquiry, Sergeant?'

'You're looking at them, ma'am.'

Victoria and Varsa looked up and then to the left, not able to believe their eyes at the vast quantity of banker's boxes of files and evidence bags laid out on the shelves both in front, behind, and high above them.

'Good god! I can't believe it,' Victoria said. 'We're going to need a pantechnicon to move this lot.'

'Well, probably not,' Keen replied. 'It arrived here in a Luton van from the ops room being used by the investigative team when the investigation was shelved.'

'You say shelved, Sarge. Was it not officially closed down?'

'No, not closed. Shelved. By Stonewall Jackson.'

'So, he was still in charge when it was, as you say, shelved? Has there been any further investigative work undertaken since then?'

'I need to look at the log, but it's unlikely. However, I will check.' He paused and then looked from the files to Victoria. 'So, what are you going to do about taking these files then, ma'am?'

Victoria thought for a moment and turned to Keen. 'We'll take them in boxes now.' She put her hand on the far side of a row of boxes. 'From here to the end of the two rows, and the rest will be collected by two of my officers as soon as we can arrange for the hire of a van. We will, of course, give you a heads up on when to expect us, if that's okay?'

'All great with me, ma'am. Hope you find what you're looking for.'

'That's the point, Sergeant, I don't really know what I'm looking for.' Sergeant Keen gave a grunt and a smile. 'Is there any chance of some muscle to help us move these into my car, Sarge?'

'Well, I'm afraid I am not at liberty to leave my post here in records, you understand. However, I could give you a hand with some of the boxes as far as the lift. I'm on my own, you see, down here.' He looked around as if checking if anyone was watching. 'Oh okay, I'll bend the rules for you both this once and help you get them into the lift.'

'Any chance of some help at the other end? Or at least the loan of a trolly so we can move them to our car?'

He tutted and drew in a sharp intake of breath. 'This is most irregular, you realise? But I am allowed to furnish you with some transportation. I'll meet you at the landing and retrieve said trolly when you've finished. Of course, this will mean closing up the records office for a short while, which is really against the rules. What would happen if another member of staff wished to gain access to the files while I am engaged with helping yourself?'

Varsa looked around the records office reception area.

'They're not exactly queuing up, Sarge, are they?'

Sergeant Keen ignored her attempt at sarcasm as he fetched a four-wheel trolly from behind a seated area. He helped them get the boxes they wanted and, as promised, met them at the top of the lift area on the ground floor entrance. Eventually, he succumbed to Victoria's charms and helped get all the boxes into her car. As the pair pulled away, Varsa looked at Victoria and they both, almost in unison, said, 'Jobsworth,' and laughed out loud.

***

Assistant Chief Constable Julie Thornton had been working late, as she desperately wanted to collate the crime figures by policing area in some meaningful way before the next day's presentation to the Police and Crime Commissioner and his team. She had just about finished when her desk phone rang. In two minds as to whether to answer it or ignore it and get herself home, she decided on the latter. She pushed her swollen feet into her patent high heels, winced a little, and stood up. She looked at the phone that was continuing to ring and began to turn away towards the door. It kept ringing and was still ringing as she reached the stairs.

She stopped and looked back at her office door. *Oh, for god's sake*, she thought, then turned and went back to answer it.

'Hello? Assistant Chief Constable Thornton speaking. How can I help you?'

'Well, get her then. The full title. Long time no speak, as they say.'

She recognised the voice immediately and sat back down, relaxing into her chair, kicking her shoes back off. 'Well, this is a pleasant surprise. To what do I owe the honour?'

'Well, I was wondering if you might like to go out for a drink or even a meal sometime? Just for old times' sake, you understand?'

'That's a nice gesture, Noel. But before answering in the affirmative, or otherwise, what do you want?'

'What do you mean, what do I want? Can't an old flame call up and ask a girl out on a date without some ulterior motive?'

'Stonewall Jackson always had an ulterior motive, I seem to remember. But having said that . . . I don't mind, so long as you're paying. You can well afford a decent restaurant on your pension. When were you thinking?'

'Well, to be honest, I was thinking of a drink this evening and we can decide how it goes from there. What do you say?'

'I say not a bloody chance. I've been at it all day. I have only just finished my prep for the PCC meeting in the morning. I'm absolutely knackered and my bath and bed are calling me with a purpose. What about tomorrow? It will give me time to make myself alluring for you.'

'I seem to remember you were always just that. You didn't get the nickname Hot Chocolate for nothing.'

Chapter 16

Julie Thornton laughed and sensed the heat rising up her neck a little. She decided to change the subject. 'So how is retirement treating you then, Noel?'

'Oh, you know, boring as hell. I've managed to fend off the desire for an allotment, but I have gone out and bought a Harley and all the leathers, although they are a bit tight. Now don't get too excited, Julie. Anyway, how are you doing? I hear you're all up to your neck in it at the moment with the missing young lad. And now a murder on top? And how's that nephew of yours getting on?'

'How did you find out about Harry? The appointment was supposed to be on the QT.'

'Hey, I did use to be a detective, you know, and you should be the first to understand that the rumour machine works overtime these days. I suspect that most of your MIT are aware he's a relative. So, how's he doing? Has he managed to solve it all on his own?'

'Adams keeps him on a tight leash. He was saying earlier today that he gets all the shit jobs. Filing, making the tea, answering the phone. She has him sorting out all the evidence from the murder victim's flat at the moment. On a positive note, however, he seems to have hooked up with Varsa Malik, the IT wizard that works for Adams. I'm not sure if they are a full-on item, as they say, but getting that way.'

'So, no real leads on either the missing lad or the murder as yet then?'

'No, I don't think so, as yet. I'm sure if there was any breakthrough, I would have been kept in the loop. Why all the interest?'

'Ah, nothing really. I suppose I miss it all a bit. What about this coffee then?'

'I see the drinks and meal have been downgraded to a cup of coffee now. I don't know, you pump me for information and then drop me like a stone. Typical Stonewall.'

'No. No, the meal is still on. You said you could make it tomorrow. What about meeting me halfway? Say that little Italian we used to sneak away to in Harrogate? If you remember?'

'How could I forget? The last time we ate there, we ended up overnighting in the Cairn Hotel, I seem to remember.'

'We are older and wiser these days, Julie.'

'Speak for yourself. Say eight o'clock?'

'Suits me, my love. See you then.'

ACC Thornton hung up the phone and felt a distinct tinge of excitement. *A date?* Julie thought. *Well, dinner at least. But who knows what we'll be having for dessert . . .*

Chapter 17

'WHAT DO YOU THINK WE should do with Strange and Leith, Jonathan?' Walsh said, jerking his thumb backwards to indicate where the two dead bodies were bumping around in the boot.

'Nothing. When we dump the car, we just leave them. It's of no consequence to us. When they find the car in Harwich, they'll find the bodies, and we'll be long gone. We've given ourselves enough time. They'll assume we've taken the ferry to Holland, and that's when they'll be alerting the Dutch police. They'll believe we've either gone as foot passengers or in another car.'

Fahey smiled at his accomplice and returned to his thoughts.

Everything was going according to plan. *His* plan. Once they had left the prison service vehicle in Felixstowe, close to Harwich ferry port, they would transfer to the second vehicle that had been organised by Walsh. They would then drive back up North to Immingham, south of Hull. The plan, although somewhat diverse, was designed to throw the hounds off the scent at each and every turn. Under their new identities, they would make the overnight crossing from Immingham in South Humberside to the seaport of Brevik in southern Norway. This ferry was one of the few still running to Norway from the UK and only took heavy goods vehicles and foot passengers. Once ashore, they would lay low for some months and decide on when to make the move to France. Well, that was the plan Fahey had made with Walsh, and, to his credit, Walsh had done everything he was asked. Although the plan entailed them both setting sail for Brevik, in Jonathan's plan, only one of them would make the overnight crossing. Only one of them would be returning. And no one would be going to live in France.

The silver Volvo V70 belonging to Wellingborough Prison was left in the multi-storey car park close to the ferry terminal at Harwich, along with its cargo of dead bodies. Fahey opened the boot of the Volvo and checked inside. The blood was now beginning to pool and spread out across the carpet in the boot. He screwed his face at the sight of the bodies and slammed it shut.

'Okay, my friend, let's have a look at the wheels you've got us to travel back up North in. I hope it's something comfortable.'

Walsh took a set of keys out of his pocket and pressed the fob. Immediately, there was a bleep that echoed around the car park and the lights of a Range Rover flashed in one corner.

'Not bad, Peter. Not bad at all. You have excelled, so far. I could not have planned this any better myself.'

'I parked it away from any CCTV and checked that we can't be seen getting into it, but we need to walk around the edge of the level to the right here.'

'Well done, you. That's excellent, Peter, just excellent.'

Walsh liked it when Fahey used his first name and liked it even more when he praised him, but little did he realise what plans Fahey had for him. If he did, he wouldn't have been puffing his chest out like the proverbial peacock, or the child who had just received a star for his homework assignment.

'My turn, I think, Peter,' Fahey said, as he held out his hand for the keys. And Peter Walsh dutifully dropped the Land Rover fob into the psychopath's open hand.

Jonathan considered for a moment how stupid Peter Walsh really was. He could be relied on to do exactly what he was told but had little in the way of initiative or any ability whatsoever to work things out for himself. The idiot hadn't even put two and two together — if the idea of swapping cars was to throw the police off the scent, surely they would pick it up again when they found the abandoned Range Rover in Immingham? He was far too stupid to understand that Jonathan would be needing that car for himself and his future plans. Plans that poor Peter didn't figure in one iota.

Chapter 17

As Fahey pulled out of the car park into the early evening dusk, he glanced at Walsh. The man had served his useful purpose now and Fahey needed to be free of him. However, his company would have to be endured for the next four hours, or at least until they were on the boat and making the night-time crossing to Norway.

The drive up to Immingham was uneventful. Peter Walsh slept most of the way there. Once awake, he talked incessantly about what their new life in the South of France would be like and how he was looking forward to learning French. Fahey thought that the chatter was only marginally less annoying than the constant loathsome snoring that reminded him of a pig grunting. From time to time, he would look down at the sleeping, fat-gutted, balding excuse for a human being and reflect on how killing him could be considered a benefit to society. Ridding the world of this, in his eyes, pointless creature should generate a knighthood, not a prison sentence. But he had seen the inside of prison for the last time, and he would never allow himself to be sent back. After ridding himself of this bundle of lard sitting next to him, he would set his sights on the pair of dykes who were responsible for his incarceration. Oh, he would bide his time, but when the time came, and indeed it soon would, the pair would be begging him for their lives and the life of their unborn child.

It was clear, in his mind, that Victoria would be his main target, along with her ex-boss, and although he had no real grievances with the good doctor Miriam, she would provide the bait to lure Victoria into his trap. If she got too much in the way, then so be it; she would go the same way as her lesbian friend. At the moment, his strategy was in its infancy, but he was in no rush. In fact, the longer he dragged out the final chapter of his revenge, the more enjoyment he would extract from it. In the warped reality that Fahey inhabited, both Victoria and her ex-boss Chief Superintendent Sean O'Neill held joint responsibility for the death of Claire. Fahey had managed to concoct a twisted reality, in which everyone other than himself was responsible for the death of his sister. Although it was he who tortured and finally killed her, the mistaken identity, the putting her up for adoption, and the secrecy around the painfulness of her early life, they were all the responsibility of others. Not him. And he had built this into a pyramid of hate directed at Detective Chief Inspector Victoria Adams.

***

Getting on board the Immingham-to-Brevik ferry was straightforward enough. Peter Walsh had been quiet for a whole ten minutes, which took the edge off Jonathan's anger and allowed him to get his thoughts together. Once the pair had secured their vehicle, they made their way to the upper deck and found the booked cabin for the overnight crossing. Carrying only a couple of holdalls, the two men had plenty of room in the two-berth cabin and both unpacked their toiletries in silence.

'Do you fancy a drink before we eat, Jonathan? Or do you want to go directly to the restaurant?'

Jonathan looked at his accomplice, doing all he could to hide his annoyance. He gave him a thin smile. The way Walsh constantly sought affirmation on everything he did, never making a decision on his own, the way he bounced around like bloody Tigger all the time, and the way he grinned, like a damn school kid... It all served to build like a volcano inside Jonathan. A volcano that was about to explode in a way that would not end happily, well, not for Prison Officer Walsh, anyway.

'Sure, let's have a drink or two before we eat. We have lots to celebrate.'

Walsh smiled yet again at Jonathan as they both stepped out into the gangway. Once in the bar, and after a couple of drinks, Jonathan suggested they go and find a table in the restaurant. His lapdog was only too eager to follow him. At the table, the one-directional chatter started again, and after they had finished their main course, Walsh asked Jonathan if he wanted a pudding.

'It's called dessert, Peter, not a pudding.'

'Oh, sorry. I didn't think it mattered what you call it.'

'Well, it does, Peter. Trust me. It does.'

Jonathan had never sat down to a meal with his accomplice before and he now watched him as he ate. *God*, he thought, *the man eats like a pig. He is uneducated, uncouth, vulgar, but above all, stupid. Not for much longer, thank god.* After they finished dinner, Jonathan pushed his chair back and stood up. 'Look, Peter, I am going to get my coat and have a short walk on the upper deck. What do you want to do?'

'Well, I was going to watch a bit of TV in our cabin. I've checked and you can put it on catch-up, I think, and I can have a look at one of those crime shows from way back. But I don't mind keeping you company on the deck for a while.'

Jonathan smiled his response, thinking he could not stand this man for much longer.

'I'll go and fetch both coats, if you like, Jon?' Walsh pandered again.

Jonathan nodded. Walsh rushed off obediently, and Jonathan made his way over to the carvery. He glanced around to check he was not being observed. All the chefs were sitting down at a round table and drinking coffee.

'Are you looking for some more food, sir?' one of them called over.

'No, just admiring your roast beef. We've enjoyed it so much, thank you.'

He waited until the cook had gone back to his conversation, then picked up one of the long carving knives. He checked again for observers and rolled it up inside a heavy, cotton tea towel used to carry hot dishes to the buffet. He was careful to fold the towel over the point of the knife. Once it was secure and safe, he lifted up his sweater and pushed the wrapped blade down inside his belt, covering it with the heavy hem of his jumper.

He took a final look and then coolly made his way out onto the weather deck. As he made his way towards the stern of the boat, Peter Walsh caught him up and handed him his Barbour coat.

'Thank you, Peter. You are most kind.'

He put the coat over his arm to help cover the bulge where the handle of the knife stuck up above his belt.

'Aren't you going to put it on, Jonathan? It's a bit brass monkeys out here.'

'Oh, I'm fine.' Jonathan replied. 'I will put it on if I get cold, hey? And thanks for getting it for me.'

Jonathan smiled and thought how he would almost miss the constant puppylike adulation from his newly found partner in crime, but only for a moment. The two men stood looking out at the wake left by the ferry as it made its way out into the North Sea, and Jonathan looked around to check they were on their own. They were the only two people on deck, as the cold breeze had driven all other passengers back to their cabins. The lights of Immingham were now only distant specs, fading to become non-existent. The ship had already passed the extensive container port on the mouth of the Humber, its bright lights now gone. Its twenty-four-hour-seven-days-per-week vibrancy and oil and gas smell that stung the nostrils had also passed. Looking back towards where the lights once shone, Peter Walsh sighed.

'It's going to be some time before we're making the return journey, hey, Jon?'

Peter Walsh didn't get a chance to say anything more as Jonathan Fahey turned to face him, smiling, and slowly pushed the long carving knife deep into Walsh's stomach. The man grimaced with shock. It was not pain on his face, but more a look of incredulity and extreme sadness. He tried to speak as the knife was twisted and pushed deeper under his ribcage. It was then pulled out, making a distinct squelching noise, and plunged in once more, this time at a slightly different angle, and up into the victim's lungs. Jonathan was standing close to his victim and looking him directly in the eyes as he pushed the knife again. Before pulling it out, he turned Walsh around so his back was resting against the handrail at the stern of the ship.

Jonathan glanced around to check they were still alone and slowly pulled out the knife.

Walsh grasped the blade as it was retrieved once more, cutting the palms on both of his hands as it slid through them. He could feel the blood gurgling up through his lungs and into his mouth as Jonathan pulled it out for the third and last time.

He now needed to hold Walsh up from falling on the deck. If he fell down it would be awkward to lift him to the height required to tip him over the rail. He managed this by propping him up against the rail and dropping the blade over the side, he turned Walsh to face the dark North Sea. Walsh was now clinging to both the handrail and his life, which he felt ebbing away, both to no avail as Jonathan heaved him over the stern of the ship. Although they were more than thirty feet above the rear cargo doors, the noise of the body hitting the water was drowned out by the heavy diesel engines of the ship and lost in the foaming waters created by its propeller blades. Jonathan wiped his hands on the tea towel and threw that over the side too.

At last, he was finished with that moron who followed him around like a lap dog. Now he could turn his mind to the real job at hand. Walsh had served a useful purpose but was redundant, and it would be good to return to the UK in the days to come without him tagging along. He'd even thought about killing Walsh on the drive back up North, but that would have alerted the police to him still being in England. Now the body was at the bottom of the North Sea with no trace, he would be free to go about his work undetected. Everything was coming together. The stupid plod would be all over the ferry ports of Belgium and Holland while he was in Norway. And nobody would expect him to strike so soon after running away.

Before turning in, Fahey put his coat on to cover the bloodstained clothing and once in his cabin, he showered and scrubbed the blood from his hands. He packed the bloodstained clothes and sealed them in a plastic bag for later disposal. Then he checked his new passport. Whoever Walsh had paid for the forgery was good. Very good indeed. And he liked the name — Michel Legrand. He would need to get used to it, but with the new ID, new haircut, and a neatly-trimmed beard, he would have little difficulty in moving freely once he returned to the UK. He could sleep well and would make the return journey on the morning ferry alone.

Once back in England, he could make his plans for revenge. And this time, he would start with the bitch who caused him all this trouble in the first place. Time to start poking her with a sharp stick. Her hormones will be running riot, and the bitch and her dyke friend would be messed up by his messages. The only problem was that if, and when, he made contact, it would alert her to where he was. And that could put the whole plan in jeopardy. But he couldn't help himself.

He decided to send her a text.

The little jibes would have to suffice until he could get within striking distance. But when he eventually did, they would regret the day they came into contact with Jonathan Fahey, more than they could ever imagine.

Chapter 18

THE CAR PARK OF THE Quarry Moor Nature Reserve was a regular stop on the night shift patrol for PC Ronnie Ogden and his new probationer PC Janice Slocomb. It was quiet, with no danger of any brass turning up, and a place to have a brew and eat a sandwich, once all the doggers had moved on at the sight of their car approaching. If the doggers didn't get the message immediately, a quick flash of the blue light would always send them scurrying.

Although Ronnie, at age forty-nine, had been in the force for just coming up to thirty years, he had spent every week of it patrolling the highways and byways of the sleepy North Yorkshire villages. He knew the countryside like the back of his hand and, for him, Ripon, with its population of almost 17,000, would be considered a large conurbation. He had worked in and around the town all of his career and by far the most aggravation he came across would be from the local garrisons of Catterick and Ripon itself, when the local squaddies, fuelled by an excess of alcohol, decided to let their hair down a little too far. He was much too long in the tooth to be easily phased and wanted nothing more than to finish his shift with nothing written in his notebook, other than his time clocking on and off, and certainly no paperwork to complete.

Janice, on the other hand, was going to set the world on fire. Although only 19, she believed she was destined for much greater things and couldn't wait to finish her time as a probationer and transfer to the West Yorkshire force or possibly Greater Manchester. She was doing a part-time degree and hoped that she would be an inspector at some stage in the next five years. Neither of them could have expected what they would stumble across, as it approached midnight in the Quarry Moor Nature Reserve.

No sooner had Ronnie Ogden turned onto the track leading to the car park when the fire became visible. The flames were a stand-out, dark orange against the pitch black of the night in the headlights of Ronnie's car. At first, there was more smoke than flames, which were steadily becoming more intense. The burning car was barely alight as they turned into the car park, but before they had got to within fifty yards of it, the flames had spread quickly to engulf the inside of the vehicle. Both Ronnie and Janice could feel the heat before their car came to a halt. Ronnie pulled as close to it as he thought would be safe and switched on the blue lights. As he jumped out and began his run towards the car, Janice was already calling the incident into control. She was standing outside their vehicle behind the passenger door and shouting over to her partner to be careful. Both of them could clearly see someone sitting in the driver's seat of the Ford Focus. Ronnie was going to attempt to get the individual out.

As he raised his hand up to his eyes, palm open to shield them from the heat, there was one almighty explosion as the petrol tank blew. It took Ronnie off his feet, lifted him a good two feet in the air, and deposited him almost back to where Janice was standing open-mouthed.

As she shook her head from side to side in disbelief, her instinct took over and she ran towards her now unconscious trainer and mentor. She grabbed him by the epaulettes on the shoulders of his jacket, hauling his upper body high enough off the ground to put her hands under his shoulders, and began to drag him away to the safety of her car door, just as a second explosion sent her rocking backwards.

She looked back at the car, now completely engulfed in smoke, and the driver now silhouetted against the bright orange flames. She looked down at her partner and checked his breathing. Nothing! No sign of life of any kind.

Ronnie's face was charred and blackened, his lips burnt away, and the skin around them pulled back against his teeth. Mouth-to-mouth was going to be little less than pointless, so she began CPR, hoping that the ambulance would not be long. She looked around in a vain exercise of searching for help. The doggers had all long since gone, but she noticed a car in the dark as it started to pull out of the car park. In a futile gesture, she shouted after it to stop and help, but it kept on moving, and once in the lane, the driver put his or her foot down and sped away.

Janice kept up with the CPR while speaking into her radio for some moral support from her control room. There was nothing else for it. She would need to use the defib machine kept in the boot of their car, for just such an emergency. Janice opened Ronnie's jacket and pulled violently at the Velcro of his stab vest until she eventually got it open. Inside the defib box, there was a large pair of scissors. Using these to cut open her partner's fleece and base layer of clothing, she eventually exposed his chest. Her training had kicked in and she quickly applied the stick-on patches, one to his left side under his arm and one to the top-right side of his chest. She powered up the machine and waited for what seemed like an age, shouting obscenities at the inanimate object.

'Oh, come on, *come on*, you bloody thing.'

Eventually, it crackled into life and the disembodied voice spoke, 'CHARGING. PLEASE STAND CLEAR. SHOCK NOW.'

Janice pressed the red button and Ronnie's body jumped in response to the 2500 DC volts being delivered.

'CHECKING FOR RHYTHM. NO RHYTHM DETECTED. CHARGING. STAND CLEAR.'

Janice waited again.

'SHOCK NOW.'

She pressed the red button again, and again, Ronnie jerked and arched his back as the shock landed.

'RHYTHM DETECTED.'

She looked down at him and his eyes twitched a little, then opened. He gave a slight cough.

'Oh, for god's sake, you had me worried there for a moment, you old bugger.'

As she was covering him up, she could hear the ambulance driving down the track leading to the car park. Although it seemed like hours before she saw its blue, flashing lights and heard its siren ripping the night apart, in reality, it was little more than seven minutes. When the paramedics came over, they checked Ronnie for vital signs and were most impressed at her work.

'Well done, PC49, you've saved this fella's life and no mistake. Not too sure about the one in the car though. He's a bit past saving, I think.' As the medics were getting Ronnie Ogden into the ambulance, they advised that Janice should go to the hospital just to get checked over. So she climbed in after her partner, who was now fully awake.

The paramedic in the back with them turned to her. 'Hey, I wouldn't worry too much. He looks a lot worse than he is. He won't have any eyebrows for a long time but he hasn't lost any sight judging by the way he can follow my torch.'

Before they pulled out of the car park, the fire brigade arrived and set about damping down the fire. It would be morning before anyone could get a close look at who it was in the vehicle, but the firefighters did manage to salvage the number plate.

***

It was 07:00 when Victoria's phone rang in the MIT operations room at Fulford Road nick.

'Chief Inspector Adams MIT speaking.'

'Oh, hello, Detective Inspector Holmes from Ripon CID here.' He paused for a second. 'I know, don't say it.'

'I wasn't going to say anything,' Victoria replied, doing her best to stifle a laugh.

'Yes, you were. Everyone always does. It's my cross in life, but anyway, it's Stuart, not who you were thinking of. Down to business. We have something you may be interested in out here in the sticks.'

'Go ahead, Inspector.'

'Well, firstly, are you missing any of your vehicles?'

'Not that I am aware of. Why do you ask?'

'Well, we have had a burnt-out car left in one of our local beauty spots, the Quarry Moor Nature Reserve, and unfortunately, there was a passenger in the driving seat. The registration number of the car, when we checked, belongs to your team.'

He read out the number and Victoria's heart sank. She immediately realised it was Harry's car. A million reasons were rampaging through her head, as to why it might not be

Harry. And, if it was . . . what the hell was he doing in Ripon? She sat down and looked around the room as if checking if he might still be there. She looked over to his desk and sank her head, putting her hand across her brow, mouthing the words, *Oh no, please no.*

She was finding it difficult to speak. She felt sick and nauseous, almost to the point of vomiting. For the moment, Victoria decided to put it down to the morning sickness she had been experiencing recently; she had to focus. She now stood up and looked at Varsa, thinking how the girl was going to take the news if it turned out to be him. The way to deal with this was to stay on track. So she turned her mind back to the telephone.

'Have you called out forensics yet and the duty pathologist?'

'We have and they are on scene as we speak. Do you want to come over? And do you think the occupant could be one of your officers?'

Victoria was now feeling even worse. It was as if a blanket of woozy, stomach-churning nausea was inhibiting her ability to think of anything other than throwing up. She put her hand over her mouth to avoid an accident and spoke in short, clipped words.

'Yes to question one. And it is unlikely to question two . . . The current driver of that vehicle would have had no reason to be anywhere near Ripon. But I need to do some checking.' She was hoping that her worst fears would not come to pass. The body in the car could have been some car thief or "twocer" whose night had ended in disaster. She could not bring herself to admit it might be Harry. He was too good a copper to be killed in that way. 'Is there anything that could identify the occupant of the vehicle?'

'No, not at this stage. I think the doc has come over from Leeds. If it turns out to be one of your guys, we will hand it over, assuming you want it. But until then, we're treating it as a suspicious death.'

Victoria was now needing the bathroom and her speech came in short staccato, two words at a time, punctuated by gulps and suppressed burps.

'It will take me forty-five minutes to get there. Just email me the location.'

'Yes, of course. You don't sound too well. Are you alright, Chief Inspector?'

'I'll be fine. Just send over the details and I will get there as soon as I can.'

She was thankful the call ended and she could replace the phone. The click of the handset was like a starting pistol enabling her to make a run for the bathroom, just in time to bring up the breakfast cooked for her that morning by Miriam. As soon as she had brought up all of it, she felt a little better, but now starving hungry. She splashed some water on her face just as Varsa came into the room.

'Wow, you look like shit, boss. What's the problem, if you don't mind me asking?'

'Thank you, Detective Constable. It's always nice to be told you look like shit. It must have been something I ate.'

'Oh . . . I just thought it might have been something to do with the phone call you just got. Seemed to cause a bit of upset. Do you want to share it?'

Victoria thought for a moment. She was not sure whether to explain. And if she did, how could she tell Varsa that her latest boyfriend might have just burnt to death in a car in the middle of nowhere?

'Well . . . the call was from the police over in Ripon, giving us some information that you all need to hear. Let's go back into the briefing room and I'll give you all a sitrep.'

Back in the office, Victoria called the team for them all to listen up.

'Okay, everyone, the phone call I just received was from a DI Holmes over in Ripon. Don't even start, Mal.'

'I wasn't going to say a dickie bird.'

'Good. Well, it appears that Harry's pool car has been found burnt out in a beauty spot outside of Ripon. Unfortunately, there was someone inside the car, who has been declared dead at the scene.'

The room fell silent and Varsa stood up with her hand over her mouth.

'Now hang on, everyone. At this stage, we do not know who the driver is.'

'What do you mean?' chipped in Pete Sinclair.

'Was. We have no way of telling who the driver was.' She let this sink in for a moment. 'However, we can't jump to conclusions about it. At this time, we just don't know for certain.'

She was not convincing the team and she was not convincing herself.

'Is North Yorkshire taking it on, boss?' Varsa asked.

Victoria detected the shakiness in Varsa's voice and took her by the arm. 'Well, they've said if we want it, it's ours. I feel we should hold on to it at least for the time being. Or until we are certain one way or the other as to the identity of the occupant. So, I'm just about to go over to the scene now. Let's not get too despondent until we know one way or the other. Okay, everyone?'

The team nodded in unison.

'Would it be okay if I tagged along, ma'am?' Varsa asked quietly.

'If you're sure you want to, Varsa? I would welcome the company. It's a bit of a trek over to Ripon.'

'Any chance of me driving, ma'am? What with all the sickness and stuff?'

Victoria reached into her pocket and tossed Varsa her keys. 'You're right. I don't feel too good. But take it steady, okay?'

'Morning sickness, is it?'

'Who the hell told you? It's supposed to be a secret. And private.'

'Don't think there's any such thing in this place, ma'am. Anyway, congratulations. We are all pleased for you and the doctor.'

'The doctor? Makes me sound like a bloody extra in Dr Who.' Victoria shook her head in a gesture of *what's the point?* 'Come on then, let's get a shift on.' As they made their way over to the car park, Victoria stopped Varsa and held onto her arm for a second. 'Had Harry mentioned to you that his car has gone missing?'

'Nope, not to me. Last time we spoke was on the phone yesterday when you and I were in Leeds. He was making a start on cataloguing the evidence from Greenwood's flat. Seemed like he was a bit on a high about something, but didn't say what.'

'If he was going anywhere, he would have mentioned it, right?'

'Yeah, I'm sure he would, boss. He normally keeps the car at his flat in town. It has CCTV, so we could check that when we get back and also have a check what time he signed out yesterday.'

'Aye. We could do that. On the way over, I'll try calling him.'

Although the pair were doing their level best to bolster each other, they were both fully aware of the high stakes here and how desperate it would all become if indeed it was Harry in the front seat of that car.

Chapter 18

***

On the drive up to Ripon, Victoria, although enjoying the North Yorkshire countryside, was also cursing how far every place was from every other place. England's largest county was truly beautiful, even in winter, but so spaced out it took forever to get anywhere. She could pick out in the distance the higher hills of the Dales, with their light dusting of snow that peeped out between the ubiquitous, drystone walls.

Later on, through the winter, this snow would become much heavier and permanent until the spring came. Swaledale sheep poked their heads through almost every rickety gate they passed, and mercifully, there were no hold-ups by farm tractors or the ever-present summertime caravans being towed at a snail's pace, which had long since been confined to their home driveways of suburbia.

The satnav took them directly to the park. By the time they arrived, the fire brigade had finished their damping down and was picking up to leave. There was a small police presence at the entrance to the car park and a young female officer lifted the tape to allow Varsa to drive under. She parked a short distance from the burnt-out wreck.

Inspector Stuart Holmes greeted their arrival with a wave of his hand and walked over once they had come to a halt. Stuart Holmes checked the pair's IDs and introduced himself, just in time for them to be greeted by the diminutive figure of Jane McCormack. As Victoria climbed out of the passenger seat, Jane looked back at the burnt-out wreck of the Ford Focus, indicating with her thumb as she began pulling off her gloves.

'We've removed the body for transportation to the mortuary, Victoria. Not really much to look at as it's been completely engulfed in flames.'

She took Victoria by the arm and ushered her to one side and a few feet away from the car. She was aware that the body in the car could well be one of Victoria's officers and was not sure how much she had passed on to her team. Jane was acutely aware of the need to allow senior police officers to run their teams in the best way they saw fit, and not let too many cats out of too many bags. As they moved out into the centre of the car park, Jane turned to face Victoria.

'The firefighters have left the plates from the vehicle and I have them in my boot. I understand that the car was normally driven by Harry Burrows. You will understand that we can't make a firm identification until we get the body back to the mortuary. However, having said this, I can say that he is the correct height and build for Harry… And we have found this.' She held up a small evidence bag containing a medal and chain. 'This was hanging around the deceased's neck.'

Victoria took the bag and looked at the charred and blackened piece of jewellery. She had no idea what it was and if Harry owned anything like it.

'Can you identify it as belonging to Harry?'

Victoria gave it a closer look and slowly shook her head. 'Looks like some form of Indian talisman or image.'

Varsa had been sitting in the car, not really wanting to get out when she noticed Jane showing something familiar to Victoria. She made her way over to where they were standing, and as Victoria handed the evidence bag back to Jane, Varsa reached out and grabbed it. Tears started to run down her cheeks and onto the collar of her blouse, streaking her make-up. She choked and gulped.

'It's Krishna, Krishna,' she said, almost as a matter of fact. 'I gave it to him. I gave it to Harry.'

She handed the bag back before turning back towards the car. Putting her hand on the bonnet to steady herself, she felt faint and started sliding towards the ground. Victoria caught her just in time with an arm under each of the young woman's armpits. Jane opened the door and the two women helped Varsa into the back seat.

***

Varsa woke up slumped in the back seat of Victoria's car, pale, drawn, and shaking.

'It's Harry, isn't it? I knew it was going to be him. I know it's him.' Varsa had yearned with all her heart that it wasn't, but she also knew now, with all her heart, that it was. She looked up at Victoria who, for once, was a little lost for words. 'What was he doing out here in the middle of nowhere? We left him sorting out evidence bags. He was supposed to be sorting out evidence bags, for god's sake.'

She made an attempt to get out of the car, but her legs would not support her and she fell back into the seat. Victoria climbed in next to her and put her arm around Varsa's shoulders. She hugged her tightly and put her face to Varsa's black hair, stroking her head. Varsa was now sobbing uncontrollably and gulping between breaths.

'I have no idea what he was doing out here, sweetheart, but we will find out and we will catch whoever did this.' Victoria, with Jane's help, ushered Varsa into the front passenger seat and helped her buckle the seat belt as she would with a child. Before climbing in behind the wheel, she spoke to Jane. 'Where will you be doing the PM?'

'I believe it would be expedient to complete it in Harrogate. They have a private mortuary we sometimes use there. It's well equipped so it will save us some time, rather than driving back to Leeds or York. I'll get it underway as soon as we get the body back, and I'll keep you informed. There'll be no fingerprints left due to the fire. However, I'm assuming Harry's DNA will be on the database. On first inspection, I'm convinced he didn't die at the scene but sometime earlier and was transported here. Looking at the damage to his head and face, I believe we will find some form of blunt-force trauma as the cause of death. The damage is so extensive that dental records are going to be of little use, so it will be down to his DNA for positive identification. The pendant will help.'

Victoria thanked her and climbed in beside Varsa. The drive back to York was going to be a long one, and she had to find the correct words to let Julie Thornton know her nephew had been killed. Victoria thought it best that Varsa should not be at home on her own. She decided to take her to stay with Miriam and herself for a few days. But Varsa was having none of it. Victoria was planning to drop off Varsa, and then go back into the office and speak with the rest of the team and ACC Thornton. However, Varsa said she wanted to be at work with everyone else. She would have all the time in the world to mourn Harry, but for now, the team needed all the numbers it could muster.

Victoria thought to herself that the next couple of days were going to be more than traumatic. Losing an officer in the line of duty was never an easy thing to deal with and this was the first time it had happened to Victoria. She thought that possibly it might help to speak with Sean, but her mind was racing. There would be no real leads as to why her newest officer was miles off-patch. There would be no forensics to speak of. And she had no idea how she was going to keep the team focused on the missing boy now they had the death of one of their own to deal with.

***

On arrival at Fulford Road, Victoria made her way up to the ACC's office only to be told by her secretary that she was still in a meeting with the Police and Crime Commissioner and the police local committee members going over the crime figures for the previous month. A message was left and Victoria made sure the secretary realised it was urgent she speak with the ACC. By the time Thornton was free of her politicians and making her way down to the MIT office, Victoria had brought Mal and Pete up to speed on the death of Harry, and both were set to work on finding what had taken him out of the office when he was supposed to be cataloguing evidence. When the ACC entered the room, the atmosphere was like one of those Wild West saloons, when the music stops and everyone looks at the person who has just pushed open the swinging doors. ACC Julie Thornton stopped in the doorway.

'What? What is it? Am I wearing the wrong aftershave or something?'

'No, ma'am.' Victoria answered. 'Can you come into my office, please? I'm afraid I have some seriously bad news.'

The pair, led by Victoria, went into the small office once occupied by Sean O'Neil, and Victoria closed the door behind them. She sat on one of the small settees and the ACC sat opposite.

'So, what has happened, Detective?'

'Well, ma'am... This morning, I received a call from Ripon telling me of a burnt-out vehicle that one of their area cars had stumbled across.'

'Yes?'

'Well, the car was registered as a vehicle assigned to our own MIT.'

'You're telling me someone has nicked and torched one of the MIT's vehicles? A bit careless of you, if you don't mind me saying, Chief Inspector.'

'No, ma'am. I mean yes, ma'am. Well, the vehicle was being used by Detective Burrows.'

'So, you're telling me Harry has lost it?'

'Not exactly, ma'am. You see, a body has been recovered from the burnt-out wreck of the vehicle and, although we are yet to make a positive ID, it could well be that of Detective Burrows.' Victoria was finding it hard to say the words that needed to be said, and she looked at the ACC, allowing the weight of the information she had just imparted to sink in.

Julie Thornton looked down at the floor, slowly shaking her head.

'No, it can't be Harry. I only spoke to him yesterday. He was in here sorting through massive piles of boxes and evidence bags. It looked like he would be tied up for a month. What was he doing over in Ripon?'

'We don't know yet, ma'am. It's possible that he turned something up from the evidence, a lead perhaps, which sent him off in the direction of Ripon, but at this stage, we really have no idea.'

'How certain at this stage are you it was Harry?'

'Varsa has identified a pendant she recently gave him. It was very unusual and of Indian origin. SOCO removed it from the victim's neck. We will have to wait for DNA to come back, but we are pretty certain the person in the car was Harry.'

Julie Thornton faced Victoria and it was clear her emotions were borderline getting the better of her. She picked up some papers that were spread out on the small table that separated the two women. She shuffled them, then shuffled them again, and replaced them in a neat pile. She then turned to look away and back again.

'You know he was my nephew?'

'Yes. We all did. It's hard to keep anything a secret in this place, and I am really so sorry.'

ACC Thornton looked around the room and then down at the floor once more and spoke this time without raising her head. 'I don't want you to treat this in any way differently than you would treat any other such case. Do you understand, Chief Inspector? I don't want the whole of the MIT running around like headless chickens chasing their own shadows. We still have this Jason Waites to find.' She looked up and directly at Victoria. 'You don't think the cases are linked, do you?'

'Well, until we dig a little deeper, we obviously don't know. But if it was some item of evidence from the murdered Terry Greenwood's flat that sent Harry tearing off to Ripon then there must have been some link. Regarding the way we follow up on any leads on Harry, of course, it goes without saying that we will treat it the same as any other case under investigation. But I can assure you, we will leave no stone unturned, and, as I said to Varsa, we will get those responsible.'

Victoria stood up, opened the office door into the main briefing room, and turned to face the rest of the team who had gathered around. Her fists were clenched and her jaw tight, and she spoke with little emotion but absolute resolve.

'Now, I want you all on those boxes. I want Varsa, if you're up to it, to check the CCTV at the station that covers the car park. And then check the ANPR to see if his car comes up on any routes. We might be able to see where and in what direction he was heading, which we may be able to link with his notes. I'll go over his desk. And, Mal and Pete, I want you going through those boxes with the proverbial fine tooth.'

The pair were emptying a box each before she could look back.

'On it, ma'am.'

Victoria tried to smile. She nodded and took her phone from her handbag, then turned to Varsa, who was already engrossed in her screens.

'Varsa, any updates on Miriam's phone I asked you to track? The one she had stolen during her assault in Birmingham? I've got another text message. I need to know, if possible, where the phone is when it's sending these messages. Can that be done?'

'Yes, I can track a location. But of course, it's not forced to be at that location now.'

'What do you mean?'

'Well, there are ways of disguising the location, but you would need some serious tech know-how to do that.'

Victoria also explained who the messages were possibly coming from. Then she handed the phone over to Varsa and asked her to keep it switched on at all times, not to reply to any of the messages, but to contact her whenever one arrived.

'What are you going to do in the meantime, ma'am? I mean, for a phone?'

'Oh, don't worry. I have a new one and will let everyone know the number in due course.'

Varsa opened the list of messages. 'Wow. This fella is a real weirdo, alright. Isn't he, ma'am? Do you think he'll actually come after you and Mr O'Neill?' She slowly read the latest one.

'Hello my dear. I hope this message finds you well and your confinement is progressing nicely. Just a quick note to say it won't be long now before I'm looking you and Miriam up again, and who knows, I might just have time to pop

along to say hello to our friend Sean. We all have some unfinished business to attend to and a lot to catch up on, don't we Victoria?' XXX Oh! I understand you two lovely ladies have now moved in together. It is, and has been for many years, one of my fantasies to experience the joys of two women at once and I hope I can do you both justice. Bye for now.

'Who knows? But we'll be ready for him if he turns out to be so stupid. Better to be one step ahead if we can, hey?' The shake in her voice told Varsa that she was not quite managing to convince herself.

Victoria turned back to the ACC, who was standing in the doorway to the briefing room.

'Once again, ma'am, my deepest condolences.'

'Sure. Sure, and thank you for bringing the news so promptly. I appreciate it, Victoria. Regarding Harry's family, would you mind accompanying myself when I go to give them the news, Victoria?'

Victoria nodded and thought that was the first time the ACC had ever used her first name, and she'd used it twice in quick succession.

'When do you want to make the visit?'

'Can we go later this evening, or do you think we should wait until we get the definite identification from the DNA?'

Just then, Victoria's desk phone rang and she answered it immediately. 'Hello, Chief Inspector Adams.'

'Oh hi, Victoria. It's Jane McCormack here. I'm just calling to let you know that we have put the DNA on fast track and pulled out all the stops as it is one of yours. And it is definitely your man Harry. I will be sending over the PM report as soon as I can get a courier, but no mistake... It's Harry.'

'Thank you, Jane, for coming back to us so promptly.'

Victoria stood up and turned to the group of officers in the room with a solemn face.

'Okay, everyone. I have just had confirmation that the deceased found in the burnt-out car was our friend and colleague Harry Burrows.'

The room fell silent until it was broken by Varsa's quiet sobbing. Although she already really knew it was Harry, the confirmation had opened the floodgates and the realisation of losing him was now hitting home. Victoria sat down beside her and put her arm around the young officer's shoulders. Varsa's sobs were becoming more intense and she buried her head into Victoria's neck and hair.

'It's okay, sweetheart. You have a good cry.'

'I really think I loved him. I really did. He was going to come and meet my mum and dad, he was.'

As the pair sat together, Victoria looked up at the ACC who also was looking close to tears. 'We can go later on today to see Harry's mother, or whenever suits you, ma'am.'

The ACC looked the other way as if making an attempt to hide her face and her feelings a little, but when she spoke, there was a croak in her voice that gave away those feelings in good measure, and the team picked up on it. 'Would you mind if we went later this evening? I want, if possible, to get the news to my sister without delay, and I would really like your assistance please, Victoria. If that's okay?'

The ACC sniffed and turned, just as Mal handed her a tissue. She took it and wiped her mascara that was starting to run.

'I'll pick you up later from your home.'

'No problem, ma'am.' Victoria turned back to Varsa, who was still clinging to her arm. 'I am going to get one of the uniforms to run you back to our place, Varsa. I'll call Miriam to let her know to make up the spare room. And don't worry, you are welcome to stay as long as you like. Okay?'

Varsa nodded between sniffs and took a tissue from the box left on the desk by Mal. She wiped her eyes and sat back in her chair. 'I'm okay now, boss. Promise.'

'Good. We need to get on with checking over these files that Harry was looking at and I'll see you and Miriam a little later.'

***

When Varsa arrived at Victoria and Miriam's home, she was warmly welcomed by Miriam, who had made up the bed in the spare room. No mention was made of Harry. She thought it best to let Varsa take the conversation there if she wanted. As Varsa was making herself at home, Miriam placed some clean clothes on the bed.

'These belong to me, pet, and don't worry if you don't want to wear them, but I think they should fit okay. I'll run you over to your place in the morning and you can pick up what you want, but these should do you for now.'

'You are really kind, Miriam. You don't mind me calling you that, do you? I really only know you as Doctor DeSilva and it seems a bit formal.'

'No, pet. That's fine. Miriam is fine.'

'I really appreciate you and the chief inspector letting me stay. I really wouldn't have fancied being alone at home right now, on my own, like.'

'No love, we both understand, and while you're here, you treat it like your own place. Okay?'

'Thank you.' As she was looking at the clothes Miriam had brought her, she spoke without looking up. 'Isn't it terrible about that Fahey creep breaking out?'

'Aye certainly is, but I'm certain they'll have him back behind bars before too long.'

'Yes. For sure.' Varsa placed her handbag on the bed and unpacked the few items she had, including her own mobile and Victoria's.

'Isn't that Vicky's phone? How come you've got it?'

'Oh, she asked me to see if I can trace the location of where he was when he was sending those bloody awful messages.'

'What messages?'

Varsa immediately realised, by the tone of Miriam's question, that she had let some kind of cat out of the bag.

'Oh, I don't suppose it's anything important, but the chief inspector has been getting some messages from the bloke on her phone. Nothing serious. I think he's just being a pest.' Varsa was now digging a hole she found difficult to climb out of.

Miriam's face was stony. 'And have you seen these, er . . . messages?'

***

When Victoria arrived home, she was greeted at the door by Miriam, who had a somewhat severe look on her face that said she should stand by for a telling-off.

'You have not been telling me the truth, have you? And now I know, you better start doing just that.' Before Victoria could open her mouth, Miriam carried on. 'When were you going to tell me what's been going on, Victoria Adams? Am I just the little housewife that needs to be protected by the big, strong policewoman? Do you see me as that? Am I such a wimpish individual that wouldn't be able to cope with the truth about what that bloody psychopath Fahey has been up to? His texts and messages, threats, and such. When were you going to tell me?'

Victoria gaped, open-mouthed, with a good degree of embarrassment, and fetched Varsa a dirty look. She was standing behind Miriam with her palms upward in a gesture of *sorry, but what could I do?* Victoria put her hands on Miriam's shoulders in a mistaken attempt to calm her down.

'Okay. I was simply trying to keep it from you until we had a better idea of where he was and what he was up to. I didn't want you to panic or get upset. I was going to tell you once we knew more.'

'But you thought it okay to confide in Varsa, but not with me?'

'I needed to tell Varsa as she was going to help with the track and trace on the phone. Nothing else.' Although it helped, it didn't help a lot, and Miriam's face said as much.

'Okay, well, now the cat's out of the bag, tell me everything. And let me read the messages from the nutcase. I'll be the judge of whether I should panic or be upset. If that's okay with you?'

The tension eased a little and Varsa asked if they would like a coffee or a cup of tea. Miriam turned to Varsa and pointed at the bottle of wine standing on the island in the kitchen, followed by an encouraging hand gesture. She turned back to Victoria and smiled at her in a way that said, *I'm angry but I love you too much to fall out over it.*

Victoria handed her the phone with the messages open for her partner to read, and Miriam scrolled through them.

'He is a right swine alright. Do we know where he is at the moment?'

Victoria took the phone back. 'Nope, we don't. But the best guesstimate is that he is likely to be heading for the continent. Probably France via either Belgium or Holland. The car used in the getaway was found in Felixstowe, close to the Harwich ferry port, with the two dead prison escorts in the boot. He looks like he is still with his accomplice, Prison Officer Walsh.'

'Isn't he the one who you had doubts about a while back?'

'Aye. I did alright and didn't take it any further. That'll teach me.'

'No,' said Miriam. 'It won't... Anyway, I've prepared an evening meal for us. Varsa has helped me with a chicken korma. It'll be ready in about thirty-five minutes, if you're ready to eat? Oh, and not too hot, she tells me.'

'I can smell it, and I'm sure it will be wonderful. Is there any chance you can keep mine until I get back?'

'You're going out again?'

'Yes. I'm sorry, but the ACC is coming to pick me up and we're going round to speak with Harry's parents. Not sure if you were aware that she is... *was* Harry's aunty?'

Just then, the doorbell rang and Victoria went to answer it.

Miriam turned to Varsa. 'It's hard to picture ACC Julie Thornton as anybody's aunty.'

Varsa turned away to check on the curry. 'Yes, I know what you mean. But Harry talked about her a lot. She's his mum's sister, and he was brought up by his Aunty Julie.'

'Oh, I see. Do you know why that was, pet?'

'Apparently, his mum and dad used to argue all the time because of her drinking. His dad left home when Harry was about twelve and he went to live with Julie. He really looked up to her as a sort of surrogate mother. The parents have got back together, but I don't know for how long, and the news of his death might kick it all off again.'

'How do you mean?'

'Well, Harry's mum never wanted him to join the police, but his dad was all for it. Harry told me that it was only the intervention from Julie Thornton that swung her round.'

'Well, you never really know what goes on in people's personal lives, do you?'

'That's right, you never really do.'

Miriam could hear the muted conversation at the front door, but could not work out what was being said. She then realised that Victoria was bringing the ACC into the house. She gave a quick cursory glance around and turned to Varsa again, and then glanced at the vacuum cleaner standing in the corner of the kitchen.

'She's invited her in and I haven't hoovered for two days. What will she think?'

'Technically, you wouldn't be able to hoover as you don't have one. That is a Miele vacuum cleaner over there. I know we use the term to describe the process, but it's wrong to say hoover unless you actually have a Hoover. You should say vacuumed the house.'

Varsa went back to stirring the curry and Miriam shook her head slowly with her mouth open. The front door opened again and quickly shut, as Victoria and Julie Thornton set off to meet Harry's parents.

'Do you mind if we use my car, Victoria?'

'No, of course not, ma'am. Just so long as you bring me back home again.'

ACC Thornton gave Victoria a thin, distracted smile, but didn't answer as she set off for the A64 in the direction of Leeds. After about five minutes, she pressed the call button on the car's hands-free telephone. A list of numbers came up and she scrolled through them, stopping at a Leeds one. She pressed the call button and the two women both listened to the ringing tone.

It was answered by a male voice after only three rings. He sounded mature but not old.

'Hello, you. Are you on your way yet, you gorgeous creature, you?' It was clearly someone that the ACC was familiar with, and already, Victoria felt somewhat of a gooseberry.

'Never mind that nonsense. I have someone with me in the car at the moment, another officer, and I'm going to have to take a rain check on the meal, Noel. I'll call you later to explain.'

She sounded apologetic and the man sounded a little disappointed, but not too much.

'Oh, no worries, my dear. These things happen. It must be something important to stand me up.'

'Well, yes. We've had some really sad news about one of our officers.' She paused and swallowed. 'His remains have been found in a burnt-out car up in Ripon, and we're on the way to inform the parents.'

'A bit unusual for someone as high profile as you, Julie, to be doing the work of an FLO?'

'Yes, but there are some special circumstances with this one, Noel.' She paused again as she indicated to take the turn for Bramham. 'At the moment, it looks like murder and... Well, this one is a little different. It's my nephew Harry. We will be making the call on my sister and her husband.'

'Oh, I am truly sorry to hear that, Julie. He hadn't been in the job that long, if I remember rightly. I really don't envy you with that one, love, not one bit. Don't forget to keep me up to date on how it all goes.'

'No, I'm not looking forward to it either, and yes, he had only just gotten through his probation period.' There was a brief silence before Julie spoke again. 'I've brought along Chief Inspector Adams with me, as Harry was one of her team. She will be able to give a bit of moral support, and she will hopefully be able to fill in the gaps, in as much as how we are proceeding.'

'And you say the lad was found in Ripon? In a burnt-out car? What was one of the NY MIT doing over in Ripon? Do you have any leads as to how he got there or anything?'

Victoria took up the conversation. 'We're not sure, as yet. The investigation is in the very early stages and we're not able to say any more on that issue. We do believe he was taken there by another person, though.'

Julie Thornton thought Victoria sounded a little guarded, wondering who this man was and why he appeared to be so interested in her case. As the ACC turned into the village of Bramham, she glanced at Victoria while ending the conversation with the man on the phone.

'Look, Noel, I'll give you the details later once we are back in York. Perhaps we can do dinner another evening this week? Same place and time? I'll call you.'

'Yes, of course, Julie. I understand entirely. See you then. Bye.'

The call rang off before Julie Thornton had time to reciprocate the farewell.

'Before you ask, he is ex-job. Now retired Chief Constable Noel Jackson. We go way back. He used to work at West York as a chief super when I was an ambitious chief inspector. Not unlike yourself, Victoria.'

For one moment, Victoria thought she was nothing like her boss, in any way. Oh, she was certainly ambitious and wanted to move up the slippery pole, but not at any price.

'You say he's retired now. Would he be the Noel Jackson that headed up the enquiry into the missing kids in West Yorkshire some years back?'

'Yes, I believe he did head up that enquiry, along with many others, of course. Why do you ask?'

'Oh, nothing, ma'am. It's just that Sean O'Neill mentioned that there might be some similarities between that enquiry and our own, so I thought there may be some mileage in speaking to the retired chief constable.'

'Aye, possibly. We keep in touch regularly and go out for a meal now and again. But I'm sure he will be only too glad to help out if he can. He split some time ago from his wife and lives somewhere over near Halifax, I think.'

Julie wondered why she felt she needed to justify seeing him, mentioning that he was available and not married anymore. She wondered also why she thought it was important to tell a little white lie about how often they got together.

The picturesque village of Bramham, known for its horse trials, three-day eventing, and show jumping, looked like some winter picture postcard. There was a hard frost which was making the pale Yorkshire stone housing glisten and sparkle, and the dimed street lights and lights coming from the Georgian bay windows on the high street only added to the effect. Julie turned her car off the main street and up a steep, narrow hill, stopping at only the second house — a small cottage.

The front door needed a coat of paint and one of the panes of glass had been replaced by a piece of plywood tacked on the outside. It was answered by a woman in her late fifties dressed in a long-sleeved, grey cardigan over a grubby-looking t-shirt and a pair of jogging bottoms. She smiled a thin greeting at Julie and immediately looked past her at the tall, impeccably dressed Chief Inspector Adams.

'Well, look what the cat dragged in. To what do we owe the pleasure? And is that the moral support you've brought with you? You sure as well fucking need it.'

She fetched a quick glance at Victoria and turned back to Julie The welcome was less than convivial, to say the least, and Victoria noted the coldness of the reception, bordering on anger. Julie seemed to expect the welcome received and, to some extent, ignored it.

'May we come in, Irene? We need to speak to you. Is George here by any chance?'

The woman in the cardigan gave a slight chuckle as she turned to go inside.

'You're having a laugh, aren't you, sis? He's not been round for ages. Last time was over a year ago now. Anyway, what the fuck do you want?'

Again, Julie Thornton ignored the belligerence and stepped inside. The woman slouched off into the sitting room and downed the dregs of white wine from an oversized glass, putting it down on a low table. She picked up an empty bottle of Prosecco and held it up to the light. 'I'd offer you a drink but I needed to get myself down to the offy and they're shut now, so I might have to go into Tad. So, come on, get on with it, what the fuck do you want?'

Both Victoria and her boss looked around for somewhere to sit and Julie nodded to Victoria to sit down on the sofa.

The room looked like it hadn't been cleaned in some time and Victoria couldn't decide if the carpet was really that colour of brown or just held a film of dog hair. The ACC noticed her looking at the floor and smiled.

'My sister isn't too house proud, but she does love her dogs, don't you, Irene?'

The sister didn't answer, other than a scowl in the direction of her younger sibling.

Julie carried on. 'Well Chief Inspector Adams and myself are really here in a work capacity, Irene, and I'm afraid we have some particularly dreadful news. Do you want to sit down, love?'

'Don't come the *love* with me. What do you want?'

It was clear that Julie's patience was wearing thin. She didn't want to stay any longer than she had to, but knew she needed to be gentle and understanding with her sister in a way that they hadn't been since they were children. When they were teenagers, although only a few years apart, the lives of Irene and Julie took different forks in the road of life that neither of them would have wanted. As children, they were inseparable. They went everywhere and did everything together. Like they were joined at the hip. But when their mother died and their father did his best to drown himself in Glenfiddich, both of them were taken into care. Although the childcare agencies did their utmost to keep the girls together, the younger Julie was fostered by a middle-class family and the older Irene stayed in care until she was sixteen. Although the pair had some contact off and on from the age of seventeen, Julie was packed off to university in Bangor and Irene was stacking shelves in the local Tesco. Their lives grew steadily apart and Irene's resentment grew. At first, Julie tried to keep contact and build bridges, but it was all to no avail, and she eventually gave up trying. Irene sat down on the sofa and Julie sat next to her.

Julie took her sister's hand in hers and took a deep breath. 'Irene, I don't want anything other than to pass on some news about Harry.'

Victoria sat opposite them and considered how was it that two sisters not many years apart in age could look so different. Oh, there were facial resemblances — eyes, noses, and cheek bones. But there, the similarities ended. Julie Thornton was the epitome of suave coolness. She was immaculately turned out, with manicured nails, perfectly coiffured hair, flawlessly applied makeup, and a uniform that permanently looked like it has just been collected from the cleaners. On the other hand, her sister looked like she really didn't care less about the way she appeared. She was overweight, her hair looked like it hadn't seen a brush in a week, and her nails, what was left of them, were almost non-existent from nibbling them away.

'Okay, go on. Spit it out. What's so bad it needed two of you to come and tell me?'

Julie looked across at Victoria as if willing her to speak first. She took the cue as it was intended and sat forward to speak to Irene. 'Well, Irene, today we attended a car fire over in Ripon, and I'm afraid to tell you that your son, Harry, was in the car when it caught fire. He was pronounced dead at the scene.'

There was a silence, and Julie gripped her sister's hand a little tighter. Irene was thinking. The silence was palpable. She pulled her hand away and turned to Victoria.

'What do you mean a car fire? Was he in a crash?' There was a false matter-of-factness in her voice like she just wanted the details, as if by getting more details it might not be true. Julie took hold of her sister's hand again and looked at Victoria to continue.

'No, Irene. We don't believe it was a vehicle collision. At the moment, we are treating the death as a murder. We are able to tell that Harry was already dead when the car was set alight.'

This time, Irene didn't pull her hand away but looked blankly from her sister to Victoria, and then back to Julie. She wanted to speak but clearly didn't have the words. Julie gave her hand a gentle squeeze before speaking.

'Do you want me to call George and get him to come over, sweetheart? Or, if he's not there, is there anyone else you would like to come round?'

Irene gently pulled her hand away again and spoke without looking at either of the two women. There was a coldness in her voice, but it was measured and calm.

'No, thank you. I will be okay. I would like you both to leave now, please.'

Victoria stood up and thought that Irene might not be alright initially, but in the end, she would survive, as most in bereavement do. She looked like a survivor who would cope in the long run.

As the two women were about to leave, Irene caught her sister by the arm. 'Well, you finally managed to take him from me, hey? I hope you're happy.'

Julie pulled her arm free and, without speaking, opened the door and let Victoria out first. Just before leaving, she turned back to her sister.

'You know I loved him too? And I'm sorry this happened, I really am.'

Irene closed the door behind her sister, and once back in the car, Victoria could not say for certain, but she thought she detected a tear creeping from the corner of the ACC's eye. On the trip back to York, the two women didn't speak more than a couple of words together, and the ACC dropped Victoria back home and was about to wave goodbye when she let her window down and spoke to the chief inspector.

'Victoria, you will let me know what is happening with Harry's case, won't you? And keep me up to speed on it?'

'Of course, ma'am. It goes without saying. It was nice to meet your sister Irene.'

Julie smiled a little. 'You sure about that? Anyway, thanks for coming with me. You were a real support. I appreciate it.

I can see why you get on so well with the team. You have real empathy. It matters. As a side issue, you will be needing a replacement for Harry. Do you have any thoughts on that?'

'Well, actually, I do. While I was over in Ripon, I managed to speak to a really competent officer called Janice Slocomb. She was one of the officers who found Harry and, by all accounts, saved the life of the other officer who was with her at the time. Unfortunately, he will be off work with the injuries he sustained when Harry's car blew up. But I would like them both as and when we could get them over. I don't think their DI will be too happy, but they seem to work well as a team.'

'I'll see what I can do, and I'll be in touch about it sometime tomorrow.'

As she drove off, Victoria was a little stunned. Not only a relatively nice conversation with the Assistant Chief Constable and a request for extra manpower agreed upon without any difficulty, but a compliment thrown into the bargain. Things were looking up.

The chicken korma for dinner was excellent, and as Victoria settled into the arms of her partner, they both looked across at Varsa who had eventually fallen asleep on the settee. They decided to put a throw over her rather than wake her up. Victoria knew she would be needed tomorrow as it would be all hands to the pumps in sorting out the boxes of files on both their current enquiry and those of the muffin man case from West Yorkshire.

Chapter 19

THE MIT OFFICE IN FULFORD Road nick was beginning to look like a self-storage unit. There were all the boxes from the flat belonging to Terry Greenwood and now, following Mal and Pete's collection from the West Yorkshire Headquarters, there were many boxes that they were spilling out into the corridor.

On the one hand, Victoria had been reluctant to bring Varsa into work, but on the other, she realised that she would be invaluable when it came to tracking down anything IT-based. They pushed their way past one of the piles of boxes, and Varsa immediately made her way to sit behind her computer screens. Victoria wanted to check for one last time that the IT wizard was okay to be in. She pushed past the same pile of boxes to stand close to Varsa's side.

'Now listen, young lady. I only want you in if you feel up to it. If at any time you feel like you want to go just let me know. Okay?'

Varsa looked back through a pair of sore, red eyes and shook her head slowly. 'No, it's okay. I would rather be doing something to help in finding Harry's killers.'

Victoria nodded a reassuring *okay*, and turned to the rest of the team, calling them into the main briefing room. Once settled down and all focused on the big board, she turned to them to speak.

'Okay then, we have lost one of our own and it has come as a blow. We all feel it. Although Harry had only been with us for a relatively short time, he had made a significant impact on all of us, and he will be sorely missed by everyone.'

Mal looked across at Varsa, who was fighting to hold back the tears. She noticed him looking and gave a thin smile in response.

Victoria continued, 'What we need to do now is focus on finding his killer or killers, and I know, although this is now personal to us, you will not allow the closeness to home, of this investigation, to let your heart rule your head. We must focus on using good police work to catch his killers, in addition to finding our missing boy Jason Waites, who at this time may or may not still be alive. And, of course, the killers of Terry Greenwood. It is likely that Jason's disappearance, and/or the death of Terry Greenwood, are linked to Harry's murder. We need to find that link.' She looked across at Mal and nodded for him to take up the briefing. 'So, Mal, what do we know about what Harry was working on in relation to the killing of Terry Greenwood and the abduction of Jason?'

Mal stood up and looked at the board with a frown that said it all. He turned to the team. 'Well, to be honest, boss, precious little. Our best assumptions are that he found something in the evidence bags and boxes that came back from Greenwood's flat that took him off to Ripon.'

Before he could carry on, he was interrupted by Varsa, 'Well, we don't even know that. Forensics and the PM point to him being killed elsewhere and brought to the car park in Ripon.'

'True. But where was he off to? And what did he find that was so urgent that it sent him off on his own?'

Victoria was reading through the PM report and stopped at the cause of death.

'It says here that death was the result of blunt force trauma to the frontal lobe, possibly inflicted by a heavy object. Something like a large, heavy hammer with a rounded head. Subsequent blows to the head would have been post-mortem as the first one would have resulted in death almost immediately. There were no defensive injuries, so he either knew his assailant or he was taken by surprise and not expecting the attack.'

Varsa stood up. 'I'm going to make us all a drink.' She left the room and went to put the kettle on. The team watched her leave until Victoria spoke.

Chapter 19

'Okay, everyone, next steps. We need to continue trawling through all the boxes and evidence bags that Harry was going through from the Greenwood scene. I have managed to get us a couple of extra pairs of feet on the ground and at least one should be arriving later today. The second, unfortunately, is still on sick leave, but I have spoken to him on the phone and he is well up for joining the team.'

'Who are they, boss?' asked Pete. 'Anyone we know?'

'PC Ronnie Ogden and Probationer PC Janice Slocomb.'

'A probationer, boss? We're scraping the bottom of the proverbial, aren't we, or what?' Mal said, shaking his head slowly.

'By all accounts, she is resourceful and a quick thinker. She saved the life of her partner PC Ogden who was blown up when the tank on Harry's car went up. The pair were first on the scene and Ogden knows the North Yorkshire highways and byways like the back of his hand. Anyway, they'll be useful, but we need to keep them on a tight leash. I'm going to have a look at the case files for the Muffin Man Enquiry this morning and probably pop over to see the guy who was running it at the time. If PC Slocomb pitches up before lunch, I'll take her with me.'

There was a multi-reply of, 'Right you are, boss,' from the team, and Victoria disappeared into her office.

***

It was gone two when Janice Slocomb arrived at the MIT offices. She knocked on the open door into the main room and was met by Mal Chambers. PC Slocomb stood in uniform with her cap tucked under her left arm and her right hand stretched out in a greeting to Mal.

'Hello. I'm Probationer Slocomb from North York. I was asked to report here this morning.'

'Ah, Miss Slocomb. Good to have you.'

'That's Janice. Not miss, please.'

Mal smiled and apologised.

She nodded her reply as Mal was turning to face his buddy, Pete.

'Mr Sinclair,' he called over. 'This here is Miss Slocomb. Are you free?' He shouted in an over-the-top caricature of the John Iman character in the old sitcom *Are You Being Served?*

Pete stood up and looked about him to the left and the right, before shouting back in the same character's voice, 'Yes. I'm free!'

And the pair sat down laughing like a pair of schoolgirls.

Janice rolled her eyes. 'You know, I haven't heard that one for at least an hour. Well, since I got into my car to drive here, that is. I was expecting a little more from a Major Incident Team.'

The two men laughed out loud, realising they had touched a nerve.

'Ooooh er, Matron,' they replied in unison.

Varsa looked up from behind her screens, not understanding what was causing all the hilarity.

Victoria came out of her office holding her car keys in her mouth while putting on her coat. 'Hi, Janice. I see you've met Tweedle Dumb and Tweedle Dee. Or is it Bill and Ben the flowerpot men these days, fellas?' Janice smiled at the pair and helped Victoria with her coat. 'Don't take your coat off, Janice. You're coming over to Harrogate with me. How is your colleague PC Ogden?'

'Oh, well, on the mend, ma'am. Looks like he'll be with us sometime tomorrow or even later today if all goes well.'

'Isn't that a bit soon, Janice?'

'Well, he's the kind of bloke that wouldn't let a little thing like getting blown up and then brought back from the dead keep him away from an investigation on what he sees as his patch.'

Victoria laughed. 'You tell him we're okay for a while. There's no need to come racing in like the cavalry.'

'I think the burns to his face have settled down a bit and he looked much better yesterday. Apparently, they were superficial, but nonetheless painful, and he hates not being in the thick of it, so to speak.'

'You did good work there that night, Janice. I hear on the grapevine you're in line for a commendation. Not many of those given out to probationers.'

Janice smiled and blushed a little. 'Yes, I mean no… Well, you know what I mean. Thank you, ma'am.'

Pete Chambers looked a question at his partner, who held out his arms, palms up, and mouthed the words, *Search me*, in reply.

Once in the car, PC Slocomb asked where they were off to in Harrogate.

'Well, we aren't actually going to Harrogate, but through it and on to Halifax. We are going to interview now-retired Chief Constable Noel Jackson. He has agreed for us to ask him some questions relating to an enquiry he headed up some years back when he was a DI in West Yorkshire. The case had many similarities with our current investigation into our missing young lad, Jason. West York gave the original investigation the title of the Muffin Man Enquiry and our friend Noel Jackson eventually shelved the case. I'd like to go over any potential suspects he had dug up at the time.'

'So, you think the cases might be linked in some way, ma'am?'

'Let's just say we'll keep an open mind, hey?'

After a long drive through the twisting, narrow lanes and moorlands of West Yorkshire, Victoria's satnav took the pair out onto the moors on the outskirts of Halifax, high above the town of Hebden Bridge, to the village of Pecket Well, eventually announcing, 'You have reached your destination.'

She pulled up outside a large, double-fronted, three-storey property. It was built around the mid-nineteenth century with an imposing outlook, set back from the road in an elevated position. It was built substantially of pale Yorkshire stone, with darker sandstone corners and a tiered, large front garden that was entered through a corner metal gate. The road outside was steep, and Victoria left the car in gear when she parked, just to make sure.

The gate was heavy and Victoria needed to put her weight behind it to get it to push open. Eventually, it gave way with a complaining screech of metal on metal.

'Best leave it open. I don't want to have to try and pull it back the other way.'

'Aye. Yes, ma'am.'

As the pair of detectives made their way up the wide, stone steps to the front of the property, the front door was opened well before they arrived. Noel Jackson stood on the porch with his hands in his pockets wearing a beaming smile.

Victoria returned the smile and followed him indoors. Once inside, he turned to Victoria and Janice and, before closing the door, called out down the long hallway, 'Sweetheart, could you rustle up some tea for the two girls here? They must be gagging for a drink after their long drive.' He turned back to the two detectives. 'Tea alright, is it? Or would you like coffee? No bother either way.'

Victoria spoke for both of them, 'No, tea would be nice, thank you. We don't want to take up too much of your time, sir. As I said on the phone, we'd like a brief chat about the Muffin Man Enquiry, if that's okay?'

'Of course it is, my dear. And don't worry about taking up my time. In retirement, that is something one has in abundance.' He led them into a large sitting room that was furnished in a classical style with Indian rugs on a polished, wood floor. The large bay window looked out across the valley of Hebden Hey, Hard Castle Craggs, and in the distance, you could see the expanse of water of the three Widdop reservoirs.

'Lovely view, sir,' Victoria said as she looked out over the countryside.

'Yes. We love it. And no need to keep calling me sir. Call me Noel.' He sat down in a large armchair, crossed his legs, and gestured to the two women to sit opposite in a chintz, two-seater settee. They duly complied, and Victoria took out her notebook, handing it to Janice.

'You don't mind if we make some notes?' She paused. 'Noel?'

'No, of course not, but can we hang on until the tea comes? I think Angela has made some scones.'

Both women smiled in acquiescence. Victoria sat back and considered the retired chief constable. Her background checks on him had thrown up that he had taken early retirement a year ago at the age of fifty-four. She could not find any information on what had prompted the retirement, but it certainly didn't look like it was on medical grounds. He looked fit, slim-waisted and muscular. He was around the same height as her ex-boss, Sean, and like him, although a little greying at the temples, he would have been considered good-looking. To heterosexual women, of course.

Chapter 19

And now I have a problem. I wish I hadn't found out about him being married. Because now I have to decide whether or not to pass on the information to Hot Chocolate. Bloody men with their brains in their pants.

What was slightly more to the point was that he must have realised she was the same officer who was travelling in the car with Julie Thornton when he called her on the phone. He didn't even flinch when his wife was introduced. Victoria wondered what kind of game this man was playing.

When Angela arrived with the tea and scones, the couple's incongruity hit home. She was small, diminutive in stature, with mousey brown hair that looked like she hadn't taken it to the hairdresser in some years. She wore a pair of grey jogging bottoms and a baggy jumper with holes at the elbows, and a look of genuine subjugation. She placed the tray of China teacups and saucers, milk, sugar, and a teapot on the polished coffee table and stood back. She then took the teapot and placed it on a metal stand that stood next to the coffee table.

'Would you like me to pour the tea for the ladies, love? I know you like to do your own.'

Noel Jackson looked up at his wife and spoke through a distinctly curled lip. 'Yes, I do, darling. Only because you have been getting it wrong for the last thirty years. And I think we can manage now.'

Angela took a step backwards and smiled at Victoria.

'Did you not hear me, Angela?' said Noel. 'I said we can manage. Thank you.' And as an afterthought, he added, 'Dear.'

She took a further step backwards and then slowly made her way back to the kitchen. Noel Jackson took one of the cups and poured the milk in first, followed by one small spoon of sugar that he levelled precisely with his finger before adding to the milk.

'I like to have my tea always milk first and the first cup. Always.'

As he was speaking, Victoria looked at Janice and rolled her eyes. When Noel had finished pouring his tea, he stirred the cup slowly three times in a clockwise direction and then three times in the opposite direction before picking it up to take a sip.

'Ahh,' he said. 'Always the first cup. Just right.'

Janice poured herself and Victoria their cups and sat back on the settee. Victoria edged forward in her seat and directed her attention at the retired officer.

'Well, Noel, you are obviously aware of why we wanted to come and speak to you.'

'Well, yes and no. I mean, well, I am assuming you think there might be some link between our investigation relating to the Muffin Man Enquiry and your current missing lad. But I do think you are barking up the wrong tree. What is it that you believe might link them?'

Chapter 19

Victoria stood and walked over to the window. She turned to face Noel Jackson. 'The main thing is that all of your missing kids played for amateur football clubs, and so does ours. Jason plays for a local York team called the Badgers. They were all around the same age, give or take a year or so. Did any of your Mispers fall into the "at risk" category? Ours was possibly gay and had some difficulties at home due to him coming out. Any of yours fall into that category?'

'Well, possibly. But it's all a bit tenuous, don't you think? Lots of kids play Sunday league football and the teams that all our three played for never actually played against each other. They never met. Their parents, coaches, and team members never knew each other. And how do you think I can be of any possible help after all these years? It's such a long time ago. You have all the notes on the cases, I believe. So there is little more I can add.'

Victoria tried a different tack. 'Were there any suspects that stood out? Any interviews that you recall that made an impact on you that may not have made it into the notes? Absolutely anything at all that you feel may be of interest to us?'

Noel Jackson took another sip of his tea, put it down on the table, and rubbed his chin with his forefinger and thumb. 'Nope. Nothing. We drew a blank at every turn, and although there were some one hundred and fifty plus interviews carried out, nothing and no one stood out as being a prime suspect in any way. Sorry I can't be of more help, Victoria.' At that, he stood up. 'Not having a scone, either of you?'

Both women shook their heads, getting to their feet.

'Thanks. That is very kind of you, Noel,' said Victoria. 'But we really need to be getting back. Please give our regards to Angela.'

Noel Jackson nodded and ushered them outside. He walked down the garden with them and stopped at the gate.

'Any movement on the case of your dead detective? Harry, was it?'

'No. Nothing as yet. We are still trying to get a handle on what he was doing over in Ripon. It looks like he was actually killed elsewhere and the park in Ripon was the body dump. The fire, we believe, was set to cover any forensics.'

'So, no leads on where he might have met his end then?'

'No, not yet, but we are still at a very early stage in the investigation. But very little to be going on. His car was serviced the day before, so we do have his total mileage for the day he died. And we have a rough idea of the distance he travelled the following day, ending up in Ripon. Not much, but something. It can give us some idea of an area of search, but at this stage, we have no idea what we are searching for.'

Noel nodded and started to turn back towards the house.

'One more thing, sir?'

He stopped and turned back again. 'Yes, Chief Inspector?'

'Well, I know you might say it's none of my business, but I seem to recall ACC Thornton telling me you were not married. Would she be mistaken?'

'Yes, you are right, Chief Inspector. It's none of your business.' His tone had clearly changed and his facial expression was set in a distinct *mind your own business* look.

'It's just that she seemed convinced you were divorced, and clearly, your wife is here making scones.' Victoria had passed the point of no return and had little to lose in pushing it a bit further. 'Also, I noticed that your conversation with the ACC was more than on simply friendly terms.'

'I think we are done here, and I would hope that you have the discretion to keep your innuendos to yourself. And that goes for your lapdog here as well.'

Victoria didn't acknowledge the request and left the gate wide open as she left.

When she climbed into the car beside Janice, they both slowly shook their heads.

As they pulled away, Janice turned to Victoria. 'Can you believe the guy? The way he spoke to his wife? If a man spoke to me that way, I'd punch his bloody lights out.'

Victoria glanced at her newest recruit and believed she was most definitely telling the truth. What was more to the point was whether she should pass on to her boss the fact her intended dinner date was hiding his wife in plain view.

Chapter 20

JASON WAITES HADN'T SLEPT PROPERLY since his incarceration had begun in the cellar of the old farmhouse, and he hadn't slept at all since the failed rescue attempt had ended in disappointment and the death of his would-be rescuer. The torchlight came on at the same time as the door above and to the right opened with a shudder and a bang. The torch came down the stairs and, for the first time since his arrival, a light switch was turned on, so he could take in his surroundings properly.

At first, he had to keep his eyes tightly shut as the brightness of the single bulb was so intense it stung the backs of his eyelids. Eventually, he became able to open them a little and, bit by bit, he began to see where he was. The room was obviously underneath some building and the walls were all brick. The floor was made of concrete, and there was a large armchair in the middle of the room with ropes laid across it. A large bath towel lay across the back of the chair and there was one on each of the arms, too. Against one of the walls stood an old bath. The type that had feet on it that stood it off the floor. It had two brass taps and the man, after placing a pile of clean clothes on the armchair, made his way over to the bath and turned on both taps, putting his hand under each, from one to the other to test how hot the water was.

He turned to Jason. 'Okay, my little muck pup, time for your bath. Time you got a little cleaned up. We have guests arriving soon and they won't look kindly on a dirty wee lad like yourself.'

Jason looked at the man, who was wearing one of those white Guy Fawkes masks.

'Why are you keeping me here? I haven't done anything to you. Was it you who hit the policeman? Is he dead?'

'Oh, so many questions you have, but unfortunately, you're not getting any answers. Now come over here and shut the fuck up. Take your clothes off and get into the bath.'

'No. I won't. You let me go, or you will be in real trouble.'

The man laughed before standing to his full height, which was considerably taller than Jason. He walked back to where Jason was standing, still defiant, and stooped to match his height with the boy. The man smiled and suddenly lashed out, slapping Jason hard across the cheek, so hard it rocked him backwards into the chair and drew a little blood from his left ear.

'Now, my lad, if you don't want another one on the other side of your face, you just do what I tell you and get into the fucking bath.'

Jason decided to do as he was told. He slowly undressed and climbed into the warm bath water. The man picked up a plastic jug that was sitting next to the bath and poured water over Jason's head. Next, he took a bottle of shampoo and proceeded to wash the boy's hair, followed by more jugs of warm water. When it was thoroughly rinsed, the man threw Jason a bar of soap and told him to finish washing.

'You make sure all your bits and pieces are nice and clean, wee lad. And don't forget to do behind your ears.' The man chuckled to himself.

When Jason had finished, the man told him to stand up and turn around a couple of times while he was inspected.

'Excellent. You look all shiny and new. No one would imagine you've been chained to a wall for over a week. You're in for a treat, my little man. You're going to be allowed upstairs for your meal. And, if you're good, I just might, and I mean *might* let you watch a bit of telly before our guests arrive. What do you say to that?'

***

Victoria was adamant that she would not divulge to her boss, ACC Thornton, that the man she was seeing had told her a lie about being single. She was a grown woman and it was up to her to see whoever she liked whenever she liked to. It would be her job to find out in her own time about his personal life. Victoria didn't like to see any woman being cheated on and found the dilemma of should she or shouldn't she tell her boss somewhat of a no-win situation for either of them, when she was brought out of her contemplating by her phone ringing.

'Is that Chief Inspector Adams? West York's CID here, Superintendent Briers.'

She recognised the voice immediately and acknowledged him with a genuine warmth in her reply, 'Hello, Superintendent. Yes, it's Victoria. How are you doing? It seems ages since we worked on the Fahey case. You know the bastard's only gone and legged it and taken one of the bloody prison officers along with him?'

'Aye, I did hear about it. And how is your . . . ' He paused as if not knowing what to say next. 'Your friend, Miriam?'

'Well, more than a friend, Superintendent, She's my wife these days. So, how can I help?'

'A number of things really. I understand you might be reopening the Muffin Man Enquiry?'

'News travels fast. Well, I wouldn't say actually reopening it as such, but we are looking over the files at the moment to check if there may be any similarities between those missing lads and our own here in York. Why? Do you have something that might be of use?'

'Well, yes and no. You see, we have had an ongoing Mispers for some months now over here in Leeds. A young lad called Thomas Walker, aged nine. He went missing at a party being held at the football club he played for.'

'So, you think this could be connected to our missing lad?'

'Well, unfortunately, ours is no longer missing. We found his body this morning on waste ground near the village of Ripley. He has been positively identified by his father today. Terrible thing. Just terrible.'

'Oh, that's awful, just awful. I suppose there might be some similarities, as they both play football, but what young lads don't these days?' She pulled a foolscap notepad out of her drawer and clicked her pen. 'So, his name was Thomas Walker, aged nine, and he went missing from his football club? When was he reported missing?'

'Four months ago.'

'And his body has only just turned up now? How far was the body dump from where he was last seen?'

'Roughly twenty miles by road. PM has been done and it looks like he had suffered some serious abuse prior to death. Cause of death is yet to be determined. Do you want me to send over the details, including the PM report?'

'Can you just hang on a moment, Superintendent?'

'Yes. No problem. Sounds a bit like you're moving offices back there.'

'Yep, just hang on a moment and I'll get them to be quiet.'

The team were shifting through box after box and banging and clattering around, making it difficult for her to hear clearly what Tubby Briers was saying. Mal Chambers was especially agitated and sifting through quantities of files and papers, spreading them out across the desk and allowing them to spill onto the floor. He had a bunch of paper in his hand and was waving it at Victoria in an attempt to attract her attention. She waved him away and returned to her call.

However, Mal was having none of it and he shouted over to her, 'Boss! Ask him what club the dead boy played for and if the club was part of any sponsorship program or trust.'

She held her hand over the mouthpiece and turned to her sergeant. 'What? Why do you need to know that?'

He stopped waving the wad of paper and put it back down on the desk. 'Just ask him please, boss. I'll explain in a minute.'

Although she was a little perplexed, Victoria turned her attention back to her phone call. 'Okay. Just be quiet for a moment.'

'What?'

'Oh, sorry, not you, Superintendent. One of my officers would like to know if you have a record of the club Thomas Walker played for and if they were part of any sponsorship program or trust?'

The phone was quiet for a second or two before Tubby Briers came back on the line.

'He played for Moor Allerton Wildcats, a Sunday league team who put out teams from ages five to six up to under-21s every Sunday, but we've no idea if they were part of any trust.'

Victoria thanked him and reminded him about the PM report, then turned back to her sergeant, who was busy tapping away at his keyboard. He waited a second then lifted his head to look at her with a face like he had just won the lottery.

'So, what's all this about trusts? And why do we think it's of any relevance?'

Mal stood up and sorted through some sheets of paper and photographs that were spread out over his desk. As he sifted them from one side to the other, he pulled out about six documents, all on headed paper, along with four photographs. He then walked over to the large table that stood in front of the big board in the incident room. Slowly and deliberately, he placed each of the photographs down on the table with some documents under each one, then turned to face the team with a wide grin on his face.

'We have the link. We only have the bloody link!' he said purposely, tapping the first photograph with his index finger. 'Right, okay. Here we go. Pin back your ears. This is an image of James McEnery. He was the first of the lads to go missing in 1998 and he played for Bradford Sharks.' He waited, watching the team's look of *what's coming next*? And then he tapped the papers that were on the table below the photograph. 'And this here is a trust agreement between the Fitz-Michael Soccer Trust and the said Bradford Sharks, to fund their teams and help out with coaching.' He waited for a response that was not forthcoming. 'Okay, bear with me.' He tapped the second photograph. 'This is an image of the second lad to go missing in late '98. Joel Sanders, who played for the Holbeck Flyers. Another Sunday League club.'

Again, he tapped the sheets of headed paper. 'And, wait for it, they too had an agreement with the same trust to sponsor their teams.'

Victoria moved closer to the table and looked at the photographs. She picked up the third one — a smiling photo of a young lad around ten in his football strip.

'And that is the third one to go missing in early '99,' continued Mal. 'A young fella called Charlie Northwood who played for Armley under-12s.'

Victoria cut in, 'And they too had a contract with the Fitz-Michael Soccer Trust?'

'You've got it, boss.' She placed the image back down on the table and Mal moved it slightly to one side to create a space.

'We don't have an image of the missing lad Thomas Walker, as yet,' said Mal. 'But I have just checked, and his team, Moor Allerton, it's the same with them. Linked to the same trust.'

The final photograph was that of Jason Waites. Victoria recognised it only too well. She looked a question at Mal and he nodded.

'Yep. The Badgers signed an agreement only last month with the Fitz-Michael Soccer Trust.'

She picked up the photograph of Jason and, as if speaking to the image, silently told it, *We just might have moved a little closer to bringing you home, young man,* while hoping in her heart that he was still alive. A ripple of applause went around the room.

'Well done, Mal, Great work, in fact.' She paused a second, looking back at him. His chest was a little reminiscent of a pigeon in a show. 'And what do we know about this trust?'

Mal turned the palms of his hands upwards in a gesture of *search me.*

She looked to Varsa. 'Job for you, I believe, Varsa. I want the full SP on them. Names and addresses of all the trustees, other clubs, where they have agreements or contacts. In fact, everything you can ferret out about them.'

'On it, boss.'

The keys on her PC were rattling away before Victoria could say any more.

Chapter 21

JONATHAN FAHEY RETURNED TO IMMINGHAM on the overnight ferry from Brevik and walked off into a misty morning with a spring in his step. He was without his accomplice and the architect of his escape from prison, Officer Peter Walsh, who now lay somewhere at the bottom of the North Sea.

Fahey had a new name and identity, and enough money in his newly opened French bank account to see him easily through the next few years, so long as he was careful. As he walked down the slipway, lost in the crowd of travellers, he felt smug and superior. He carried a small holdall and a plastic carrier bag containing a few bottles of duty-free alcohol and some cigarettes.

But most of all, he carried with him an overwhelming, burning desire for revenge.

He thought about how he would seek it out on the hapless police who had contrived his downfall. But he would bide his time and take revenge when it suited him. He would make all those who treated him like a pariah and told lies at his trial eat their words in more ways than one.

The Range Rover had been left in an overnight car park close to the Immingham ferry port used by the seamen who worked on the many ships that came and went each day. No one took any notice of him. No one considered him a threat. And those he was about to hunt down had no idea where he was or when he would strike. Although he was eager to finish his work in York, he would need time to plan it fully as he had no intention of being caught for a second time. It would be best, he believed, to find somewhere close to York where he could hole up and use it as a safe house. Not a hotel, but possibly a small B&B or select guest house, if possible.

By the time he had negotiated the Humber Bridge and the outskirts of Hull, it was past eleven in the morning. He decided to hang on for his lunch until he was closer to York. Jonathan knew of a small hotel — or a large B&B — called the Black Bull, in the village of Escrick, only six miles to the east of York. Fortunately, they had vacancies. The winter months kept the holidaymakers away and, other than himself, there was only one couple booked in, and they were, he found out at dinner, leaving the following day. The wi-fi worked, the food was more than acceptable, the staff were polite, and best of all, they didn't ask too many questions. As a bonus, the owner and landlord, Vanessa, was relatively attractive and even a little flirtatious.

Yes, he thought, the Black Bull would do fine as his safe house. At least until his work in York was done.

***

Varsa had only been pounding her keyboard for a few minutes when she stopped suddenly and sat back in her chair. The abrupt silence made the rest of the team stop what they were doing and look over their computers at her.

'What is it, Varsa? Do you have something?' Victoria called over.

'You're not kidding I have something...'

She paused for a moment, only to be interrupted by Pete Sinclair. 'What, for heaven's sake? What have you got?'

'Well, I've been looking at the register of UK trusts and pulled up the list of the trustees connected to the Fitz-Michael Soccer Trust.'

Again, Pete couldn't contain himself. 'And?'

'Well, the treasurer is Lord Donald Fitz-Michael the fourteenth, Marquis of Highbury himself. I believe he is a hereditary peer with a seat in the Lords. Other trustees include his brother, the right honourable Jeremy Hugo Fitz-Michael, who is MP for a constituency in Lincolnshire, Alexander Farquhar, OBE, another MP for somewhere in the southwest, Howard Sefton, MP and CBE, two senior police officers, one of the rank of ACC in the MET, and another who is a chief superintendent in the MET. There's a Mr Jerry Hardcastle, OBE, famous for playing records on the radio and running a kids' TV game show in the seventies and eighties. By all accounts, a bit of a national treasure. And a Mr Grahame Hortense, MBE. No background on him so far. There are also a couple of judges, minor TV celebs, and a smattering of general nobodies.'

'Wow! They've got more gongs between them than the bloody rank organisation,' Mal chipped in.

But Varsa hadn't quite finished. 'Hang on there. You will not believe who the chair of the board of trustees is.' She paused again, doing her level best to build the tension for effect. 'The most interesting one by far . . . Only our dear friend retired Chief Constable Noel "Stonewall" Jackson, CBE. Now who would have thought it?'

Pre-empting Victoria's next instruction, Varsa immediately sent the document to print, and the printer jumped to life.

'What do you reckon to that then, boss?'

Victoria was already at the printer and reading a copy of the list. 'Wow! Now this lot certainly pack a punch, no mistake. All with some considerable influence. Erm . . . ' While still reading the list, she spoke without looking up. 'Meeting in the briefing room in twenty minutes, everyone. I need to speak with Hot Chocolate ASAP. In the meantime, I need background checks on all of them. Pick a couple each and dig into their histories, big time. No stone unturned.'

She was out of the room and on her way upstairs as the team turned away to get busy.

Victoria had only been gone a minute or so when PC Ron Ogden entered the room. Only Varsa looked up to see Janice greet him with a big hug that was a little too tight, causing a wince and a, 'Steady up there,' before he pulled away. 'I'm still convalescing, you know,' said Ron. 'We'll have less of this rough stuff, if you don't mind?'

Janice laughed and turned to introduce him to the rest of the team — acknowledgements all around before Mal went to make him a drink.

'Sorry about not being able to save your lad in the car.'

'No worries, mate,' replied Pete for the team. 'I hear you did your level best, but apparently, we've since learned that Harry was most likely dead before the car caught fire.'

Pete was interrupted by Varsa. 'It didn't catch fire. It was deliberately *set on* fire.'

'Sorry, Varsa. That's what I meant.' Pete glanced at Ron Ogden and held up his hands in a gesture of surrender. He stood up and walked over to where Ron and Janice were standing. Holding onto Ron's arm, he whispered in his ear, 'Varsa was going out with poor Harry when he was killed. They were quite involved. An item, as they say these days.'

When Mal returned with a coffee for the newest member of the team, Ron sat down on the edge of Janice's desk, taking a sip before speaking. Varsa was checking the list of names and assigning who would check out which. Ron picked up the sheet when she laid it on the desk. He read down and stopped; one of the names jumped out at him.

Chapter 21

'Well, well, well, Grahame Hortense. Who would have thought it?'

'Why? Do you know him, Ron?' Varsa asked.

'Well, yes and no. Top striker in his day. He was one of the best United ever had, back in the day, of course. Never actually met him, but certainly watched him play fairly often.'

'Is that Manchester United?' Varsa was making an attempt to show off her knowledge of football and actually showing off her lack of it.

'Hardly. He was good, but not that good. No. He played for Leeds United back in the eighties. He had a bit of a chequered career but then went into coaching and talent spotting. Ended up playing a few games for Doncaster Rovers before officially retiring, as far as I remember. So, what can you start me with, anyone? As the new boy, I don't mind getting on with anything, so long as it doesn't involve too much chasing around.'

Varsa picked up the list and circled the name Grahame Hortense.

'Well, you may as well start with Mr Grahame Hortense MBE, as you are already somewhat aquatinted with him. You already have some background, I mean. We need as much as possible on him going back, say, over the last ten years or so? Or further, if you think it's relevant. Family, work, any convictions etc., addresses then and now. All the usual stuff.'

'What's he been up to then?' Ron asked as Varsa began walking away.

She answered without turning back. 'Well, at this moment in time, we aren't sure. We're just establishing if there're any links with the cases of the missing kids in the nineties and our own today.'

Janice came over and brought her partner from Ripon up to speed on the investigation, talking him through the big board. She pointed out the images of the three missing boys from West Yorkshire and explained why there was a gap left for the image of the young lad whose body had recently been found. At the side was an image of Jason Waites, and, close by, an image of Harry.

Varsa was busy filling in the links and listing the names of the board of trustees who managed the Fitz-Michael Soccer Trust. As she got to the last name, Retired Chief Constable Noel Jackson, Ron laughed out loud.

'Not old Stonewall. How's he mixed up with this lot?'

Janice explained the links and how he had headed up the original Muffin Man Enquiry before it had been shelved.

'Had you worked with him before then, Ron?' she asked.

'Worked for him, you mean. No one worked *with* Stonewall Jackson. You were told what to do and you just got on with it. He was always the boss and woe betide anyone who ventured to believe they could think for themselves. If you tried to voice an opinion, you were firstly made to look stupid, and if your impudence persisted, you were off his team quicker than a rat up a drain.'

'Well, I'm sure Victoria will have a chat about that with you and anything else you can tell her about him. We did go and visit him and he sent us packing with our tail between our legs.'

'Sounds like Stonewall alright.'

***

Up in Hot Chocolate's office, things were about to get heated.

Victoria knocked and went straight inside. 'Can I come in and have a brief word please, ma'am?'

'Well, you're already in, Chief Inspector, so I suppose you should go ahead. Take a seat.'

'No thanks, ma'am. I'm only here to pre-empt a warrant request.'

'You don't really need my permission, Chief Inspector. Just submit it in the usual way and I will see it when it comes back from the courts. I'm sure it will all be in order. No need to warn me of it.'

'Yes, I know, ma'am. I just really wanted to run it past you before doing it formally.'

'Carry on then, spill the beans. Give me the details. Who, where, and why?'

Victoria paused, looking at the assistant chief constable, then placed the warrant request on the ACC's desk and waited for her to pick it up. ACC Thornton looked at both sides, carefully considering the list of names, and put it back down on the desk. She looked up at Victoria, eyes wide in complete amazement.

'Are you serious? Do you know who these people are?'

'Yes, ma'am. I am fully aware of who they are, and I'm fully aware of the seriousness of the case that I believe them to be involved in.'

Julie Thornton pushed the piece of paper over towards Victoria. 'Not a cat in hell's chance, my dear. Not a cat in hell's chance. A judge will not sign this off without some cast-iron evidence of involvement. And by the looks of it, you will need at least mine or the chief's recommendations to get this through. And I think you will be waiting some time for that.'

'Well, ma'am, it's not quite as simple as that.'

'Simple? There's nothing simple about this.' The ACC gave Victoria a look that said she was standing firm. She glanced again at the list of names and the request and slowly shook her head. 'Nope, nope, and a third nope, Chief Inspector.'

'Well, with or without your recommendation, I will be pushing it over to the duty magistrate to sign it off. But, you see, the warrant includes the search and seize at the home of a close friend of yours, and I wanted to give you a heads-up before taking it further.'

The ACC picked up the application once again, thinking she had missed something. Reading down the list, she stopped. This time, a name jumped out at her.

'What in god's name are you thinking, Chief Inspector? I'm beginning to think you really have lost it.'

'Yes, ma'am. I could see how you might come to that conclusion.'

Julie Thornton slowly shook her head, looking at the name of Noel Jackson with wide-eyed astonishment. 'What on earth do you want to search Noel's home for?'

'Well, ma'am, we believe he may be connected to the disappearance of Jason Waites, and possibly linked to the disappearance of more young boys back in the nineties.'

The ACC was still shaking her head in complete bewilderment.

'What absolute nonsense. I know Noel Jackson personally and I have known him for years. For god's sake, we were on the beat together. I know more about him than anyone. No way is he involved in anything like that.' She stood up and walked over to look out of the window, before turning back to face Victoria. 'What on earth has brought you to such a conclusion? Do you have any evidence, or is it little more than *one of your hunches?*' The final four words, she delivered in a mocking tone. 'You know where your hunches have gotten you in the past? Into deep trouble, in more ways than one.' She handed the warrant request back to Victoria. 'No, my answer is definitely no. Without some clear evidence to link him and the rest of those on the list to these crimes, you will not be getting a warrant to search any of them, let alone seize any property.'

Victoria was not going to give up without a fight.

'Well, ma'am, we do have substantial evidence, although much of it is circumstantial, I grant you.' She paused to get her mind into gear before continuing. 'One. He headed up the Muffin Man Enquiry into the three missing teenagers in the nineties and he was the prime instigator in the investigation being kicked into the long grass. Two. He is the chair of a trust that sponsors young people's soccer clubs in Yorkshire. This trust actively sponsored *all* the clubs where the missing boys played, including Jason Waites's club. Three. There is no mention in the Muffin Man files of the links between said trust and these clubs. And there is also no mention in the Muffin Man files of the links between said trust and Noel Jackson himself. At the very least, you would have expected some note of a conflict of interest to have been identified. But no. I believe that only by looking closer at Noel Jackson and the others on this list will we potentially uncover more in the way of hard evidence.'

Victoria sat down and watched ACC Thornton, who was twirling her pen and again looking out of the window.

'Listen to me, Victoria. I would normally trust your judgement unreservedly. However, as I said, I know this man well. For heaven's sake, I'm having dinner with him later this week. He is not the type of man to be involved in the abduction of young boys. I can assure you of that. And before this gets any more bizarre, I think we need to call it a day. Could I just put three thoughts out there for you to consider? One. Have you checked if there are any other clubs that this *trust* is sponsoring where young lads have not been reported missing? Two. Are there any young Mispers of young boys in Yorkshire that have no links to football clubs? And finally, Noel Jackson in his time on the job has put more murderers, rapists, and child molesters away than you, me, and Sean O'Bloody Neill put together. To barrel into his home on such a flimsy pretence would be an outrage. So nope, and nope again.'

She picked up the warrant request and looked at it once more.

'No, Victoria, I'm sorry to say that both myself and the chief constable would openly oppose any request for a warrant to search the homes of these men.'

She returned it back to its place on the desk.

Victoria didn't move and held the ACC's gaze. She was not about to let go and decided to have one more stab at it.

'I take all your points, ma'am, and I know that your opinion of Noel Jackson is based on years of experience. But I know for a fact the man is a liar, and that always makes me suspicious.'

'Now steady on, Victoria. You can't go around making accusations like that. I think you should explain yourself. What makes you say he's a liar?'

Victoria looked away from her boss, not really wanting to answer.

'Go on. Explain yourself! Why do you think he's a liar?' She gave Victoria a questioning look, eyebrows raised in the centre of her forehead. Julie Thornton knew Noel Jackson well enough; he could be a little economical with the truth. So she was genuinely intrigued.

'Well, it's personal, ma'am, and it would be somewhat inappropriate for me to comment.'

The ACC was not having any of it and pressed her again. 'I don't give a monkey's fig how inappropriate you think it is. Come on. You've made the accusation. Why are you calling him a liar?'

Victoria clearly didn't want to answer, but the ACC was not going to let it drop. She had little option other than to explain. She girded her loins before doing so.

'Ma'am, if you recall, when we were on the visit to the home of Harry's parents, you had a phone call from Noel Jackson?'

'Yes. I remember. I may be somewhat older than you, but I'm not senile, well, not yet at any rate. Go on.'

'You explained to me that you might be seeing him in a social context?'

'Yes. And?'

'Well, you went on to explain that he was not married, and I think you mentioned he had been divorced, or separated, and therefore single for some years now.'

'Yes, I remember. He has been separated for some time now.'

'Well, when myself and Officer Slocomb called to see him, to get some background on the Muffin Man Enquiry, we had tea and scones with him and . . . ' She paused for a second. 'And his wife, Angela.' Victoria sat on the edge of the chair and let it sink in for a moment. 'I know it's a personal matter, and you might say it's none of my business, but he clearly is, at best, economical with the truth, and, at worst, a seasoned liar, which simply makes me distrust him.'

The ACC was considering what she had been told. She sat back in her chair, arms folded across her chest, with a slight "let me think for a moment" frown. Before speaking again, she relaxed her face and looked at Victoria.

'So, you think because he told me a lie about his marital status, he is involved with the abduction of children? That is one massive leap, Chief Inspector. One massive leap.'

'No, ma'am. I just think it is indicative of the man. That's all.'

The ACC stood up and walked to the door. She opened it and gestured to Victoria that the meeting was over.

'Thank you, Chief Inspector. That will be all. I am sure we will speak again soon. You are correct about one thing, however. It is a personal matter. And it is certainly none of your business.'

As Victoria was leaving the room, somewhat disappointed and a little aggrieved, she knew it was unlikely that her ACC would have gone for it in the first place. Although left wondering where to take the enquiry next, she was certain that retired Chief Constable Noel Jackson would figure in it.

As Victoria entered the corridor, Julie Thornton relented a little and felt the need to build some damaged bridges. She called Victoria back in.

'Victoria, you are undoubtedly one of the best officers I have ever had the pleasure to work with over the years, and as I said before, we need to tread extremely carefully with this case. We both know how the Yew Tree Enquiry eventually went tits-up, and how the force ended up with egg on its face. Not to mention how many lives we managed to bugger up with all the wrongful arrests. The press will be all over this, if and when it breaks, and I don't want us to end up being the baddies again. Before we send in the cavalry searching homes and taking away computers, we need to be on much firmer ground. If that's okay with you?'

Victoria nodded her reply but was in no way convinced. She believed that the team needed to act fast, and although she was uncomfortable about bringing up such a personal matter with her boss, it needed saying. However, on the plus side, the ACC now had some idea of the man's easy ability to lie.

She went again to leave then turned back. 'I do take your points about all of that, ma'am. But we also need to consider how inaction only allows those involved to hide or dispose of evidence. And we should never forget the harm caused by our inaction, allowing the likes of Savile, Glitter, Harris, and others to carry on doing what they were doing.'

Victoria turned to go. Julie Thornton closed the door behind her. She paused, then picked up her telephone and dialled a familiar number. It rang for four rings before being answered.

'Hey! Hello. How are we doing?' she said.

'Hi! How are you doing, gorgeous? I am really looking forward to dinner. It will be just like old times.'

'Yeah, me too. So,' she said, hesitating a little, 'you didn't tell me that Chief Inspector Adams called to interview you. How did that go?'

'Well, I wouldn't call it an interview. More of a wee chat. She just wanted some background on the Muffin Man Enquiry. Don't know if you remember that one I headed up way back? I said I really couldn't help her much at all, so she left.'

Julie considered his answer, and although she was willing to give him the benefit of the doubt, she was not quite convinced he was telling it as it actually happened. Her feelings for Noel were still strong and she more than wanted him to come clean about his personal circumstances. But she decided, on this occasion, to allow him to expand on his account.

'Anything else you think you might want to tell me, Noel?' She paused for a second, giving him time to think over what he would say next. 'About the meeting, that is?'

'Like what? Tell you about what?'

He was becoming defensive, she noticed. 'About her visit. Anyone else there?'

'Only her sidekick. I don't know if you were aware. She only brought a bloody probationer with her. I must say, Julie, you've got to be scraping the bottom of the old barrel using probationers as CID officers. It would never have happened in my day.'

She felt his attack on her competence. Before defending herself, she thought that perhaps this side stepping was typical of him, but nonetheless unwelcome. Julie didn't answer straight away. She decided to let it ride and push a little more. Although he was once her mentor, he had no place belittling her choice of who operated and who didn't on her patch. However, there would be no point in showing her displeasure. He was clearly not going to mention his wife. Julie decided to bring it up herself and take it from there. She would not be bamboozled by his rhetoric. But at the same time, she did not want to end a relationship before it had begun.

'Aye, yes, we are struggling at the moment. It's all hands to the pumps, as they say. More to the point, Noel.' She took a deep breath before moving on to the sixty-four-thousand-dollar question. 'Victoria tells me that she met your wife, Noel.' She let that sink in for a second. 'And I thought you told me you were divorced?'

Without letting him speak, she launched into a staccato of options, none of which she was really interested in hearing the answers to. They were more directed at making him feel uncomfortable.

'So, what is it? Divorced? Separated? Living together? Open relationship? Married, or what? I hear open relationships are de rigueur right now.'

Now she gave him the option to say something. He didn't speak for a second or two, obviously trying to marshal his thoughts into some form of coherent answer. When he did manage to say something, it came out in a slightly shaky, nervous reply that was calculated to portray him as the victim in all this. Or at least deflect the questioning on to a more favourable line.

'Well, we have never really got around to actually getting a divorce. In the legal sense. What with the properties we jointly own, it would be a field day for the lawyers, who would clean up. It was a long time ago that we separated, after she had an affair, but we don't live together. We haven't for around, oh . . . ten or eleven years now.'

'So why was she at your house?'

'What is this, the Spanish Inquisition? She just came round to sign some things relating to property we still own together. But look, if you want to call our dinner date off, it's up to you, Julie. Just let me know.'

'No, nothing like that, Noel. But I'm not the kind of woman you can take for granted and lie to willy-nilly, you know. No way will I become your bit on the side. I'm worth more than that.'

There was another pause until he came back to her.

'Of course you are, Julie. And I would not treat you any other way. I would never treat you like that.'

She was not convinced by his answers. But Julie decided to give him the benefit of the doubt, for now. It would be best to proceed with caution. He was definitely not telling her the full story. Yet she always knew he was a bit of a rouge. She remembered the tales surrounding his relationships with women while he'd been in the job. In many ways, although she was attracted to Noel Jackson, she didn't really trust him. But sometimes living on the edge was more interesting. It wouldn't hurt, to bring a little excitement back into her life.

'So . . . ' said Noel. 'Are we still on for dinner?'

Julie thought for a moment. She decided she would use the dinner to bring up the questions relating to his involvement with the trust. She would do it surreptitiously, but nevertheless try to ascertain what his involvement was.

'Absolutely. Looking forward to it.'

'Me too,' he oozed down the phone, almost Terry-Thomas-like.

Julie wished him all the best and he blew a kiss down the line that she didn't reciprocate. As she put down her phone, she noticed that Victoria had left the search and seizure request on the desk. She thought for a moment then picked it up. Opening her desk, she placed the document inside and closed it.

Chapter 22

One week before Christmas

"But Jesus said, suffer little children and forbid them not, to come unto me: for of such is the kingdom of Heaven."
Mathew 19:14

Jason felt warm and comfortable in his clean underwear and the warm, towelling dressing gown wrapped around him. The gown was a little rough, but not unpleasantly so, and it smelled like the towels did at home after his mum had done the washing and let it dry outside. He relaxed in front of the television and was watching some of the *Game of Thrones* series when the man brought him in a mug of hot chocolate. Jason took it from the man, cupped his hands, and had a sip. The taste was comforting and consoled him somewhat, relieving his anxiety just a little. He let the steam drift up from the mug and scent his nostrils.

Chapter 22

When the man spoke, Jason put the mug down on a small table at the side of his armchair.

'What do you say then, you ungrateful little tyke?'

He looked at the man and quietly said, 'Thank you.'

The overwhelming feeling he had was that of loneliness. He missed his mum and dad, and also his big sister. He thought about them constantly. About how worried they must all be. And he wondered if they were missing him as much as he was missing them. He didn't think about his friends that much, as he didn't really have any close ones, other than Terry. That was the only friend he had.

As he watched the man sipping from a can of what looked like lager, he wondered what had become of Terry.

'What the fuck are you looking at? The pizzas will be here soon. I got you a pepperoni. If you don't like it, tough shit. I'll have it.'

Jason turned away and took another sip from his mug of chocolate. He plucked up the courage to speak. 'No, I mean, yes. I like pepperoni.' He paused and again spoke more quietly. 'Thank you.'

The man tutted and burped, almost at the same time, without putting his hand to his mouth. Jason went back to watching his programme as there was a knock on the door. The man jumped up to answer it and Jason considered calling out for a moment. If it was the pizza delivery, he could shout out and the delivery man might hear him and go for help. But as he was considering this as an option, the man stopped in the hallway and turned around to look back into the room. He looked at Jason and wagged his index finger at him, as if he knew what was going through the boy's mind.

'Now don't you get any ideas, little man. Don't you even think about shouting anything out. You know what happened to your policeman friend. Not a pretty sight, hey? I don't want any trouble from you, or you can go straight back down into the cellar. Okay?'

Jason nodded slowly and took another sip from his mug of hot chocolate. He could smell the pizzas before the man returned with the two boxes, which he dropped onto the small table that stood in the space between Jason's chair and the settee where the man sat down. He opened the first box and closed it again, throwing it over to Jason.

'That's yours. Pepperoni. Do you want a coke with it?'

'Yes.'

'Yes what? You little sod.'

Jason wondered what the man wanted him to say, and then remembered his mum always asked that too.

'Yes, please,' he said quietly.

'Well, get of your fucking arse and go and get one.'

Jason looked a little bewildered.

'Out in the corridor, turn right and first on your left is the kitchen. Fridge is in the corner and you can fetch me another beer while you're at it. And don't try anything stupid like running off anywhere.'

Chapter 22

Jason was surprised that the man was allowing him to move around the house on his own for the first time. There was a sort of ambivalent relationship developing between the two of them, and Jason, although worried and on edge most of the time, felt oddly secure when the man was around. Even remembering how the man had killed his would-be rescuer and knowing that he was on the edge of constant danger, much of the acute anxiety was subsiding. He was in some ways beginning to trust that the man would not do him any harm.

As he walked down the corridor and into the kitchen, he could never have believed what harm was about to befall him. Not at the hands of the man he was about to fetch a beer for, but at the hands of the so-called guests who were yet to arrive.

Jason eventually made his way back with the drinks, and handed the beer to the man. As he was about to let go of the can, the man caught hold of his hand and squeezed it gently. Jason pulled it away.

'Now come on, little fella. We both know what you are, don't we? Your friend Terry told me all about what you got up to in his flat. So don't come all coy with me.'

Jason felt scared, his anxiety building once more. He quickly sat back down, curling his legs up under himself.

'Anyway, enjoy your pizza.' The man checked the time on his mobile phone. 'It won't be long until our guests arrive, and then you can start earning your keep.'

The man stuffed a large slice of pizza into his mouth and laughed out loud, spitting food onto the carpet. Jason had no idea what the man meant by "earning his keep," but it didn't sound like it would be anything pleasant. His mind was racing. The apprehension put him off eating.

The man looked into Jason's box. 'Not like it then? Or just not hungry?'

Jason shook his head slowly, and before he could answer, he heard the front door opening and men's voices in the hallway. They sounded well-spoken and a bit like that of Mr Barnes, his headmaster at school.

The man who licked his fingers, stood up, and went out into the hall.

Jason curled his legs up under him a little more.

'Everything ready, I hope?' one of the voices said. Jason could tell this was not the younger man who had been looking after him, but he could not see who was speaking.

'Yes, all ready. I've set everything up in the big room. I've checked the lighting and run the camera a little, just to make sure it's working properly. All the other stuff is in the room — ropes, hoods, and towels, all ready and waiting.'

'And the boy?'

'Cleaned up, fed, and ready to go. Well, I say ready to go. I've put the stuff in his cocoa so it'll be a few minutes before it takes effect, and, of course, he hasn't got a fucking skooby about what's going to be happening to him.'

There was a pause and Jason heard the other man speak again, this time a little louder to overcome the noise of other people walking down the hallway.

'God, you are so uncouth, Jimmy. So damn common. My guests don't do that sort of language, okay?' The same man then made a *tut, tut, tut* sound.

Jimmy, Jason's pizza eating buddy of sorts, burped and laughed at his telling off. 'What?' He laughed again. 'I've heard them effing and shouting when they're getting down to it. You are all a bunch of sick bastards, if you ask me. So don't come with the uncouth here. I have more on you than you could realise. Don't be high and mighty with me.'

'Now watch your tongue, Jimmy. We pay you handsomely to do your stuff, and don't you forget it. You look after the *arrangements,* I pay you, and the guests have their fun. That's how it works. Now let's get this show on the road.'

Jason could feel himself becoming a little groggy. Not so much that he wanted to fall asleep, but enough to build a level of euphoria that wasn't too unpleasant a feeling. More a relaxed warmth, like being covered in a warm soft blanket. He put his drink down when one of the men entered the room and gestured for him to follow. Jason looked at the hooked finger beckoning and felt a shiver run down his spine. He was wearing one of those Guy Faulks masks he had seen people wearing on TV, and he thought this man to be the one who was telling Jimmy off about his language.

'Come on, young fella. This way.'

Although Jason had no real idea what was about to happen to him, he knew it would not be pleasant. As fear took hold, he began to shake a little. He stood up from his chair and looked past the man who was standing in the doorway. He could see three more men outside in the hallway. They were wearing the same masks as the beckoning man, and as he moved towards them, he felt his knees buckle slightly. One of them took him by the arm. Jason shook his head in a vain attempt to clear his thoughts, but it was little help; the fog of nausea enveloped him in an ever-thickening cloud.

He was led along the corridor by the man holding his arm. They turned right into a room he had not been in before. The three other men followed, and although Jason found it difficult to focus, he could see the space had little furniture, other than a single square table in the centre. There were four spotlights, one in each corner pointing at the table and he could make out the ropes across its surface. His fear was mounting, not from what he knew what was about to happen, but from the unknown. He did think about resisting in some way, but as the drugs took a tighter hold, it was never going to happen.

Jason was led to the table and it became apparent that he was the centre of attention as those in the room began to circle, taking photos with their phones and laughing loudly. The bright lights shining down from all four corners of the room, and the wooden table with its ropes, all looked reminiscent of some kind of medieval torture chamber. As Jimmy attached one rope to each of Jason's writs, Jason looked at the man, willing him not to continue, but knowing that he would. Two more ropes were tied to Jason's ankles, and then all four ends were attached to the four legs. When the ropes were pulled tight, it had the effect of spread-eagling him, face down on top of the table.

He could hear the men in the masks laughing and drinking and tried to look around, twisting his head from side to side. Jimmy checked the ropes and squatted down in front of Jason's face. He gave him an almost apologetic look that Jason found difficult to interpret. And although the drug was making him feel relaxed, it did nothing to take away the fear he was feeling. His legs had given way, and if not for his wrists and ankles being secured to the table, he would have slipped onto the floor.

The beckoning man then moved centre stage, before speaking. 'Okay then. What are you lot waiting for? You've paid good money for this evening, so make the most of it. Just remember, Jimmy here will be the *only one* taking any more pics. So phones away please, gentlemen. We need to keep a lid on this. All the photos will be circulated in the usual way, so please be patient.'

This was the worst part for Jimmy. He had to both endure the proceedings and also ensure that they were well documented on both video and stills. It was always the same — don't show anything that could link any of those taking part to what was happening, get lots of the kid, and distribute on the secure system they had set up. The fat bastards would be shown enjoying themselves, and bugger the poor bastard who was tied down on the table. Oh, it was okay to show as much of the boy's anguish as possible, but never anything to link those taking part.

While he was moving around the room, the scene would take him back to his own ordeal all those years ago. It would give him flashbacks for weeks, following one of these sessions. Flashbacks to his own identical trauma at the age of ten. In this very same room. In this very same house. There was no escape for him, and the only way out would mean the same fate as that of little Thomas Walker — a star of one of their best-selling snuffs.

Jimmy was sickened by what went on in this dingy, old house. So sickened that sometimes it was difficult keeping the camera rolling and making sure the images were in focus. He kept thinking about how Thomas Walker had died. He remembered the threats he himself constantly received from "the boss."

During the evening's ordeal, when the guests were deep in their visceral pleasures, Jimmy made a conscious decision. If anything were to befall him, he needed a get-out-of-jail-free card. Something he could use to barter for his life. He had been thinking about this for some time now. He remembered how his boss had been quite willing to dispose of the body of the cop and set fire to it, not even batting an eyelid. He thought about the way they had gotten rid of

Terry Greenwood and how his boss didn't like loose ends. Increasingly, Jimmy was feeling like one of the loose ends. He needed something that would ensure these men could not harm him. Something he could hold against them if the crunch came. If that cop could track them down, then so could others.

So, that night, he decided to ensure he had a level of self-protection insurance that could bring them all down if need be. The problem was that they all looked the same. Same blue overalls, same stupid Guy Fawkes masks, same blue, latex gloves. Any images would never be identifiable in a court of law.

Then he noticed something.

One of the guests had taken his glove off to wash his hands as he was waiting his turn with Jason. Jimmy noticed the man was wearing a distinctive ring. It looked gold, and it had a dark stone with an emblem that looked like one you'd see on a castle gate. He had never seen one like it and knew that it must be something important. Jimmy focussed the zoom on the ring and took the photo. He then noticed that the same man was wearing a pair of heavy, brown and white shoes. Again, he thought this was very unusual. They had lots of little holes in the leather, a bit like those worn by older men. Again, he focused and clicked.

Now his eye was tuning in to the tiny minutiae of how these men might be identified. As the cuff on the wrist of one man pulled back, Jimmy noticed a small tattoo just above the wrist bone. It showed what looked like writing in a foreign language. It reminded him of something he had once spotted on a flag somewhere. Once again, he focused and clicked.

He then turned his attention to "the boss," who was busy fixing himself a whiskey. Jimmy moved around the room until he could get a shot of the man now lifting up his glass in a toast. He waited until he lifted his mask up to take a drink from his glass. The man took a large swig. Jimmy clicked the shutter. The image could not have been more incriminating if the man had actually posed for it. It clearly showed Jason tied to the table in the middle distance, and his abuser, retired Chief Constable Noel Jackson, standing right behind the boy.

Chapter 23

BACK IN THE MIT OFFICE, the team were like a pack of coiled springs. Varsa especially. She was sitting on the edge of her desk, reminiscent of a cat shuffling its back legs about to pounce on unsuspecting prey.

'Okay, you lot,' said Victoria, entering the room. 'I've got some good news and some bad. Which do you want first?'

No one spoke until Varsa, not able to contain herself any longer, jumped up. 'We're not too bothered, ma'am. Just tell us when we can go and rattle those bastards' cages.'

The rest of the team, including the new blood, Janice and Ron, looked at the young Asian woman in surprise. No one had ever heard Varsa use language like that, and the look of full-on vengeance in her eyes was almost primaeval.

'Well, the short answer to your question, Varsa, is . . . we're not. Well, not at this time, at least.'

Mal swung around on his chair and threw his head back. As the chair settled back in its original position, he looked around the room, catching the eye of Pete Sinclair.

'I knew it. I bloody knew it. So, what's going to happen then, boss?'

Before Victoria could speak, Varsa was on her feet and prowling the room like a tiger in a cage too small for a wild animal.

She turned to Victoria before speaking. 'What do you mean, ma'am? You mean we aren't going to do *any* searches on these bastards? The longer we give them, the more time they have to cover their fucking tracks.'

There was a perceptible silent shock that made its way around the room at Varsa's use of the F-word. She'd either been drinking or gone through some form of metamorphosis.

'Calm down, Varsa,' said Victoria. 'I know how much this means to you, and all of us on the team, but the ACC has said she will not sanction any form of search and seizure at the homes of these people at this time. She has a point. A judge will look at the evidence and agree with her that there it is insufficient to issue a warrant. If we go bowling in there at the crack of dawn with the cavalry, teams of SOCO, and all guns blazing, and then draw a blank, these people, with the influence they have, will have us over a barrel and, more importantly, waste our time dealing with accusations of harassment.'

Varsa hit her forehead with the palm of her hand in complete exasperation and disbelief. The sound of the smack was loud enough to make Victoria turn to face her.

'Something wrong, Varsa?'

Varsa walked away towards the big board. Without turning, and in a slightly mocking tone, she replied, 'No, of course not, ma'am. Absolutely nothing wrong.'

'Good. Now can I carry on?'

There was silence until Varsa turned again to face the group.

'So, what you're really saying, ma'am, is that it's one rule for them and one rule for the rest? Because of who they are, they get special treatment and possibly get away with stuff that the rest of us would go down for?' Varsa was like a dog with a bone. Her injustice-hackles were well and truly up. 'It's Savile all over again. Can't touch them because they supposedly do *so much* for the community. Household names, national treasures, and such, while all the time abusing and murdering children and possibly police officers, to boot.'

'I said calm down, Varsa. And that goes for the rest of you. If we're going to ever get a warrant, we need more to go on. We need chapter and verse on the lives of all these individuals, their backgrounds, their home life, their bank accounts, social media. Absolutely everything. And . . . ' She paused. 'We need twenty-four-seven surveillance.'

Mal was holding up his hand to speak.

'Yes, go on, Mal.'

'And the surveillance, has that been sanctioned by those that must be obeyed?'

'What do you think?'

A sigh went around the room alongside a lot of head shaking.

Janice Slocomb held her hand up slightly to one side of her face.

'Yes, Janice. What is it?'

'So, if it hasn't been sanctioned from on high, that's going to mean we won't get any extra bodies to cover all these people twenty-four-seven. And there's only six of us. How will that work out?'

Pete Sinclair made his way over to the board, looked at the list of names, and turned back to the team. 'Well, in effect, as we usually run surveillance ops in pairs, we really only have three teams if there's no help around.'

'That's right, Pete,' said Victoria. 'So we need to reconsider, twenty-four-seven being out of the window if we try to cover more than one suspect. If we are to do a thorough job, we need to seriously prioritise our resources. We can realistically only follow one of those on the list effectively. Before we make the decision of who that will be, we'll split into three teams so we can do round-the-clock surveillance. It would make sense for Ron and Janice to work as a team. Mal and Pete together, of course. And Varsa, you can ride shotgun with me. I might even let you do some of the driving.' Varsa gave a thin smile. 'Now, who to target? Any ideas?'

Pete, who was standing next to the board, drew a circle around the name of Noel Jackson. 'Well, it's got to be this bugger,' he said. 'He's the one who was in charge of the original enquiry. He's the one responsible for kicking it into the long grass. And he was instrumental in setting up the trust in the first place.'

Victoria made her way over to his side and took the board pen from him.

'I agree, Pete, he is definitely a prime mover in this organisation. But he is also an ex-copper who knows how to cover his tracks. He'll probably spot surveillance from a mile away. I don't want to waste any more time chasing up dead ends.'

She put the cap back on the pen and tapped her teeth with it while thinking. Varsa came over to the board and rubbed out the red circle around the name of Noel Jackson, then tapped the name of Jerry Hardcastle.

'What about him, boss? He lives relatively local. He's, by all accounts, a bit of a national treasure who may think he's beyond the law, and certainly not expecting any kind of investigation. The kind of individual who may slip up.'

Victoria picked up the background notes on him and skim-read through the two pages.

'I see he lives over the other side of the A64 in the village of Elvington. That's close enough for us to make the changeovers without too many problems. And I agree, out of the whole bunch, he is probably the most likely to make mistakes. Of course, that is, if there are any mistakes to make.' She drew a double circle around his name in red. 'So, Mr Jerry Hardcastle, we will start with you.' Victoria turned to Janice. 'Janice, will you draw up a rota for the three teams, please? Round the clock, seven days per week. You can start with me and Varsa, kicking it all off at six o'clock this evening. Are you okay with that, Janice?'

'Yes, ma'am. Right away.'

'In the meantime, everyone keep digging on the rest of this group of so-called trustees. Let's get on with it.'

The team, although very unhappy not to get a shot at a warrant to search, now believed they had something they could get their teeth into.

***

As ACC Julie Thornton was sending a text to Noel Jackson confirming their dinner arrangements, Victoria and Varsa were settling into their first night of surveillance on the home of Jerry Hardcastle. They had parked in a convenient pull-in only twenty yards from the driveway to his house. Varsa had brought a flask of coffee along with half a dozen homemade samosas.

Suddenly, Victoria sat bolt upright.

'Oh shit. Shit, shit, shit. What a complete bloody idiot I am. Don't answer that, Varsa Malik.'

'What is it, boss? What's the problem? Have I gone and dropped the proverbial bollock again?'

'No, not you, Varsa. Me.'

Varsa sat up and gave her boss a perplexed look, while Victoria took out her frustration on the steering wheel.

'We're sitting here staking out the home of our friend Jerry when we don't even know if he's in the bloody house. How stupid is that?'

Varsa again realised that this was not a question she needed to answer.

'I've got an idea, ma'am. What if I go and give that nice Merc parked on the driveway a good old nudge? It's bound to be alarmed. And when it goes off, the man of the house is bound to come out to see what's up and switch it off. How's that sound?'

'Sounds good to me. But don't come straight back to the car. He might spot you coming over and it could spook him. When you set it off, go hide yourself in those bushes across the road. Watch to see if he comes out. If and when he appears, wait until he goes back inside, then come back to the car.'

'Sounds like a plan, boss,' Varsa said, as she climbed out of the passenger seat and into the damp night air.

It had started to snow a little, well, more like sleet, but before Varsa could get over to Hardcastle's driveway, the sleet had already started to settle. Victoria watched her enter the driveway and then disappear from view. But only a couple of seconds later, the shrill tone of the car alarm started with its annoying *BEEP, BEEP, BEEP.* Varsa only just managed to get herself across the road and into cover before a large, overweight man of well over six feet, with matching girth, emerged on the driveway. He was wearing pyjamas and a dressing gown and stood looking left and right up the street. Fortunately, there was a street lamp outside his property and Victoria could identify him as Jerry Hardcastle.

She slipped down into her seat so he would not see her sitting in the car, but not so far that she couldn't see him. 'Gotcha,' she mouthed, as she watched him return to the warm and dry of his front porch. As she was making a note of the time of identification, Varsa pulled open the passenger door and slipped inside.

'Did you see him, ma'am? It was definitely him alright.'

'Aye, Varsa. Now the boring stuff starts. We sit and wait.'

'They've got decorations and a tree in the front room, lights on and the curtains open on the bay window. I think I spotted a woman when he came out to check on the car.'

Victoria made no comment and Varsa poured them a couple of coffees from the flask.

'Do you want a samosa, boss? You can have chicken or vegetable, your choice.'

Victoria shook her head and gave a wave of her hand; she would forgo both, on this occasion.

The night dragged on and on with absolutely nothing happening. No one went into the house or left it. The pair decided there was no point in them both staying awake, so they took turns sleeping. Two hours on, two hours off. After the first four hours, it became apparent that while one was asleep, the other found it far too hard not to join them, so they both decided to stay awake. Varsa told Victoria about every member of her family, what they did for a living, how many children they had, their kids' names, where her family came from in Punjab, and the history of the Sikh religion. Victoria listened and made a real attempt to show some level of interest, hard that it was. Varsa stopped now and again and Victoria breathed a sigh of relief, only for Varsa to kick off again. As the night wore on it was becoming harder to fain interest, so when a car approached from the opposite direction and Varsa actually shut up, she said a little prayer of thanks. It was still dark. The car slowed to a halt and pulled alongside their own. Victoria was about to get out of the passenger door when Varsa wound down her window. They were met with the wide grin of Mal Chambers.

'You two okay? We can take over from here, if you like. You both look like shit, by the way.'

Victoria leaned across Varsa from the driver's side. 'You don't look so good yourselves and you've been in bed all night. We'll be off then. Don't forget to monitor any visitors. And if he makes a move, follow him. Okay?'

Mal nodded his reply and waved a hand as Victoria started the engine and pulled out of the small layby.

***

The Carin Hotel was, in its heyday, quite the place to visit. It had looked after many politicians and celebrities throughout the years. To this day, it was thought of in the area of Harrogate, and much of North Yorkshire, as a relatively up-market place to be seen. It had lost much of its Edwardian ostentatiousness and now relied mainly on the conference trade and visitors to the various book and antique fairs in town. The food was thought of as modern but not silly, and the restaurant sported four stars, along with an array of culinary awards Just the place for a romantic dinner for two. And an excellent spot for an individual to show off and do a bit of overt flirting.

When Julie Thornton arrived at the restaurant, she was shown immediately to a table in one of the smaller booths that ran along one wall. Noel Jackson was already seated. He stood up as she approached and kissed her on the cheek.

'You look absolutely stunning, Julie. You haven't changed a bit since we last met all those years back.'

They both sat down opposite each other and smiled in welcome.

'And you haven't changed one jot also, Noel. Still got all the old blarney. I'll swear you spend most weekends kissing it until your lips are sore.'

He laughed and took her hand. 'Anyway, it's great to see you again. I have taken a bit of a liberty though.'

'What, already? And we haven't even ordered.'

He laughed again. 'Well, what I mean is that I've taken a bit of a liberty and already ordered. Chateaubriand for two, medium rare, just like you used to have it. I hope you don't mind, Julie?'

On the one hand, she hated being led along by people making decisions for her, but on the other, she would probably have ordered it herself. So, what was the problem?

'Aye, that's fine, Noel. And some wine?'

'The first bottle of Merlot is on its way as we speak.'

When the wine arrived, the waiter offered Noel to taste the first glass. He waved him away, asking the man to just pour it. The waiter filled Julie's glass first. As she looked across at Noel, she thought how, although some years her senior, he was still in great shape and quite good-looking. The problem was, he was well-known for playing the field in and around the various nicks he'd worked. Even when he moved into the higher echelons of the job, he never passed up an opportunity to have his cake and eat it. This, she knew first-hand, being in the past, one of his "fondant fancies."

There was no doubting it; she was attracted to Noel Jackson. But who wouldn't have been? And plenty, she surmised, probably still were.

They didn't have to wait long for the food to arrive, and, as expected, the fillet was excellent. The conversation was trivial, but never too far away from a flirtatious glance and compliment about how clever she was or how much she deserved her rank and status. She thought, at times, how adept he was at the flirting game. He knew just when to turn it on, give a cheeky smile and flash of his teeth. She couldn't help but notice the laughter lines and small creases at the side of his eyes that only added to his attractiveness. As Julie was polishing off her last spear of asparagus, Noel put down his knife and fork and took a sip from his glass.

'So, Julie, tell me. How's the case going?'

'Which one?'

'The one we were discussing the other night. The missing boy, the death of your man Harry? I see you have re-opened the Muffin Man Enquiry?'

Julie wondered why he was so interested. He was clearly a little agitated. She initially put this down to his damaged professional ego, or more likely the damage to it if the new enquiry opened up any more mistakes or omissions in addition to those already identified by Victoria. Julie thought she would give him a little more rope, just a push to see where it went. She thought he always did have an ego the size of the Empire State and it never did any harm to bring him down a peg or two.

'Why, what's your interest?'

'What do you mean, sweetheart? I'm just showing a bit of professional curiosity. I did work on that enquiry for some years, you know. I was just thinking about how I might be able to help your team, give them some ideas. So long as they shelve any ideas of shafting me over, if you catch my drift. That Victoria Adams is a little too direct for my liking. I don't really trust her too much.' He gave the side of his nose a little tap, tap, with his index finger in a gesture that said *keep an eye on that woman.* His arrogance was venturing into the offensive, and he seemed totally oblivious to any offence he might cause by insulting a member of Julie's team. After all, it was she who recommended Victoria for promotion to the chief inspector. She began to think this dinner might not have been such a great idea. Still a little taken aback by his choice of words, she waited until her mouth was empty before placing her knife and fork down carefully. Picking up her napkin from the table, she dabbed the corners of her lips with it, making sure her lipstick wasn't smudged, and then leaned forward before replying.

'Now I am aware of your prowess with us ladies, Noel, and I am more than aware of your background knowledge regarding the case you worked on. As far as I am aware, the Muffin Man Enquiry is not being re-opened. Victoria is looking into the backgrounds of the missing boys from back then to see if there are any links with the current lad who disappeared.'

'And has she found any links?'

Julie's radar was now becoming tuned in to Noel's constant questioning about the case. On the one hand, he was saying he didn't really rate Victoria as a copper, but in the same breath appeared overly interested in how she was conducting the investigation.

'Well, actually, I have had, all on, to stop her and her team raising a warrant to search your property, seize computers and the like. Not only you. But all the other trustees of the Fitz-Michael Soccer Trust. She has a point too.'

His face turned pale. Julie noticed he had stopped eating and was holding his knife and fork so tightly that she thought he might crush them.

'What the fuck? A search warrant, are you kidding me? The woman has gone stark raving mad. I can see the headlines now. "Homes of community-conscious philanthropist Lords and MPs raided." For *nothing*. She's a complete nutter. No mistake.'

The harshness of his response took Julie by surprise. She decided now would be the time to get out in the open what she had been debating with herself since earlier in the week.

'Okay, Noel, calm down. I told her that the warrant would not get passed the magistrate and neither I nor the chief constable would sanction it. So don't choke on your steak.' She eyed him now with some degree of suspicion. His outburst was, to say the least, over the top. But she needed to satisfy herself that there was nothing other than his damaged ego going on here.

'Okay, good. At least someone's got some sense in York.' And he went back to eating.

Julie thought for a moment as she was chewing on her food. How could she bring up the concerns and circumstantial evidence that Victoria had laid before her? It was clear that when she mentioned the possibility of a search warrant, he became more than rattled. It could be no more than a simple case of *how dare she?*

She decided to push him, just a little more. 'Well, Chief Inspector Adams has some questions that will, in the near future, need some answers.'

With a look of exasperation, he finished eating and placed his knife and fork down on his plate in the customary way. As the waiter came over and made a move to collect his empty plate, Noel waved him away and folded his arms, tightly, in a show of defiance.

'Is that right, sweetheart? Such as?'

His direct challenge was loud enough for those on adjacent tables to hear. Julie placed her cutlery down, glancing around to check no one was eavesdropping. She leant forward, speaking in a confident yet non-confrontational way and using her fingers to denote the points she was making.

'Well... Firstly.' She raised her thumb. 'Why did you never declare your links to the trust when you were carrying out the original investigation? Secondly.' Her index finger joined her thumb. 'Why is the trust not even mentioned in any of the case notes? And thirdly.' Her middle finger was now added. 'Why is it not mentioned anywhere in all the reports that all three missing boys played for clubs that were sponsored by this trust? And that's only for starters. We haven't even touched on the little wifey thing. Oh, and don't call me sweetheart. Unless I decide to call you sweetheart, of course.'

He looked across at his date and frowned. He had no idea that the MIT had uncovered so much background. He didn't like it. Noel had two options, he thought. Either he could brazen it out and say, "So what? So the original investigation was a bit slack," or he could grovel and admit how poor the investigation had been, then congratulate Victoria and her team on discovering so much. In the end, he decided on a bit of both. Although clearly taken aback, he soon recovered his composure.

'Look, Julie . . . I grant you the original investigation was a bit suspect. We should have dotted all the Is and crossed all the Ts, but we were short-staffed, and in addition to the Muffin Man stuff, there was a double murder in Chapeltown, a serial rapist on the knock, and a shooting in Ilkley all in the same few months. Regarding the non-disclose of my links to the trust . . . ' He paused and Julie recognised the tell-tale signs of some concoction about to come forth. 'Well, it didn't seem to be so important. We hadn't made the link between the trust and the clubs, so the so-called conflict wouldn't have arisen. Would it?'

She laughed, not out loud but more an inner laugh of complete incredulity. She looked at him and shook her head slowly. He was now quite rattled and doing his level best to hide his annoyance and concern, both in equal measure.

'What?' he protested. '*What?* Now look, I've got nothing to hide and neither has any of the members of our trust.'

This time, she laughed so he could hear — a scornful jibe of a laugh that was meant to hit home. 'You are joking, aren't you, Noel? Come on, for heaven's sake. If, like you say, you have nothing to hide and, along with the other trustees, have no involvement in any of it, then give me one good reason why I should not allow the search warrant to go ahead?'

He didn't answer. She looked around for the waiter so she could order some dessert. When she looked back, Noel was staring at his phone and hitting the buttons with some urgency.

'Problem?' she asked.

'No. No problem. I just need to answer this message.'

She attempted to peer over the top of his phone. He noticed and tilted it more towards his chest so that she was unable to see.

'I didn't hear you get a message.'

'No, it's on silent.'

'Well, I didn't hear it vibrate either.'

She thought he was being a little more than secretive. But when she looked across at him and into those blue eyes, he looked up and smiled. *How can he be involved in something like this? It's absolutely impossible. Why would a man like this have any interest in boys of any age? Preposterous.*

But still, she could not shake off that he was most definitely hiding something. She wanted him, just the same way she'd wanted him when they'd worked together. He was always going to be the man a woman fancied, rather than the one a woman settled down with. He was exciting and handsome, but any relationship with Noel Jackson was always going to be a proverbial rollercoaster. She bit her lip and decided to give him one more chance. *This is becoming a bit of a habit,* she thought. Clasping her hands together on the table, Julie looked straight at him, wondering what was suddenly so important about his messages. After delivering his smile, he went straight back to his phone. It was becoming a little intolerable.

'I have to ask, Noel, am I boring you? Or do you need to be somewhere else?' He looked up with the surprised-little-boy look that said, *I'm sorry for being caught out doing something I shouldn't have been doing.* He smiled again, this time a little less effectively.

'No, sorry. I just needed to check that message.' He put the phone down and turned his attention back to his date, taking her hand across the table. He was about to speak when the waiter brought over the dessert menu. Julie pulled her hand away. She ordered cheese and biscuits and Noel shook his head. 'Nothing for me, thanks.'

The waiter nodded, leaving them sitting in silence.

Julie was about to speak. She leant forward to say something when Noel abruptly stood up. 'I'm so sorry, Julie, but you will have to excuse me. Something has come up and I need to go home urgently.'

She was completely taken aback. 'Is it something to do with your wife?' It was as if he didn't even hear her. As his phone pinged again, he once more began to scroll through the messages. 'Well, is it? Is it your wife?' She paused to let him respond. But he was too engrossed in reading whatever messages were arriving all the time. The phone continued to vibrate and ping. '*Noel*, tell me what the fuck is going on.' He didn't react to the request. 'You're going to have to explain yourself, Noel. That is if you wish to see me again. I'm not going to put up with this. Not for much longer.'

He sat back for a moment and turned his phone face down. It continued to receive messages. Noel raised the palms of his hands in a gesture of capitulation.

'I can't really say anything at the moment, darling, other than I can't let this go. I need to deal with something urgently.'

'Yes. You've made that abundantly clear, Noel, and I'm doing my level best to understand. But if you can't make it any clearer, then I'm afraid that's it. Over before it got started.' And as a bit of a toxic ending, she gave a sneered, '*Darling*.'

Noel made no reply. He opened his wallet, took out a bundle of notes, and dropped them onto the table. She sat back and watched him put on his jacket and leave, just as the waiter brought over her cheese and biscuits.

'Will your friend be wanting any coffee, madam, and will he be returning?'

'Nope, and I hope not... And he's no fucking friend of mine.'

Chapter 24

ON HER DRIVE BACK TO York, Julie Thornton's mind was racing. Her emotions were up, down, and sideways, all at the same time. On the one hand, she was more than angry at the way she had been treated by Noel Jackson. Just running out and leaving her in that way... *How dare he?* On the other hand, she was still struggling with the thought that he could be involved, in any aspect, in the case of the missing boy in York. She found it almost impossible to think he was linked to any cover-up of the original Muffin Man Enquiry. It was clear that he was rattled when she mentioned the likelihood of a search warrant, and she didn't believe for a minute the cock and bull story he came up with when she asked about his conflict of interest in the initial enquiry.

What's he playing at?

She reflected on the search warrant request sitting in the top drawer of her desk. If Victoria was right, and these so-called public figures were involved in some elaborate paedophile ring, she, the bloody assistant chief constable, had just alerted them to the investigation. Her dilemma was palpable. She felt herself building towards a decision. As she entered the outskirts of York, Julie made up her mind. She would grant the warrant.

If Victoria was correct, and this lot did have some involvement, she had provided them with the ideal opportunity to start the process of destroying evidence. If, on the other hand, Victoria was wrong, then it wouldn't matter. She had made her decision not to see Noel Jackson socially again. She was no longer a young kid with her head in the clouds, and she should not let her hormones take over her brain. She drove straight to the office, and before she had climbed the stairs, a plan had been formulated.

***

Varsa and Victoria arrived home just in time to catch Miriam leaving for work.

'You okay, hun?' said Miriam. 'You look like death warmed up.'

'Gee, thanks for the compliment. I love you too. You, on the other hand, look fantastic. I hope you take care of those nails while cutting up those bodies today. Me and Varsa are going to try and get some shut-eye for a couple of hours and then get back to the office.'

Varsa had already gone to put the kettle on as Miriam turned back.

'Hey, I forgot to tell you. Sean's son Matt is up and planning to spend Christmas with his dad, so Aggie has invited us out for a meal this weekend. Will you be up for that, what with everything that's going on?'

'And Varsa?'

'Well, they didn't mention Varsa, but I'm sure she'll be welcome.'

'Can we have a think about it, love? I am absolutely bushed. We can make a decision later. Okay?'

'Sure, no worries.' Miriam kissed her on the cheek and waved goodbye as she climbed into her car.

Varsa and Victoria were back inside before it pulled away.

'I'm going to have a shower before settling down, Varsa, and I don't think I really want a drink of anything.'

'Sure thing, boss. If you don't mind, I'm going to crash on the settee.'

Victoria had already left the room and begun to climb the stairs when her phone buzzed on the kitchen worktop. *Oh, for god's sake. Give us a break.*

She shouted down from the top landing of the stairs, 'Can you pick that up for me, Varsa, and see if it's urgent?'

Varsa picked up the phone and looked at the caller name. Pete Sinclair. She swiped and said hello.

'Oh, hi, Varsa. I really wanted the boss.'

'Well, I'll have to do, I'm afraid. She's in the shower. What is it?'

'We have updates at the Hardcastle house. He's on the move and we're following. Don't think he's clocked us, but I've asked Ron and Janice to come out and join so we can interchange the cars.'

'Good idea. I'll pass it on to the boss. One sec.'

Varsa ended the call and ran up the stairs two at a time. The shower was fully on and Varsa had to shout through the bathroom door to make herself heard.

'That was Pete, boss. He says that Jerry Hardcastle is on the move and he and Mal are following—'

She was about to explain about Janice and Ron helping but was cut short by Victoria, wrapped in a bath towel, who stepped out onto the landing. 'I can't do much about it like this, can I? Tell them to keep in contact, and don't lose him, for god's sake. We'll get to help as soon as we can.'

'Pete says he's called in Ron and Janice for the time being, so they can change over the cars, like.'

Well, well, well. Actually showing signs of a bit of initiative, Victoria thought. 'Tell them that's fine, but keep us posted on where he's off to. I'm going to finish off my shower. Can you make us a coffee? And when I'm dressed, I'll scramble us some eggs. You sort the toast out?'

Varsa nodded and shot up a salute. Victoria gave her a half-hearted grin, thinking how much more confident Varsa had become over the last year or so, and then went back to her shower.

Varsa passed on the information to Pete and Mal. She felt jealous, wishing she was out, still tracking the bad guys.

When she finished her shower, Victoria came down to the smell of burning toast, the aroma of fresh coffee, and a snoring Varsa on the sofa. She put a coat over Varsa to help her sleep and returned upstairs to continue dressing. It was unlike Victoria to select any clothes that didn't say she was the boss, but on this occasion, she wasn't in the mood for smart suits and designer shoes. Instead, she opted for a pair of stretch denims and Nike trainers, a t-shirt, and a warm sweater. All matching, of course. She had only just started cooking the eggs when a bleary-eyed Varsa came into the kitchen.

'I thought I'd let you sleep, love. You look like you need it.'

'Oh, cheers for that, but don't we need to get back, what with the stake-out and all?'

'After we've had something to eat. The others can deal with it for the time being.'

Victoria began whisking some eggs with milk, and she put more toast on.

Vasa yawned and looked at her boss. 'I don't know how you do it, boss. I feel like death warmed up and look twice as bad, and you come down looking like you've just stepped out of Vogue. It's not fair.'

'The shower has perked me up a bit, but stand by when it comes to this evening. When I hit that pillow, you won't be able to shift me with an atomic bomb.'

When the eggs were ready, the pair demolished them just in time for an update from Pete Sinclair, who relayed the information that Jerry Hardcastle's Merc was travelling east along the A64 and turning off onto the A169, heading for Pickering. They added that they had handed over to Ron and Janice, who were now the lead car. Mal and Pete were two cars back.

'Sounds like an episode of NCIS, hey, boss?' Varsa said, once again unable to stay still, reminding Victoria of Tigger.

Victoria ignored the excitement and picked up her phone and bag. She was about to place it in the small phone compartment when it began to hum and vibrate. She swiped the screen. It was the ACC Crime.

'Hello, ma'am. What can I do for you?'

'I need to speak to you back at Fulford. There have been some developments that may result in you getting your warrants.'

'Sure thing, ma'am. We'll be back soonest. See you in about twenty minutes.'

Victoria ended the call. Turning to Varsa, she gestured for her to get a shift on. 'Come on, you. We're going into the office. The ACC wants to speak with us. Maybe, just maybe, there might be some movement on the warrants. We can coordinate the action from back at Fulford. In the meantime, you can be getting on with trying to find out where Harry was off to in such a hurry.'

'Are we not joining the chase then, boss? I don't want to miss out on any of the action.' Varsa looked distinctly disappointed at having to return to the office.

'Two things, Varsa. So far, there is little to be excited about as it's not a chase. We have no idea where Hardcastle is going or why. This is merely a follow, look, and see op, and at this time, our efforts would be better placed going through the evidence boxes from both Terry Greenwood's flat and anything else we can dig out from the original Muffin Man Enquiry. If that's okay with you?'

Varsa was suitably deflated, puffing out her cheeks and giving an exasperated blow.

On the way to Fulford nick, Varsa's phone kept pinging with messages from Mal and Pete updating her on what was going on, which she related to Victoria. It only served to fuel her disappointment at not being on the chase, as she put it.

By the time the pair arrived back in town, it was almost eleven, and they had only just made it to the office when the ACC stuck her nose around Victoria's door.

'You alright, ma'am?' Victoria enquired. The ACC was still in her going-out clothes. Her hair was somewhat array and she still had her make-up on from the previous night. 'You look like you've been up all night, ma'am. Working, I mean. Not *out* all night, that is.' She realised she was digging a hole and decided to change tack. 'If you're looking for an update, there is very little happening, ma'am. Sergeants Sinclair and Chambers are working on a lead we dug out of the original enquiry, and I've got PC Ogden and Slocomb doing a follow-up on some of Jason's close friends.'

This was all lies, of course, and Varsa was burying her head low behind her screens in the hope she would not be brought into the conversation and expected to support the untruths.

Victoria then added, 'What was it about the warrants you wanted to speak about, ma'am?'

The ACC handed Victoria a piece of paper. It was a list of all the names and addresses of those on the original warrant request with names and ranks of officers and their telephone numbers. Victoria looked at the list with some shock and amazement.

'Well, you can call them all back in if their work isn't crucial. I have your warrant for search and seizure at the homes of all those on your original list. So, if you want to be getting on with it, there's no time like the present.'

Victoria was shocked. She wasn't sure what had prompted the change of heart, but it didn't really matter. They had the warrant. She picked up the phone to start the ball rolling with the search teams.

The ACC stopped her from making the call with a hand on Victoria's arm. 'Who are you calling, Chief Inspector?'

'Just rallying the search teams, ma'am. We need to be contacting Cumbria, West York, and the Met. This lot are spread wide and far, and I would like to crack all the search locations at the same time if possible. And there are a fair few.'

'No need, Chief Inspector. I have taken the liberty of putting teams ready to go at the addresses of the eight trustees of the Fitz-Michael Soccer Trust, including the home of Noel Jackson. That's what I've been doing all night and early this morning. They are ready to roll at your command. Just give the shout and they'll be mobile in thirty minutes. It would help if you could co-ordinate the operation, ideally from here. But I see no reason why you shouldn't take the lead on one of the searches.'

She looked at the clock on the wall and back to Victoria.

'As it's now gone eleven, I don't think we can expect to set the dogs loose until possibly sometime after twelve. They should all be in place by then.'

Varsa stood up from behind her screens with her jaw still on the desk. She was as much stunned by the ACC's change of heart as Victoria, if not more so.

'Well, that's great, ma'am,' said Victoria. 'Erm, thank you, for all that.' She was still somewhat stunned and stumbled over her words a little. 'I think I'll be going out to the home of Lord Donald Fitz-Michael, the fourteenth Marquis of Highbury. Might as well start at the top. I think I might take the lead on that one and coordinate from there. What do you think?'

The ACC nodded and turned on her patent heels to leave the room.

Victoria called after her, 'Can I ask? What prompted the change of heart on the warrant, ma'am?'

The ACC kept on walking and answered without turning around, 'You can always ask Victoria. You can always ask.'

Obviously, at this time, the reason for the U-turn would belong to ACC Julie Thornton and her alone. That much, Victoria did know.

She followed anyway and caught the ACC just before the stairs.

'Whatever it is that changed your mind is your business, ma'am, but thank you again.'

'No need, Chief Inspector. No need.'

The ACC sounded a little detached and less than interested as she began to ascend the stairs. Then she stopped and turned to Victoria before speaking again. It was more of a thought out loud than a statement. 'When I was reading through the list, I noticed Lord Fitz-Michael lives out Rosedale way.'

'Aye so he does, ma'am, but so do lots of other folk. Any special reason for saying that?'

The ACC was rubbing her chin and looking the other way, clearly considering her reply.

'Well, it's just that the day Harry went missing, he was in the MIT office going through the evidence boxes and I came in to have a wee chat with him. Nothing heavy, just checking how he was doing, you understand.' She was still thinking and appeared to be choosing her words carefully.

'Yes? Go on, ma'am. And?'

'Well, I noticed that Harry's notepad was on the floor and I picked it up and gave it back.' Victoria was beginning to think that getting the ACC to finish what she was saying was akin to pulling teeth. 'Well, written on the pad was a location in Rosedale. It was the name of some farm and it had a six-figure grid reference. I thought he was planning to do some walking up there. It's a great place to go rambling.'

Victoria threw her head back in disbelief.

'I'm sorry, ma'am, but let me get this straight. You're telling me that on the day Harry went missing and before he left for god knows where, he had written the location of a farm in Rosedale on his notepad? And you are only *now* telling us of this? Didn't it occur to you before now that this farm may have been where he had set off too?'

Varsa had overheard the conversation and come out into the corridor to join Victoria and Julie Thornton. They both looked at ACC and Varsa, wide-eyed spread her arms out in a gesture of complete astonishment.

'Even I would have known that there was real significance in that, ma'am. I can't believe you have been so stupid.'

Victoria butted in before Varsa got herself sacked. 'Okay, Varsa, there's no need for that. Go back into the office. I will speak to you later.'

Varsa turned and retraced her steps to the MIT office, tutting and shaking her head.

Victoria turned back to the ACC. 'She has a point, ma'am. Why didn't you mention this before?'

'Now look, Chief Inspector, I genuinely thought Harry was planning to do some walking. I was rushing to get to a meeting with the chief constable and it completely slipped my mind. We can't all be Little Miss Perfect, can we?'

Victoria realised instantly that her boss was severely on the back foot. She had been found to be lacking and was clearly feeling ashamed.

'Well, ma'am, we know now and we have the chance to put it right.'

She was angry with her boss, but there was no point in crying over spilt milk. What mattered now was to act quickly on the information they had. It could just be a coincidence, of course, she thought. But Victoria never liked coincidences. She decided to press her boss a little more.

'So, you recognised a grid reference as being in Rosedale. That's quite some memory, ma'am, if you don't mind me saying. What made you think it was in Rosedale?'

Julie Thornton gave Victoria one of her *are you doubting me?* frowns, before replying. 'I am a walk leader in our local ramblers group and it's an area we frequent more than often. I didn't recognise the whole six figures of the reference, obviously. I'm not Wonder Woman, but I did recognise the four figures that denote the grid square it fell within. When I recognised it, I just said it was an excellent place to go walking, even in the winter.' Victoria thought for a moment.

'I don't suppose you can remember the reference, Ma'am?'

'What do you think I am, Chief Inspector? Not a chance. I can remember it would be on the North York Moors East sheet though. That's the one we use.

'How do you know the reference was on the east sheet?' It felt like she was now interrogating her boss and it was hard to conceal her contempt.

'Well, the six numbers were prefixed with a letter E, meaning east. The North York Moors ordinance survey maps are divided into two. East and west. Although Rosedale is mostly on the west sheet, the dale does cross over onto the east side of the map for a short way, which means there isn't that much ground to cover, if you stick to the dale itself. You know, I think I might have a west sheet in my office.'

'Can you get it for us, ma'am? This may be the lead we were looking for.'

'Of course.' Julie Thornton strutted up the stairs, and once in her office, she began pulling out drawers and cupboards, looking for the map. She found it hard to conceal her anger at herself for this massive lapse in basic police work. How could she have been so stupid? Why didn't she question Harry at the time about his intentions? If she had perhaps he might still be alive. In the meantime, Victoria was on the phone with Mal and Pete.

'Hi, Mal, change of plan. We now have the warrants for the search and seizure at all of those on the list of trustees. So you, Pete, and the other two, might as well make your way out to Rosedale and hang on at the home of Lord What's-his-chops, as that's where we'll be door knocking first.'

'Well, actually, we're already there, boss.'

'What do you mean?'

'We were following our friend Hardcastle and that's where he's taken us. Right to the front door of the Fourteenth Marquis of Highbury. And you'll never guess who else is here.'

'Go on, who?'

'When we arrived, there were a number of cars on the driveway. All quite posh ones. So we did some PNCs on them. We have the chair of trustees, Noel Jackson, the two Fitz-Michaels, the ex-footie player, Hortense, and, of course, our friend Mr Hardcastle. Possibly some kind of board meeting. Do you want us to make the knock, or wait for you?'

'Just stay put. Stay out of sight but keep an eye out. I don't want any of them making a run for it.'

'No worries, boss.'

'Great. We'll be coming out to join you and bring the warrant with us. But I'll let you know when to expect the cavalry when we get mobile. In the meantime, don't let them out of your sight.'

When the ACC returned, the open map was flapping around in her right hand. She gestured for someone to clear a desk. Varsa cleared one of the tables and Julie Thornton spread the map out across it. She took a sharpie pen and highlighted the area covered by the Vale of Rosedale, making a long, oval shape in yellow.

'Well, that's Rosedale running from north to south. Most of the dales run that way. The village of Rosedale is just to the west of the abbey. That's the area I thought Harry was going to go walking in.'

'And you can't remember anything other than that, ma'am?'

Julie Thornton was looking up at the ceiling as if some divine intervention would bring back something to mind.

'Anything, ma'am. Anything?'

Suddenly, the ACC flattened out the map with both hands, smoothing it from edge to edge.

'Yes!' she exclaimed. 'Yes. That's it, that's it.' She stabbed her index finger at a point on the map. 'That was the name on the notepad I gave back to Harry. Jack Daw's Farm. Jack Daw's bloody farm.'

'You're sure, ma'am? Are you?'

'Positive. I can't remember the full grid reference, but I can remember the name of the farm at the bloody grid reference.'

All three women looked closely at the map and Varsa ran the edge of her hand across it to make it flatter.

'Well, who would have thought it?' Varsa pointed out. 'It's only a stone's throw from the Fitz-Michael Estate. Isn't that his home there? Where that big house is marked in brown?'

Victoria and Julie looked a little closer.

Chapter 24

'Absolutely correct, Varsa,' said Victoria. 'It's one of those stately homes open to the public.' She turned to her boss. 'Well, as we're going up there to issue the warrant on the Fitz-Michaels, we might as well take in the pleasures of Jack Daw's farm and check out why Harry was interested in it.' She looked up at the ACC. 'Are you coming, ma'am?'

The ACC shook her head. 'No. It's your call, Chief Inspector. Your call. It could be nothing to do with anything connected to any of the cases. Just make sure that you keep hold of old Stonewall Jackson until they have completed the search on his place near Harrogate.'

Victoria nodded a wilco and gestured for Varsa to come with her.

Varsa picked up the map and both women were on the road within minutes. Once in the car, she reached inside her bag for her phone and dialled the number to set all the search teams in action. Simultaneous searches began knocking doors in London, Cumbria, and across North and South Yorkshire. Normally, these types of operations would have been carried out first thing in the morning, catching the occupants while they were half-awake. But this time, there was no time to waste.

Chapter 25

IT ONLY TOOK THIRTY-FIVE MINUTES to reach Rosedale. Victoria had used the blue light once on the A64 and, thankfully, most of those out and about were more than willing to move over and let the police car through. As they drove up into the valley of Rosedale, Varsa thought how right the ACC had been when she'd described this place as being the prettiest of dales on the North York Moors. The road twisted and turned, never letting you see more than a few hundred meters after each bend before coming to the next. Sometimes the bends negotiated a stone hump-backed bridge traversing across the proverbial babbling brook, or beck as it would be called in North Yorkshire. The houses were predominantly built out of Yorkshire stone and there were even a few thatched cottages still surviving. The hedge roads bristled with holly and hawthorn contrasting with the deep red of the holly berries. The map showed the entrance to Jack Daw's farm being just off the road before you entered the village itself. However, although the pair of detectives drove up and down the main road three or more times, they could still not see any signs for the farm.

Victoria pulled up outside the village pub.

'Fancy a drink, Varsa?'

'Shouldn't we be getting on to the search at the Fitz-Michael home, ma'am? The cavalry will have arrived by now, and Mal and Pete will be chomping at the bit.'

'You're right. We really should. But I'm convinced there is more to this place where Harry was planning a visit than meets the eye.' while standing next to the car Victoria called Mal Chambers.

'Hi, Mal. Look, I've given the search teams the go-ahead at all locations, but Varsa and I are a little tied up at the moment, so I need you to take over at the big house. I really need Varsa with me at the moment.' The look in Varsa's eyes was reminiscent of a puppy wanting to be hugged and being told no. She really wanted to be in on this operation and Victoria recognised her young detective's desire to get involved. She handed Varsa her keys to the car, opened the boot and took out her wellies. She changed her shoes and wished she had also brought thicker socks, but she certainly felt better with more appropriate footwear on. Then she turned to Varsa who was about to start complaining again.

'Aye. Go on then. Get yourself up to the house before it's all over, and don't get in the way of the SOCOs while they're dismantling everything. I'm going to try and find this bloody Jack Daw's farm. Some of the locals here should be able to direct me. And don't leave me stranded out here with these country folk. I've seen *Deliverance* so I know what they're capable of. I want you back to collect me in one hour sharp. Okay, Varsa? One hour, and don't be late. It's turning bloody cold.'

'Deliverance, boss?'

'Never mind. Just don't forget to come back. Okay?'

Varsa had no idea what her boss was on about, but she took the keys and was driving away before Victoria could get into the pub. Once inside, it was like one of those scenes in a Wild West movie, when someone walks into the saloon and the music stops and everyone looks at the stranger. On this occasion, there was no music, but the dart players stopped to look around, and the four older men propping up the bar turned in unison to clock her as she walked into the room.

As Victoria moved closer to the bar, the four men parted to allow her to speak to the lady behind it. The woman was imposing, to say the least. Anyone drinking in this establishment would be in no uncertainty about who was in charge. She was probably in her mid-to-late fifties and certainly dressed to impress, even for the lunchtime drinkers. Her close-cut, bobbed, dark hair, bright red, full lips, and plunging neckline certainly gave the punters something to look at, and her engaging smile would only serve to make the regulars feel at home. Her black dress revealed an ample bosom, which she propelled towards Victoria while polishing a pint glass.

Chapter 25

'Now then, miss, what can I get you?' The broad Yorkshire accent was on show, and Victoria wasted no time in flashing her ID.

'I'm sorry, my dear, but I'm not really here for anything to drink. It's more information I'm after.'

'Oh aye. And what would that be then, my dear?'

The jollity of the initial greeting had now moved on to a more business-like approach, and the four men once standing shoulder to shoulder on each side of Victoria had suddenly moved to sit at one of the tables, taking their pints with them.

'Well, I'm looking for a farm that is marked on an Ordnance Survey Map, but it doesn't seem to be in the place it is shown on the map.'

'Well, what's the bloody name of the farm, lass?' called out one of the men who were previously standing but now seated.

'It's called Jack Daw's Farm, and it should be somewhere off the main road into the village.'

The four men chuckled and Victoria wondered what the joke was.

'Did I say something funny?'

'No, love,' said the woman behind the bar. 'It's just that we've had quite a few people wondering where it is just lately. You see, it's not a farm any longer. Hasn't been a farm since... Let me think...'

One of the men then chipped in, 'Since the early sixties, about sixty-two.'

Then one of the other men, shaking his head, added his tuppence worth. 'No, you're wrong, Alf. It was back end of sixty-one.'

This was followed by a third, much older man, arguing, 'No, you're both way out. It was start of sixty-three.'

This pointless argument wasn't helping Vitoria find the farm.

'Look, the four of you, just tell me where it bloody well is.'

The older man stood up and gestured to her to come out to the front of the pub. As they stood outside, he pointed to an open gate a couple of hundred yards up the main street on the opposite side of the road.

'That's it there, love. No need to get your knickers in a twist. It belongs to the Fitz-Michael Estate.'

'Thank you. And what did the lady mean when she said you have had quite a few people looking for it?'

'Well, a week or so back, a young fella came wanting to know 'bout it. And there 'as bin a lot of comin' and going' lately. Looks like the Lord Fitz is doin' it up as a shooting lodge, like.'

'And you say it's not been a working farm since the sixties?'

'Aye, that's correct, love. Isn't sixties when cold war was going' on, the place was gonna be used as one of them bunker things? They had all the cellars soundproofed and made strong, like, with air ducts and stuff. When it came to it, they never used it. House was left to go a bit.'

'So as far as you're aware, no one actually lives there?'

'Well, no. Lord Fitz leaves a lad there who looks after the place. Sort of a caretaker, like.'

'Do you see much of him?'

'Now and again, when he comes into the shop. Never comes into the pub though. Keeps himself to himself, like.'

'Cheers. You've been a great help, Mr . . . ?'

'Aye, that's right, I am a mister.'

He turned and went back inside to return to his pint.

Victoria looked both ways up and down the main street. *The friendly face of Yorkshiremen*, she thought, and crossed the road. It was turning colder and starting to rain a little, almost sleeting but not yet. *Won't be long though*, she thought, and turned up her collar. She noticed a couple of horse boxes being towed by four-wheel-drive cars heading up onto the moors, and a tractor slowly turned up the lane opposite the pub.

Victoria made her way up the slight incline towards the open gate that had been pointed at by Mr Yorkshireman. The gate was open and she looked up a wide, gravel driveway towards what looked like a slightly dishevelled farmhouse. There was a sign on the gate telling whom it may concern that the place was the property of the Fitz-Michael Estate, and reminding any trespassers that they would be prosecuted. She was glad she'd put her wellies on before leaving the car with Varsa. Although the path was well gravelled, it had some large potholes filled with rainwater.

As the path turned in front of the main entrance to the house, she could see a small van, similar to the one owned by Greenwood. This one had its engine running, and as she approached it, a distinctly uneasy feeling came over her. So much so that she unsheathed her expandable baton and slipped it into the pocket of her Barbour jacket. Instinct told her that she also might need her handcuffs. She undid the press stud that held them in place so as to make them more easily accessible.

There were three wooden steps leading to the front door of the farmhouse, which was wide open. Through it, Victoria could hear singing coming from inside. She could not quite make out the words, but it sounded like a nursery rhyme. Stepping onto the front step, she stopped to listen.

'Here comes the Muffin Mann,
the Muffin Man,
the Muffin Man.
Here comes the Muffin Man
Who lives down Drury Lane.'

Vitoria stepped back down, turned to the van, and switched off the engine, putting the keys in her pocket. When the engine stopped, so did the singing. A young man in his twenties appeared in the doorway.

Chapter 25

'Who the fuck are you then? What gives mucking about with my motor?' He looked over Victoria's shoulder. 'And what the fuck have you done with my keys?'

He was a slim, rangy young man wearing dirty jeans with holes in the knees and an even dirtier sweatshirt that was an indistinct grey colour, and also covered in holes and stains. He really needed a good wash. But most importantly for Victoria, he was holding in his right hand a large, ball-pine hammer.

'I won't ask you again, missy. Who the fuck are you and what are you doing trespassing on this 'ere estate?'

She pulled out her ID, held it up so he could clearly see it, and stepped a little closer to him, all the time keeping an eye on the hammer.

'Chief Inspector Victoria Adams, North Yorkshire Police.' She let that sink in for a few seconds before continuing. 'I believe one of my officers recently visited the farm here, and I was wondering if you had met him at any time?'

He looked her up and down and considered his options. She was at least six or seven inches taller than him. She looked athletic and could probably handle herself. But at the end of the day, he thought, she was a girl, copper or no copper. He decided to bluff it for the time being and decided to answer in the negative. After all, there was no evidence he had been there, so what could she do? His only concern was Jason down in the cellar.

'Nope. Never met him.'

She looked at his eyes, twitching like he had just told the biggest lie of his life.

'And you are?' She gave him a further moment to answer. He seemed to be thinking of something to say, which was a little beyond him. 'It's not a hard one, sir, is it?' She spoke slowly, in single-syllable words. 'Who are you? Your name will do.'

His face became a little distorted and his eyes twitched once more, darting to the left and right — a clear sign that he was not sure whether to select flight or fight mode.

'Can I show you a photo of the officer in question?' Victoria continued. 'And ask if you have ever seen him around? Possibly a week or so ago?'

She held up her mobile phone with an image of Harry on it. Without looking, he answered while fixing his eyes on the lane and the gate. Victoria sensed that flight mode had been selected. She moved to block his escape. She re-slung her shoulder bag across her body to make sure that, if she needed to run, she wouldn't be forced to let it drop.

He shuffled his feet a little; he was about to make his move.

As he lurched into a run, he shouted out his name in the vain hope it would distract her sufficiently for him to make a sidestep and get up some speed before she could block his way out.

'Jimmy! Jimmy McEnery,' he shouted, as he pushed past her and began his sprint for the gate.

Chapter 25

He was fast, and Victoria, although making a grab for him as he passed, would never have caught him in a month of Sundays. That was if he hadn't slipped in one of the puddles. She closed in on him and noticed, just in time, that he was still holding tightly onto the large hammer. He jumped to his feet and cried out at the same time. It was obvious he had injured his ankle when he fell and could not bear weight on it. Also, he realised that his running days were now limited to a hobble, so decided to stand his ground with this woman who stood a little over six inches taller than him.

'You stupid fucking bitch. Give me my keys or I'll fucking do you. I swear I will.'

She gave him a little distance and held up both palms in a gesture of peace. Jimmy, on the other hand, was clenching his free fist and gripping the hammer tightly, shaking with the head of the hammer less than a meter from her face.

'Okay, Jimmy, Just take it easy, okay? Why don't you put down the hammer?' She paused and thought about where she had come across that name before. 'Jimmy McEnery, you say. I think I've heard that name before somewhere, but I'm not sure where.'

He appeared to calm down a little and she put her hands inside her jacket pocket and took hold of the handle of her baton. She was trying to think where she had seen his name before. It suddenly dawned on her. '*Jimmy.* I know who you are, son.'

'What do you mean you know who I fucking am? You don't know me. You're just trying to fuck with my head. Now just give me my fucking keys, or I swear I'll cave your fucking head in.' He waved the hammer again, right in front of Victoria's face, and she took a small step backwards out of his reach.

'Jimmy. You were abducted in nineteen ninety-eight in Leeds. You were taken away from your family all those years ago. Your family have been looking for you ever since. You were only nine years old. So that would put you at around thirty-two now, son.'

She could see the slow realisation developing behind his eyes, and a sadness crept across his face. Although he was a grown man on the outside, inside, he was still a little boy.

Victoria waited for a response. She expected him to buckle and burst into tears at any moment. But the opposite happened. Just in time, she noticed his right hand clasp the hammer shaft more tightly, and he came lunging towards her with the weapon held high in the air. Just as it came down only a few inches from her forehead, she sidestepped him and, in one fluid movement, struck the metal baton on his wrist with considerable force. Sufficient enough to hear an audible snap. The hammer fell to the ground. He clutched his wrist with his free hand, balancing on one leg and crying in agony. She considered giving him another smack on the arm but instead decided to go for his standing leg. She caught him just above the kneecap, and he fell into a heap on the wet ground.

As Jimmy lay yelling and screaming in pain, not knowing whether to hold his knee or clutch his wrist, Victoria was on him in an instant. She flipped him over onto his face and had one side of her handcuffs on his likely-broken wrist in a split second. She hauled him to his feet, using the handcuff that was clipped tightly as a lever to put him in a wrist lock. This would have been painful enough with an undamaged wrist and arm, but in Jimmy's situation, it was excruciating. She marched him over to his van and opened the driver's door.

'You're fucking hurting me, you bitch. Do you fucking understand? You've broken my fucking wrist.'

Victoria wondered if it was possible to get more of the copulation adjectives into a sentence, but wasn't really listening. All she was interested in was having a look around this farmhouse. To ensure her captive wasn't going anywhere, she clipped the other end of the handcuffs onto the steering wheel of his van and went back to retrieve the hammer. The sleet was still falling. She pulled a pair of blue forensic gloves from her pocket, slipped them on, and picked up the hammer, gingerly holding it by the end of the handle with her thumb and forefinger. Walking over to the porch on the front of the house, she carefully placed the hammer down, out of the elements.

Jimmy had turned his legs around into the van and was sitting out of the sleet and rain. As Victoria walked over to him, she could see he was crying. Long sobs and full tears streamed down his cheeks. He looked like a child. Head on the steering wheel, his whole body lurched with each weep.

She called Varsa on her mobile and waited for her to answer.

'Oh, hi, boss. Do you want me to come and pick you up at the pub? Hope you're nice and warm and dry there?'

'I do need you to come and pick me up, but I'm not in the pub. Now listen carefully.' She gave Varsa the details of her location and told her to bring over some of the search team and SOCOs. 'I have one IC male in custody here who will need transportation to York, along with an ambulance. I think he may have a broken ankle and wrist.'

'Wow! You certainly know how to make an arrest, boss. I hope I never cross you.'

'Just get them over here quick as you can. I'm going to have a look inside now.'

'Do you think that's wise, boss? Before we make sure it's safe, like?'

Victoria didn't answer but ended the call and stepped up onto the porch. Before going inside, she looked back at Jimmy handcuffed to the steering wheel.

'Jimmy,' she called out, and he lifted his head up, eyes sore from crying.

He tried to say something that Victoria couldn't make out, so she stepped down and walked over to him.

'What did you say, Jimmy?'

'I said sorry. That's all. I didn't mean to do it. I didn't mean for him to die. Honest.'

'You didn't mean for who to die, Jimmy? Who are you talking about?'

'The copper. The copper. I didn't know what to do.'

'Okay, Jimmy. We'll talk about it later. Is there anything I need to know before I go looking around the old property here?'

Jimmy began to sob again. 'He's in the cellar. The keys to his locks are on my car key ring. I never hurt the kid. I never would. You've got to believe me.'

'Who's in the cellar, Jimmy?'

'Jason. The young lad. You've got to believe me. I didn't mean to kill the copper, honest.' There was a pause. 'And I would never hurt the kid.'

He started crying long sobs again.

Victoria clutched the keys in her pocket and made her way into the building. She found the light switch on the wall and, thankfully, when pressed, the lights came on. The only closed door off the hall was locked. Quickly, she sorted through the keys until she found the correct one. She stopped herself at the top of the stairs, feeling the wall for another light switch. There wasn't one.

She called out into the darkness, 'Hello? Is there anyone down here? I'm Chief Inspector Adams from North Yorkshire Police. If there is anyone down here? Make yourself known. Come out and show yourself.'

There was no reply. She took a few steps down into the darkness.

'Jason? Jason, are you down here?'

She was not prepared to go any further without some light, so Victoria retraced her steps into the hall and shouted out to Jimmy.

'Jimmy! Is there a torch anywhere?'

Jimmy shouted back that there was one in the kitchen at the end of the hall. Once found, it was back to the cellar steps. As she began her descent for a second time, she thought she heard what sounded like a chain being dragged across a stone floor. She shone her torch in the direction of the sound.

The light missed him at first and he shouted out to her. 'Over here. Over here!'

She aimed the torch back in the direction of the shout and settled on his face. He looked dishevelled and filthy, chained at the ankles and wrists, but he did manage to raise a hand. He held it up in front of his eyes to shelter them from the beam. Victoria obliged by angling it slightly off, just enabling her to see him without blinding the young lad.

Her relief was palpable. She couldn't contain her joy at the sight of him.

'Jason? Is that you?' She immediately felt somewhat foolish at the question. *Who else could it be?* 'I'm Chief Inspector Adams from the police. Don't worry now, son. We're going to get you out.'

She was down at his side in seconds, and he put up both arms in a request for an embrace. Victoria let him hug her and he began to cry — long sobs interspersed with choughs and chokes. He pulled back from her arms and looked over her shoulder. He was grasping her shoulders tightly and staring past her towards the stairs.

'You need to watch out. The bad man might come back. He did before and hit the other policeman.'

'He won't come back, Jason. Don't worry.' This did little to reassure him and his eyes widened, all the time looking at the open door at the top of the stairs. 'I promise he won't come back, Jason. I have him handcuffed upstairs. Don't worry.'

She flashed the light around until she found the padlock that was securing Jason to the chain. It was apparent that one of the keys she took from her captive upstairs would fit the lock. She found it, and in a split second, Jason Waites was free. He had been kept in the most appalling circumstances. The smell of urine and faeces emanating from the open bucket used for a toilet was overpowering. Victoria struggled, at this point, not to run upstairs and punch the living daylights out of Jimmy McKendry. Her anger at these men was focussed on Jimmy, and he needed to come clean about what had taken place at this farmhouse, and quickly. She took Jason by the hand to encourage him to follow her, but he stopped short of the stairs and looked up once more.

'Come on son, it's okay.'

Before following Victoria up the steps, he bent down and picked up what looked like a jacket from the ground. 'The policeman gave me this to keep me warm. I want to give it back to him. Do you think that would be okay?'

'Yes, I'm sure it will be, Jason,' Victoria said, and wrapped it once more around his shoulders.

When they emerged from the farmhouse, the sleet had stopped falling and Victoria was relieved to see the cavalry had arrived. Varsa had brought along Mal Chambers and was busy unlocking Jimmy from the steering wheel. She looked up and stared in shock at the boy with Victoria.

'Is that who I think it is, ma'am?'

'Yes, this young man is Jason Waites, and he's going to spend this Christmas with his Mum, Dad, and big sister. He's going to get spoiled rotten with presents and have a wonderful time. Aren't you, Jason?'

And Victoria gave him a big hug to confirm she meant it.

Chapter 26

JASON WAS SEATED IN THE ambulance and Victoria climbed in with him. He was still clinging to her and only let his grasp loosen when they reached the A&E at York District Hospital. While he was being checked over, he asked if Victoria could stay with him. Only once did he relent — when she had to stand outside his cubical and make the phone call to Mr and Mrs Waites.

Sam Waites answered the phone. 'Hello, Sam Waites here. Who's speaking please?'

'Hi, Sam, it's Victoria Adams speaking. Can I have a word with your mom?'

'Sure, I'll get her for you.'

Victoria could hear Sam calling for her to come to the phone. 'Is there any news about Jason?' he asked afterwards.

'I really need to speak with your mum first, Sam, if you don't mind.'

'Why, what's happened? Have you found him? Is he . . . okay?'

Chapter 26

Before Victoria could answer any of the questions, Mrs Waites came on the phone. 'Hello, Victoria. Is it about Jason?'

'Yes, Molly, we've found him.'

She let the news sink in for a second.

'How? I mean where? Where is he? How is he? Where is he? Have you seen him?' She blurted the words out, never realising she was asking the same questions over again. 'Is he alive?'

'Yes. I was the one who found him. He's safe and well and in the A and E department of the district. I'm with him and I will wait here until you can get down.'

'A and E? Is he injured? What have they done to him?'

'I don't think he's injured, but it is always wiser to err on the side of caution, so he will get a thorough examination. We need to take his clothing for forensic examination so he will need a complete set of clothes to go home in.'

'Examination! What do you mean examination?'

'Well, it may help us to ascertain how he might have been treated while held. Then we can build a case against his abductors. So don't forget his change of clothes when you come down.'

Victoria wasn't sure if Molly had registered any of what she had said, and she waited for her to speak again.

'Oh my god.' She almost whispered it down the phone, then shouted to her husband. 'Paul. *Paul!* They've found

Jason. He's okay. Oh my god, they've got him. They've got him. Sam, he's coming home.'

Paul Waites then came on the phone. There were no introductions or niceties when he spoke, with a distinct abrasiveness in his voice. 'Who's the bastards that have had him then? I'll fucking kill them when I get my hands on them. You better warn them. I swear I'll do time for them, I will.'

'Okay, Mr Waites. There's no need for that. Jason will need peace and quiet, not anyone making things worse for him. He'll need his mum and dad at home. Not one of them in prison.'

'Have you got anyone then?'

'We are holding someone in custody for certain offences connected with the disappearance of your son, but that's all I can say at this time. So calm down and think about looking after your son rather than any vigilante bravado nonsense. Okay?' He rang off before she could say any more, and she wondered if he would be likely to cause trouble at the hospital.

In the end, it all went well. By the time Jason's parents arrived with his sister, all the forensic checks had been carried out and his clothes were off to the lab. At the police's request, the examination was carried out by Miriam, who was more than sympathetic in her approach to Jason. The subsequent medical report wasn't what you might call bedtime reading. It showed evidence of multiple anal rape, ligature damage to his wrists and ankles, and significant bruising to his genitals and penis. The boy had been to hell and back in the time he had been held in captivity, but later tests would be inconclusive with regards to DNA and any other traces of who might have been involved in the abuse. Jimmy McKendry had done an excellent job of cleaning up, and the forensics knowledge of Noel Jackson had been used to good effect, rendering all the scenes of crime empty of any useful or useable evidence.

His family took him home later that evening, and although his bruising and superficial wounds would soon heal, the deeper psychological trauma he suffered at the hands of this group, who believed themselves to be above the law, would take a lifetime to repair—if indeed ever. With the right counselling, his condition would improve. But it was doubtful if Jason would ever be able to reconcile his ordeal.

Chapter 27

THE SEARCHES AT THE VARIOUS homes belonging to the trustees of the Fitz-Michael Soccer Trust turned up little in the way of hard evidence to link them to any paedophile ring, and nothing to link them to the abduction, imprisonment, and sexual abuse of Jason Waites. Or indeed anyone else, for that matter.

All computers, when scanned, had nothing incriminating on them. In fact, there were actually pitifully few electronic devices removed at all. When the top tech boys at Scotland Yard pulled them apart, they were unable to find any incriminating images, texts, or emails on their hard drives and believed it was likely that, if indeed this was an organised paedophile network, they had been tipped off; they'd had time to destroy the computers containing any incriminating evidence.

Both Victoria and ACC Thornton were aware of how the latter had most likely been responsible for inadvertently tipping off Noel Jackson. although Victoria was not the sort of officer to go behind her boss's back and report her for the likely breech, she had lost all respect for Assistant Chief Constable Thornton and would find working alongside her in the future more than difficult. Fortunately, as both their careers were about to take major turns in the road, this was not going to be so much of a problem.

The case would eventually hinge on the testimony of James McEnery, who had confessed to the murder of DC Harry Burrows. Harry's blood was still on the hammer that killed him — the same hammer McEnery was threatening Victoria with when he was arrested. Harry's blood was splattered down the stairs to the cellar, and traces were also found on clothes belonging to Jimmy. Along with his confession, there was ample evidence to charge him with murder, and he would eventually be given a sentence of life imprisonment with a minimum term of thirty years. Paul Waites cheered at the trial and shouted, 'I hope you rot in there. So help me god, I hope you *rot* in there.'

Initially, the CPS were more than a little reluctant to accept any charges against the others involved as all the evidence, in their view, was circumstantial. Although Victoria and her team were not happy with the decision, there was nothing they could do about it. The main problem would be getting these cases to trial in the new year.

No one, at this time, had much idea about the virus spreading around the UK and the rest of the world at an alarming rate from a little known city in China called

Wuhan. One lockdown after another would result in delays to the criminal justice system that no one working in it could have imagined. The real breakthrough came with James McKendry's testimony. Although McKendry's lawyers advised against him testifying, as it would obviously incriminate him in the violence, by association, he *was* willing to identify Noel Jackson as an accomplice in the disposal of Harry's body. Jackson was eventually charged and convicted with conspiracy to murder and perverting the course of justice. He received a sentence of twenty years, but would not admit to any charges of abduction or rape. Indeed, he and his co-defendants, who were charged with the abduction, imprisonment, and abuse of young boys would go unpunished for over three years.

Noel Jackson failed to implicate Julie Thornton as the person who let slip how the team were closing in on the paedophile ring, but she knew only too well how this lack of initiative and protocol had possibly contributed to the death of her nephew Harry. She would have to live with this burden, and this burden would contribute to her eventually leaving the force.

Because of the sensitive nature and the high profiles of all the defendants in the investigation, the cases would eventually be handed over to the Met's Child Protection Unit based at Scotland Yard. And it would be them that finally brought justice for Jason and the other boys who went missing. During the time waiting for the case to come to court,

Hardcastle, like most people in his position, thought of himself as above the law and he continued with his abuse of young boys in other countries. On one of his visits to Goa in India, he was arrested by the local police in a hotel room with a young boy of eight years old. He had a laptop that contained thousands of images of children, some dating back to his crimes in Yorkshire.

Hardcastle was subsequently charged with possession of these images and his links with others in the ring were followed up. The unit began a nationwide investigation, steadily working its way through Hardcastle's contacts, that would rival anything previously undertaken by Yewtree. All files appertaining to both the original Muffin Man Enquiry and the enquiry undertaken by Victoria and her team would be handed over to Scotland Yard who would pursue the paedophile ring for the next eight years. This investigation would involve police forces across four continents. But in reality, only the tip of the iceberg would be uncovered. The irony of it all, in the final analysis, would be that the only person to be given a full life sentence for their crimes was himself an abused child who knew little else other than the life of an abused child and the subsequent life of an abuser and murderer.

No one was ever charged with the murder of Terry Greenwood, or that of the boy found dead in Leeds, Tommy Walker, the young boy incarcerated for a time with Jason. Their cases remain "open" to this day. Both killings were linked to the second Muffin Man Enquiry and both were put down as deviant sexual acts that had gone too far. The crime scenes and body dumps threw up no evidence that would stand up in court, and although detectives working the case were convinced that one or more of the paedophile ring were involved, there was insufficient evidence for the CPS to proceed on any one of them.

It was James McEnery's testimony that would put retired Chief Constable Noel Jackson behind bars. The image taken by Jimmy at the scene of Jason's abuse would be damming in the extreme. Jackson received an eighteen-year custodial sentence spent mostly in isolation. An ex-copper and a nonce, the two most detested crimes by those in prison, ensured his years were not spent reading books and watching television.

Jason returned to his family and spent a Christmas that, on the face of it, was a happy one. His dad tried to ask him what they had done to him and would constantly push the boy for answers, eventually causing him to run away from home on a number of occasions. Jason would never really get over the trauma he suffered, and in later life, took to alcohol and drug abuse, on two occasions attempting suicide.

Victoria, on the other hand, returned to a hero's welcome. She was given the accolade of saviour and, for a few days, enjoyed the spotlight. The celebrations, held as always in the Blue Bell Pub on Foss Gate, were self-congratulatory, but on this occasion somewhat muted, due to the loss of

Harry. Julie Thornton showed her face and bought a round of drinks before setting off.

As she was leaving, Victoria took her by the arm and led her out into the street. 'Might I have a quick word, ma'am?'

'So long as it's quick. I'm having dinner with the Police and Crime Commissioner in an hour and I need to get home to change.'

'It won't take long, ma'am. I just wanted to ask you something.' She paused and looked at the ACC square on. 'Why on earth did you not tell us sooner about where Harry was possibly buggering off too? If only you had put two and two together, he might still be here having a drink with us now. We might have got Jason out sooner and closed these sick bastards down straight away. It beggars belief. And what on earth were you thinking of, passing on to Noel *fucking* Jackson the details of what we were doing? I have been considering if I should pass this information on upstairs. At least it might settle my mind.'

'And will you?' Julie Thornton asked quietly. 'Pass it on upstairs?'

'No, I won't. But if you had an ounce of integrity, you would be dealing with it yourself.' Victoria let go of the ACC's arm and looked her in the eye. It was clear that the comments had hit home.

As she watched her boss walk away to her waiting car, Victoria wondered what the future would bring for the two of them. She returned to the muted festivities and the adulation of her peers. The best thing was spending some time with Miriam. She sat next to her and linked arms and listened, embarrassed, to the team singing, 'For she's a very food fellow,' for the umpteenth time.

However, all the adulation, pats on the back, and congratulatory handshakes would not save her from what was about to befall Victoria on Christmas Eve.

Chapter 28

23rd December 2019

"Then Herod, when he saw that he was mocked of the wise men, was exceeding wroth, and sent forth, and slew all the children that were in Bethlehem and its vicinity who were two years old and under, in the time he had learned from the Magi."
Mathew 3:16

Varsa was sitting outside on the patio. She was well wrapped up, and cupped her hands around her coffee cup watching the steam rise into the night air. Her thoughts were wandering in and out of scenarios that variously saw her and Harry in different places, doing different things together, but always enjoying themselves. Her mind jumped around from being on holiday, living together, shopping and kissing and laughing, holding hands, and just looking at each other. She sighed into the cup in her hands. Harry was the first real boyfriend she had ever had; his death still weighed heavily on her. She had been so looking forward to spending time with him and him alone this Christmas. Although she had agreed to take him round to meet her mom and dad, and she knew they would've liked him, it was always going to be difficult — her going out with a boy who was not Sikh. But it didn't matter now.

She would be going home on her own; she would never be seeing him again.

Varsa was so engrossed in her thoughts and dreams that she hadn't noticed the man standing on the footpath at the end of the garden.

Sharing with Miriam and Victoria had been so very helpful in getting over her loss. Varsa wished there was some way she could repay them both. Perhaps she could babysit for them? She would like that. Taking another sip from her drink that was rapidly losing its warmth, she watched her breath as it turned to vapour on the night air. Living here, in this idyllic village with its views over the Hambleton Hills and the castle, was the best of places to live. Even having to contend with the ramblers who always peered across their back garden as they shuffled in groups and couples along the path at the bottom of the lawn was no big deal. Most just said morning or afternoon as they passed by. Miriam thought that, when she retired, she might sell teas and scones to them, but managed to only think of this idea for a moment before common sense got the better of her. The last thing she wanted was crowds of strangers wandering all over her garden and demanding to be served.

This public right of way at the back of Miriam and Victoria's garden separated all the rear gardens of the twelve properties on High Street in Sheriff Hutton from the now derelict and fenced off fourteenth-century Sherriff Hutton Castle, which was set in its own large, two-acre site, surrounded by a high fence. The footpath was well-kept with wooden benches set in small rest areas for ramblers and locals alike. It was a favourite of the local groups, and the fence made of wire and wooden posts provided some security, keeping any prospective vandals out of the castle grounds and some level of privacy for the homes that had their boundaries along it. Miriam and Victoria had thought about building a more secure screen across the bottom of the garden but decided not to, as it would only obscure the views. The garden dipped down towards the path and the pair loved to sit out looking across the Howardian Hills to the north and York to the south, with York Minster clearly visible some ten miles away.

Varsa looked up from her thoughts for a second and thought she saw something move at the end of the garden. She stood up and stepped off the wooden decking, down the three steps and onto the lawn, peering into the darkness. It was very late for someone to be out walking, she thought. *Possibly just a deer.*

She was about to take a few more steps when Miriam called out to her. 'What are you doing out there, love? It's absolutely freezing. You're letting all the heat out and we're not made of money, you know. You're going to catch your death.'

Varsa ignored her for a moment and took a couple of steps towards the fence, before shouting out her reply, 'I think there's someone or something at the end of the garden looking up at the house.'

'Oh, for heaven's sake, Varsa. Come in out of the cold. It's probably a deer or something.' Varsa didn't move and turned to look back at the house.

Although Miriam and Victoria were concerned about the convicted killer Jonathan Fahey being on the loose, they didn't want to alarm Varsa. And even if he did harbour intentions to harm them, it was unlikely he would make a move while there were three of them in the house together. There had been sightings of him all over the place, both in the UK and abroad. All had been checked out and none had resulted in any meaningful outcome. Still, Victoria had thought it right they should take precautions, locking doors and windows, not opening the door without checking who it was, and having new alarms installed.

Varsa turned back again and took a few more steps towards the fence. She clearly noticed — it was a man facing the house. She turned and walked back quickly. Then, just before making it to the decking, she turned back again.

He had gone. When she opened the sliding glass doors, the warmth of the kitchen distracted her for a second. She slid the doors closed and clicked the catch down.

'Now sit yourself down, Varsa,' said Miriam. 'We're having homemade soup with some crusty French bread and brie. How's that sound?'

'Great, lovely,' Varsa said while turning back to look out of the now closed patio doors. 'But I'm sure I saw someone at the end of the garden looking up at the house. I'm sure I did.'

'Well, if it helps you feel better, we'll lock the doors.' Miriam turned the key in the door lock, checked the handle, and turned back to Varsa with a broad smile. 'Now, is that better?'

Varsa was now a little more settled. She turned to make a start on the soup Miriam had placed in front of her.

Victoria came into the kitchen and pulled herself onto one of the bar stools at the end of the breakfast bar. 'Wow! This smells good, sweetheart. Thanks for doing the honours.'

Miriam gave her own cheek a tap with her index finger inviting a gratitude peck from her wife and where it should be planted. Victoria obliged.

'Small price to pay for the cooking, cleaning, and everything else you do, love.'

'I know. I'm a saint, aren't I?' Miriam replied, and she gently kissed the nape of Victoria's neck. It had the effect of sending a shiver of excitement down Victoria's back and causing her to shake her shoulders in response.

Chapter 28

'Okay, you two, knock it off and have your soup, for god's sake,' said Varsa. 'I'm fed up playing gooseberry. At this rate, you'll be happy to see the back of me tomorrow so you can have some alone time together.'

All three women laughed. Varsa sliced herself another chunk of bread from one of the baguettes on the table and spread it liberally with a slice of brie.

Miriam turned to Victoria. 'So Varsa reckons she saw something or someone at the end of the garden.'

'Not at the end of the garden but in the lane over the other side of the fence. I thought they were looking up at the house.'

Victoria got up and went over to the sliding doors. She peered out into the darkness. It was sleeting again, and she couldn't see anything other than the silhouette of the castle against a moonlit sky.

'Well, I can't see anything, but it is dark. Could have been a dog walker, stopping to let the dog have a pee . . . or worse. I wish people would clean up after their animals. Anyway, they've gone now, so no worries, hey?'

She thought the idea that Fahey might be stalking around outside in this cold weather was more than unlikely, but she also thought she wouldn't put it past him. Victoria didn't want to alarm the others, but made a conscious decision to remind them about checking the doors and windows before bed time.

She closed the curtains and went back to her meal. Victoria had made the point of telling both women, many times, that while Fahey was still on the loose, it was imperative they checked who was at the door before opening it.

'All it takes is a quick look through the bay window after turning on the light in the porch,' she told them once more. And they both nodded. 'Keep all the doors and windows firmly locked.'

They nodded again, and this time Varsa added, 'Yes, ma'am,' throwing up one of her silly salutes.

'I've arranged for a drive-by to start tomorrow. The local plod have agreed to drive past twice each day. Once during the day and once in the evening.'

'Do you think he might come after us?' Varsa said, at the same time as buttering her fourth slice of crusty bread. Victoria put down her spoon and placed her hands palms-down on the table.

'Look, Fahey is no fool. He's probably long gone. He's made his break and it looks like from all the reports that he's high-tailed it abroad, so let's not over worry this, hey?'

Varsa and Miriam settled down into finishing their soup.

None of the three women had any idea of the ensuing danger about to befall them, and it would not be coming from some night stalker at the end of the garden taking his dog for a pee. None of them had noticed the man settling down in his sleeping bag in the Range Rover parked a hundred metres or so down the street. If they had, they would not have been laughing, chatting happily, and sipping the chilled Chablis Miriam had just opened.

In the Range Rover across the street, Jonathan Fahey was opening his flask of coffee and plotting his next move.

Chapter 29

24TH DECEMBER 2019
CHRISTMAS EVE

"In Rama was there a voice heard, lamentation and weeping, and great mourning. Rachael weeping for her children, and would not be comforted, because they were not."
Mathew 3:18

ALTHOUGH VARSA HAD AGREED WITH her parents to spend the Christmas holidays with them and the rest of the Malik clan, she was definitely not looking forward to it. Going home was always somewhat of a trauma for Varsa, especially when her brothers and sisters were there. She would have to endure her mother telling her how well her older sister was doing as a chemist and put up with the constant questions about how many children she'd be having once she found a suitable husband. And why was she still playing at cops and robbers?

'Your sister Shaadi now has three children and you don't even have a husband. And your brothers all have beautiful children as well. When are you going to give me a grand-child? And when are you going to leave that silly job. It is no place for a young lady, you know.'

Just the thought of it all filled Varsa with dread. That, and how her younger brother would be constantly rabbiting on about how many dead bodies she had seen. It was all too much. But she had agreed to go home, and as Victoria drove her to the station through the sleet so she could catch her train back to Bradford, she wished she hadn't agreed to the bloody ordeal.

The sleet was now turning to heavier snowfall and starting to settle on the verges.

Victoria was contemplating how nice this Christmas would be. She and Miriam, spending their first Christmas together and possibly a white Christmas in the bargain. What with a baby on the way, nothing was going to spoil it.

The drive didn't take too long, and after waiting for the line of taxis to clear, she dropped Varsa at the entrance to York Station under the ornate Victorian canopy of the entrance hall. She jumped out to open the boot. Varsa picked up her weekend bag and leant forward to give Victoria a kiss on the cheek. Victoria accepted and gave her young detective a hug.

'Merry Christmas, Varsa. I'm sure it won't be as bad as you're anticipating.'

'Oh, it's likely to be much worse, boss. Much worse. But thanks to you and Miriam, I'm slowly managing to come back a little after Harry. I wouldn't have been able to face it without you two. I owe you so much, I really do. You're both the best, the very best, and thanks for putting up with me.'

'Oh, give over. You're always welcome to come and stay. Hey, and you're not emigrating to the other side of the bloody world. You're only going home for a couple of weeks. It's Bradford, not bloody Afghanistan.'

Varsa laughed and gave Victoria another hug.

'Cheers, boss, It means a lot to me.'

She turned to go and Victoria watched as she joined the throngs of people all making their way home for Christmas. She turned around and climbed back into her car. As she drove away, she didn't see the forlorn figure of Varsa Malik, holding her bag in one hand and wiping her eyes with the damp sleeve of her jacket, standing looking back at the car as it pulled away out of the station concourse.

The drive out of York was uneventful, and as she left the suburbs of the city, the snow started to stick on the road, covering the verges and making the central white lines more difficult to see. The lack of traffic was allowing and even encouraging the snow to settle and become fixed to the road surface. By the time Victoria was out on the road up to Sheriff Hutton, she could barely make out where the road ended and the soft verges began. Due to the lack of traffic, it would not take too long to get back home, but the lack of gritters out on the road meant she had to take it steady. She thought it would not be long before the short hill up to Sheriff Hutton became impassable and was so glad to have made it back safely.

When she turned into the village main street and pulled up outside her home, Victoria was so glad, in fact, that she took little notice of the van parked across the road opposite the house. She switched off her engine, locked the vehicle, and made her way carefully down the snow-covered path, searching her handbag for the front door keys.

The lights were on, and she could see the Christmas tree with its lights flashing through the front bay window of their lounge. She could almost feel the warmth inside reaching out to her as she continued the search for her front door key. Her senses immediately became heightened when she put the key in the front door; it opened without her turning the lock. The door swung open with the slightest of pressure and she stepped into the hall. The hall table had been knocked over, and the plant that once sat on it was strewn across the hall carpet, leaving a trail of soil and compost. Now alert, Victoria moved slowly towards the kitchen. She stopped at the stairs and, looking up, called out her wife's name. There was no reply. Her apprehension doubled.

'Miriam?' she called out again. 'You in here?'

Again, no reply. The resulting silence brought on a feeling of nausea. She took a deep breath and steadied herself. Knowing something was not right and turning a thousand different scenarios over in her head only served to build her trepidation. The door into the lounge was open and she glanced inside. Nothing was out of place. The fire was roaring away and the tree lights still blinked on and off. She could feel the contrast of the warmth of the living room and the blast of cold air from the open front door. *Next stop, the kitchen.* Although she was walking at half-speed and placing her feet down slowly and carefully, not wanting to make a sound, she made the door of the kitchen in four strides. Cautiously, she eased the door open.

'Miriam. You in here? Are you okay?' The words came out shakily and a little too quietly. 'Miriam?' she said once more.

Victoria entered the room and thought for the first time that, compared to the rest of the house, it was probably overlit. As she fully entered, the first thing she noticed was a smear of blood across the kitchen island. *Blood always looks worse than it often is,* she thought. *Always looks more than it actually is, especially when it's been smeared.*

She told herself to be calm and think clearly, but it didn't seem to help. As she turned to her right, her first sight of Miriam took her breath away. She gasped, putting her hand to her mouth. Miriam was sitting in the corner of the kitchen, slumped to one side, only supported by her head, which was jammed into the corner of the open cabinets. The corner cabinet door was hanging off its hinges and looked like it had been used to trap Miriam's head into the corner. There was a large smear of blood that ran down the island unit, across the floor, and disappeared under her wife. She had a large wound to the side of her head and two massively swollen eyes. Her blouse had been torn open, and her breasts were visible through the open bra that hung below them. The whole of her torso was soaked in blood. It looked like it had originated mainly from her nose and head wounds.

In two steps, Victoria was at Miriam's side, kneeling down and pulling her in tight. 'Oh Miriam, darling!'

A quick check over told Victoria that her partner was still breathing, though very fast and shallow, and thick blood continued to ooze from her deep head wound, matting her hair and sticking it to her scalp and forehead. Victoria stood up and picked up the house phone to dial 999. She realised immediately that it was less than pointless; there was no dialling tone.

She had left her phone in the car and was about to run out and get it when she turned to face the room. She replaced the handset slowly and looked into the far corner. Sitting there calmly on one of the kitchen stools was Jonathan Fahey. She shivered and her stomach did a couple of involuntary somersaults.

'Well, glad you could make it, my dear. We were wondering where you had got to, weren't we, Miriam, my love? Oh, sorry, you can't speak, can you? Not at the moment anyway, not with being unconscious and having a broken jaw and all.'

He chuckled to himself and grinned at Victoria.

***

When the doorbell rang, Miriam was in the middle of taking her second batch of mince pies out of the oven. She pulled off her oven gloves, which were made to look like cats, and placed them on top of the breakfast bar. *What on earth has she forgotten now? She's only just bloody left.*

As she walked down the short hallway, she called out, 'I'll put money on your keys, or is it your phone again? Poor Varsa is going to miss her train at this rate.'

Although Victoria had repeatedly told her to always make sure the outside porch light was on, and to look through the bay window to check who it was before opening the front door, it completely skipped her mind to do this. She fully expected her wife to come barrelling through the front door looking for her phone and complaining about being late. She was not expecting an uninvited guest. When she opened the door with a wide smile on her face, she was greeted by it being violently pushed backwards into her face. The heavy frame hit her square on the forehead, knocking her backwards into the hall table, sending the plant on it crashing to the floor. Just before she passed out, she could feel blood running down her face from the gash on her forehead and the back of her head being bumped along the hall, as she was dragged by her feet into the kitchen.

When she awoke, her head was pounding and she was tied face down on top of the kitchen island. Her wrists were bound with cable ties and ropes that ran over the edge of the counter top and secured on to the drawer handles that ran on either side of it. Her ankles were similarly bound to handles further back down the sides of the unit. This had the effect of spread eagling her legs and stretching her body both from end to end and side to side, with her face pressed down on the counter. Her skirt had been pushed up above her waist and the intruder had removed her pants. There was sufficient free movement in her upper body to just allow her to move her head from side to side. Miriam looked around the room as best she could, trying to see who had done this. Her head thumped, and she could feel bile rising in her throat. As she tried to rest on her chin, a man's face came starkly into focus only inches from her own. She winced as he grabbed her by the hair and pulled her head back, stretching her neck violently.

'Hello, Miriam, my dear. Surprised to see me, are we?'

She recognised him instantly as Jonathan Fahey. Her anger spilled over into some attempt at contempt; she managed to raise enough adrenalin to spit at him from very close range. It hit him in his right eye and only served to infuriate. He retaliated by slamming her face down on the hard surface. She cried out loud as she felt her nose break against the granite. Salty blood ran down into her mouth. Fahey lifted her head again and this time slammed it down even harder, hitting her jaw against the counter and surely either breaking it or causing a dislocation. He heard her jaw bone crack violently, sending four of her lower teeth across the floor. He contemplated hitting again and lifted her head for a third time. Fahey looked at her now vacant face, eyes rolling in their sockets, and let the head drop down. He contemplated abusing her some more but decided it was pointless while she was unconscious. There was little fun in it if she couldn't feel the pain. So he untied the wrist restraints and let her fall backwards onto the floor.

When she hit the tiled floor, her head swung backwards and crashed against the tiles with a hollow thwack. He then cut the ankle restrains, pulled her by the ankles into the corner of the kitchen, and propped her up against the cupboards in a sitting position. As he stood back to look, she began to slowly slide down, eventually settling on her left side, lying in the foetal position. He glanced around the room, settling his eye on a bottle of opened white wine. He had to step over Miriam so he could help himself to a glass, and perched on a kitchen stool.

Now, he had to wait until his main prey returned home. Taking a large gulp of the Chablis, his mind turned to the depravity he had planned for Victoria.

Chapter 29

***

Victoria's mind was racing. She glanced from side to side in the kitchen, settling her eyes on the knife block that sat on the side worktop, equally distanced between her and Fahey.

He looked at her and to the knife block and then back to her.

'Well then, are you going to make a move for it, or not? I tell you what, I'll give you a fighting chance and let you choose one of the knives. Which one would you like to pick? Let me guess, the big meat knife? Too big for you to handle easily? But it would put a little more distance between us.'

He stood up slowly and began to walk around the kitchen island like a big cat stalking its prey, all the time grinning at Victoria. He had his hands on the granite as he walked sideways around it and stopped when he reached the centre. He was now only a couple of feet from Victoria and could have reached out to her across the kitchen island.

She glanced at the knife block once more; it was now much closer to her than him. In fact, he had no chance of getting to it before her. *Why has he allowed this to happen?*

Victoria pushed herself slowly of the counter and followed the edge of the worktop. Never taking her eyes off Fahey, she reached back with her left hand until she felt the knife block, slowly pulling out one of the large meat knives. Then she quickly changed hands and pointed it in Fahey's direction. Her grip on the handle would have crushed a bone. She could feel her temples throbbing as the adrenalin coursed through her.

Fahey grinned. 'Now that's more like it, my dear. But what are you going to do with it? You are going to have to come round here, up close and personal, as they say, if you want to use it. Unless you fancy yourself as a knife thrower, that is?'

He laughed out loud and she got the distinct feeling he knew something she didn't. He was in no way worried by her holding the knife, and he showed it. This had the effect of setting her mind racing yet again. What trick had he in hand? What subterfuge was he was planning.

'Just piss off and leave us alone for fuck's sake, why don't you? You bastard. Just fuck off and crawl back under whatever stone you were living under.'

Still holding her knife tightly and never taking her eyes off the man, she started to move closer to Miriam, who still sat slumped in the corner of the kitchen, unconscious and with an ever widening pool of blood spreading out onto the tiled floor.

'If you don't make up your mind what you're going to do soon, Victoria, poor old Miriam there is going to bleed to death before your very eyes. And then how could you live with yourself? Leaving the little one with only one mummy would not be good, now, would it?'

He was attempting to goad her into some action, she knew that. But glancing at Miriam, Victoria could see her chest moving. Although unconscious, she was still breathing, albeit more rapidly. Sometime, Victoria would have to make a move on him. She edged a little closer. He stood upright and folded his arms across his chest in a show of defiance.

'Go on then, you can have first go, Vicky, my dear. I know you would love to plunge that knife deep into my chest. So be my guest. Have a go.'

He dropped his arms to his side and spread them in an invite. Victoria was frozen to the spot. She didn't move her feet but held the knife tightly and waved it in front of him. 'I will shove this into you with great pleasure, you murdering bastard. So help me I will.'

Just then, Miriam moaned and shifted her position. Her voice came in wheezes as she propped herself up on her elbow. 'Victoria . . . Is that you?'

Victoria glanced down at her wife. It was only a split second, but before she could look back, Fahey was on her. He brought the heel of his right hand up under her chin with such force Victoria thought her neck might have broken. But she held firmly onto the knife. She managed some level of retaliation, even though the pain in the back of her neck was excruciating. It felt like she had been hit by a train.

She plunged the long-bladed knife towards Fahey's abdomen. It hit its desired target but she felt an unexpected resistance to the point of the blade. The bastard was wearing a stab vest. She recognised it instantly. It was a thin one but a good one, giving protection against even large blades. She should have realised he was far too compliant.

Raising the knife high above her head, she intended to bring it down on his face or neck, but she was too late. He blocked her arm and headbutted her square in the face, breaking her nose and almost rendering her unconscious. As the knife fell to the floor, Fahey grinned and laughed out loud.

'Not as quick as you thought, are you, my dear?' He might have said something more, but the next blow to the side of her head with his clenched fist rendered her unconscious.

Victoria woke only minutes later, finding herself tied down on the top of the kitchen island. She was tied in a similar way as Miriam had been before, but this time on her back, with Fahey looming over her.

He had taken off his stab vest and removed all his clothes. He was completely naked. Victoria noticed, in addition to the tattoos that covered almost all of his torso, how well muscled he was. The tattoos were mainly of religious symbols — Christian crosses, images of Christ, Jewish Stars of David, and the Muslim star and crescent moon. There were biblical quotes, some written in English and some in Hebrew. He turned his back on her and stretched out his arms in an exaggerated showing off. She looked at the images on his back and upper arms. Spreading out his fingers like the limbs of a tree, he slowly turned back to face her.

Chapter 29

'Now then, my dear Victoria, now the fun will start.' He spoke in a higher than normal voice accompanied by a slight ripple of laughter. As he moved down to Victoria's side, she could see he was holing a thin-bladed knife. A scalpel.

He began to remove the buttons of her blouse, one by one, using the small blade to cut through the material of the garment, slowly opening it as he went. Once the blouse was open to her waist, he pushed the sides wider apart to reveal her bra.

'I will never understand why you dykes bother with all the alluring underwear. I could see the point if it was done for a man, but for another woman? Beats me.' He grinned again.

As he walked slowly around her, Victoria could see the images on his body extending down his back and onto his buttocks. On his lower back, descending below his waist, was a scene of the crucifixion intertwined with a scene of the nativity, the infant Jesus nailed to a small cross. He looked down at her and stroked her breasts, letting his hands move gently across her stomach and between her legs. He then leant forward and caressed her stomach with his lips.

Looking up, he asked in a concerned yet matter of fact way, 'Have you chosen a name for the little one yet, my dear?'

Victoria didn't answer, but she did noticed he was becoming aroused. She looked the other way. Her breathing was heavy, heart pumping like a steam hammer. She tried to keep him in her line of sight, but he would sometimes move just a little too far to one side. Although her hands were bound and tied to the handles of the drawers, her feet were a little more loosely attached to the island itself. She had some movement in her legs. But as she gave a slight tug on the ropes she realised they were tied securely. There was little or no chance of escape.

He stopped his pacing and moved to the end of the island. When he stopped, Fahey climbed onto it and sat astride Victoria. Even with his weight bearing down on her, she could still squirm and shift herself a little under him, but had no chance of getting out, and no possibility of retaliation.

Is this how it will end? she thought. She and Miriam butchered by this bastard in the house where they'd hoped and dreamed of bringing up their child together?

She felt the need to cry, but managed not to, and racked her mind for a way of escape, however pointless. Although she was gripped by an all-encompassing fear, there was still part of her in fight mode. She began to twist and squirm again under his bulk. All this resulted in was more grinning and laughter.

Fahey looked her directly in the eyes. 'You thought you had put me away for good, didn't you? You thought you and your dyke girlfriend over there were set up for life. Well, I have some news for you, deary. That life is about to come to an end. Yours, your wife's, and of course, the life of the little one jumping around inside you. It's all about to end for the three of you. But which one of you will be first? Now let's see.'

He jumped off the worktop and knelt down beside Miriam, grabbing her by the hair.

'I think we'll start with little old wifey here.'

He gave her a slap across the face to make sure she was awake. Once he was sure she was, he re-tied her hands around her back and then tied her ankles together with more cable ties. Walking across the room, he reached into a holdall bag he had brought with him. Fahey took out a piece of thick rope roughly three meters long. Running the rope under Miriam's arms from behind, he tied a slip knot and pulled it tight. He then took a loop of rope and passed it around her neck, carefully leaving it loose enough for some movement, but not enough so she could shake free. Next, he ran the rope over the top of the kitchen door. From the other side, he hauled Miriam up so that she was suspended by her shoulders, with her feet just off the floor, but not so far that she couldn't support herself by standing on her tiptoes.

There was no possibility of escape. Any movement only resulted in a tightening of the rope around her neck. If she tired of holding herself up on her toes, which she would eventually, she would asphyxiate herself. Miriam sobbed and called out for Victoria. The pain in her armpits as the rope was pulled tighter was excruciating.

'I'm so sorry, Vic... I'm so sorry. I love you, sweetheart. Please remember that.'

'Aw. How touching? All a bit late though now, girls.'

Once the rope was secured to the door handle on the other side of the door, visible from the hall side, and Miriam was securely suspended, he came back into the kitchen and picked up the scalpel. Kneeling down in front of Miriam, he made an incision in Miriam's left calf of about three inches long. She cried out in pain. He then repeated this on her right leg. Blood began to steadily flow out onto the tiles of the kitchen floor.

Waggling the scalpel in her face, he spoke to Miriam in a mocking tone.

'Now then, Miriam, my dear, you will probably last a few hours, but the steady blood loss will eventually get the better of you. As I'm sure you know, as your body senses the loss, your brain will *increase* your blood pressure to pump an ever *decreasing* amount of it around your body. Although your heart will beat faster to push the lost blood to your vital organs, eventually your brain will be starved of its life-giving oxygen. In due course, you will die. We both know that the brain will try all it can to sustain life. But we also both know that all its efforts will eventually be in vain. There is some consolation, however. You will be alive long enough to watch me cutting your beloved Victoria here into small pieces.'

And he laughed out loud. He climbed on top of Victoria once more and pressed his naked body onto hers. She could feel that he now had a full erection. She thought she was about to be raped.

He looked her in the eye and recognised the fear he had seen many times before in other women's faces at this moment.

'Oh! Don't fuss now, deary. I'm not going to fuck you. Well, not yet anyway.'

Chapter 30

VARSA HAD DECIDED TO SIT out her wait at York Station on a bench on platform nine. It was colder than the waiting room, but she didn't have to put up with the Christmas Eve celebration on display from at least three office parties, whose alcohol-fuelled revelries were too much for her. Especially in the mood she was in.

As she sat there, the station Tannoy made a disembodied announcement.

'Unfortunately, the twenty-one thirty-eight train to Bradford calling at Leeds has been delayed due to unforeseen circumstance and will now not arrive until twenty-two forty-five.'

Oh, for heaven's sake, that's all I need.

Standing up, she decided to have a walk up to the bridge that straddled the main line out of York. She thought about how much she missed Harry. How much she was not looking forward to her mother's ramblings. And how much she was going to not enjoy her Christmas.

Chapter 30

Once under the bridge, she turned and made her way back to her empty bench. Varsa looked down at the stone paving under her feet and wished so much she was somewhere else. She looked across at the party underway in the waiting room, and then back down at her feet. They were playing Christmas music.

Her eyes filled. She thought how bloody worthless the world was and put her head in her hands, not noticing the man who had just sat down beside her. When he spoke, she almost jumped out of her skin.

'Sorry. I didn't mean to startle you. You just look like you're carrying the world on those shoulders. It's Christmas, you know. You're allowed to be miserable at Christmas, I understand, but only a bit and certainly not that miserable. I have it on good authority. You can be fed up, but not fed up enough to cry over it.' And he smiled, a massive set of white teeth sparkling through a huge, thick, black, curly beard. She couldn't help but smile back. 'See, that's better. Are you off home for the holiday? Student, are you?'

She looked him up and down and noticed the three stripes on the front of his hi-vis jacket. 'No, I'm a police officer, just like you. Detective Constable Varsa Malik from the North Yorkshire MIT. At your service, Sergeant.'

It was his turn to look surprised. Varsa took her ID from her handbag, showed it to the sergeant, and they both laughed together.

'Well, sorry. I hadn't realised you were on the job,' he said, looking at Varsa's ID before going on to introduce himself. 'Sergeant Ashif Mohamed, at your service, ma'am. British Transport Police.'

Varsa nodded her reply. 'No worries, Sarge. I see you've drawn the short straw and copped for the Christmas Eve shift.'

'Correct. However, being a Muslim and not celebrating, I'm not missing much. The wife and I do buy the kids presents and we have a big dinner and all the trimmings, but the whole church thing . . . Well, it's not for us. Where are you off to this Christmas Eve, Detective?'

'Call me Varsa, Sarge. I'm off home for Christmas. We're Sikhs, and although we don't celebrate anything to do with Christ and the nativity, we certainly know how to party. Mum and Dad make a big thing of Christmas dinner. All the family come round and the ritual goes on most of the day.'

'So, why so glum? Why the long face if you're going home to see your folks?'

'Well, that's just it. I don't really want to go home for Christmas. I'd much prefer to spend it with my friends who I work with.'

'Well, why don't you? It's a free country. Well, I think it is, sort of, up to a limit, of course. But as far as I understand it, you're still allowed to spend Christmas with whoever you like. So long as they'll have you with that miserable look on your face, that is.'

Varsa smiled at Ashif, and then looked across at the revellers in the waiting room who were busy getting a conga line organised.

'So, who are these friends then?'

'I've been staying with my boss and her partner for a few weeks now, ever since my boyfriend . . . ' She stopped.

Ashif recognised that something had happened to the relationship. 'Go on,' he encouraged.

'Well, he was killed while on duty. We were not so serious but it was getting that way, and my boss, the chief inspector has been letting me stay at her place since it happened. But I decided to let them have their Christmas alone without me playing gooseberry. Oh, they offered for me to stay and I wanted to, but I decided to go home.'

'And now you feel you've made the wrong choice?'

'Yes. Completely.'

'Well, where do your boss and her partner live? Here in York?'

'No, they live out in a village called Sheriff Hutton. It's about ten miles north out of town.'

'Why don't you go back and tell them you've changed your mind? You can telephone your parents and let them know. You could tell them the trains have been cancelled and you can't make it. Perhaps you could go see them all in a few days?'

Varsa shook her head slowly, but her mind was telling her that what Sergeant Ashif Mohamed was saying made absolute sense.

'You can get a taxi outside if they're still running. Remember it's double fare on Christmas Eve.'

Varsa stood up, just as the conga line was exiting the waiting room and snaking its way out onto the platform. Ashif also stood up from the bench.

She looked up at him and gave him a peck on the cheek. 'Thank you, Sarge. You've made up my mind. I'm going to spend Christmas Eve with my friends.'

Sergeant Mohamed looked at the conga line and ushered Varsa out of their way. He walked with her to the taxi rank and said his goodbyes. Outside the station concourse, Varsa could feel the frost and see it on her breath. She spoke to the driver of the first cab in line. The snow had stopped falling but had settled on the roads, and the light traffic was giving it a chance to settle. There was a little negotiating with the driver as he didn't really want to drive ten miles out with little chance of a return fare. But when Varsa told him she would give him an extra twenty pounds, he quickly put her case into the boot and set off for Sheriff Hutton.

Chapter 31

FAHEY EVENTUALLY SLID HIS NAKED body off her, releasing her like a boa constrictor leaving its prey. Once standing, he scanned the room once more. Victoria turned her head to one side, not wanting to look at him pacing their kitchen. She glanced over at Miriam and could only watch in quiet horror as her partner's blood ran down her legs and spread in an ever-increasing pool on the floor. But now it was Victoria's turn to suffer.

Fahey picked up the bloody scalpel. He was about to come over to her when he spotted the CD player sitting on a shelf with a rack of CDs on a slightly higher shelf just above it.

'Anything Christmassy, Victoria, my love?'

He ran his bloody finger along the row of CDs and settled on something that read *Christmas Cracker Compilation*. He flicked open the tray and placed the first CD into the machine, which duly obliged by sucking it into its mechanism. Fahey waited a moment and Mariah Carey's "All I want for Christmas" came on.

Chapter 31

'Wow! Don't you just love this track, Victoria? Don't you just love it . . . *Not?* But it certainly gets us into the festive spirit, no mistake. Makes you want to get up and dance, hey? Oh, sorry, you can't, can you? Being tied up and all.' He laughed loudly.

Victoria thought that he was becoming more insane by the minute, if that were possible. She contemplated her and Miriam's fate and how everything they had built up together was about to end. She could do nothing to stop it. For a moment, she let her defences drop and began to cry softly.

Fahey shouted across to Miriam, who was barely able to take in what was going on.

'Hey, Miriam! You need to watch what I am about to do to your dyke wife here. You, being a doctor, can give me a critique when I've finished. Assuming you're still in the land of the living, that is.'

He took one of the small kitchen knives and tested its sharpness by running it across Victoria's abdomen.

'Not sharp enough,' he muttered. So, he picked up his scalpel. Fahey tested it on Victoria's arm with a cut of around an inch or so. 'Ah! Much better. The right tool for the right job,' he said to himself.

His first cut into her abdomen was made about two millimetres deep and about ten centimetres below her navel. It stretched across from one hip to the other, but even at this superficial depth, the blood flowed freely, pooling under her waist, and eventually running over the kitchen work surface and onto the floor. He made the incision neatly and carefully and stepped back to let it open fully. Victoria winced under this new pain, and Miriam's look of complete horror caused Fahey to stop for a moment.

'Yes, my dear Miriam. You've guessed it. I'm going to perform my first ever caesarean on good old Victoria here. I know I'm a rank amateur, but hey-ho! We can give it a go.' And he laughed out loud at his rhyming. 'Now, you need to watch carefully while you still have time and you're still able. If you like, you can give me pointers as to how I'm doing.'

'No, you bastard. *NO!*' Miriam was sobbing deeply.

Victoria said nothing. She squeezed her eyes tightly shut and held her breath. What was the point? *He will do what he does.* Her only defence was defiance, however pointless. She opened her eyes and looked at him. Through a clenched jaw and teeth, she spat out her words. 'Go on, you bastard. Get it over with. If you think I'm going to plead with you, forget it. You are a fool if you imagine I am intimidated by you. Just fucking do it.'

'Ah . . . Belligerence. The last vestige of those full of fear, who know they are beaten.'

Victoria's vitriol served to hide her fears to herself. But she knew all was lost. This was where her life would end. Both she and her unborn child of only two months would die here at the hands of this monster.

Fahey looked down at her, now angered by her defiance. He was about to make a deeper cut when he stopped and looked across at Miriam.

'Oh, I am aware, my dear, that we may not be able, at her stage of confinement, to find much of a little person in here, but hey! Whatever we find, we can remove. What do you say?'

He pushed the scalpel deeper this time, into the left side of Victoria's stomach, following the line of his initial cut just below the navel, then pulling it across to the other side, finishing almost at her hip bone. She gritted her teeth and bit down hard. She was determined not to scream or shout out. Fahey had to stand clear of her stomach contents as they emptied themselves onto the floor. The blood loss was immense. He found himself standing in the thick, sticky darkness that covered his bare feet and stained his lower legs. At least, Miriam thought, it would not be long before Victoria lost consciousness and not be able to feel the pain.

A further cut was made in Victoria's uterus and he leant forward over her body, using his fingers to search for the embryo of the child. All the while, he sang along to "All I Want For Christmas." So engrossed in what he was doing, Fahey didn't even notice the diminutive Asian woman standing behind him holding a large kitchen knife.

***

As Varsa arrived back outside Victoria and Miriam's house, the snow was crisp underfoot and a heavy frost was settling in. She paid the taxi driver and thanked him for taking her in this weather. He wished her a, 'Merry Christmas,' and was gone before she could get through the gate. As she approached the front door, she could hear music coming from inside. Mariah Carey was telling us all she wanted for Christmas was you, and Varsa thought it unusual for the women to be playing the song so loud. It was not like Miriam or Victoria, who preferred peaceful atmospheres.

She wondered if they were having some sort of party. And she hadn't been invited?

At the front door, she noticed it was slightly ajar. Carefully, she pushed it open a little wider. Varsa stepped inside the hall and, immediately, the hairs on the back of her neck stood up. There was blood smeared on the walls and door leading into the kitchen. A plant had been knocked over and the remnants of it were halfway along the hall carpet. Things were not right.

A thousand thoughts raced through her head. There was a light on in the kitchen. As she moved slowly towards the door, the music grew louder. She noticed a rope tied to the kitchen door handle. There was a dark stain creeping under the frame and blackening the carpet. Lights were flashing in her mind. She could feel her anxiety levels rising, the adrenaline pumping. There was danger behind this door.

She had no idea what it was, but she knew she would have to face it, and quickly.

Instead of swinging the door open, she stood to one side, enabling her to peer through the gap. The kitchen door faced the end of the kitchen island. Nothing could have prepared her for what she was about to confront. Hanging on the back of the door was the body of Miriam tied with a rope that went under her arms around her neck, over the door, finishing on the handle on the hall side. Her body weight was hanging on her armpits. As she became slowly exhausted, the pressure on her neck would increase. Varsa could see Miriam's lips already turning blue.

At Miriam's feet, a large pool of blood spread out across the tiles, eventually reaching the heels of a completely naked man who stood leaning over the island worktop. Tied to the worktop, Varsa could see the body of a woman lying motionless with her legs spread apart The whole surface was covered in blood that ran over the edges and dripped onto the floor, soaking the man; he was totally engrossed in what he was doing. This woman, she assumed, was Victoria. Varsa hoped in hell that she was not too late.

She did a silent retch at the sight and smell and put her hand across her mouth in an attempt to keep what little food she had inside her remaining that way. She realised she would need to summon up all her resolve, and more, if she was going to save her friends and colleagues. The man was singing along with the music, totally oblivious to her presence and close proximity to him. He was pressing down on Victoria's lower abdomen. Varsa didn't want to contemplate what he might be doing.

She scanned the room quickly and noticed, just to her right, a large carving knife lying on the counter. Silently, she slid her hand across the surface and grasped the handle of the knife. Its blade was at least ten inches long and, at its widest, around three inches. She let it sit in the palm of her hand for a moment, grateful for its weight and length. A weapon she could use to full effect. She gripped the handle and it bolstered her confidence for what was about to come next.

The music suddenly stopped. The man stood upright. She tensed and gripped the handle of the knife so tight her knuckles turned white. The next song came on and the man bent back down, now singing along to Wham's "Last Christmas."

This was Varsa's moment. She would only get one chance. If she called out to him to stop, it would give him a chance of sorts, and the element of surprise would be lost. Then she would have to tackle him face to face. Something she was not ready for. He would stand head and shoulders above her and she could see the muscles in his back and upper arms rippling and tensing as he worked on Victoria. There was only one course of action.

She raised up her hand holding the knife as high as she could and closed the distance between the man's back and herself in two steps. He was still singing along with George and Andrew as she plunged the blade into his back. She was aiming for the top of the crucifix in the middle of his shoulder blades. Although he was totally unaware of *her*, he certainly became violently aware of the knife. It was driven home with such force that it came out through his lungs, the tip showing through his chest, only just missing his heart in the process. Fahey immediately jerked bolt upright and screamed out in pain, coughing dark, red blood from his lungs across the room.

Varsa gripped the handle of the knife again. With both hands, and before he could turn around, she had pulled it out and plunged it in for a second time. This time, both she and Fahey felt it passing through his ribs, separating them, and eventually settling in his heart. He coughed again, more blood directly into Victoria's face, as he slumped down on top of her. This time, Varsa left the knife in and waited for a moment before she heaved his body off Victoria, letting it fall to the floor.

Now the full extent of Victoria's injuries became apparent. Varsa was frozen to the spot. She realised the lives of her two friends hung in the balance. Only she could tip it in their favour.

The expanse of Victoria's abdomen was laid open and Varsa could make out tears to the muscles and intestines. Her first aid training kicked in almost at once, and remembering where all the towels were kept, she was about to run and fetch some. But quickly looking around the room, she noticed the laundry basket. It contained an assortment of bath towels that would help to stem the flow of blood and give some vital minutes before help arrived. She took the top one, folded it, and pressed it down across Victoria's exposed mid-section. *This is, on its own, not going to stop the bleeding, but might just slow it down a little.*

In less than two seconds, the towel was completely soaked red. Varsa placed further towels on top, holding them down with one hand. She then cut the wrist and ankle ties away and told Victoria to hold the towel on her stomach while she called 999.

Victoria was losing consciousness rapidly, but still managed to hold onto the towels. They were now little more of a thick, bright red mash of cotton, mixed with her stomach and intestines. It seemed like an age before the woman on the end of the 999 service answered.

'Emergency. Which service do you require?'

'Ambulance and police.'

'Can I take you name, address, and nature of the emergency please?'

'Oh! For god's sake … Detective Varsa Malik from the North Yorkshire Major Incident Team. Two officers have been assaulted and have suffered major trauma injuries. Plus one individual at the scene who is already dead. You need to get here fast, and I mean in the next few minutes. The officers are both having difficulty breathing and lapsing in and out of consciousness.'

The phone was quiet for a couple of seconds while the operator took in the information.

'Yes, Varsa. Please stay on the phone and let us know what is happening with the casualties. We will task the ambulances now and keep you updated on their progress. You mentioned a third individual who you say is now deceased. Can I ask how you can be sure about this? And are you in a position to perform CPR?'

'I know he's dead because I've just pushed a knife into his back and killed him. And no, I have no intention of performing CPR or anything else on the bastard. Don't forget the police.'

Chapter 32

THE DOORS OF THE A&E department at the district hospital crashed open, and the first of the ambulance emergency stretchers carrying the results of Jonathan Fahey's handywork from the scene at Sheriff Hutton came bursting through. On the first one lay the body of Chief Inspector Victoria Adams. She had monitors attached to the length of her body, saline drips in both arms, and an orderly riding on the frame of the trolly performing CPR and shouting out the timing of the chest pumps—*one, two three, four, five*—as she pressed down hard on Victoria's sternum.

The trolly made its way at speed towards one of the waiting trauma rooms. Two doctors, one either side of it scooted along like a pair of crabs doing a sideways shuffle, barking orders to the other members of staff as they went. The older of the two shouted at one of the staff nurses to prep theatres one and two. 'There's another one on its way. This one's for theatre one and the other lady into two please,' he shouted.

The staff nurse disappeared, shouting further orders as she went.

Bringing up the rear was the young paramedic who first attended on scene. He was reciting a list of information on the patient's condition and what treatment he had already administered to the now completely unconscious and non-breathing Victoria.

As the trolley passed, distraught Detectives Mal Chambers and Pete Sinclair stood aside to let it get by. As it moved on past the pair, they returned to a side-by-side position blocking the corridor. The look of anguish and helplessness on their faces told it all. Mal stood clenching and unclenching his fists and rubbing his palms together, while Pete Sinclair couldn't stop wiping his dry mouth with the back of his hand. They looked at each other, then back to where the trolly with their boss on it had just disappeared through another set of doors, leaving them in a silent limbo.

The silence was broken by the second casualty to arrive, Miriam DeSilva.

Mal and Pete stepped aside again, just in time to let the medics pass. Miriam was attired in similar fashion to her partner, minus the orderly attending to CPR, as she was breathing under her own steam. Her journey towards the same doors her wife had just passed through left a trail of blood and swabs down the corridor, leaving Mal and Pete once again anxiously wringing their hands and searching for something to say. A nurse approached and ushered them down to a waiting area, explaining that the trauma teams would be doing everything they could to save their colleagues. They were not to worry; the two women were in the best hands possible. Of course, this did little to allay their fears.

They sat, then they stood, then they sat again. From time to time, they looked through the glass window of the waiting area, down towards the trauma rooms. Just waiting for news. Although they usually had too much to say, now didn't seem the time to say anything.

They paced up and down for what seemed like ages, drank copious amounts of coffee, and every now and again stood outside the small room, which was becoming somewhat claustrophobic. They had no idea how long they had been waiting when the door opened. ACC Julie Thornton entered. She took Mal chambers by the arm and ushered him to sit down.

'What the fuck happened, ma'am? How did it all end up like this?'

'It looks like Miriam opened the door to Fahey by accident. When Victoria came back from dropping Varsa off at the station, he attacked her. The doctors are saying the pair have lost a lot of blood, but hopefully they're going to make it. He made an attempt at performing some kind of caesarean operation on Victoria. We think he may have aborted the foetus.'

Pete put his head in his hands.

Chapter 32

'We heard on the grapevine that Varsa saved the day?' said Mal, his hand on Pete's shoulder. 'Any idea of where she is, ma'am?'

'She's under arrest. She's been handed over to internal investigations for the time being.'

The shock and surprise on the faces of the two detectives clearly showed.

'*What?* She's been arrested. What the fuck for?' Pete was clearly angry. Mal tried to placate by putting his arm around his shoulder and ushering him to a seat.

'She's been arrested because she plunged a carving knife into Fahey's back.' Thornton paused. 'More than once, so it seems. So there needs to be an investigation into the circumstances of his death. You pair should be aware of the procedure when an officer kills a suspect.'

Pete went to leave the room, then turned back to face the ACC. 'He's a bit more than a fucking suspect . . . ma'am. The bloke's a murdering fucking psychopath. If Varsa did this then she did the world a favour.' He then stormed out of the waiting area and slammed the door, almost breaking its glass panel.

'Sorry about that, ma'am,' Mal said, trying to sooth the situation. 'He really liked, I mean likes, the boss. If she doesn't pull through, he'll be devastated.' He paused for a second. 'And so will the rest of us.'

'Look she's a real fighter. She and Miriam will not give up easily. They have every chance of pulling through.' She gave a thin smile in Mal's direction in a vain attempt to instigate some hope, but knew full well it would fall far short of the mark. She began to leave the small room and turned back. 'Look, there's nothing to be done here. The pair will be in theatre for some time and we will know how they are doing before too long. Perhaps you and Pete need to go home to your families. I'll stay on here and contact you, if and when there are any developments.'

Mal nodded and went to find is partner. Before getting very far, he turned back to the ACC. 'I've just had a thought, ma'am. Has anyone told Victoria's mum and dad? Or any of Miriam's relatives? They should really be informed.'

'I've done all that. Miriam's mother is on her way from Leeds, and Victoria's mother and father are driving up from Birmingham.'

'Oh, okay fine, ma'am.' He paused for a moment. 'Any problems if I give Sean O'Neill a call and let him know what's happened? He would want to know, like. Him and Aggie and the boss, they're best mates.'

'No, you do that, Mal. I'm sure he will want to come down.'

Mal made the call to Sean and left to spend the rest of Christmas Eve with his family, as did Pete Sinclair. Both agreed it would be a strange Christmas, and before going home, they decided to go back to the station to check on how Varsa was fairing up.

Chapter 32

Varsa had been questioned by the IOPC officers for hours after volunteering herself. She had her police representative with her the whole time. She had been advised to say very little but wavered any rights she might have to say nothing. Instead, she explained what had happened. She was asked why she didn't call for back-up before tackling Jonathan Fahey. Her answer was clear and to the point.

'Wait for back-up? If I had done that, Victoria's doctors would be now trying to piece together her various body parts, not just putting her stomach back in the right way round.'

***

Miriam's mother had arrived shortly after midnight at the hospital in York. She had travelled over from Leeds with Miriam's friend, Jane McCormack, and both women looked pale and somewhat disoriented. Jane was doing her best to console Mrs DeSilva and point out that, medically speaking, her daughter had every chance of making a full recovery. Of course, Miriam's mother was doing her level best to go along with this, but it wasn't working out, and she remained anxious and apprehensive in the extreme.

Sean and Aggie arrived shortly after getting the call from Mal Chambers. They were greeted by the ACC, who explained what had happened and updated them on any progress made by the two women. It was not until around four in the morning when Victoria's parents arrived. They looked worn out from their non-stop drive from Walsall in the West Midlands, and, like Miriam's mother, whom they sat with, they were anxious and apprehensive about the condition of their daughter and her partner.

All were formally greeted by Julie Thornton, who had arranged accommodation for them at a nearby hotel, the cost of which would be met by her department. After all the introductions had been made, one of the nurses came across to the group and told them that the consultant in charge would be over to speak with them shortly. Victoria's parents were led away to a private family room and true to the nurse's word, the consultant arrived. He sat opposite them both in the family room with the young nurse standing behind him. Wearing a clean set of scrubs and a flowery-printed head scarf, he looked in his late fifties and was carrying a clip board in his right hand.

'Hello. It's Mr and Mrs Adams, is that right?'

Mrs Adams nodded and looked up at her husband. She looked back at the consultant before speaking. 'Yes. But you can call us Frank and Margaret, if you like.'

'Sure. My name is Dr Rafferty, Michael Rafferty, and I am in charge of your daughter's care. Well, we have some good news for you. I can tell you that all the surgical procedures carried out early this morning and late yesterday evening have gone much better than expected. Victoria looks like she will eventually be able to make a full recovery.'

Mr and Mrs Adam's gripped each other's hands in relief.

'However,' continued Dr Rafferty, 'the not so good news is that, unfortunately, we were not able to save her pregnancy. The foetus had aborted before we were able to treat her. The miscarriage was almost certainly a result of the trauma she suffered before her arrival at A&E.' He let that sink in for a moment, before adding, 'We are truly sorry about that.'

Mrs Adams began to sob gently while her husband put his arm around her shoulders and fought back his own tears. The doctor let the sobs die down before carrying on.

'Although she is back from theatre, she is still sedated. She's in our intensive care ward. I will arrange for Nurse Jacobs here to take you up to see her. Victoria is young fit and very strong, which all bodes well for a quick recovery from the surgery. Although her injuries were extensive, there was no real damage to major internal organs. If you would you like to ask any questions, please do.'

Both Mr and Mrs Adams shook their heads and Dr Rafferty stood up, offering his handshake. Both parents shook his hand in turn, then followed him out into the corridor. The young nurse took Margaret by the arm and led her over to the lifts, as her husband was thanking Dr Rafferty again. Once Victoria's parents were in the lift and on their way up to visit their daughter, the doctor walked back across the waiting area to the other family room containing Mrs DeSilva and Jane McCormack, and Victoria's friends, Sean, Aggie, and ACC Thornton.

He went through the usual introductions then asked if he could please speak with Mrs DeSilva alone.

'It's okay to call me Jacinda,' she replied. 'And it's okay to speak with my friends here. They are all close friends of Miriam and I will only need to pass on the information after you have said whatever. And I most likely will get it wrong. So please, how is she? Can we go and see her?'

Just then, another young nurse entered the room and closed the door carefully, steadying it with the palm of her hand so it didn't bang shut and make a noise. Mrs DeSilva looked up at the nurse, whose face was solemn and deadpan. Mrs DeSilva then turned her attention to Dr Rafferty whose face was also sombre and serious. She put her hand to her mouth and jerked her head from side to side in a frenzied shake, in the hope that what she was thinking would somehow go from her mind. She looked at Sean and Aggie, then back to the doctor.

'What?' she said. 'What? What are you saying?'

Of course, he hadn't said a word, but everyone in the room knew what was coming. It could only be one thing.

'I'm afraid I have some terrible, terrible news for you, Mrs DeSilva.' He took a deep breath before continuing, followed by a swallow. 'Unfortunately, Miriam died in theatre this morning, during an operation to remove a blood clot on her brain. The clot was caused by a blow to her head sustained during the attack. We are truly, truly sorry, Mrs DeSilva.' He let the news sink in for a moment. 'The clot was extremely large. I'm afraid there was nothing we could do. Attempts to revive her were ineffective and she died peacefully at three this morning.' Again, he paused before adding, 'If you would like to go and see Miriam, the nurse here will show you where. It is also fine for you to take your friends along with you. If you wish.'

The room was completely silent.

No one knew what to say. Only Aggie was able to move, and she moved over to Miriam's mum and sat down beside her. She put her arm around her shoulder. Jacinda DeSilva sat looking into the distance, a blank stare that simply said *disbelief*.

Eventually, Jacinda, along with Sean and Aggie and Jane McCormack, made their way to the chapel to visit Miriam. They all stood outside while Miriam's mum could have some time with her daughter, then took their turns going in to say their last farewells. Aggie and Sean agreed that, perhaps, it was not a good idea for Jacinda to be alone in a hotel room. They offered for her to stay with them, if she wanted. Jacinda accepted.

Back upstairs in the family room, Mr and Mrs Adams had returned. They received the news about Miriam from ACC Thornton. It hit like a shockwave. Neither of them had words. Neither could bring themselves to find the right things to say.

Eventually, Mrs Adams gave a slight cough before speaking. 'Who's going to tell Victoria about Miriam?' She asked in an almost matter of fact way.

The ACC did her best to answer. 'I am sure that would be best coming from someone close, but I wouldn't envy the person responsible. Not one bit. I wouldn't relish the prospect at all.'

'Do you have children, Mrs Thornton?' asked Victoria's mum.

'Never actually managed to get round to it, and it's a bit late now.'

'It's amazing that no matter how old your kids grow to be, they are still your kids. The worry is no different from when they were babies.'

'No,' said ACC Thornton, 'I can see that.'

***

Back downstairs in the chapel, Sean sat next to Jacinda and Aggie sat holding his hand.

'We are so sorry, Jacinda. Miriam was such a bright light,' he said, 'She would light up the room with her smile and infectious sense of humour. We all loved her so much.'

Jacinda glanced down at the pair's hands with their interlocking fingers, and she wished she too could have someone to hold onto at a time like this. She reached out and took his other hand in hers, and squeezed it, placing her head on his shoulder and letting the tears flow.

Chapter 32

Who is going to tell poor Victoria? First the baby, and now this.

Eventually, the ACC agreed to drive Mr and Mrs Adams back to their hotel. She stayed to have coffee with them while they ate some breakfast. The hotel was surprisingly busy for Christmas Day. Most of the rooms were booked, and the staff were preparing for Christmas lunch, which was fully booked up. Over coffee, the ACC reminded the pair that they were not to pay for anything — to simply charge it to her account.

'We haven't met you before, have we, Julie?' Mrs Adams asked.

'No, that's correct.'

'So, how is our Victoria doing at work? We don't hear much, well, she never tells us anything. Oh, we knew about that business when she caught that nutcase a while back, the one who was going around killing women. But she never gives us any details.'

'Not sure we want details about that kind of thing,' her husband added.

The ACC took a sip of coffee and put down her cup on its saucer. 'Victoria is highly thought of Mrs Adams. Both by her superiors and her team. The man she apprehended in the case you are referring to is the same man who is responsible for the attacks on Victoria and Miriam. He had escaped from prison and was out for revenge. Like most, if not all, psychopaths, he thought himself somewhat invulnerable and somehow in the right to exact his revenge on those who had been instrumental in putting him behind bars.'

'And have they got him? Or is he still at large? And if he was in prison, how did he — '

The ACC held up her hands in a gesture of surrender. 'It's a long story, Margaret. Suffice to say, he escaped, and set out to get his revenge on Victoria. Sadly, Miriam was probably in the wrong place at the wrong time. The man responsible is now dead. Killed by one of our officers. It appears that if Varsa hadn't come back when she did, he might have killed both women and made his escape once more. However, at this time, I can't go into any of the details of that. Victoria also recently rescued a young fourteen-year-old-boy who had been kidnapped. I can't really say any more about that also. But she is certainly a real asset to us all.'

Mr and Mrs Adams sat back proudly as their breakfasts arrived. The waiter asked the ACC if she would like anything to eat and she ordered a tea cake to have with her second cup of coffee. When the tea cake arrived, Mrs Adams put her knife and fork down on the plate and looked across at Julie Thornton.

'How much do you know about our Victoria, Julie?'

'Well, I know she's a good cop. Intuitive, persistent, and above all, courageous. But I know little about her personal life. Other than being married to Miriam, of course. I mean, I know what's in her file, but there is little of personal background in there.' She took a bite from her tea cake before continuing. 'Why do you ask?'

'Well… I don't suppose Victoria ever told you she was adopted, did she?'

'No. Never,' the ACC said. 'It's not something we ever discussed.' She was slightly taken aback, but also a little intrigued, and wondered why Mrs Adams was mentioning this. 'There would have been no reason for her to give me such personal information. And anyway, these days, it isn't such a monumental issue. Many people are adopted. Did she know she was adopted, Margaret?'

'Oh yes, of course. We told her when she was a young girl. About five or six, and we reminded her as often as we thought best as she grew older. She never asked to find her birth mother or father, and although we knew who the mother was, Victoria never did. We kept in contact with her over the years and we are able to contact her now. But we're not sure if we should without asking Victoria first. I was just thinking, what with the news about poor Miriam, that if anything were to happen to Victoria, heaven forbid, her birth mother should know. She should have the opportunity to come and visit.'

Mr Adams looked at his wife. 'Oh really, love, there's no need to be so pessimistic. The surgeon said everything is going to be okay now.'

'Yes, but what about the loss of the baby? She should be told about that, surely? And her birth mum doesn't even know Victoria got married, let alone now lost her wife.'

The ACC looked across at the parents.

'Mr and Mrs Adams, it may be better to allow Victoria to fully recover before broaching the subject of her birth mother again. And, as the surgeon said, she is likely to make a full physical recovery before too long. Perhaps she should make the decision about whether or not to tell her birth mother about the baby. It will be a tremendous blow to Victoria when she learns, not only about the loss of the baby, but also the loss of Miriam. That will be a lot to deal with.'

'Yes, I suppose you are right in all that,' Margaret said. 'We just thought, as Victoria is so poorly, we should tell her birth mum.' She paused. 'There is, also, one more thing.'

Mr Adams raised his palm to his wife in a gesture to stop her talking.

'Please forgive my wife, Ms Thornton. She is a little tired, what with the travelling and all this happening to our daughter.' He looked across at his wife. 'I don't think the assistant chief constable wants to hear about the comings and goings of the Adam's family. I'm sure she's not in the least bit interested.' And he turned and smiled at Julie in the hope of agreement.

Julie Thornton said it was okay and put Mrs Adams's rambling down to the need to say something, or anything, when you realise you have little control over what is happening around you.

'It's okay, Margaret, Go on, if you want to. I don't mind,' Julie said, taking a further sip of her coffee.

'Well, when Victoria was born . . . ' Mrs Adams looked to her husband. 'She had a twin.'

Julie Thornton looked up again. 'A twin, you say?'

'Yes, a twin sister who was also adopted. I know, even back then, it was unusual not to keep twins together. But the authorities allowed it on this occasion. The problem is that we have no record of where she went or who adopted her. We never told Victoria about her twin sister but just wondered if we should try and trace her at this time? We just wanted to make sure she could see her sister. Before anything happened, if you know what I mean?'

'Look, love, nothing is going to happen to Vicky now. She is going to pull through this. Isn't she, Julie?'

There was a pause before Julie spoke again. 'Yes, I'm sure she is, and again, I would think this should be Victoria's decision, Margaret. I am sure she might want to do this at some stage. But I don't think it would be a very good idea to pre-empt that decision. Do you?'

Mr Adams took hold of his wife's hand and shuffled his chair closer to hers. 'You see, love? No need to worry the poor lass at the moment. She's going to get better and we can — '

He was cut short by his wife. 'We thought poor Miriam was going to get better as well.'

Chapter 33

25TH DECEMBER 2019
CHRISTMAS DAY

"And she brought forth her firstborn son, and wrapped him in swaddling clothes, and laid him in a manger; because there was no room for them at the inn."
Luke 2:7

IT WAS LATE AFTERNOON WHEN Sean called the hospital to check on how Victoria was doing. He was told that she was now awake, and although still very poorly, her vital signs had all stabilised. But she was not really able to see visitors, other than close family.

Jacinda DeSilva had taken Sean and Aggie up on their offer to stay over. After taking some sleeping pills, she had eventually drowsed off into some kind of fitful sleep.

Chapter 33

Sean called the hotel where Victoria's mum and dad were staying, and he was told they had left for the hospital. He thought there was no point in going until Victoria was able to speak to visitors. That would be some time yet, he assumed. His thoughts were centred on how she would take the news about Miriam and the baby; if asked, he would not shy away from the responsibility.

At around eight o'clock in the evening, Sean's phone rang. It was Frank, who told him that Victoria had come round from the anaesthetic. She was still in intensive care and not really able to speak. He said that the hospital staff thought Victoria might be able to come out of intensive care in a couple of days. Then it would be okay for him and Aggie to visit. The staff also said that perhaps it was not yet a good time to mention Miriam or the baby. But to wait until she was a little stronger.

Three days passed and Sean rang the hospital again. This time, they were much more ebullient about Victoria's condition. He was told she was fully awake and had been moved into a private room. Now she would be up to short visits. He and Aggie headed straight over.

When they entered the room, Victoria, still attached to a drip and monitors, turned her head towards the pair and smiled.

'How's Miriam?' she asked. 'Is she well enough to visit? I don't think they will let me go anywhere for a while. They won't tell me anything. It's like . . . Well, I don't know what, but they could all get good jobs in MI5, this bloody lot. All the secrecy is . . . ' She stopped and looked from Sean to Aggie and back to Sean. 'Well, I'm beginning to fear the worst, Sean.' She looked back to Aggie. 'Can't you find out what's going on? If it's bad news, I want to hear it. Do you understand? I *want* to hear it.'

Sean gave her a smile. He realised no one had told her about Miriam, or the baby, yet. He just didn't have the words to tell her. She could see by the pain and confusion on his face, something was not right. So she asked again.

'How's Miriam?'

He took hold of her hand and squeezed it gently.

'Well, I'm not sure how to say this, my love . . . '

He stopped, and Aggie took Victoria's other hand and held it tightly. Before Sean could say any more, Dr Rafferty entered the room. He realised immediately the atmosphere was somewhat tense, to say the least. He was nothing if not direct.

'Hello, Victoria, How are you feeling?' he asked, as he picked up her notes from the end of the bed and ran a check of the monitors she was hooked up to. 'You are one strong lady, my dear. At this rate, you'll be going home in no time.' She did her best to sit upright so she could look him in the eye. She slumped back and Aggie put her arm around her to hold her. She knew what was coming and wanted to give the support she knew would be needed.

'Never mind that. How's Miriam?' She looked across at Sean and Aggie, then back to the doctor. '*So?* How is she?'

Dr Rafferty nodded at Sean and Aggie to leave, but Victoria held onto Aggie's hand. 'No. I want them to stay. They are my friends and I want them here. What's wrong?'

The doctor cleared his throat before speaking. 'Well, I have some very sad news for you, Victoria.' He paused, and Victoria looked at Sean. She knew what was coming next but hoped her instinct wasn't true.

'Is she not well? Has she taken a turn for the worse? What is it?'

The look of anguish on the doctor's face said it all.

'I'm afraid to tell you that Miriam has died of her injuries,' he eventually told her. 'She had a brain haemorrhage we could not treat, and she has passed away.'

'When? How? Why? No. No, she wasn't hurt as bad as me. She was conscious at the house and only bleeding from her legs.' Victoria didn't really want any answers and began to sob uncontrollably. 'No. No, not my Miriam. It's not fair.'

The sobs turned into convulsions, and she let out a mournful cry, lighting the blue touch paper of tears. Sean and Aggie began crying in unison. The doctor stood back and allowed Aggie to put both her arms around Victoria's shoulders. Dr Rafferty gestured to a nurse outside the room to come in. He said something to her that no one could hear or, indeed, had any interest in. The nurse left and came back quickly with a sedative for Victoria.

She knew straight away what it was and pushed the nurse away.

'I don't want any of that. All I want is my Miriam back. Sean, Aggie, this is not fair. Why has this happened? We were going to have our baby.'

She convulsed into more sobbing and eventually allowed the nurse to administer the sedative. It was fast-acting and knocked her out in a couple of minutes. The nurse made her comfortable and checked over the monitors, before retracing her steps out of the private room.

Dr Rafferty turned his attention to Sean and Aggie, who stood sniffling, looking down at the sleeping Victoria. 'It might be better if you take a break. She will be out for some time now, but it might help if a face she recognises is here when she wakes up.'

The doctor smiled at Sean. Aggie took Sean's arm, and they left the ward to have a coffee, telling the staff nurse they would come back later. They were joined by Victoria's mum and dad, and they explained that their daughter was now aware of Miriam's death, but not yet of the loss of the baby. Mrs Adams's angst was overwhelming. She had no words, not now or later. This was more than she knew how to deal with.

***

It was New Year's Eve before Victoria was in a state where she could put up with visitors again and willing to say a few words. Although her mum and dad and Sean and Aggie had visited each day, little was said. There was no mention of either Miriam or the baby. The New Year's Eve celebrations were in full swing on the ward. Victoria had never felt so lonely.

Her mother and father had spent most of the day with their daughter. As the evening wore on, they sat alongside her bed, watching the Jools's Holland Hootenanny. They drank tea and ate some Christmas cake. Victoria was in no real mood to eat it, let alone enjoy it. She managed a smile at her dad, as he managed to drop a slice of cake into his mug of tea while falling asleep.

By ten to midnight, she was able to drink some tea from a cup, so long as she had assistance. Although feeling very tired, her speech was improving, and the pain she felt in almost every organ of her body was masked by copious amounts of painkillers. These painkillers, although making her constantly drowsy, did enable her to sit up a little and take in what was going on. But the medication could do nothing to remove the pain of losing her beloved wife.

As they sat watching the cheering and whoops and shouts as the clock on the TV struck midnight, Victoria turned to her mum. 'I've lost everything, Mum. Just everything. I know the baby's gone. I can feel it. I know it's not there anymore. And Miriam . . . She would have known what to do, what to say, how to deal with this. We could get past the loss. She isn't going to be here. What am I going to do, Mum?'

And Victoria started to cry. Not long sobs or crying-out-loud sobs, just an inward cry of helplessness. One that Mum or Dad could not resolve or make even the slightest bit better. Between sobbing, Victoria gasped out little words and phrases, none of which was too coherent.

'The baby... We've lost our baby. What's the point? Not happening... Surely. Not right. Not right.'

And the tears began to flow more freely, running down her cheeks. Victoria tried to stem the flow. But the more she tried, the more she coughed and sobbed. Her mum held her hand. Dad was awake now, and put his arm around her shoulders, hugging her tight and close. He leant across and kissed away some of the tears. Although Victoria knew they loved her, and wanted to make it all go away, they would never be able to do that. She was on her own.

All the hugs and kisses in the world would never replace her wife and lover.

The three of them sat and lay in silence until well into the New Year. A year that would bring all manner of problems for everyone, not least Victoria—how she would set about overcoming her loss. But also for the rest of the population—how they would overcome the onslaught of the Covid-19 virus.

***

Victoria was going to need more surgical procedures over an extended period of time to put right the physical damage resulting from her encounter with Fahey. But it was going to prove to be a long time before she would be in a position to manage the mental scars that she would carry for many years to come. She would burst into tears on and off for months after her discharge from hospital. She began a course of counselling to help her deal with the flashbacks of the encounter with Fahey, as well as the loss of both Miriam and her unborn child.

Victoria had a reluctance to speak of the losses. Although her friends would give her space to talk about it all, she found it was only her counsellor whom she could really open up to. The woman in her fifties called Anita Montgomery, appointed by North Yorkshire Police, would also be responsible for compiling a report that would eventually set a time when Victoria could return to work. Before this, Victoria would need to attend a full course of counselling and be able to demonstrate she was mentally well enough. Physically, she was improving in leaps and bounds, and as soon as she was fully discharged from hospital, she was itching to get back to work — and its distractions.

However, her counsellor had very different ideas. Following Victoria's discharge from hospital, and during the two weekly sessions, it was apparent that Victoria was acting out the part of being psychologically well. She knew the right answers to give and thought that, by giving them, she could go back to work sooner rather than later.

From Vitoria's point of view, she saw the counselling sessions as hoops she needed to jump through. And while this attitude persisted, it was not going to happen that way. Anita Montgomery was not so easily fooled. She always found the question that would open up a chink in Victoria's armour. There was no way she would allow a police officer to get back on the job before they were ready. And all the wishful thinking on Victoria's part would do little to hasten it.

It was a good six months after her discharge that Victoria decided she would look in on the team. She decided to call into the station to say hi to everyone, merely for a catch-up. She was desperately lonely at home. Other than visits to the shops, she had not really spoken to anyone other than her counsellor, her parents, and Sean and Aggie for months. When she arrived at Fulford nick, she was disappointed to find an almost-empty MIT office.

Covid had forced everyone to try and work from home, and contact was mainly via video links and team Zoom meetings, although, at times, they would need to come together in the office. On the day Victoria came in, she found the only person actively working was the ACC, who welcomed her and invited her up to her office.

'Sit down, Victoria. I'll make us a coffee and you can tell me how things are. How are you getting on?'

'Not sure, ma'am. Not sure at all. I want to get back, but the bloody counsellor says I'm not over it. She says I need to give it more time. I know I'm okay and ready to come back. I just need to convince her.'

'Well, you look well, Victoria. You really do. But rather than doing your upmost to convince her that you're well, it might be more productive to put the emphasis on *getting* well.'

Victoria sat down in one of the comfy armchairs in her boss's office. Julie set about preparing the cafetiere and putting the kettle on to boil.

'Oh! I'm glad you popped in, by the way, Victoria. I have some things here for you.' She pointed to a large, brown cardboard box in the corner. 'Varsa had to go over to the mortuary a couple of weeks ago for an autopsy on a suspicious death, and the assistant over there had cleared out Miriam's desk and locker. He's sorry it took so long. But they weren't sure if you were going to come in and do it.'

'I had totally forgotten about it. Sorry, ma'am.'

'No need to apologise. But the assistant was not sure if there might be some personal stuff you'd want to keep.'

The ACC then walked over to the corner of the office and picked up a brown, cardboard bankers-box that was sitting on the floor. It appeared to be a little heavy, and she set it down on the desk, then gestured for Victoria to come and have a look inside it.

'Varsa was planning to drop it off for you at home, but it sort of got left here. I think she was unsure if it would be okay to call round. You know what she's like.'

Victoria stood up, took the lid off the box, and looked inside. It was full of mainly papers and notebooks, some small, framed photographs, some items of clothing, and a small parcel wrapped in white paper with little teddy bears on it.

'Thanks, ma'am,' Victoria said. 'I'll go through it at home if that's okay?'

However, in the end, she was not able to close the lid without looking at what was in the small parcel. She took out the package and read the attached card. It was written in Miriam's handwriting. *"To the pregnant lady I live with, who is going to be the best mummy in the world. And this is for our little new arrival and not for her to cuddle. That's what I'm here for."*

Victoria slid open the end of the package and looked inside. It was a small teddy bear wearing a blue and pink bow around its neck. And a little tag read, *"Just hedging our bets. XX."*

Victoria could not contain herself. She let out an almighty howl of pain. So sharp and visceral that it almost made the ACC drop the coffee mug she was carrying.

'What is it, Victoria? What is it, love?'

Victoria slumped down into the armchair and sobbed her heart out. She knew, at this moment, that the counsellor was right. She was nowhere near ready to return to work.

Epilogue

THE MUFFIN MAN ENQUIRY, ALONG with all the notes and files from the MIT's enquiry, had been handed over to the team from the MET soon into the new year. The team, while Victoria was in convalescence, would be temporarily led by Sergeant Mal Chambers. PCs Ronnie Ogden and Janice Slocomb were drafted onto the team, now as permanent members, and things were ticking over nicely. Varsa had been told that no further action would be taken over her stabbing of Jonathan Fahey, as it was found to be in self-defence and a justifiable killing under the extreme circumstances she found herself in.

She was glad to be back on the team but worried about how Victoria would be coping. Unsure as to whether to call round and say hello, she had at least managed to visit at the hospital before Victoria was discharged. The whole team were somewhat disappointed to have handed over the case. But they realised the size and complexity of the investigation was likely to go ballistic and end up way outside of their remit. They got down to their day-to-day solving of crimes, and eventually, after almost twelve months, Victoria arrived back at work in the December of 2020.

On the face of it, she was back to her usual professional and proficient self. But the whole team detected a somewhat more distant Victoria. One who they could still speak to and confide in, one who was totally professional and committed, but one who was not quite as interested in them as individuals as she once was. This was to improve as time went on, and as they saw out the year and moved into 2021, Victoria was getting back to herself once again.

During the early part of 2022, with the covid restrictions improving, Varsa managed to arrange for a night out and she convinced Victoria to come along. It was somewhat of a turning point. Eventually, Victoria began to open up about how she felt about the loss of Miriam and the baby. Sean and Aggie had asked Vitoria if she would like to accompany them on a holiday to Italy in the spring of 2023, as all but a few of the covid restrictions were being progressively lifted at home and abroad. She was contemplating saying yes and even looking forward to it a little.

She was still desperately lonely and had taken the plunge and gotten herself a cat and called it Frank. When she was little, her family always had cats, and her dad would always give them human names. No Tiddles or Smokies, only Brian's, Margaret's, and the occasional Peter. So, to continue the tradition, she called this one Frank. She had begun to have long conversations with Frank about the planned holiday, and work in general, and wondered why she had never thought of getting a cat before. He did appear to listen to what she was saying and best of all, never interrupted her, and of course, she could swear he understood every word she was saying to him.

As the year moved into 2023 and spring turned yet again, into what now seemed to be the norm of baking hot days in April and May the team had become one again. The new recruits had become well embedded in and the routine of day-to-day policing had a firm grip on all activities. ACC Julie Thornton had been promoted sideways into a training position and a new ACC had taken over. He was on temporary loan from the Canadian Police, youngish tall and relatively approachable. Only time would tell if he was to fit in. For once there was little in the way of major crime for the MIT to sink their teeth into and on a balmy Friday at the end of April the team were heading off to the Golden Ball Pub in South Bank, which had become their watering hole of choice. They were about to leave the office when Victoria's mobile rang.

It was a number she didn't recognise.

'Hi, Victoria. It's Matt O'Neill You remember? Sean's lad. Have you got a moment to speak?'

'Sure. Nice to hear from you, Matt.'

'Privately?

She knew instantly from the tone in his voice, and the way he used the word 'privately', that this call was something other than simply calling to say hi.

'Yes of course.' She left the office and stood in the corridor. 'What can I do for you, Matt? And how's your dad, by the way? You know he and Aggie have asked me to go on holiday with them this year?'

'Oh, he's fine, and so is Aggie. No, I didn't know about the holiday. But hang on before you accept. He doesn't know I'm ringing you, by the way, and we need to keep it like that, if at all possible?'

'Sounds a bit cloak and dagger, Matt. But nothing more than I'd expect from you lot. Go on then, spit it out.'

'Well, I can't say much more on the phone, but we have a case that we would like your input on . . . Well, more than just your input actually.'

He paused for a second and Victoria jumped in. 'Sounds intriguing. Are you going to give me any more information?'

'We need you to take an active part in a case. Something we are working on has taken a turn we weren't quite expecting and you may be able to help.'

'And?'

'Well, you know how it is, Victoria. I mean, you know how it is with us down here. We need you to come down for a briefing at our offices in The Strand. No one else. Just you.'

'I see. Well, I don't see why, but when do you need me to come down? Can it wait, or is it something I need to deal with immediately?'

'Sorry. No, it can't. We need you to come down tomorrow actually, if you can make it, that is. We have cleared it with your Chief Constable and your new ACC. I know you don't have too much on so you have been booked on the six-thirty train tomorrow morning. First class. I'm emailing you over the details. You'll be met by a driver at Kings Cross and brought to our offices. Is all that okay for you?'

'Well, as you put it like that, it sounds like I don't really have a choice, does it?'

'Well, you do. But save the decision until we've given you the details of what we need you to do. So, we'll see you sometime before lunch tomorrow then?'

She was about to answer in the affirmative but the line went dead before she could.

At the pub, Victoria sat back into one of the leather armchairs and listened to the rest of the team recounting tales of daring do and villains caught. Mal was mansplaining to Janice why the new coms system was rubbish, and Varsa was doing her utmost to explain to Ronnie Ogden how simple it was to circumnavigate the firewalls put in place in the average PC. As she sat listening to the team, Victoria looked at the empty seat next to her and wished to be able to turn the clock back and have one more night with Miriam. She eventually managed to shake off the feeling of melancholy as a second G & T arrived, and Varsa plonked herself down in the empty chair.

'Everything okay, boss?' Varsa asked.

'Yep, all fine,' she replied, and smiled.

Throughout the evening Victoria continued to listen to the stories of her team. She remained somewhat preoccupied with what Sean's son Matt might want with her. But most of all, she thought about Miriam, and how much she missed her. Yet another year looming ahead on her own. Well, not quite. After all, there was Frank, who was always happy to see her.

Other books by David Kirk

- Without Conscience
- Here Comes the Muffin Man
- Doppelganger (Due out late 2023)

Please visit my website **David Kirk — Author of the North Yorkshire MIT trilogy** (*davidkirkauthor.com*)

For more information about locations and characters.

About the Author

Although now retired, the author's background is that of an ex-serviceman who has spent time in the Army and Royal Marine Commandos. After leaving the military, he worked with ex-offenders and looked after children in the care of the local authority. He has a first degree in Applied Community Studies and a master's degree in Criminology. He has lectured in Law, Crime and Deviance at undergraduate level and on aspects of criminal law and deviance to prospective and serving police officers. His main area of academic work includes looking at the phenomenology of violence and homicide in the UK and how perpetrators seek — or don't seek — to justify their actions. Without Conscience is David Kirk's debut novel and forms part of a series featuring the work of The North Yorkshire Major Incident Team led by Chief Inspector Victoria Adams. Having lived in North Yorkshire for much of his life, David wanted to capture how the seemingly outward rural tranquillity of the North Yorkshire landscape can often, simply by scratching the surface, reveal a much more disturbing reality. In this book, he exploits his intricate knowledge of police procedure, crime, deviance, and law, to achieve this.

Printed in Great Britain
by Amazon